Myst, Titan and the Outcasts

A Novel by

Robert C. Aultman
and Rex Torres

authorHOUSE®

AuthorHouse™
1663 Liberty Drive, Suite 200
Bloomington, IN 47403
www.authorhouse.com
Phone: 1-800-839-8640

First published by AuthorHouse 9/8/2008

ISBN: 978-1-4389-1473-2 (sc)
ISBN: 978-1-4389-1474-9 (hc)

Library of Congress Control Number: 2008908432

Printed in the United States of America
Bloomington, Indiana

This book is printed on acid-free paper.

Contents

Dedication

This book is dedicated to every child that has ever wanted to be a superhero. Every child who has pinned on a beach towel and pretended to fly, deflect bullets, or just simply dreamed of saving the day. This book is for the child in all of us that yearns to be that hero in our everyday lives.

Robert Aultman would like to dedicate and thank:

This book is being dedicated in loving memory of Brandon E Rathbone. Born May 5, 1988 and tragically taken from us March 21, 2008. Brandon, you always believed in me, no matter what. You stood by my side, you fought for me, you even fought with me. My little brother becomes my guardian angel. This world is such a cold place without your smile, and laugh. I am always thinking of you. I love you, my little brother. Thank you for being simply YOU! There has never been and never will be anyone quite like you. That is why, in this book series, you will forever be immortalized within its pages. I owe you my love, honor and respect. Those three things are yours for the taking. I miss you bro, we all miss you. Please watch over us. This book is for YOU! "Heaven's Newest and Mightiest Guardian Angel!" I love you!!

First of all, I would like to thank God for his direction in my life. Without Him, there would be no heroes, no imagination, and nothing to look forward to. God gave us the mightiest hero of them all, when he gave us his son Jesus Christ. To him we owe it all.

Next I would like to take the opportunity to thank my lovely wife Celina, and my boys Mathew, Michael, and Madison. Thank you for the patience and understanding that I have needed throughout this endeavor. Celina, thank you for putting up with the late nights and heated debates on how this book should progress. Boys, thank you so much for letting a dork like me be considered your Step-Father. You boys mean the world to me and have given me hours of laughs and good times. Celina, again I want to thank you for loving me, and supporting me on this crazy journey. I could not have made it without you.

Koren Taylor: Thank you my brother, my blood, for all the brainstorming sessions that we would have at Mrs. Mary's expense. You are the inspiration for the passion in Myst's life. Every time someone sees you on stage, or in life itself, I hope they see the artist within. Thank you for being a muse in the darkness.

Billy Gowin and My God Sons: Without you my brother, I would not have made it this far in life. You have stood by my side, even when I was wrong, just to kick my butt back into gear. In addition, my little rays of sunshine. This book is really for you.

Rex Torres' dedications

First, I would like to dedicate this book to my father, Rudy Torres, who always supported me financially ever since I was a student. As a young boy, I was drawing cartoons on notepads and writing short stories and articles in the high school newspaper. He paid for my education at the University of Arizona, where I got my Bachelor's Degree in Management Information Systems, but I had also taken some classes in Media Arts, Marketing and English. These courses had sparked an interest in writing fiction, even if it meant just starting out with writing short stories at first.

Next, I would like to dedicate this book to my mother, Apollonia van Vuurden, who has taught me to always be honest, humble, open, and up front about everything and with everyone. I guess these characteristics shine through in my writing, because I also like for my main heroes in my stories to be honest, humble, open and up front about everything as well. This is especially true for Titan, who was my main character throughout this story. I don't have any children of my own but if I did, then I would have raised Jake Knight the same way that my mother had raised me. That's why I want to dedicate this book to her as well.

Acknowledgements

We would like to thank the following individuals for their inspiration, encouragement, patience and support during the past nine months, as we labored on this story. Now that you have the finished product in your hands, we can feel confident when we can claim that this is our longest and best work we have ever written! This is our masterpiece! We hope you will enjoy reading it as much as we have enjoyed writing it.

We have spent long hours thinking, discussing, arguing, pondering, dreaming, writing, typing, talking, and wondering about our characters in this book, and what they would do or where they would go. We spent countless hours chatting online, e-mailing one another or talking over the phone, brainstorming the next heroic scene for our heroes. It has been nothing short of a miracle seeing this little narrative balloon into this massive book, which is now in your hands. This is our story, and it is written from our hearts because we care deeply about our characters, and we hope you will, too.

In the midst of all this, many of you have e-mailed us, chatted with us, and written us. You have been very patient, while you waited for this book to arrive. The long wait was worth it, and the book is now here! For some of you, this book could not have come a moment too soon.

From Rex:

I would like to thank all my online friends, first of all, especially all those friends on Yahoo! Instant Messenger and MSN Messenger, who chat with me on a daily basis. I would also like to thank all the Yahoo! Group members who have joined the various groups I own. Let's not forget the members on my MySpace page, Hi5 page, DeviantArt page, and the Facebook group as well. Lastly, I want to thank all those who have visited my superfantasystories.com web site.

I made a lot of friends online during the past five years. These are guys like Bill Handy from Connecticut, who came down to help edit the text during his vacation, and Thomas O'Donnell, my friend from England who is actually a character in the story (He is rescued by Titan). I also want to thank Daniel Patrick Borg and Mark Julian Borg, the twins from Malta, who are always asking about the book. Then there is Tom Nichol from Tennessee, who has been there ever since I started writing stories in 2003, always giving words of encouragement and support, and an occasional (bad) joke here and there ("It is ten o'clock. Do you know where your brain is?" Ha ha!). I would also like to thank Marc R. from Spain, who started writing the Superboy Jamie stories during my absence from the group. He was a constant source of encouragement and inspiration, especially with his stories and photo manipulations.

Next, a huge "thank you" goes to Forest McNeir for his writing and his editing. Forest has penned some of the most wonderful scenes in this book, including the first meeting between Jake Knight and Genny Williams in Diablo Rojo, Arizona, and Titan's amazing jumbo jet rescue scene. Forest's knowledge of airplanes – due to his experience in the Navy - has allowed him to write these scenes with such a technical level of detail, that you can almost visualize Titan rescuing the plane while you're reading it. Truly, Forest is the only person who was capable of bringing that quality of writing to our book!

Furthermore, a big word of thanks goes to Niño Harn Cajayon for his stunning cover illustration. He took our character descriptions and came up with a drawing which included the main heroes of the story, Myst and Titan, and the faces of Zhango-Rhe and Thadius Malcolm in the background, without having read the story. What a remarkable feat! Truly, we could not have asked for a better illustrator than Niño.

Next, I would like to thank all my friends and co-workers at the Florida Department of Education here in Tallahassee for their support. They had to listen to me talking about this book for the past nine months and now, finally, they will see the finished product. So, to all of you who have listened to me talking about this mysterious book (I know it is impossible for me to list all the names, but I can't get away without mentioning David, Nikita, and Karen, who had lunch with me in the Eatz Cafeteria on the sixteenth floor every day) I say: "It's finally here!"

I couldn't write this without mentioning Mr. Barry E. Pitegoff, the Vice President of Visit Florida, who asked me every day how things were going with the book. He provided great ideas and suggestions for the final product, including how to market and promote the book once it was finished.

Last, but definitely not least, I want to extend a HUGE thank you to Rob Aultman, who truly is our real-life "Myst". I can never tell when I can get a phone call or a text message from this mysterious man, or when he may pop up at my front door with the entire family in his tow. When he says he will come over, he truly arrives at my house in no time at all, even though he clearly lives on the opposite side of town (he teleports!). He has an unlimited imagination and he has come up with practically all the characters in the book. Truly, it has been great fun working with "Robbydoo", and we have come a long way from the Superboy Jamie Yahoo! Group till the creation and publication of this book. Even though we have known each other for over a year, we have become "blood-brothers", just like Jake and Robby in the story! So, the story has been written, the artwork is done, the editing has been completed… And Robby has already written the first scenes for the second book! Amazing… This man is a "Myst"…

Robert would like to thank:

Thanks to all those that made this possible for Rex and I to do. I would like to thank Bill Handy, for all his heated debates on how our boys would be portrayed here in this completed work. Bill I never get tired of arguing.

Forest McNeir, Man what can I say? You knew a diamond in the rough when you saw it. Thank you so very much for standing by Rex, and myself throughout the writing process. You have made a huge impact on both of us.

Niño Harn Cajayon: A friend that "sees" this the way I imagined it. You are a credit to your craft. There is no other like you my friend. We will continue the debate on who is taking Bruce's place soon (ha ha).

Rex Torres: My friend and co-author. Without you, this fifteen year dream would not be complete. No matter our differences of opinions, we always seem to do the RIGHT thing for this book, and for our friendship. Thank you for all your tireless effort and pushing the envelope to the limit with me. You are a true TITAN!

Lastly I would like to thank all of my co-workers at Alltel Wireless for their support. I can honestly say that "I got my bidness socks on!" Thanks Dimitri Barlas, Elizabeth Decent, Lauren Greene, Jessica Moreen, Jason Tucker, Adnan Shakil, Gina Rossi, Chivonne Carter, Ateasa Holland, Robert Pflueger, Felicia Hardnett, and Carlos Gant. Gov Square ROCKS!

Rob Aultman and Rex Torres, August 2008

Myst, Titan and the Outcasts

**Robert C. Aultman
and Rex Torres**

www.superfantasystories.com

Cover illustration by
Niño Harn Cajayon

www.craftycomix.com

Prologue

Three hundred years ago, there was an evil that the universe had never seen or endured before. An intergalactic despot reined his brand of terror throughout the galaxy. Planet after planet, galaxy after galaxy fell under the vile gaze of an evil entity. Thadius Malcolm, a reckless, malevolent and vile being traveled the galaxy leaving a wake of terror behind him.

Zyrton, a normally peaceful planet, fell into Malcolm's sights. Zyrton was a technologically advanced world, full of natural resources and bustling with life. Zyrton had not known anything but peace for centuries. There were no wars, famines or plagues in recorded history for over three-hundred years.

As Malcolm traveled the galaxy, his plans had been to enslave and destroy any planet that he targeted. He drained the lifeblood, the natural resources of every world he saw fit to target. He would strip any valuable minerals, gems, and metals away, leaving the planet a lifeless uninhabitable rock adrift in space.

There was no stopping this madman, however this time, Malcolm met his match. Zhango-Rhe, general of the Zyrtonian defense force, stood in the way of Malcolm's prize. Even though known for their peaceful nature, Zyrtonians were also known as skilled and honorable warriors.

The epic battle ensued. Malcolm and his forces landed upon an almost unsuspecting planet, eluding all eyes but the mighty Titan known as Zhango-Rhe. Both military forces all but obliterated each other as Malcolm and Zhango-Rhe fought endlessly.

The fate of Zyrton however was sealed. The planet was abandoned, uninhabitable and an extinct rock. The battle raged on throughout the universe. Galaxies after galaxies were affected, until they arrived in the Milky Way and the only life-supporting planet, Earth.

The two beings landed upon earth and the battle continued. The scales, however, tipped in Zhango-Rhe's favor. As their spacecrafts crash-landed on earth, Zhango-Rhe had been given an amazing gift. He gained powers beyond all belief. He gained the ability to fly, along with unlimited strength, plasmoidal blasts, and enhanced hearing and vision.

Zhango-Rhe fought Malcolm to what he thought was the death. Believing that he had defeated Malcolm, he started his life anew as Earth's first guardian. As a precaution, Zhango-Rhe made a techno-genetic copy of himself to pass down to a rightful successor. That successor would have to be pure of heart and posses the sterling character to rightfully deserve the mantle of Earth's guardian and protector.

The time has come for that successor to rise up and become a hero. This, actually, is the tale of two young people with intertwined fates, who will become Earth's mightiest champions, battling to save an unsuspecting planet from a gruesome fate. The amazing thing is they are not even old enough to drive.

This is the account of Titan, the most powerful being to grace the planet, even more powerful than Zhango-Rhe himself. It is the chronicle of Myst, the most powerful mutant who has ever lived. This is how these two boys became Earth's mightiest defenders.

Chapter 1

It was late summer in the year 1999. Dr. Charles Knight, a world-renowned archaeologist, had made a startling discovery at an archaeological dig in the Nevada desert. His Team had been working tirelessly, night and day, to unearth the treasure lying beneath the sand. Excitedly, Charles called home to share this news with his wife, Nancy, and his five-year-old son, Jake.

"Hey Nancy, its Charles... Honey, we've hit pay dirt. I am not sure what it is, but I am almost positive it is extra-terrestrial. Yes, it is fantastic. No, honey, we have not released any findings to the government. OK, sweetheart. Is Jake there? May I talk to him please?"

"Hi, son, how is my little guy? Yes! Mom is serious. I think the team and I have found something from outer space. Can you believe it? I can't wait for you to see it. You bet, Tim is picking you up from the airport, my little man! He can't wait, and neither can I. Talk to you then!"

Dr. Knight closed his flip style cell phone, and beamed with pride. His son had always had a keen interest in his expeditions. Jake would always bounce into the lab while his father was working and studying the ancient artifacts that he would bring back. On a couple of occasions, Jake's deeply insightful questions had led Charles' investigations and research into directions he might otherwise have overlooked!

The next afternoon Jake's plane landed in Nevada. Tim Marshall, Charles' assistant and family friend, went to pick up the youngest member of the Knight clan in Jake's all-time favorite vehicle, a bright yellow Hummer SUV. Tim waited patiently for the plane to arrive, glancing periodically at his watch and then back at the flight arrival board. He was fiddling with his PALM Treo cell phone when he felt a tugging at his shirt.

"Get outta here! You snuck up on me again, tiger!" laughed Tim as he reached down to pick Jake up off the ground.

"Hey Tim!!!!" five-year-old Jake Knight squealed, as he hugged his dad's assistant and right-hand man.

Jake was a thin, wiry-built boy. He had a crop of sandy brown hair adorning his youthful head. His eyes were a stunning almost-electric blue. They contained a very innocent and inquisitive nature within their cerulean gateways. He was dressed comfortably in a pair of khaki cargo shorts and light-blue t-shirt.

Tim reached down and picked up Jake's carry-on backpack, and corralled his young protégé towards the exit of the concourse. He looked down at Jake with almost fatherly pride. He too was happy that Jake had joined the team for the remainder of the excavation.

The whole team was like family and Jake was no exception. Jake had always thought of Tim as his big brother. He flashed a mega-watt smile as they made their way to baggage claim where they milled around waiting for Jake's bags to arrive.

"Hey Tim, did you bring the Hummer?" asked a wide-eyed Jake.

"Sure did sport, did you think I would let you down?" chuckled Tim as he looked down at the skinny kid at his side.

"YAY!!!" cheered Jake.

Tim grabbed Jake's bags and escorted his young friend out to the waiting SUV. The ride out to the dig site was quiet. The normally exuberant and loquacious Jake was awestruck by the stark wild beauty of the Nevada landscape. He had seen the scenery on the educational channels at home and in photos in his dad's study, but never had he personally observed anything like this up close and personal.

Tim drove past the Airport Embassy Suites where his dad had told him they were staying, without stopping. Jake looked back at the hotel as it faded into the distance. He turned his attention back inside the cabin of the Hummer.

"Tim aren't we gonna stop at the hotel to drop off my stuff?" asked the blue eyed youth.

"Well sport, your dad has a surprise for you that will not wait" responded Tim with a grin.

"OHH OHHH OHHH What is it? Tell me tell me tell me Tim, Please!" pleaded Jake excitedly as he jumped up and down in his seat.

"Settle down kiddo, you will see soon enough what you got in store for ya" reassured Tim.

After half an hour's drive, Tim pulled the Hummer off the paved road onto a dirt path that lead to the dig site. He navigated the winding path down into a remote, deep rugged ravine, leading down into a canyon in the middle of the dessert. He came to a complete stop, put the large vehicle in park and shut down the engine.

"Well, here we are. You can leave your bags in here, kid, my assistants will get them for you later, for now we go and find your pops" said Tim.

"YAY!!!!! Dad has been gone too long!" squealed Jake.

Tim led the youngster into the middle of the canyon where the team had been diligently working. Right away, Jake spotted his father standing by a large tent. He set out running at full speed and leapt into his happy father's waiting arms. Jake squeezed his father in a loving embrace.

"Jake!!!! Hello son!" Exclaimed Dr. Knight as he held his son tightly to his chest.

"DADDY, I have missed you so much!" said Jake with a huge grin on his face.

"I have missed you too, kiddo!" exclaimed Dr. Knight, as he set his young son's feet gently back on the ground.

"Tim said you had a big surprise for me Daddy, what is it?" asked Jake excitedly.

Dr. Knight looked over at Tim with a smirk. "Tim has a big mouth," he laughed.

"But yes, son, I do. I have wanted to take you camping for a long time, but I have been so busy with work," Charles said. "So I figured that if you were coming to visit me out here, that we would make this a camping trip," he continued.

"REALLY? YAY! I've always wanted to do that like the older kids! Thank you, Dad!" exclaimed Jake.

"I'm glad we could do this together, son. I'm so glad you're finally out here with me! I've missed you so much, Jakie!" replied Dr. Knight.

Tim's staff brought Jake's luggage to the tent. Charles came into the tent and showed Jake to his cot.

"Thanks, Dad. This is gonna be awesome," exclaimed Jake.

Jake spent the rest of the afternoon settling in and exploring the campsite with Tim. Dr. Knight finished some documentation of the current dig findings. Then he took time out to join Jake and Tim to continue as the official tour guide of the dig site. They had saved the best for last, the discovery! This, of course, had been the pinnacle of the young man's curiosity.

Charles, Tim and Jake entered the cave, the focal point of the investigation. They ascended far below ground and made their way to the actual excavation site. Jake was studying the pictures that adorned the caverns as they winded slowly downwards to the depths of the cavern.

"Daddy, these pictures, they are hieroglyphs, aren't they?" asked Jake.

"Yes sir, they sure are, very good! Now if only we could decipher them." replied Dr. Knight.

"Well, I think I can help. I believe they're coded instructions."

"What? How do you know that?" asked Jake's father.

"I dunno, Dad... I guess it's just something about the patterns that made me think 'instructions' or something. See right here, the long sections in short blocks of pictures, in like burst form? If it was like a sentence or something, don't you think that there would be some longer sections of pictures? This looks like it's giving us instructions."

Dr. Knight was extremely impressed with the analytical perceptiveness of his young son. He was proud of his son's curiosity and recognized the boy's instincts as incredibly sound for one so young. He had all the makings of a great field archaeologist, or perhaps a forensic pathologist. He had the mind to do and be whatever he wanted. In fact, Jake's "intuitive leap" was probably correct, given their location on the artifact.

"Some of the planes and helicopters I have seen pictures of have stuff like that grouped together on the sides of them, dad. Like the area at the back of a plane that warns people 'Beware of Blast'. I think this is something like that," explained Jake with an innocent grin.

It never actually crossed Dr. Knight's mind that Jake might actually be able to decipher the arcane characters that were so unlike any other ancient language known to man. He looked at Jake with a bewildered and amazed gaze.

Jake had understood more than he'd let on to his dad. He knew exactly what the inscriptions said. He was not sure just how or why the characters that had so eluded the encryption experts would be so easy for him to decipher. He doubted they would take anything that he said as the truth, seeing as though it came from the mouth of a child. Jake understood very well that he SHOULD NOT be able to read alien glyphs. The fact that he could, made him both a little afraid and very excited. He decided to keep his own counsel for the present and bide his time. He started to play his PSP video game, as his dad continued to work.

Later that afternoon, Dr. Knight took Jake to the artifact collection area. He showed him where the other scientists had been working all day. Charles began pointing out all the wonderful items that the team had uncovered so far.

They made their way back to camp to relax for the rest of the evening. The two Knights played around wrestling and picking on one another. Jake laughed uncontrollably; basking in the warmth of his father's loving attention. Charles was not only Jake's father; he was his ultimate hero. They laughed, joked, and chattered for most of the evening until, exhausted, Jake started to yawn and rub his bright blue eyes. Charles just smiled and stood up. He stepped over to the flap of the tent and zipped it shut.

"Time to get ready for bed, sport" suggested Dr. Knight.

"Yes sir. I'm pretty sleepy anyway," retorted Jake. "It was a long trip from DC, Daddy," continued Jake.

"Yes, it sure was son," smiled Charles. "You've been up since early this morning, and you've had a very long day. I'm just so glad you're out here with me. I've really missed you!"

Suppressing a yawn, Jake smiled back at his dad. "I've missed you too, Dad. Thanks for the surprise camping trip, daddy. We are going to have a blast."

Jake changed into his pajamas and climbed into his cot. His father walked over, and tucked him in gently. He bent down and kissed him compassionately on the forehead.

"Good night daddy" said Jake.

"Good night Jake," responded Charles.

Dr. Knight sat there and watched in awe as his only child fell fast asleep. He smiled to himself marveling that this bright-eyed inquisitive youth loved him so much. Dr. Knight loved his son more than he loved his own life. He was happy. Happy to be a father, happy to be a husband, and happy to be right where he was at that moment with his son safely next to him.

Dr. Knight took a few moments to send a short e-mail to his wife and to let her know that everything was going well. He told her that by the end of the summer, the excavation of the unknown craft would be finished. He closed his laptop and took off his glasses. He turned, rose from his chair, and staggered wearily over to his cot. Then he climbed into his sleeping bag and slowly closed his eyes. Within a few short moments, he was sound asleep.

Chapter 2

It was four AM, when Jake bolted straight up on his cot, wide-awake. He glanced over at his father, who was sleeping rather restlessly. Jake climbed out of his sleeping bag, and off the cot. He pulled on his shorts and quietly put his shoes on. He cautiously unzipped the flap of the tent and stepped outside into the crisp early morning air.

He looked up at the pre-dawn sky, wondering to himself whether what his father had uncovered was really, in fact, an alien spacecraft. Jake breathed in deeply, allowing the cool night air to inflate his lungs. A mischievous grin crossed his youthful face.

"I wonder what that thing dad found looks like" Jake said to himself.

Jake started to walk towards the dig site. He had noticed earlier in the day that armed security guards had secured the site. He glanced around and noticed that the guards were conspicuous by their absence. He slowly and quietly made his way to the cavern entrance.

The dig crew installed massive floodlights to help in the early morning and the waning evening hours. Jake noticed that the lights were not on, so navigating the cavern entrance might become a little tricky. He then located a flashlight resting on top of the generator. He reached out, grabbing it, and switched it on. He grabbed a hard hat, and put it on, as his father had taught him always to do at a dig site. Then he cautiously entered the cave opening, not sure what he was about to find. Little did he know that his life was about to change dramatically.

Jake made his way back into the massive expanse of the cave that contained the "Alien Artifact", as his father called it. He took more time and actually read the strange hieroglyphic-type writing that adorned the path towards the main site. He did not know how, but he could read and actually understand everything that had been inscribed on the rocky surfaces that he passed.

Jake continued to read, he learned that what his dad had discovered was the last vestige of an alien civilization, now extinct. Every man, woman and child had perished in a massive global war. Jake shuddered at the magnitude of this cataclysmic event that had claimed so many lives. Bitter sadness gripped the young boy's soul as he considered what these long gone people must have had to deal with before their utter and total demise.

Jake ventured deeper and deeper into the cavern, until he stopped dead in his tracks. He was face-to-face with what appeared to be a space ship. His jaw dropped as he stared at the thing that he thought was only possible in science fiction movies and books. He now saw that those things of fiction were not too far off from the truth.

Cautiously, he approached the craft. He made note of a diamond shaped symbol emblazoned on the hull. Variations of this diamond-shaped emblem had recurred throughout the cavern, spread among all the hieroglyphic inscriptions. Their significance had been less apparent to Jake than the hieroglyphic inscriptions. This diamond symbol, however, was different. It seemed to be essentially calling out to him.

The diamond symbol began emitting an audible hum as it pulsated with soothing blue aura. Jake, feeling drawn to the aura, traversed the rocky path to the ship. He walked right up to it, and stood firm at what he deduced was the source of the sound. His youthful curiosity had overpowered his better judgment.

Casting aside all caution, Jake boldly approached the symbol, reached out with his hand and touched it. Suddenly he froze in place. The humming tone silenced, the faint blue aura died away, yielding to near total darkness. The only light remaining was the faint glow of the small electric torch that he dropped as his body seized motionless by an unknown force.

The boy was frozen and scared as he faced the alien vessel with a mixture of fear and excitement. Slicing through the darkness radiated a dazzling blue three-dimensional hologram. It flashed its massive appearance directly in front of Jake, and peered down at the young child that stood before him.

The image addressed the boy by name.

"Greetings, Jacob Knight."

"Wha? How do you know my name?" stuttered the terrified little boy.

"Ah, my young Jacob, it was my ship that sought you out. This vessel, which contains the stores of my knowledge, brought you before me now. The computer in the ship scanned your mind. I have learned quite a lot about you," responded the image.

"Who? What are you?" asked Jake.

"My name is Zhango-Rhe, last descendant of a long dead world," answered the holographic image.

"Young Jacob, you have nothing to fear from me. Please, little one, do not be afraid. I have chosen you to continue my legacy here on earth. When I arrived here three-hundred years ago, I became guardian of this world. Here I was able to do what I could not accomplish on my own world. I became an unstoppable defender of this world and all her inhabitants," explained Zhango-Rhe as he smiled soothingly at Jake.

"What? You want me to do that? There is no way! I am just a kid," rebutted a far less frightened but very skeptical Jake. "Why me, anyway?"

"Why you? That is a good question, young Jacob. I chose you because of your heart and kindness. You were chosen because you have been destined to become my successor since the day you were born," replied Zhango-Rhe.

"Since I was born, how long have you been watching me?" inquired Jake.

"I have known of your family line since its present incarnation came into existence" replied Zhango-Rhe.

"What do you mean?" asked Jake.

"I have watched your family for generations. Keeping a watchful eye, or scanner, on you from afar" said Zhango-Rhe with an almost electronic laugh.

"Where are you now, inside your space ship? Can't you just come out here and talk to me?"

Zhango-Rhe smiled ruefully. "My apologies Jacob, but my body has been dead, for near a century now. My essence, my powers, my thoughts; all my knowledge that I have accumulated over the years have been stored within the technology that composes my ship. For the lack of a better term, the ship is me," explained the shimmering hologram.

"You see young Jacob, when I came to this solar system; I gained powers and abilities that I could never have imagined on my home world. Unlimited strength, the ability to move at blinding speed, the ability to gaze through solid matter and great distances, and the ability to emit powerful streams of energy from my hands." continued Zhango-Rhe.

"WOW!" murmured Jake.

"I was also granted the ability to defy gravity. You could say that I had the ability to fly" smiled Zhango-Rhe.

"Fly!? That is awesome!" exclaimed Jake. "OK, so you can like fly, without a plane or helicopter or anything like that?" asked Jake as he continued the interrogation.

"Yes Jacob, completely out of sheer willpower. All this and more is what I want to pass on to you. These are dangerous times. Your world needs you now. I have waited many a year to see you as Earth's guardian," explained Zhango-Rhe.

"You want to pass that all onto me? You want me to become Earth's protector?" asked Jake.

"Yes, my young friend, I do. Your people desperately need hope. They need someone that they can believe in, and who in turn believes in them. They need someone who will stand up for the weak and powerless. They need a champion who can bring those who operate above the law to justice. The duty that I ask of you will not be easy. The burden will be heavy at times. Never again will your life be your own. Little one, all the gifts I bequeath to you, come with great responsibility. You will become the strongest, most powerful being on this planet. You will be amazingly fast, and virtually indestructible, with keen senses and a powerful intellect. I am asking that you allow me to make you my gift to the people of this world. You'll become a continuation of the protection that I once offered to this planet" expounded Zhango-Rhe.

Jake stood there, still frozen in place, no longer paralyzed by Zhango-Rhe's alien technology but by the overwhelming implications of this alien's words. He attempted to digest and assimilate all of what the alien before him had begun to explain.

"Jacob, I cannot, however, do this without your wholehearted consent. This path is not an easy one. You can trust that I speak from earned experience in this matter. As a planetary guardian, you will face the full gamut of human behavior and emotions. You will see humanity at its best and do all that you can to aide it at its worst. As you serve the people of this world, you will find, as in any world, including my own beloved and long-dead Zyrton, there will be those who will break your heart and those who will uplift your soul and spirit beyond the highest heaven. All of this can and will happen, sometimes within the span of a single day! Jacob, you must understand, if you accept the offer that is yours alone, you can never repent of your decision. The powers and the duty I would give will be with you until the day you die. There can be no going back. Do you understand this clearly, little one?"

Jake did not answer right away. He pondered everything that was told to him before answering.

"Sir, may I ask a question before I answer?"

Zhango-Rhe nodded. "Yes, of course."

"What if something happens? Like what if I turned out bad? What would happen then? There wouldn't be anything that could stop me. From what you are telling me, I would be able to conquer the world" inquired Jake.

Zhango-Rhe answered. "Little one, this morning when you got out of your bed, you did not even know of my existence. You could not have known that your path would bring you to me, to this place, to this decision now thrust upon you. Here I stand, asking for your trust and your faith, not only in me, but in essence, within yourself. Once these gifts have been imparted to you, nothing in this world could stop you; nothing that is outside yourself. Many of the freedoms you and anyone else in this world have enjoyed will be lost. You must control your passions. You must be on your guard unceasingly. Don't you see, dear Jacob, the very fact that you asked this, is proof that you will be a champion, nothing more and defiantly nothing less. So young you are, but your first thought was not of the powers you will gain, on the contrary, your concern is with those powers, for you might pose a danger to others. I have asked that you to put your faith in me. In all actuality, I need you to have faith in yourself, as I do. And so, young Jacob, do you accept the gift and the burden that I offer you?" asked Zhango-Rhe.

Jacob bowed his head as he murmured, "Yes Sir. I will try. I promise that I will do everything I can to be the best guardian that I can be" replied Jake as he nearly bowed in reverence to the entity that was asking the world of him.

Zhango-Rhe spoke again. "Little one, your stature is very small; too small to accommodate the strength and powers that will soon be yours. I must alter your body structure. It must grow in stature, in muscle and bone density, to proportions more in keeping with those of a planetary guardian, even one so young as yourself. I will be frank. These changes will be painful. No consolation that I could offer would ease the searing pain that you must endure. However, this is part of the process. Once your powers take hold, the pain will subside. I can only ask you to be brave. In addition, as you endure the pain, try to think of all the good that you will do for the people of this planet. Moreover, I will be with you, Jacob, in your mind. I do not ask you to endure anything I myself would not endure by your side."

Jake looked up at Zhango-Rhe. "I won't lie to you sir. This is scaring me. I just don't want you to go through it, too. So please, sir, I'd rather do this on my own."

Zhango-Rhe shook his head. "I cannot, little one. I could not bear to witness you going through pain that I have instigated! I cannot allow you to proceed with the changes without my guidance and direction. With all the pain and anguish that I have seen in this world, I ask that you would spare me the burden of your suffering in solitary agony. Allowing me to endure this with you would not be an act of cowardice, young Jacob. Under the circumstances, it would be an act of mercy."

Reluctantly, Jake agreed, as he bowed his head in submission to Zhango-Rhe's request.

"Be brave, little one! This will be over soon. Be warned, after you reach your thirteenth year, you will undergo another massive growth spurt, after which you will be even stronger and more powerful," continued the alien.

Jake took a deep breath and nodded gravely to Zhango-Rhe. "I'm ready, Sir. Anytime you are."

"OK Jacob, take a few steps back, and a few more deep breaths, and we will begin your journey. A journey of personal and physical transformation" directed Zhango-Rhe to his young protégé.

Jake did as instructed. A fiery red glow bathed the cavern in its shimmering light. The young guardian-to-be was just a little apprehensive, but that was mixed with anticipation and burning curiosity. In this respect, Jake was still his father's son, with a keen and analytical mind.

A bolt of red light lanced out of the hull of the craft and slammed into little Jake Knight's frail chest. He clenched his fist and gnashed his teeth, trying to suppress a scream.

In his mind, the boy heard Zhango-Rhe, speaking gently to him. "Jacob, try not to hold it in. You will not be able to. I couldn't. No one could. You've got to let it out!"

"YYYYYEEEEEAAAAAARRRRRGGGGGGGG!" Jake howled like a wounded animal as he succumbed to the force of the transformation's awesome power.

He fell to his knees as the transformation began. His shirt began to constrict his torso as his chest, shoulders, back and arms began to grow. Slowly his body began to adapt to the powers that it was accepting.

The pain in Jake's head pounded mercilessly, as his body continued its violent transformation. His DNA morphed from Terran to Zyrtonian, giving him all the wonderful powers and abilities that Zhango-Rhe had promised. His body weight had increased by at least twenty pounds in a matter of seconds, as layers of muscle packed onto his formerly small frame. His height remained about the same, but his muscularity had increased dramatically. The short, skinny stripling first-grader quickly morphed into a strapping young athlete.

Jake fell to his knees, as an intense tingling coursed through every muscle in his body. His arms grew thicker, making room for the unstoppable strength that would soon be at their young master's command. The muscle in his calves and thighs became rock-hard and shredded like the legs of a professional athlete, giving him the power to run like the wind.

His fingers tingled. Zhango-Rhe informed his successor that he would now be able to fire directed energy bursts from his hands. He would be able to fire it with laser pinpoint accuracy and cause massive damage with a wide spread blast. With the density of his now massive musculature, he had become invincible. Jake gained a form of auto-telekinesis. This amazing ability would allow him to move his body in any direction he saw fit. In essence, this particular gift would grant him the ability to fly.

Jake closed his eyes for a moment and shook his head. The tingling stopped just as abruptly as it had started. The pain had abated. The crimson energy beam that fed his body faded slowly as the transformation session ended. He opened his eyes and raised his head; he looked around the cavern with a newfound amazement for his surroundings. The normal colors of his eyesight failed him, only replacing it with an eerie red hue.

"I don't get it, why can I only see this weird red color?" asked Jake as he continued to look around.

"That, my boy is another one of your new gifts. You now have the ability to see heat signatures. It is, what I believe, your scientists call 'infrared'. You will be able to hone this gift so well that you can almost see with clarity that would rival most heat scanners," explained Zhango-Rhe.

Jake's body felt heavier and more powerful. He did not yet fully grasp the full range of his newly acquired abilities, but it was immediately apparent that things had changed dramatically. He did not have a mirror to tell him what his mind had already conceived. He grinned wildly as he began looking at his newly expanded arms, legs and chest. He felt omnipotent. He was not far from the truth.

"Arise, young Jacob. You will forever been known as Titan…" Zhango-Rhe said to him. "You have been granted all my powers, strength and abilities. Now you are the guardian of the earth. Young people all over this world will look up to you. The elderly will cheer you. Titan, you will lead them to a better tomorrow. A word of warning, you are not their master. Your destiny is not to rule, but to serve. That is why I chose you, for your servant's heart."

Gravely, Jake regarded his alien benefactor. Solemnly he repeated Zhango-Rhe's injunction.

"I am here to serve, not to rule. I will remember. I will never forget. I promise that on my body and my soul."

"I just have one question," he said.

"Yes, young Titan, what question would you ask of me?" replied Zhango-Rhe.

"How do I control all these powers?" asked Jake as he hoped in his heart, that Zhango-Rhe would have answers for him.

"Don't worry, young hero" Zhango-Rhe replied. "You must begin your training. You will need someone to guide and teach you how to use your abilities, for there are many. You are far more powerful than you can even begin to imagine at this moment."

"OK, so what are my abilities exactly?" Jake asked inquisitively as he flexed and relaxed his now massive young muscles.

"Yes, my young champion. You now possess the ability to run great distances in mere seconds. You can will your body to travel unassisted through the air. With your newfound strength and body structure, you can bend steel, lift countless weight, and stop a train with your bare hands. Your body will be resistant to practically all forms of harm. The energy projection that I had told you about before, will be able to level an entire city if you so choose" Zhango-Rhe explained to the boy.

"I don't want to destroy a city! What about all the people? I just wanna know how to control it! I sure don't want to fry a city by accident!" Jake exclaimed.

"Your father, he is the one who found my ship, correct?" the alien asked the young hero.

"Yeah, he's the archeologist who found this site! His research team discovered this cavern and your ship," Jake answered.

"Bring your father to me please" Zhango-Rhe instructed. "I must pass on to him all the knowledge he needs so that he can train you..."

"OK, I will go get him!" Jake announced. "Hang on; I'll be right back!"

The boy turned around and in a flash, made his way out of the cavern. Once clear of the entrance, he sprinted to his father's tent. He arrived in less than a second and stopped on a dime. To the normal eye, there would have been a faint blur, followed by Jake's seeming materialization at the entrance to his father's tent. Fortunately, Jake's sudden arrival had gone unobserved.

Chapter 3

"Whoa! Dude!" Jake murmured to himself, when he realized how quickly he had run the distance of two football fields. "I can't believe this. Did I just run that fast?"

"I gotta try that again. There is no way!" He thought to himself. Jake took off in a flash; as the world seemed to freeze in place. From Jake's perspective, the world around him had come to a virtual stop. To an outside observer, there would have been a barely visible blur and a "whoosh" as he flashed past, faster than the normal eye could follow.

"WOW!" he exclaimed to himself. "This is so awesome!"

Jake glanced at his digital watch, making careful note of the time. Then, he ran back to his father's tent, over two hundred yards away. As he arrived, he stopped and glanced at his watch.

"Two seconds?" he gasped. "I just ran all that way in two seconds! I don't think I was even running as fast as I could! Weird!"

He just stood there, his mouth agape. "This is amazing! I can't believe this. Zhango-Rhe gave me all this, I can't wait to see what else he gave me!" Jake exclaimed.

The boy opened the flap of the tent where his dad lay sleeping.

"Dad! Hey Dad!" Jake whispered to his father. "Wake up, daddy!"

"What is it, Jake?" Charles said groggily, as he rubbed his eyes.

"Quick! You have to come with me to the space ship!" Jake said excitedly. "Something's happened! I saw a strange thing there!"

Charles opened his eyes and stared at his young son, who now appeared very different.

"What? What are you talking about? What's happened to you? What strange thing are you talking about, son?"

"I got zapped by this ray from the space ship and now I've become really fast and really strong! This man from the ship kept calling me 'Titan.' He told me to bring you to him so he can tell you what you need to know to train me to use my powers! I'm supposed to be this 'planetary guardian!' And you're supposed to be like my trainer or something!" Jake said in one breath as he finally drew in a breath.

"Whoa, slow down, Jake," Charles said, as he got up. "Jake! Look at you! Your arms! Your legs! Your shoulders! Everything! You've grown! Your muscles are huge! I'll bet you're nearly as strong as I am!"

Jake looked into his father's eyes. "That's just it; I'm stronger than you and everybody else now! You have to come with me, dad!" Jake insisted. "You need to come back with me to the space ship, right now!"

Gently, Jake took hold of his father's hand, taking care not to crush it with his mind-blowing power. He turned dashed toward the cavern. Fortunately, Jake's grip had been gentle and has father's hand had slipped from his grasp. That was fortunate because otherwise, the sudden acceleration would have dislocated Charles' shoulder at the very least.

From Charles' perspective, Jake had quite simply vanished, reappearing over two hundred yards away at the cave entrance in the blink of an eye. "Oh my God..." Charles murmured. "How did he do that?"

Jake raced back to the tent, rejoining his father.

"Sorry Dad! I'm just starting to get used to this! I didn't mean to run off and leave you like that."

"Son? What has happened to you? What you did, it's impossible! If I hadn't seen that with my own eyes, I wouldn't have believed it. But, I'm still not sure I believe it. Jake, you need to start from the beginning. We are not going anywhere until you explain this to me."

Gravely, Jake looked into his father's eyes. "Dad, I'm sorry, but there is no way I can explain it on my own. That's why you've gotta come with me now. Zhango-Rhe is waiting for us. He told me he'd explain everything. Please, Dad. Just trust me. You have to do this."

When Charles appeared to hesitate, Jake snatched his father by the waist, tucked him lengthwise under his arm and dashed off to the cavern entrance. He ran the distance much slower than he had on his own, careful not to subject his Dad to the horrific acceleration forces that his own super powered body had endured with no ill effects.

Jake arrived with his dad at the cavern entrance, proceeding through the network of subterranean chambers to the alien spacecraft. He set his dad upon his feet, apologizing, "Sorry, Dad, but we've gotta do this with Zhango-Rhe before everyone else wakes up and we're running outta time."

Charles looked around, realizing that he was standing in a dark cavern alongside the alien space ship, a bright blue glow emanating from the hull. A holographic figure shimmered into view and addressed Charles in a rich baritone voice.

"Greetings, Doctor Knight..." Zhango-Rhe said to Charles. "Thank you for coming with your son to meet with me! I must pass my knowledge to you so that you may instruct young Jacob in the usage of his powers and abilities so that he can become Titan, the global guardian of this world."

"Titan? Instructions? Training?" Charles stammered aloud, as he gave the figure a confused look. "I don't understand..."

Zhango-Rhe replied, "I have given your son great powers. He is now and forever, the most powerful force on this planet. However, the knowledge he needs I give to you. I could give this knowledge to Jacob, but wisdom comes only with age and experience. Jacob is still a boy and, powerful as he is, he still needs a mentor. He still needs his father. He needs you, Charles Knight." A red beam lanced from the ship's hull, striking Charles between the eyes. After about twenty seconds, his eyes glazed over, as he collapsed to the ground and convulsing slightly.

"DAD!!!!" Jake cried, as he dashed to his father's side.

Jake knelt alongside his dad and cradled his head in his arms. Tears began to well up within the young, yet mighty, five-year-old's eyes.

"Dad! Dad! Dad! Please, wake up, Daddy!"

The boy looked up at the alien holograph. "Mr. Zhango-Rhe! My dad!"

"Your father will be fine. I have transmitted an enormous amount of knowledge into his mind. He needed to lose consciousness as his brain assimilates and organizes the information I have given him. He will regain consciousness shortly. And please do not be alarmed if he is slightly disoriented at first."

Charles slowly regained consciousness. Just as predicted, he showed a disoriented appearance. Jake, forgetting Zhango-Rhe's reassurance, continue to cradle his father's head in his arms. "Daddy! Daddy! Are you alright?"

Coming to himself, overcome with awe, Charles gazed up at Jake. He reached out and touched Jake's cheek with his right index finger.

"Oh my God…" Charles said in a soft voice, as he passed his hand over Jake's arm.

"What is it, daddy?" Jake asked, his voice quavering with worry. "What's wrong?"

"Oh goodness, this is incredible…" Charles continued. "I cannot believe what he has done to you! He's transformed my little boy into the most powerful being on this Earth! Jake, you have no idea how powerful this being has made you. Maybe you think you know, but you have no clue. No to mention what he's done to me! I've learned more in the past minute or so than in my entire previous lifetime! Part of what Zhango-Rhe has given me, is everything I need to serve as your mentor!" Charles addressed Zhango-Rhe's holo-image. "But why didn't you just give all of this knowledge directly to my son?"

Zhango-Rhe smiled at Charles, and addressed him telepathically, as to not alarm Jake, "Because, as I have stated before, if I had done so, I might've created a monster instead of a young hero. Imagine a child of Jacob's age in possession of all of the knowledge he would need in a lifetime but with the wisdom of a child. No, Charles Knight, powerful as your son is, he needs YOU, his father. More important, he needs to KNOW he needs his father. Perhaps this approach is unnecessary. How better to ensure that a boy who can fly, will keep his feet on the ground, other than to keep him tethered to his father, at least until he is old enough to decide things for himself. I could not have chosen a better father-and-son team, than you and your son."

"Is something wrong, dad? Is there something wrong with me?" questioned Jake.

Charles hastened to reassure his son. "No, son, nothing's wrong. It's just that I'm a bit overwhelmed. This man has made you the most powerful being, indeed, the most powerful force of any kind on this planet. He has just imparted to me all of his knowledge and experience, and I do mean EVERYTHING, accumulated over his entire lifetime. The scientific breakthroughs we'll gain because of this, to say nothing that the world has just been given its greatest guardian-hero in over three-hundred years! And Jake, that hero is you! You can trust that I'll be right here to guide you, step-by-step, as you learn to master the skill of controlling your powers. When the time comes, we will introduce my baby boy to the world as 'Titan', its guardian and champion."

"Yes, Dad, Zhango-Rhe told me that I'm going to be guardian and that I should call myself 'Titan.'" But, you were right a minute ago when you said I don't really understand any of this."

"Jake…" Charles explained. "You're practically omnipotent."

"Omni… Ommi… Ommipo…" Jake stuttered. "Omni- What?"

"Jake… That means you're invincible!" his dad continued. "Nothing can hurt you! On the other hand, you'll be able to help a lot of people with these new and fantastic powers!"

"Powers?" the boy wondered. "What all can I do?" he prodded.

"You already used one of your powers when you ran outside at super speed, Jake! Nobody can run that fast; well besides you, that is! Not to mention, you have strength that is almost unlimited! You can lift incredible massive amounts of weight, and you can leap to incredible heights. With your powerful lung capacity and diaphragm strength you could generate hurricane-force winds!"

"You are practically the immovable force that the Myth and Legends speak about," continued Charles.

"I'm just a little kid. I don't know if Zhango-Rhe really made such a good choice. I guess the powers are kinda cool and all, but what if someone gets hurt?"

Charles looked deeply into his son's eyes, "Son, you've been chosen out of all the young boys in this world because of your heart; because Zhango-Rhe believes in you, and because I believe in you. Trust me son, once we've completed your training, you will believe in yourself too." Charles said as he attempted to reassure his young son.

"So, when do I start my training, daddy?" asked Jake as the excitement started to well up within him.

"Well, we've already started! You just learned your purpose! Now you need to learn how to control your powers!"

"Like I said, Jake, you are almost unstoppable, but even you have your limits. These limits may be difficult to understand, especially when you realize that you are not like all the other people on earth now. You've always been different, Jake; far more intelligent than average and exceptionally athletic. You have to understand that now your physiology has been so radically altered that your abilities, both physical and mental, are so amazing, that you are going to need to learn your body all over again.

"So, I can do anything?"

Charles laughed. "I wouldn't go quite that far, little man. Let's just say 'ALMOST' anything. One thing you need to be aware of, notice I said 'aware of,' not 'worried about.' I said nobody can hurt you and that's pretty much true except for one thing. You can encounter plutonium with no ill effect, even though its radiation is deadly to every other living thing on this planet. However, there is one thing you need to watch out for."

"What's that, Daddy?"

It's an element not natural to Earth. It is from Zhango-Rhe's home world, Zyrton. It was a rare element, even there, but its radiation is deadly to you. Once exposed to it, you will feel immediately weaker, and prolonged exposure will kill you. Fortunately, not only is the element exceedingly rare, you must be close to this element for it to have any ill effect, not less than fifty feet. Within about fifty feet, you will start to feel the effects. As you get closer, its increase in toxicity is very non-linear."

"Non-linear? What do you mean dad?" Jake asked.

"Yes, Jake. You know, like the Richter Scale." If you were twenty-five feet away from the Zyrtonium instead of fifty feet, its effect on you would not just be twice as strong; it would be more like ten times as strong. The effects increase at a more or less logarithmic rate as you approach it."

Jake nodded gravely. "OK, I get it now. Well, I'll try and make sure I never get near that stuff."

Charles nodded. "One good thing though. Once you get away from the material, assuming it hasn't killed you, you'd recover from its effects fairly quickly. Even if you were to have been knocked down by the Zyrtonium, your body would still be indestructible. So it's not like some bad guy could drop you with Zyrtonium and then shoot you with a pistol. Even if you were suffering from the effects of Zyrtonium poisoning, the bullets would still bounce off of you."

"Well, I hope I don't ever run across any of that stuff!" Jake sighed. "What happens if I do?"

"For now, I don't expect you have anything to worry about. You certainly wouldn't want to broadcast your weakness to the world. For now, Jake, this should be our little secret. As long as we keep this under wraps, you should be safe. Moreover, if you ever encounter this element, you'll know. Just get away from it as fast as you can. Remember, the radiation increases exponentially the closer you are to it. However, the effects of the radiation weaken substantially the further you get from the stuff. And, as I've said, this element is extremely rare here on Earth."

"OK, Dad. Well, so now what?"

In addition to your speed and great physical strength, there are your other powers. You have the power to project hi-energy, highly concentrated plasma blasts from your hands. These directed energy beams can be used as weapons or as tractor beams to lift and move, objects of any size and weight. Oh, and Jake, you should really like this. You can fly!"

Jake cocked his head, and raised an eyebrow skeptically. "What? No way, Dad! I don't have wings. So how am I supposed to get up in the air, dad? I don't have a rocket pack like they do on the cartoons! I thought that birds and airplanes are the only things that can fly? Well except for bugs" exclaimed a puzzled Jake.

Charles explained. "Well, strictly speaking, what you'll be doing isn't actually 'flying.' You're right. Flying requires a wing and in human cases, some form of propulsion. Actually, your ability to move through space at will, in any direction, up, down, left, right, forward, backward, at supersonic speeds, without walking or running, is actually auto-telekinesis. You will your body to move in a given direction, and your body simply moves in that direction. And you can stop on a dime!"

Jake still wasn't convinced. "Aw c'mon, Dad. You're telling me I can just wish myself into the air and..."

Even as Jake was speaking, his body lifted into the air and began to drift forward. "Whoa!" Jake exclaimed. As soon as he noticed he dropped like a stone, landing flat on his butt.

Charles rushed to his son's side. "Jake!" he cried in anguish. Charles asked, "Jake! Are you hurt?"

Jake looked up at his dad and flashed an ironic smile as he answered, "Not at all, dad."

Charles even laughed too, "Of course you're not hurt! You're indestructible now! Old habits die hard, son. Even though you're the most powerful being in this world, indestructible or not, you're still my little boy and it's hard not to worry."

Jake had always been a happy kid with a great sense of humor. Thanks to his upbringing by two loving and affirming parents that, without being egotistical in the least, he was secure enough in his sense of self that he was not afraid to laugh at himself. Although more than willing to laugh at his own, he would NEVER have laughed at another's misstep. Instead, he would rush to their side to offer his hand to help them to their feet. In that way, Jake was very much like his father.

Jake made multiple attempts to lift off the ground and touch back down. He would giggle uncontrollably every time he tried. Charles joined in the laughter too, as he watched his baby floating around the cavern like a giant puppet on a set of invisible strings.

After setting back down and gaining his bearings and getting the feel for his flight power under control, Jake stood to his feet, brushed himself off and said to his dad, "I think I got this now. Let's try that again."

This time he lifted off the floor of the cavern and hovered about six feet up. He and his dad locked eyes with each other, both completely in awe.

"Dad, dad, look I can't believe this! I'm flying, I am actually flying!"

Charles looked up at Jake as he corrected him. "Well, son, right now, actually. You're floating."

"Jake looked down at his dad with an all-boy, wide-mouth grin. "Well, let's see if we can get some forward motion into the mix."

The boy reoriented his body to horizontal, as if he were lying down in mid air and begun to move toward the cavern entrance.

Charles followed Jake on foot as far as the cavern entrance, but gave up the chase once Jake had left the confines of the cave, realizing that he could not possibly keep up with his ultra mobile son. As soon as Jake had cleared the cavern entrance, he shot forward like a rocket as he put on an aerobatic display of loops, dives and spirals that would have made the Blue Angles or the sport pilots at Oshkosh green with envy!

Charles just stopped and looked up and marveled at a flying boy who was his son, now flying in wide lazy circles above the large open field. He resolved to guide his son as Zhango-Rhe had instructed, to be a force for good for all humanity. Charles was understandably proud that it had been Jake, among all the possible choices in this world, which Zhango-Rhe had chosen to, endow with these marvelous powers.

Charles could hear his boy laughing and cheering as he was learning how to control his flight abilities. He thought back to the time when he was a young boy, how he had wished to have the ability to fly. Now he would get to live that dream, if only through his son.

"Whooohoooo!" Jake cheered, as he continued to spiral above the field, flying higher and higher. Eventually, he shot straight up, climbing high above the clouds, before coming and descending for a low pass right above his father's head.

"What's up daddy?" Jake cheered, as he flew over Charles' head, causing his hair to blow in his wake turbulence. Then Jake slowed to a halt, hovering in midair.

"That's great, Jake! Now, you need to land!" Charles said.

"Uh, land?" Jake asked a little disappointed. "Why would I want to land if I can fly?"

"Are you planning on remaining aloft for the rest of your life?" Charles asked him, as he folded his arms across his chest.

"Uhhh… That would be kinda hard to explain in school, huh?" Jake responded affably.

"Yes, it would…" Charles said with mock sternness. "Now, are you ready to come back down to earth?"

"Yes, Dad… I guess so…" the flying boy conceded. "So, now how do I land?"

"Well," Charles answered, "You've got the first part right. You're hovering in place. Just reorient your body from horizontal to vertical and just will yourself down to the ground."

Jake did has his father said, reorienting his body from horizontal to vertical. Then, gingerly, he descended earthward to a soft landing.

"There! I landed! I did it! Yay!!!" the boy cheered, as he raised his arms above his head. "I've just made my first flight!"

"Very good, Jake…"

Jake giggled. "Thanks for taking me through the approach and touchdown, Dad!"

"Give me a hug, champ…" Charles said, as he embraced his son. Presently, he felt his feet leave the ground.

"J-j-Jake! What are you doing?" Charles stuttered as he looked at his son in shock. As father and son embraced, Jake had unconsciously lifted them into a hover about one hundred feet above the ground.

"Oh, Daddy! I'm sorry! I didn't even know I was doing that. I'll hafta work on my control."

Charles agreed. "Yes, but in the meantime, why don't you work on getting us back down on the ground? I could break my neck if I fell down from here."

Jake murmured. "I'd NEVER let that happen, Daddy. You're not heavy at all and there's no way you COULD fall from here. Not as long as I've got a hold of you."

Charles answered, "OK, I trust you, Son." Charles said calmly. "But it's getting light now and people are gonna wonder why we're floating around up here."

"Oh, I guess I'd better set us down on the ground, huh?" Jake agreed.

"Yes. We need to keep this just be just between us for now. You need to master control of your powers."

After they had touched down, Charles continued, "I'll do all I can to help you with that. Zhango-Rhe has given me everything I need for that and more besides! But you must never permit anyone to observe you using your powers, at least not until you have mastered your control of them. And we need to have a disguise for you. Once you've mastered control of your powers and are ready to begin your work as 'Titan,' you will follow Zhango-Rhe's example, performing your powerful feats ONLY as Titan. You must never been seen using your powers as Jake. You might think it's cool now, showing your school mates and friends what you can do. Nevertheless, before too long, you'd regret it. You'd never have a minute's peace. There will be times when you'll just wanna be 'Jake' and lay your 'Titan' persona aside. But if your secret is blown, you'll never have that option ever again! The Paparazzi would be all over you, 24/7."

"Not to mention, they will bother you and mom to death too!" Jake added.

Charles nodded, gravely. "Yes there's that too."

"OK, Daddy. I'll be very careful," Jake promised.

"I know you will, Son. You'll be Titan when you wear that suit, when we get one made for you, that is. You'll always wear it, even under your street clothes, even when you go to school. That way, you can quickly assume your 'Titan' persona in case of an emergency. One challenge will be PE. We cannot have you changing clothes in the dressing room. No privacy there. We'll have to get a permission slip for you to be excused from PE. In addition, you cannot go out for sports. As powerful as you are now, you'd have an unfair competitive edge. There's not a professional athlete in this world who could challenge you in any sport. You are that powerful now."

Jake lowered his eyes, obviously disappointed. Gently, Charles asked his son, "What's wrong Jakie?" Charles only used 'Jakie' at their most intimate moments, usually when dealing with disappointments or hurts and such as that Charles used that name to tell his son, that it was alright for him to speak his mind.

Jake looked up at his dad. "It's not fair. I've always enjoyed sports, especially soccer and baseball, more than anything!"

Charles nodded. "I know that, and you've always been an especially gifted athlete. It is something that you will have to get used to. Nothing comes without a price Jake; at least nothing worthwhile. You'll feel left out sometimes, and it hardly seems fair that, even while you've become the guardian over all of us, in some ways now, you're an outsider. However, if I let you play, one of your friends could be very badly hurt. You wouldn't mean to hurt them, but in the moment, you might easily forget yourself. Would that be fair to your friends?"

Meekly, Jake answered. "No, Dad. I guess not."

"And with the physical advantages you have now, you could win every game all by yourself because you're so much stronger and faster than all the other boys your age. Would a game like that, where you have all the advantage, really give your opponents a fair and sporting chance? Would that be fair?"

Again, the boy answered. "No, Dad. It wouldn't be fair at all. It'd be like I was cheating."

"And you wouldn't wanna be a cheater, do you, Jake?"

This time, Jake's answer was more emphatic. "No Dad! If I hafta win like that, I would not want to play at all?"

Charles nodded, satisfied that his son understood.

"Jake, there are compensations. Not only can you help others with your powers, you can do things no one else could even dream. Once you've mastered your powers, you'll be able to fly yourself anyplace on Earth within a matter of minutes. The things you will see, the experiences you'll have," Charles chuckled softly. "In a way, I'm just a little jealous of you, little man."

Jake laughed too. The thought of his dad, the man he looked up to more than anyone in his life, being jealous of him struck him as funny. Father and son walked back to the tents together.

None of the other members of the archaeological expedition suspected anything unusual had happened.

Chapter 4

It was a beautifully hot summer day in the bustling metropolis of Boston Massachusetts. Everywhere you turned there were parks and playgrounds full with active children and adults. Some were at the lakes and swimming pools frolicking in the water, while others crowded around the little league baseball diamonds watching the under-ten team play America's favorite past time.

Today, however was a special day for one of the members of the under ten Boston Bobcats. Robby McCloud was about to celebrate his fifth birthday. His mother, Susan had set up a surprise birthday party for Robby after the game.

"Come on Beth, we have to get all the stuff set for Robby's party!" stated Susan McCloud.

"You got it Sue, I have the cake in my van, along with the plates and forks" replied Beth McCloud, Robby's aunt.

"Great, is Richie bringing the ice cream and presents?" asked Susan.

"Sure is, just got off the phone with him" responded Beth.

"Awesome!! I am so glad that Richie could make it, Robby is going to be a little disappointed that his father couldn't make it, so I am really glad that you, Petey, and Richie could make it," said Susan.

"We would not miss our favorite nephew's birthday. Not to mention Petey would not stop bugging us about it," chuckled Beth as she nodded over to the field at her blond headed son, standing next to a fiery red headed hotshot baseball player.

Robby McCloud was a very active young man. He was into everything at the tender age of five. In the fall, he played soccer. In the summer however, he played his favorite sport, baseball. All the dedication to sports showed on the young man's body. He did not have an ounce of fat upon his entire form. He was not the biggest kid, but he was strong as an ox and agile as his team's namesake, a bobcat.

This day, he knew, was going to be special. The team was going to be doing well from what his coach had told his mother. The other team was tough but did not have the heart that the Bobcats possessed. The whole team huddled up to listen to the coach give his "Go get 'em boys!" speech.

Robby loved the summer. He loved the smell of the fresh cut grass that adorned the baseball diamond. His brain electrified by the smells of the concession stand, with its peanuts, popcorn and fresh grilled hot dogs. This was his favorite time of the year and his favorite place to be.

"Hey!!!! Wake up baseball boy!" exclaimed Petey, as he stirred his cousin out of his daydream.

"Ha ha ha! Sorry Petey!" replied Robby as he came back to the here and now.

The other teams had cleared off the field, as Robby and the Bobcats took the field to warm up. Petey came out to practice with the team before first pitch. The coach made special arrangements to make that happen, because Petey loved baseball, and detested Tee Ball, played by the other kids his age.

Robby started to warm up by running in place, He continued by stretching thoroughly, carefully warming up his shoulders and rotator cuffs. Robby used his training, in knowing that if he did not take care of himself, he could be more prone to injuries. As Robby continued to warm up, his mentor and personal hero, Brandon Rathbone, looked on as his protégé continued his stretching and calisthenics. Brandon was the one instrumental in inspiring young Robby's interest in baseball. Brandon had taken Robby under his wing, coaching and encouraging him along the way.

Brandon stood about four feet eight inches tall. He possessed a lean, muscular, and athletic frame. Being just over a year older than Robby, he was a little taller and heavier than his protégé. He had sandy blonde hair and deep piercing brown eyes that could peer directly into a person's soul. He had a kind and warm demeanor about him. Brandon had taken Robby and his friend Derrick under his wing, but always felt closer to Robby. He and Robby were as close as brothers were.

"Good job kiddo, you have learned a lot over the past year," Brandon said as he smiled down at his young pupil.

"Thanks B. I owe it all to you, I never could've come this far without your help" replied Robby as he returned the smile.

Robby had always thought Brandon was the coolest kid on the planet. His best friend, Derrick, his cousin Petey and he were inseparable. Brandon was a year-and-a-half older than the other boys were. He was also an early bloomer. He had grown tall and relatively strong early in his life. His parents had encouraged his interest in sports. Katherine, his mother, was always pushing him to stay physically active instead of playing video games, like the mass populous of children these days. They had strictly rationed his television and internet time, insisting he spend his leisure time outside with other kids in games and competitive sports. As a result, he was exceptionally strong and agile for his age. All the kids in the neighborhood looked up to Brandon. But to Robby, Brandon was more than just an older friend. He was more like an older brother. Brandon returned Robby's affection regarding him almost as a younger version of himself.

"Pay attention Petey. See how Robby stretches, warming up his muscles before the game?" This is really important to avoid injuries, Brandon explained as he patted Robby's cousin on the shoulder.

Petey watched in awe as his favorite person in the whole world, his cousin, prepared himself for the game. From the very beginning, Petey had been an avid fan of Robby's short but very successful little league baseball career. Robby and his team mates practiced every day after school. Petey looked up to his cousin both for his natural talent, his serious dedication and iron willed self-discipline. He had sensed that Robby was an exceptional child long before even his own parents.

While warm ups were underway, Richard McCloud sneaked into the ballpark with ice cream and birthday gifts. He made his way over to his wife, greeting her with a kiss. He placed Robby's Birthday presents in Susan and Beth's care, as he quickly ran the Rocky Road ice cream over to the concession stand before it could melt.

The opposing team took the field to warm up with the Bobcats. Even though they were heated rivals, or as heated as an athletic rivalry could be among five and six-year-olds, they nevertheless conducted themselves with respect and sportsmanship.

Robby, although he was one of the smallest kids on the field, at age five, was best at batting, and fielding. The umpires took the field and called the coaches to the mound to decide who was going to be up at bat and who was fielding. The coin was tossed, and the Bobcats took to the dugout since they made the choice to be up at bat.

Derrick Malone, Robby's best friend on the team was always the first to bat. He stepped up to the plate. The ball was pitched to him with a slight curve. He swung the bat with all he had.

"STRIKE ONE!!!" The umpire yelled from behind home plate.

"COME ON DERRICK!!!!" screamed Robby at the top of his lungs.

"Yeah COME ON DERRICK!!" Petey followed, as he yelled encouragement to his cousin's team mate.

"Derrick! You better take this guy out man, he is nowhere near as good as you and Robby are, you keep your eye on his shoulders, watch his movements" bellowed Brandon.

Derrick gritted his teeth, gripped the bat, and stared the pitcher down. The pitch was thrown, straight and fast. Derrick coiled like a snake and swung the bat with all the power he could muster in his little body, and the reward was a straight line drive to earn him a second base run.

All the parents and other spectators cheered. They were on their feet for this six-year-old dynamo. With lightening speed, Derrick sprinted to second base. He bent over at the waist resting both hands on his knees to catch his breath and regain his strength.

"Way to go Derrick" cheered Brandon through the fence, congratulating him on his two-base hit.

"Now go and get 'em Red" Brandon called to Robby as he gave the red-headed baseball phenomenon a stern look of encouragement.

Robby grabbed his batting helmet and strutted out into the bullpen. He took a few practice swings and walked over to the plate where he took a few more warm up swings. The pitching coach knew this was going to be trouble. Robby was well known in the league, not only for his athletic conditioning, but also for the fact that he had never been struck out. He had never had a strike called on him. He would swing and connect with some of the most improbable pitches ever. What irked this thirty something pitching coach little-league dad was that his pitcher was about to be out psyched by this five-year-old phenomenon.

Robby glanced at Derrick and gave him the thumbs up sign for a job well done. He stared down the opposing team's pitcher and concentrated as hard as he could. For some reason it was as if Robby could sense what the coach was going to throw at him. He allowed a wry smile to play across his lips, confident that he was about to best his opposing team's best pitcher.

The ball was thrown rather hard by little league standards. This kid really had a rocket-arm on his young frame. That did not faze Robby McCloud. He ground his heel into the dirt and swung the bat with devastating accuracy.

"HOME RUN!!!!" The announcer yelled from the Little League press box.

"MOM, Robby did it! He hit his first Homer of the game!" squealed Petey.

"ALRIGHT SON, WAY TO GO!" Susan yelled her approvals to her son as he and Derrick rounded the bases.

"Way to go, Robby!" added Beth and Richard in unison.

"That's my boy!" yelled Brandon.

Brandon smiled, beaming with pride as he watched his best friend round the bases. He scanned the ball field stands, noticing that everybody was on their feet for this young man. Brandon's pride originated from the time he spent teaching the finer points of baseball to Robby. Brandon was so proud of Robby's accomplishments. He watched him grow as a player and a friend.

As Robby crossed home plate, the scorecard changed to two to zero, in favor of the Boston Bobcats. His entire team was waiting to heft the red headed bomber onto their shoulders in congratulations.

"Wow, what a great birthday so far" thought the fiery-headed youth.

The rest of the game, the Bobcats maintained a marginal lead. It was the last inning and the opposing team had caught up with the bobcats. Robby climbed out of the dugout and faced the pitcher. He knew that there was something inside him that would help him beat this person one last time. He smiled at the pitcher and looked back at Petey.

"This one is for you Petey, It's my birthday, but this is your home run," Robby cheered confidently.

Robby knew that he was going to hit the home run he had just honored his cousin with the dedication. It was as if he could read the thoughts of the opposing team's pitcher.

"He is gonna throw a curve ball at me! How am I hearing this?" wondered the cardinal-haired youth.

The pitch was thrown, and just as Robby had known it would be; a curve ball. He was ready, and put the bat to the ball.

"ANOTHER HOME RUN FOR NUMBER 18 ROBBY MCCLOUD!!!" The announcer bellowed.

"HOLY COW ROBBY!!!! HOW DID YOU KNOW!!!" yelled Petey.

"WOW kid I never thought that you would have gotten this good! Two homers in a row!" screamed Brandon.

The whole Bobcats dugout and fan section were on their feet cheering their hero. Little Robby McCloud had pulled out the win for the Bobcats.

Robby's mother, aunt and uncle, and Cousin Petey all stormed the field, hoisted the red headed baseball star onto their shoulders. They paraded him around the field as onlookers applauded the kid's effort. Brandon kept his distance as he stood in the shadows and watched his "little brother" enjoy his accolades.

Finally, the team cleared the field. Robby and his family made their way over to the picnic area of the ballpark. Robby sensed that something was up with his family.

"Hey, what is with the surprise party?" asked the inquisitive youth.

"How do you know that we were planning a surprise party for you Robby?" asked Susan.

"Just call it a hunch," Robby grinned as he nudged his mother in the ribs. "Today is my birthday ya know?" Robby continued with a smile.

All the family and friends gathered around the table for the cake and ice cream. Robby was so happy, yet something was not right with him.

"Hey you alright little bro?" asked Brandon as he glanced at the red headed birthday boy.

Brandon, Robby, and Derrick could read each other like books. Brandon, being the eldest of the three, knew something was not right with his "little brother". He kept a keen and concerned eye on Robby as he awaited his response.

"Just not feeling too well man" responded Robby wearily.

He looked around as if someone was talking to him. No one was directly speaking to him, but he could hear them talking about him. The "sound" was becoming more than he could handle.

While his mother was busy getting the cake and presents set up, Robby politely excused himself to the restroom. As he quickly made his way away from the crowd and rounded the corner, Robby doubled over in pain. He grabbed his head and fell to the ground.

"Unngghhh!" he grunted as he fell.

He laid there for about a minute. It sounded as though twenty people were babbling at him at once. He could barely make out what any of them were saying, he just knew he wanted it to stop.

As he sat up, one of the voices inside his head broke through the massive sea of nonsense. It sounded like his cousin Petey. He seemed concerned, wondering where his hero had gone off too. He also sensed that he was slowly approaching him. He panicked!

"Oh man! I can't let Petey see me. Not like this, I need to get to the bathroom!" Robby thought to himself.

In a split second, Robby McCloud found himself surrounded by a cloud of mist. Shortly, as the mist cleared, he found he managed to teleport into the boys' restroom. He had not made his way there on his own, or so he thought. One moment he had been just outside the restroom. The next moment, he was inside. Robby stood perplexed, thinking of how this could have happened.

"What the heck?" Robby exclaimed.

He was an avid comic book fan. He murmured, "I did NOT just TELEPORT myself into this bathroom! That did NOT just happen! There is NO way I just did that! No Way!"

Robby slowly made his way to the sinks and reached out for the handle. He opened up the faucet, running the cold water on his hands. He then slashed the cold liquid on his face, in a vain attempt to clarify his present situation.

"Well at least I am not hearing all those voices inside my head, anymore, I can sort of make the....." he trailed off.

Robby stopped dead in his tracks when he realized that was he was doing was keying into everyone's thoughts and feelings. He stood there looking into the mirror, dumbfounded at what he just realized.

"I can read minds? That is how I knew what the pitcher was tossing my way. It has to be," Robby murmured aloud.

Worried, Robby thought to himself, "I gotta try this stuff; I have to know what is happening to me!"

As the boy faced the bathroom mirror, he began to concentrate as hard as he could on his mother. His emerald green eyes slowly began to darken until nothing but onyx black was visible, no whites or the familiar emerald green. Robby bolted upright with a huge startle as his eyes shifted colors, but he continued to concentrate.

"Mom is wondering where I ran off to," he realized.

Robby did not want to worry his mother. He felt a sharp pain in his stomach as he began to realize that his absence at the party was causing her, and the rest of his family concern. He, again, realized that he was feeling something from another person.

He closed his eyes and concentrated on teleporting back to the place where he had come from. His eyes remained black as coal, as a cloud of warm mist surrounded the delighted red headed youth.

Within another split second Robby McCloud was standing back, where he had began his journey of self-realization. He remained entranced in thought. He had read about this in his comic books. There was a word for people with powers like this, "MUTANT." He realized that in the comics some people thought of mutants as heroes, while others feared and even hated them.

Robby made a crucial decision. He could not tell anyone what was happening to him. He did not fully understand it himself. He hated the fact that he was going to have to keep something from his parents. It hurt even more to have to hide this from Petey, Derrick and especially Brandon. All he knew was, he could read a person's thoughts, feel a person's emotions, and teleport from place to place with a mere thought. He was worried what people would think about him if they found out.

"I have read all about this in my comics," thought Robby solemnly.

"I am kind of scared, but it's also kinda cool!" he mused.

Robby made his way back to rejoin his family and friends. He concentrated on keeping the voices in his head quiet so he could get through the rest of his birthday party without going insane. By the time he'd returned to the party, he'd mastered control of his mind reading power.

He deployed a filter to keep out the unwanted mental noise.

Robby's friends brought the gifts up one by one for the birthday boy to open. He greeted them all with a smile as he sensed their sincere feelings of admiration and affection for him.

The last gift was from his aunt, uncle and Cousin Petey. All three walked up and handed him a manila envelope, and a box. Surreptitiously, Robby peered into their minds and hearts. He felt the love that they had for him and he sensed how much Petey looked up to him.

"There ya go champ, I hope that you like what we got ya." said his uncle Richard.

"Thanks Uncle Richie, I am sure I will, especially if you guys got it for me," replied Robby with a sly grin.

With his "scan" of their minds, Robby had known what his gifts would be. There would be no more surprising this young man. He chuckled to himself, thinking that his coolest birthday present were his special "gifts".

He tore open the box first. He looked up with feigned amazement in his eyes. His aunt and uncle had given him a very expensive pair of baseball cleats. These were the top of the line and he could not have been happier.

"Thanks Aunt Beth! Thanks Uncle Richie!" He cheered as he hugged them both appreciatively.

"You're welcome sport!" responded Richard as he ruffled the hair of his only nephew.

Peter walked up to his cousin and draped his arm around him. He patted the envelope on the table.

"Ya might wanna open my present next cuz!" giggled Petey.

Robby slowly and methodically tore the flap of the envelope open. He had already known what it was, but could not let on and ruin the thrill of the surprise. He slowly pulled a comic book from its confines.

"WOW!" This is Marvel Man # 2. This is where Marvel Man learns how to control his mind powers! Robby exclaimed.

"See Mom! I told you he would like it!" squealed Petey.

Robby looked over at his cousin and could not help but laugh to himself. He thought that this issue, out of any issue, could prove to be very helpful to him. After all, he is trying to learn how to control his own abilities as well.

Brandon coolly walked over to Robby with a box in his hand. He wrapped it in a paper bag. Brandon had never been one for flash and flair when it came to gift giving. He was all heart when it came to the gift itself though.

"Here ya go little brother. This is something that I think you will really love "smiled Brandon.

Robby quickly tore the paper open on the small box. He pulled out a silver beaded chain, and a metallic dog tag. His eyes lit up when he saw what was on it. He quickly put it on and slowly made his way over to Brandon.

"Brandon, you gave me your dog tags, the ones that your dad had made for you. That is so cool," said Robby amiably as he hugged his mentor.

"Dude you are so worth it little brother" replied Brandon as he returned the embrace.

"Are you ok? Brandon asked.

Robby sighed. "Not really, I'm not feeling well at all," Robby replied as he turned to glance back at his mother.

"Son, are you ready to go home now? You've had a very big day with the game and the party. Maybe it's time for you to call it a day?" asked Susan.

"Yeah mom, I am pretty tired and my head kinda hurts" Robby answered with a sigh.

Everyone was having fun, and he hated to cut it short. Nevertheless, he desperately needed to get away. His control over this new mental "gift" was still very tenuous and his ability to stave off the voices had started to waver. He wanted to get home and read the comic that his cousin Petey had given him in hopes to gain the knowledge of how Marvel Man handled his new mental powers. Maybe that would give him some clues how to deal with his.

Susan loaded herself and her son into the van and headed for home. Robby knew that she was worried. He could read what she was feeling only. He could not sense what she was thinking for some reason. He opted to ease her worry.

"Mom I am sorry. I just have a little headache and I did not want people to keep fussing over me," Robby explained. "If I can just lie down in my room for awhile, I'm sure I'll be just fine."

"Kid you have to be a mind reader, I was just thinking of why you wanted to leave so early," grinned Susan.

Robby, glancing over at his mother, had a frightful feeling, creep into his soul at his mother use of the term "mind reader." He worried that she might have guessed the truth about his abilities. He scans his mother's mind. She had a feeling that she was joking, much to Robby's relief. Little had she realized how close to being very correct, she had been.

Chapter 5

Charles and Jake remained at the excavation site for one more day, Charles wrapping up with the onsite crew and Jake staying as close by as he could without interfering with his father's work. Other kids might have been inclined to run off and play, away from the work of these grownups, but Jake had always been keenly interested in his father's work and dearly loved passing the time with his dad.

That evening, their last evening at the site, they turned in for the night. However, as Zhango-Rhe had predicted, Jake no longer needed more than thirty minutes to an hour of sleep. After Jake was sure the other members of the archaeological expedition were asleep in their tents, he slipped out of his sleeping bag and stepped outside. Quietly, he made his way to the edge of camp, carefully surveyed the area to make sure no one could see him. Once he was satisfied that the coast was clear, he lifted off the ground and took to the sky. With his enhanced vision, he had no trouble discerning the terrain features. From an altitude of about 500 feet above ground level, he took careful note of them, making sure he would be able to find his way back to camp. Then he soared skyward, leveling off at about eighteen thousand feet above sea level. He scanned the horizon in all directions, searching for aircraft. He saw an eastbound Southwest Airlines flight passing overhead at twenty-three thousand feet MSL (mean sea level). Aside from that one aircraft, there was no aviation traffic for miles in any direction.

Jake flashed over the horizon, headed due west. As he was passing over the tiny community of Diablo Rojo, Arizona, a faint cry attracted his attention. He slowed to a stop, using his super sensitive night and distance vision, searching for the source of the cry. He saw it, a cat, or more accurately, a kitten. He was perched on a tree limb, high above the ground, obviously terrified. His meowing was the most pitiful cry Jake had ever heard.

He streaked earthward and slowed to a hover, arriving alongside the kitten, a red tabby. Jake grinned, "Hello there, little fella! Looks like you could use a hand." The kitten answered with a tentative "meow." As Jake reached out for the kitten, the little animal leapt right into his arms. Jake giggled.

"Whoa there, little guy! You sure are ready to be rescued, aren't you?" As the kitten settled into Jake's arms, he began to rattle, purring contentedly. Jake had always had a special way with animals and tonight was no exception. Softly Jake landed on the lawn at the base of the tree. Presently, he heard a voice, a human voice this time. It was a little girl, she was calling, "Jake! Jake! Where are you Jakie?"

Jake wondered, "It's a girl! How does she know my name?"

He saw the little girl trotting down the street, flashlight in hand, calling out his name. Suddenly, she spied Jake, still holding the kitten in his arms! She trotted alongside. "There you are, Jake! I've been looking all over for you, you silly cat!"

Then it hit him. The kitten's name was Jake, too! She spoke to Jake, the boy this time. "Oh thank you! You found my cat. I've been looking all over for him! Where did you find him?"

Jake smiled as he handed Jake, the kitten, over to the little girl. "Well, I guess in away Jake found me! He jumped right into my arms!"

"The little girl giggled. Why am I not surprised? Jake never met a stranger. He loves up on everybody. The little guy loves to roam too. We try to keep him inside, but he got out. And I've been looking all over for him."

Jake smiled again. "Well, all's well that ends well. But, gee, you shouldn't be out her all by yourself at this hour. Where are you parents?"

The girl let a crossed look spread across her face as she glanced over at Jake. "Me? What about you? Where are your parents?" she questioned.

"Well," Jake answered, "They're around. I am just glad that I could get your cat back to you safe and sound. C'mon, I'll walk you home."

As they walked, the little girl chattered away. She finally decided to introduce herself. "I'm Genny, what's your name?"

Jake answered as he laughed. "You wouldn't believe me if I told you."

"Try me." Genny answered.

"Well, um, no foolin', my name is, Jake! When I heard you calling, at first I thought you were calling out to ME! And I was wondering, 'how does this girl know my name?'"

They both laughed. Jake asked. "So how did little Jakie here get his name?" As he spoke, Jake reached out and stroked the kitten's head, just behind his ears. The kitten turned his head and rubbed his whiskers against Jake's fingers. "My uncle's name is Jake. He gave him to me so I named Jakie after my Uncle Jake! I see he likes you, the cat I mean, not my Uncle Jake, even though I'm sure he would if he met you."

They arrived at Genny's house. She smiled at Jake, "Well, this is my stop. Thank you again, Jake. I guess I'd better get inside and, come to think of it, what're you doing out this late?"

Jake grinned, "Let's just say I couldn't sleep. Just thought I'd take a walk but you're right, I guess I better get back. It was nice meeting you! Oh, and you too, Jakie," Jake stroked the kitten once again.

Genny asked, "I've never seen you around here and we know everybody around here. So where are you staying?"

Jake had not anticipated this question. However, he had spied a Motel 6 alongside the highway as he had descended to little Jakie's rescue.

"Oh! We're just passing through town. We're staying at the motel on the highway. We're leaving first thing tomorrow morning."

Genny sighed. "Aw, that's too bad. So I guess I won't be seeing you again."

Jake smiled. "Oh I don't know, Genny. Maybe we just might meet up again." He flashed and even broader all boy grin. "And if I have anything to say about it, we WILL meet again."

Genny giggled as she dropped her gaze. "I hope so, Jake. Thanks again for finding Jakie. Good night."

Genny turned and made her way to the door to her house. She slipped inside, quietly trying to avoid discovery by her parents. She spun on her heel, waving out at Jake and silently closed the door.

Jake turned and walked back to the street. Smiling, he thought of the first good deed that he just did. He thought back to what Zhango-Rhe had said. The thought of no deed would be neither too small nor too large for Titan to handle.

Cautiously he looked around and once again made certain that no one could see him, he took to the sky. Letting the wind whip his cropped mop of golden brown hair, he aimed his body, out of memory, back towards his father and the dig site.

Chapter 6

Later that night, as Robby lay in his bed, the headache that had plagued him all afternoon began to subside. He wondered how it was that the intruding thoughts that had tormented him had abated, leaving him in peace.

"It's quiet, I wonder if it's because I am not around a lot of people? That has got to be reason" Robby thought to himself.

He sat up suddenly as he contemplated the prospect of telling his parents about his newfound abilities. How would they react? Would they accept him?

The front door opened to the McCloud home, announcing that Bob McCloud, Robby's father, had come home from work. Robby knew even without reading his thoughts that he had been disappointed that he had been obliged to miss his son's birthday party that afternoon.

He overheard him greeting his mother. Then he heard his father's thoughts. More accurately, sensed his father's visceral mistrust of mutants and aliens. Heartsick, Robby faced the hard truth; his parents' love was NOT unconditional. At least that was the feeling that he was gleaning off his father. They would never accept a mutant as their son. He must bury his secret, never ever trusting it to anyone. Just like his comic hero Mr. Amazing.

His father had hidden the truth from his family for years. He had told his parents, wife, and son that he worked for the FBI, in the international computer crimes division. When in all actuality, he worked for a clandestine group that monitored mutant and alien activity in the United States.

Robby felt, what he thought was his father's hatred and mistrust of the beings that he policed. The thought of what his father might do to him were he to discover that his only son was a mutant made his blood run cold.

He heard his father's footsteps on the stairs. He quickly rolled over and played possum, feigning sleep, hoping to avoid having to face his father who would possibly hate him if he knew the truth. Bob opened the door to Robby's room, seeing his son apparently asleep. He looked over at him and knew that he was not about to let his son's birthday go by without a good tiding from him. He sat at the foot his bed and gently shook his son, attempting to wake him.

"Robby, hey Robby. Wake up champ" Bob said tenderly.

"Hmmm MMPPHH. Oh hey dad" replied Robby feigning a groggy mumble.

The mutant boy rolled over to face his father. He looked into the eyes of this man who had loved him so dearly but who would surely hate him if he knew what his son truly was, a despised mutant freak.

"I am so sorry that I couldn't make it to your game or your party, champ," confessed Bob.

"Daddy I understand, your work is important," replied Robby sheepishly.

"Nothing is more important to me than you or your mother son. I just could not get away from the project that I was working on," said Bob.

"Daddy I understand, and thank you for the presents that you and mom got me." Robby forced a smile.

"You are so welcome, son" smiled Bob.

The man reached down and embraced his son. Robby knew that his father loved him more than anything. It would devastate his family if the secret of his abilities ever got out. He feared that the hatred that his father felt for "his kind" would most likely outweigh the love for his son. He hoped that he was mistaken, but he was not willing to risk everything on that slender hope.

Chapter 7

The next morning, Tim drove Charles and Jake to the airport. Charles left the recovery of the alien artifacts, including Zhango-Rhe's spacecraft in Tim's capable hands. Jake mused at the irony. He would be flying home to Washington, DC in a commercial jet when he could easily have flown himself and his father home in less than half the time and at no cost.

As they winged their way eastward, Jake looked forward to the time that he could take to the skies again without the feeling of being stuck inside a metal tube. He understood the necessity of making this flight via commercial air, but understanding the need certainly did not mean he had to like it.

Charles and Jake arrived in the Dulles International Airport main terminal. They made their way to the baggage claim area, where they collected their luggage. Quickly they made the trek to the long term parking garage and their awaiting vehicle. They loaded up and drove home. The busy cityscape was a comforting sight to both of the Knight men. Charles breathed a sigh of relief at the realization that he was finally home.

Most of the way home, neither Jake nor Charles spoke much. "Jake, we have to tell your mother about all of this," Charles said as he broke the eerie silence.

Jake nodded. "How do you think we should break it to her?"

"Well I am not sure son, but no matter how she takes it, we have to tell her," reinforced Charles.

They pulled into the driveway in front of the house. Charles jumped out of the van, dashed to the house. He had already spoken to Nancy on the phone and let her know that they were on the way home. She was expecting them to arrive and was impatiently waiting on them.

Charles made his way to the front door, reached for the handle, only to have the door opened before he could touch it. Nancy reached out and wrapped herself in a warm embrace with her husband. She kissed him softly and hugged him again. Nancy pulled away and began to look around the yard and at the van.

"Where's Jake?" she asked him.

"He's coming with the luggage," Charles explained.

"What? Well don't you think you'd better get over there and give him a hand? How is an almost-six-year-old gonna carry all that luggage into the house by himself?" she laughed. "I know you're glad to see me and all, but get out there and help your son, you beast!"

"Naw," Charles answered. "I think Jake can handle it."

Puzzled, Nancy looked at her husband. He grinned, "Just wait and watch."

Shortly, Jake stepped around the back of the van, carrying two huge suitcases, one in each hand. He handled them as if they were empty. He gingerly set the suitcases down on the sidewalk, looked up at his mother, and smiled.

"Hi mom!" he cheered. "We're back!"

"Jake what happened to you? You look so different!" Nancy gasped, as she caught the first glimpse of her phenomenally transformed son. She stood in amazement as she continued to look her son over from head to toe. She thought back to when Jake started his vacation as a skinny kid. This is not the small child she remembered, that stood before her. Jake's face was starring at her from a muscle-bound body.

Charles, sensing her mood swing, proceeded to explain to her how Jake had met Zhango-Rhe at the dig site, and that what they had unearthed was in fact an alien spacecraft. He continued the explanation with the change that had taken place in their son. Charles told her about the powers that Jake now possessed and the mission that Zhango-Rhe bestowed upon him.

"Look at you! You're a little muscle-man!" Nancy gasped, as she bent down to give Jake a hug. "You've grown so much and you've gotten so heavy! Your shoulders are so wide now! Look at your arms! Look at your chest! You're like a little gymnast!"

Charles nodded. "But unlike a gymnast, he can fly, not just high jump, I mean FLY, literally, like a bird or a plane! He can run with lightning like speed, and he can see in the dark," Charles explained. "No weapon can harm him, he can fire directed energy bursts from his hands and there is no practical limit to his physical strength!"

Charles explained that the alien Zhango-Rhe, or rather his computer-generated hologram, had lured Jake into the cavern to his spacecraft and passed the powers that he had in life to their boy. "He has made Jake Earth's 'planetary guardian,' the role he had about three-hundred years ago. He is long dead although he stored a copy of his conscious essence in the memory core of his spacecraft computer just before he died. Zhango-Rhe's powers didn't grant him immortality, nor have they made Jake immortal. Jake can expect to live a normal, or perhaps slightly above normal life span. The fortunate thing is that it's highly unlikely he could ever die of something other than old age."

Jake had waited patiently through his father's explanations up until now. However, he interrupted his dad's narrative as he leapt off the floor into his startled mother's arms, wrapping her up in a loving embrace, giving her a powerful but gentle hug. He bussed her lightly on the cheek as he said, "I missed you, Mom!"

She responded, "Well, my little muscle-man, I've missed you too!"

The love shared in this family was defiantly universal. There was no guessing that they all loved one another unconditionally. There had always been some kind of soothing warmth that emanated from the Knight family, and all who had the pleasure of knowing them could agree with those feelings.

Charles explained to Nancy, "I'll have to convert the basement into a lab for me and workout and training facility for Jake. Zhango-Rhe has given me the knowledge of Zyrtonian technology that I need to devise physical strength and agility training devices for Jake, suited to his preternatural strength, as well as metering equipment that will enable me to monitor and chart his progress. I should be able to fashion these devices from off the shelf items from electronics and hardware stores. One of Zhango-Rhe's more simplistic devices is a computerized garment synthesizer. Just think about this one, honey. No more buying school clothes for him anymore. It can even create imitations of the clothes that you have been drooling over for years. The most important thing about this device is that it will create a nearly indestructible uniform for Jake to wear when he is Titan. It takes the stress off you having to create a costume for the world's greatest hero after he destroys it in his little romps as Titan!"

"I can't believe this, our son a super-hero?" Nancy exclaimed, as she stood there trying with all her might to process this news. She was still in shock by all the changes that were taking place. "That sounds dangerous Charles! He could get hurt!"

"No way, Mom!" Jake exclaimed. I'm nearly indestructible! And I'm super-strong!" Jake said, as he hovered three feet above the ground. "See? I can even fly!"

Nancy's mouth dropped wide open as she witnessed her five-year-old son floating three feet above living room floor. She continued to stare at her son as he hovered, trying to ease her unsettling mind.

"Look, mom! Watch this! I can lift the sofa!" Jake exclaimed, as he drifted over to the couch, settling alongside and easily hefting one end single-handed. He positioned himself under the sofa and hefted the far end toward the ceiling. Nancy sputtered, utterly speechless at this amazing feat of strength by her six-year-old son!

In a quavering, tremulous voice, Nancy demanded, "Charles, what have you done to our son? He's, he's..."

Nancy's voice trailed off. Then, to herself, she murmured, "He, he isn't human anymore. My baby, my baby is a ..." Her voice trailed off again.

She dropped to the floor and wept.

Jake was mortified. Never before had he witnessed his mother cry. In all actuality, he could not recall a time that he had seen either of his parents shed a tear. He crept up to his mom, reaching out to touch her. In this solemn moment, Jake was not "Titan." He was just Jake, a little boy reaching out to comfort his mother. His mother flinched at his touch. She had not meant to recoil at the feeling of Jake touching her, but she had. Jake felt as if a knife had been plunged into his heart and he felt his own tears welling up. He choked down a sob and held his ground. He reached out again, touching his mother's cheek. With his hand, he turned his mother's face to his. Gently but firmly, he spoke. "Mom, I am NOT a monster."

Nancy started to protest that was not what she had meant to say but Jake cut her off.

"No, Mom. It's OK. I know this is an awful lot to take in. I mean, what mom has her kid come home and lift the sofa clean off the living room floor or levitate off the ground or weird, freaky stuff like that?" Jake ventured a wry smile. "You can honestly say that you are the only one Mom!"

Jake continued, "In a lotta ways, things will never be the same. My life is going a different way now than I guess we all thought it would. But the things that really matter haven't changed; not one bit. I am still your son." Jake pointed to Charles. "He's still my dad. And you're still my Mom. And I love you both, more than anything. And Mom, I promise I will never, ever do anything with these powers that you could not be proud of. I really need for you to know that."

Nancy sniffed and then reached out to hug her son. "I know, baby. I know. I'm sorry I made such a scene like this. I shouldn't have."

Jake laid his finger to his mother's lips. "Shhh. I said It's OK. It's OK!" He kissed her cheek and then looked up at his dad.

Charles was next to tears himself. Everyone thought Jake to be more mature than his age. However, this display of understanding and sensitivity from his son made a firm believer out of Charles that his young hero was defiantly growing up fast. He doubted he would ever be more proud of his son than he was right then. He did not say anything to Jake, but father and son communicated with their eyes. Jake backed away from his mom as Charles stepped in, sat down next to her, hugging her tight.

He released Nancy from his embrace and looked into her eyes. "Our little boy of all the little boys in this world has been chosen to fill this role of guardian of Earth. This happened for a reason! He is a magnificent child. Even with all his gifts and a terrible burden he bears, he's still our little boy. Only now, he needs us more than ever! Nancy we are about to embark upon the most amazing life adventure imaginable. I know this has come to us all of a sudden but Jake's destiny is really our destiny too. The world is indeed fortunate to have our dear son as its guardian. We've been blessed with the incredible honor of raising him to manhood, to prepare him for his role as guardian of this world.

Nancy knitted her brow as she answered her husband. "I want to be a good mother. I've always tried to be a good mother, to protect Jakie and to meet his needs the way a mother does. But what does Jake need from me now? He is so powerful. Compared to him, I am nothing!

Jake interrupted. "Mom! You are not 'nothing'! I may be able to fly and I know I'm strong and all that. But I am not all grown up yet. I'm still just a kid. I can't do this without you!"

Nancy didn't answer in words. She just hugged her son, holding onto him as he relaxed into her embrace, hugging her as tight as he dared. Nancy felt a slight release in emotions as she held onto Jake, as if clinging to him for dear life.

Nancy looked up at her husband. "How can we do right by our son as his parents now? We know nothing about raising a boy with powers like Jakie's."

"Don't worry about that, Nancy, I have been given a full run down on Jake's strength and powers and believe me… He is strong! There are very few things in this world that can hurt him right now…" he assured his wife. "Our little boy has truly become a 'Titan' in every way!"

"I know…" Nancy said, as she turned back to her beloved son and walked up to Jake, who was still floating in the middle of the living room. She reached out and passed her hand over his arms and chest. "And you're right, Jakie, no matter how strong or powerful you've become, you'll always be my little boy…"

"I love you, mommy…" Jake murmured, as gently he drifted into Nancy's arms and embraced her.

"I love you too, my little Titan," Nancy said to her son.

The family hugged and spent the rest of the evening watching TV, before they went to bed.

Chapter 8

Jake slept in his room that night for the first time since receiving his powers from Zhango-Rhe. It was that first night that he awoke and realized that he had been floating in his sleep. He mused, "I gotta get control of this. If I ever spend the night with friends, this secret is blown. I'll ask Dad about it in the morning. I sure hope I don't hafta sleep with a boat anchor tied to my ankle!"

The next morning, Charles and Jake set to work on the basement lab and training facility. First came a few trips to a nearby electronics store, the hardware store, and an office supply store. When they arrived home, Charles backed the family van into the garage, clicked the remote to close the garage door and pressed the button to release the rear hatch. He and Jake got out and stepped to the rear of the van. Charles started to reach into the van to pick up some of their purchases when Jake gently grasped his elbow. "No Dad, I got this."

Within minutes, Jake had unloaded all the heavy essential items of the day. Charles had set up half the basement as storage for the supplies. Charles instructed Jake to construct a partition designed for the sole purpose of concealing the rear half of the basement. It would not fool a professional carpenter, but to a passing glance, the partition would certainly go unnoticed.

After the secret interior entrance had been fabricated, Charles and Jake began the delicate process of building the machines that Zhango-Rhe placed inside his head. Charles knew that no matter how strong Jake would get, he could always use training to make him stronger and faster. The very first machine constructed was one that Jake would become overly accustomed with. This machine was an electromagnetic powered weight-training station. The main function of this machine was to help Jake increase his mind-blowing strength to new heights.

After father and son had worked side by side for the better part of four days, the "Sanctum" was ready. Every security measure was intact. The monitoring and control station powered on and registered operational. The satellite-imaging center came on line without a single glitch.

The time had come for Jake to begin his official stint as Earth's Guardian. Charles had prepared the device that he had informed his wife of as he led Jake to the replicator and began passing on instructions to his son.

"Son, the device will perform a full head to toe body scan. We'll start with you facing the machine. The replicator will direct you when to turn. Just follow the instructions from the device. Once the scan is complete, the replicator will fashion a uniform for you to wear as Titan. You can chose your own design and color scheme once your measurements have been take by the scanner. Or you could leave it all up to your subconscious mind. The scanner will read and take into consideration what your inner most thoughts have to say regarding the uniform's appearance."

Jake thought briefly, weighing the two options carefully within his mind. He decided quickly to let the machine dig into his inner thoughts in order to fashion just the right look for Titan. As the machine initiated its initial sweep of Jake's frame and mind, several images flashed across the monitors. Images of Zhango-Rhe and what he must have look like in life. Images jetted across the screen of the cavern where the archeological had found the space ship. Quick images of the design from the hull of the spacecraft repeated one after the other. Suddenly, and without any warning, the machine ceased its activities and revealed the findings of young Jake's mind.

Standing on the computer monitor, was an image, not of Jake, but of Titan. Jake smiled as he looked at his picture staring back at him. He was adorned in a tight red bodysuit, accented by blue trunks and blue piping on the sleeveless top. Metallic gauntlets with matching gloves, which he would later find out, would serve as a conduit for his plasma blasts. To complete the uniform, was a pair of white knee high boots, highlighted with the same blue as his trunks.

The scan took mere seconds to finish. What was frustrating Jake, was waiting for the fabricator to complete the construction of his Titan uniform. Jake and Charles both waited impatiently as the machine attempted to complete its task as quickly as it could. Finally, ten or so minutes later, the machine had produced one form fitting super-hero uniform. A uniform tailor made for Titan, the youngest, and most powerful hero the earth will ever know.

Jake snatched up the costume from the fabricator's storage tray. Within a split second, the transformation was complete. There in the center of the room, stood Titan at last. Jake smiled from ear to ear as he looked to his father for approval.

"Well? Whatcha think dad?" asked Jake. "Do I look like a hero?" he pressed.

Charles, overcome by a deep flush of pride in his young son, answered simply, "Like the super-hero you are destined to become!"

Jake stepped over to the mirror and studied his reflection. He was well satisfied. He murmured to himself, "I'll make Mom and Dad and Zhango-Rhe proud of me. I'll never do anything that would upset them, or make them look bad."

To his dad he cheered, "Awesome! I'm ready, Dad! I'm ready to be a super-hero!"

Charles briefed his son. "OK kid, here is your flight pattern and patrol route. Start north of the city in St. Georges County, Maryland; make your way as far south as Loudon County, Virginia, and then fly back home. Look for anything out of the ordinary, anything that looks wrong. Remember; don't take the law into your own hands. If you happen to see something going on, help out the police as best you can. Understand, son, that you are not the law. You are an extension of it. You are here to protect and serve, not to rule. If you apprehend someone, just turn him or her over to the nearest police officer and explain what they've done and then be on your way. Keep it short and sweet, without telling them too much."

"Okay, dad…"

"Jake, you are very powerful, and you may get it in your head that you can do what needs to be done, regardless of what others may think. You have to remember that you are still mighty young as well. Mind your manners, and address people appropriately. You do this, along with helping people; you will earn the respect, and even the love of the masses."

Jake had listened intently to his father's instructions. He answered "Alright, Dad. Mind my manners, check! Patrol area, check! OK, wish me luck!"

Father and son hugged one another before Charles and Jake made their way upstairs to the balcony.

Jake and Charles stepped out onto the balcony. Jake looked up into the clear star-filled night sky and gazed intently at the moon.

"Thank you, Zhango-Rhe… Just a few days ago, I was just an ordinary kid. But you have given me many awesome gifts, and fantastic powers. You've named me 'Titan.' You've given me a great purpose in life, to help people in need or in trouble. Now the time has come for me to put this strength and these powers to good use, and to introduce the world to Titan. Well, I'm here, Zhango-Rhe, and I'm ready to carry forward your mission to serve as guardian of this world as the new Titan. I promise, Zhango-Rhe, I will do my very best."

Jake extended his arms and lifted into the sky, soaring high above the ground as Titan for the first time. Right away, people on the ground spotted an unidentified flying object. Little did the citizens of Washington DC know it was actually an unidentified, soon to be identified boy. Jake knew that for as many people that looked up into the night sky on his maiden voyage, there would be talk spreading across the nation's capital like wildfire.

Suddenly the sound of police sirens broke the calm silence of the night. Metro DC police were engaged in a high-speed pursuit of a flaming red BMW Z-3 Roadster. The crazed driver made a rash attempt to lose his police shadow, the perpetrator drifted his Bavarian speedster into a residential neighborhood. Jake's heart skipped a beat. "Omigosh! This is not good! People are bound to get hurt!"

Titan scanned the surrounding area with amazing speed and accuracy. A couple, taking a mid-evening walk, pushing their newborn daughter in a stroller with them, made their way down the street, and right in the path of this wheeled madman.

"Oh no!" Titan thought to himself. He knew that he needed to act fast. He aimed his muscular frame at the speeding car, and became a pre-pubescent missile.

Titan streaked towards the rear of the out-of-control car. He reached under the rear bumper, grasped the frame and firmly planted his feet back on the ground, gradually slowing the car. The driver tried in vain to keep his speed up, but against Jake's irresistible power, all he managed to do was to burn rubber until Jake lifted the wheels clear off the pavement. Jake pulled the car to a stop just as the driver removed his foot from the accelerator and attempted to jump out of the car.

He was a wiry, slender young man of medium height, in his late teens or early twenties. He saw the source of his problem. A six-year-old muscle-boy, in blue and red tights, was holding his stolen escape vehicle aloft by the rear bumper. He panicked. The police were nearly upon him. He sprinted down the street trying to escape from the approaching squad car and to put as much distance as possible between himself and this apparition in the form of this impossibly powerful boy-child. Jake gently lowered the rear tires of the Beamer to the pavement and flashed after the fleeing young man. As he caught up to the criminal, Jake grasped the man's belt from behind and gently pulled him to a stop. The young man looked over his shoulder and seeing Jake, decked out in his Titan gear, exclaimed in abject terror, "Please! Please don't hurt me!"

Jake had already considered how to play this. He answered as calmly and as gently as he could, "I'm not here to hurt you or anybody else. But you hafta answer for what you've done here, driving through this neighborhood like that. Did you know that there was a couple and their baby walking on the street in the next block? By stopping you, Mister, I might've saved you from killing someone today."

By then the police cruiser had pulled to a stop just behind the Beamer. The two patrol officers alighted and approached Jake and the perpetrator. One of the two immediately handcuffed the young man as the other demanded of Jake, "Who are you? WHAT are you?"

Jake answered, "I'm Titan. And I am Guardian of Earth. I'm just here to help the best I can. But I hafta go now."

"Wait!" The patrol man pleaded. " What??? How???" he sputtered, not quite sure how or where to begin with his questions. Jake answered, completely empathetic to this man's predicament, "I know, Sir! This is freaking me out nearly as much as it is you. But, I promise, very soon, I'll be making a public announcement about who I am and why I'm here. Just know for now that I'm a friend. And I'm just here to help. And I mean no harm to anyone."

With that, Jake lifted into the air and, at low altitude, flashed over the horizon, as he continued on his first patrol.

"I must be dreaming!" the officer murmured. "That kid just stopped a BMW with his bare hands, apprehended this punk, hopped up into thin air and freaking flew away!"

The patrolmen returned to their police cruiser, their collar in tow. One of the officers sat the perpetrator in the back seat, taking care to guide his head through the door. Once the perpetrator had been settled onto the back seat, the patrolman proceeded to read the man his Miranda rights as the other called the arrest into headquarters. He ended the radio transmission and then explained to his partner. "I'm not saying anything about that flying muscle kid until we get back to Headquarters. This isn't something that needs to be broadcast over the air. All we need is some civilian listening in on a police scanner getting wind of this. We need to bump this up to Headquarters. Maybe they can figure out what we're dealing with here."

They drove to DC city lockup, turned over their prisoner to the jailers and then drove straight to police Headquarters. Their shift was less than half over, but they had to report in on the flying boy and they had known very well that a report over the radio could easily be misinterpreted, maybe even causing mass public panic. At first, their division sergeant didn't believe their hair-brained tale. But a replay of the video tape from their cruiser-cam quickly corroborated their unbelievable report. It clearly showed Jake flying into view and stopping the fleeing Beamer with his bare hands, apprehending a fully-grown adult single handedly and then self-levitating into the air and flying away!

The division sergeant called the section lieutenant who viewed the tape. Finally, the word had made it all the way through the chain of command to the Metro DC police Commissioner, who, after viewing cruiser-cam video, returned to his office, telephoned the Pentagon, and demanded an immediate face-to-face meeting with the Secretary of Defense.

Meanwhile, Jake continued on a northerly course, heading for St. Georges County. His mind wandered aimlessly as he thought about the out-of-control car. "How could anyone be that careless?" he thought to himself.

Beneath him, with his impossibly keen eyesight, Jake spied two armed masked men who had ambushed an armored car just as two security guards had exited the vehicle with deliveries of cash to a DC area bank. The guards had no time to reach for their weapons before they found themselves staring down the barrels of two AK-47 assault rifles. They had no choice but to surrender the cash.

The two masked gunmen dashed to their getaway car. Their accomplice was waiting in the get-away vehicle with the engine running. One of the gunmen yanked open the rear door and he and his partner dove in. Seemingly, from out of nowhere, the young Titan flashed into view, blocking the getaway car as it began to pull away from the curb. The driver lowered his window glass, with his left hand aimed his pistol at the young hero, and demanded, "Move it, kid or I'll blow you away."

"No!" Jake replied, simply.

The driver squeezed off a round, aiming for Jake's chest.

Jake's synapses fired, many thousands of times faster than that of an ordinary human, warning him of the shot. His heart skipped a beat. His first instinctive thought was, "This man has just killed me!" He had known better. Indestructibility was one of his powers, as he had known very well. However, old habits and attitudes sometimes seem to die hard. From the boy's perspective, the bullet seemed to float along a leisurely trajectory, aiming straight for him. He could easily dodge. On the other hand, he could allow the round to hit him. It would simply bounce off his harder-than-diamond chest like a harmless marshmallow. Where would the slug ricochet? Would it hit one of the perpetrators or even an innocent bystander? Jake could not permit that.

With his right hand, quicker than the normal eye could see, he reached out and snatched the bullet out of the air, palming it into his left hand, standing ready to intercept the gunman's next shot. However, the driver never fired the second shot. Their weapons drawn, the armored car's guards had recovered their wits and approached the getaway car, one on each side. The man on the driver's side aimed his weapon through the window at the driver and ordered. "Drop your weapon, take your foot off the gas and shut down your engine or I'll splatter your brains all over the dashboard."

On the other side, the second guard tapped on the rear passenger window, with his pistol. The perpetrator stepped out of the car with his hands up. The gunman on the other side opened the left rear door, shouldered aside the guard and broke into a dead run. Jake shrugged and sighed.

"Here we go again." He lifted into the air, only inches above the street and floated after the fleeing bank robber. From the perspective of the guards and the other crooks, it looked as though Jake had simply vanished, blurring back into view immediately behind his target. Jake snatched him by his jacket collar and lifted him clear off the pavement. He floated at a much more leisurely pace back to the guards, the bewildered crook dangling helplessly from his fist.

The guards were every bit as bewildered at Jake's abilities as the bank robbers. Jake handed his captive over to the guards and took to the sky without as much as a single word.

Chapter 9

A lonely middle-aged man, dressed in old, worn clothing stumbled onto the Francis Scott Key Bridge. It had been dark for some time, and it had rained earlier that evening so there was still a low overcast. Staggering towards oncoming traffic, he fidgeted for something in his tattered jacket. Hours ago, he had used his last few dollars to buy a pint of whisky from an all-night liquor store. He was homeless with no family. He was all alone in the world, care and concern for this poor soul had long since faded into the past.

He stumbled across the bridge; fatigue, hunger, and the influence of the alcohol were having their effect on his balance. He staggered off the sidewalk into the roadway falling flat on his face. Unable to keep his balance, nor his wits about him, he lurched towards the bridge's railing. Disoriented and scared he tried to regain his bearings. He could not remember where he was going, or where he came from. Frantic revelations struck the man like a ton of bricks, as he realized that he was standing on a treacherous structure. With a frightened groan, the man grabbed for the rail of the bridge moments before he would have toppled over the edge and into the menacing Potomac River below.

Titan was flying above the city, occasionally setting down on the rooftop of a building just to enjoy the view. He kept a sharp eye out on the unsuspecting people below. Neither dark, nor the overcast sky would keep young Titan from his first night on duty.

As he overflew the bridge, Titan immediately spied the man as he almost fell over the edge of the bridge. He pondered what to do as he slowed to a stop, hovering dead overhead. "What's going on with this guy?" Titan wondered to himself. He kept a keen and sympathetic watch on the man. Compassion had always been one of Jake's strong points, and would defiantly be seen exuding from him as Titan. "That poor guy. There has to be something wrong here, no one would just walk out on a busy bridge like that. I better stay close by" he expressed mentally.

Like a guardian angel, Jake hovered overhead as the man swayed back and forth, tripping toward the guardrail for about the fifth time. "Wow! He looks sick! What is going on here?" He asked himself as he continued his keen observation. The height mixed with the alcohol had sealed the confused and intoxicated man's fate. For the last time, he fell full-force into the railing. His momentum carried his body over the railing this time. Titan saw the accident swooping in, like a bird of prey and plucking the man right out of the air.

"Gotcha!" a friendly voice said.

Like a guardian angel, Titan had saved this man's life. He extended his muscular young arms, and accepted the old man's sickly form into them with heart-felt compassion. Titan pulled the man to his chest and held him close as he halted his decent into an almost certain death.

The man murmured. "I may be nine sheets to the wind, but you are flying. How is that happening? And you are a kid too, a big kid at that!"

"My name is Titan" the boy replied. "You don't look too good, sir. Do you want to go to a hospital? Or how about I take you someplace where it's nice and warm?"

"What are you? Who are you? Are you an angel?" asked the frantic alcoholic as he grazed the back of his hand across Titan's cherub-like face.

Titan flashed a half smile, "Well, I guess you could say that. Let's just say that right now I am your guardian angel."

The man looked into the crystal blue swarm that composed Titan's eyes. Love and warmth was all that he could feel from him. Gently he touched Titan's thickly-muscled arm in an attempt to make sense of what had happened.

Titan laughed to himself as he watched his cargo pinch himself in the arm repeatedly, and shake his head trying shake out the cobwebs that cluttered his mind. He could not help but wonder what caused this man to end up the way he is.

"Son, I must tell you, I may want to rethink my life," stammered the man.

"Whatcha mean, sir?" asked the young hero.

"I need to do something to clean up my act, seeing as I was just snatched from the jaws of death by a flying angel!" exclaimed the thankful man.

"Well, just make me a promise, sir"

"Sure son, what is it?" asked the man.

"Promise me that when I get you to safety, you will get some help, and stay off bridges!" pressed Titan.

"That I can do, errr, what was your name again?"

"Ja…Uhm….Titan!" he replied as absentmindedly as he almost told the man his real name.

"Well Titan, I give you my word, I am headed to rehab, and I am NEVER walking across this bridge again" promised the man as he raised his right hand as if in court.

"OK sir; let me take you over to the emergency room. Maybe the doctors can help you get somewhere safe and sound," said Titan as he aimed them both towards the closest hospital.

After landing and helping check-in the man, he walked back to the room where the emergency room technicians took his "patient". Titan pulled the curtain back and walked to the bedside. He stood over the man as he waited for him to speak.

"Titan, son, I owe you my life, and my thanks" said the grateful man as he placed his hand on Titan's shoulder.

"You are more than welcome sir," responded Titan.

"My name is Bill, I never got the chance to tell you that before, son."

"Well, Bill, nice to meet you" said Titan.

Bill reached out and grasped Titan by both shoulders, drawing the young hero into a thankful embrace. "I can honestly say that I will never forget you Titan."

Titan's tanned face turned a slightly rosier shade as he blushed. "Bill, I will be watching, and if you need me, I will be there. Please take care of yourself." smiled Titan.

"I will!" exclaimed Bill.

Titan said his farewell to his new friend, and walked out as the doctor came into the room. He made his way to the parking lot. He looked up into the black night sky, and forced himself to take off. Titan aimed his body towards his house as he streaked back home from a very eventful first night.

Jake breathed a deep sigh of relief. His emotions were running on overload, and he needed to call it a night so that he could collect himself. His heart longed to be with his parents. Jake knew that if there was anyone that could help him make sense of the madness that he witnessed today it would be his mother and father.

Throughout the metro DC area, news reports were hitting television sets all over the city. An attractive field reporter spoke with bewilderment to the general population. "Two incidents in metro DC have authorities mystified. Reports have been pouring into the local police department dispatch centers all evening long. It seems that earlier this evening, a high speed chase through a residential neighborhood ended when what appeared to some as a young boy flew onto the scene and stopped a stolen sports car with his bare hands..." the young woman smiled into the camera. "I am sure that as of now you don't believe me. Well I don't blame you. I wouldn't believe it either. But seeing is believing and you will believe too once you've seen this video from a DC Metro Police cruiser-cam." The television faded to the video showing Titan flying into view ahead of the police cruiser, right behind the fleeing sports coupe, bringing it to a dead stop with his bare hands, apprehending a fully-grown man and flying out of the picture. The view switched back to the newsroom where again the anchor smiled into the camera, "A picture is worth a thousand words. But I have to say that I for one am almost speechless."

The female newscaster continued, "In the second incident at about eight PM this evening, three masked gunmen attempted a holdup of an armored car as it was making a delivery to the Midtown Bank on the corner of Pearl Harbor Street and Franklin Boulevard. Just as the men were about to make their escape, they were stopped by the same costumed figure who had assisted police in apprehending the carjacker earlier in the evening. As the boy blocked the perpetrators' escape, the getaway car driver fired directly at him. It appeared to the security officers as if he reached out with blinding speed and caught the speeding bullet in his bare fist! The armored car guards managed to surround the getaway car, taking two of the perpetrators into custody. The third man exited the car and attempted to flee the scene on foot. As with the carjacker, the boy apprehended the fleeing suspect, a fully-grown man. Then, in the blink of an eye, he took to the skies. Pay close attention to the video to follow. This video is from one of the bank's external security cameras. We apologize for the poor quality of the picture but you can clearly see the boy overtaking and stopping the perpetrator, handing him over to the security guards and then flying away."

The man Titan had rescued stared at the television and exclaimed, "Hey! That's Titan, that's my Guardian Angel!"

The screen flashed a news update over the monitor. The commentator looked at the camera in abject horror as she began to recount the grave news story.

"This just in," the newswoman announced. "A twin engine Cessna Crusader, en route to Washington Reagan Airport, has issued a distress call, reporting that it has experienced complete engine failure of one of his engines and is losing power from its other engine. The pilot has reported that he is having difficulty maintaining altitude and the control tower has issued a straight-in approach through normally restricted airspace into Washington Reagan. Crash crews are standing by at the airfield to render assistance."

"OH My Lord, I hope that my new friend can help!" exclaimed Bill as he watched in fright as the events unfolded.

Titan ascended above the city, and scanned the horizon. He had heard a mass of sirens heading in the direction of the airport. He had only thought that he was going to call it a night early. Titan then attuned his ultra sensitive ears to listen for the emergency radio traffic below him. He gained all the information that he needed. He squinted his eyes and strained even his keen eyesight as he searched frantically for the disabled Cessna. He spotted an anti-collision strobe and then focused his infrared vision on the aircraft. Using the beacon as a starting point, he scanned the area, locating the crippled aircraft. Its flight path would take it right into the capitol dome. Jake could see clearly the infrared "shadow" of the pilot through the skin of the aircraft. He was struggling in vain to maintain altitude.

Titan streaked toward the stricken plane, and positioned his body underneath the airframe, allowing its weight to balance on his back. Spreading his arms and legs, he stabilized the wounded aircraft so that the pilot could guide his plane to a safe landing at Reagan National. He had considered alerting the pilot of his presence but decided against it. Titan reasoned to himself, "The pilot has all he can handle just trying to keep this thing in the air. I wanna help him, not scare him to death. I'll just let him fly, while I play like I am the engine."

In spite of the seriousness of the situation, Titan allowed himself a half-smile. Looking ahead, the young hero flattened the angle of descent, enabling the aircraft to continue along a direct course to a safe landing at Reagan National Airport. The Cessna crossed the runway threshold as he slowly descended the aircraft to a safe touchdown. He shifted his position from underneath the airframe, moving to just above the tail which he grasped pushing the Cessna clear of the duty runway onto the main runway. A crash truck pulled up alongside as Titan released his hold on the vertical stabilizer. He waved the crash crew in before ascending back into the night sky, headed for home.

Jake, exhausted and proud, softly lowered his body back onto the familiar balcony of his house. He tried to quietly open the sliding glass door, and slip in undetected, as to not wake his parents. Jake all but succeeded, as his father looked up from the data he had been compiling. Charles knew that his son would be using the sliding door that resided in his office. He smiled at the sight of his massive, heroic son.

"Well, I don't have to ask how it went. It's been all over the news tonight. Looks like you've had your hands full for your first time out! A carjacker, an armored car heist, and rescuing an airplane?" Charles smiled again. "Not bad for a rookie!"

Jake replied gravely, "Well, with the armored car thing, I was scared to death, dad! One of those men shot at me! For a second, I thought I was gonna die!" his voice quavered.

"But, you're indestructible!" Charles exclaimed.

"I know," Jake replied. "But just for a second, it happened so fast, I guess I forgot."

Suddenly with all the pent-up emotion and excitement of his first day as "Titan," Jake broke down in tears. Charles stood to his feet and embraced his son who, notwithstanding his almost limitless power, was still a six-year-old boy. He was a six-year-old boy that needed the reassurance from his father.

"I-I-I was so scared, daddy... But it happened so fast..." Jake sobbed. "Before I could do anything, he shot at me. What kind of man shoots people?"

Charles then pulled away and looked Jake in his tear-filled eyes.

"They were afraid of you, Jake... You were in their way. When you're the good guy and you're trying to stop the bad guys, the bad guys will sometimes try to hurt you..."

"Oh... I guess I was lucky, huh?" Jake said, as he wiped the tears from his eyes.

"It wasn't luck. You're indestructible. And the news reported that you snatched the gunman's shot right out of the air, making sure it didn't ricochet off your chest and into someone else! That was quick thinking, son. I am very proud of you!"

"I guess it was instinct as much as anything else, Dad."

Charles answered, "Well, if it was instinct, that just proves that you are cut out for this hero thing!"

"Why don't you take a shower and get some sleep, so you can be fresh and rested for school tomorrow morning."

Although with his powers, Jake should not have felt tired, however he was emotionally spent from his first time out as "Titan."

Jake flashed an ironic smile, "I know Zhango-Rhe said I shouldn't feel tired, but I do. A shower and bed sounds really good right about now."

"Well, it's official... You're a super-hero now!" Charles announced. "You completed your first evening on the job."

"Thanks to you.... I love you, daddy!"

Charles ruffled his son's sandy brown hair as he walked out of the study and towards the bathroom. Jake started the shower and pulled his uniform off. He stepped into the shower and let the warm relaxing water run over his face and body. He quickly washed up and got out. He dried off, dressed for bed, and made his way to his room. Jake relaxed his heavily muscled frame on his bed and quickly dozed off.

Chapter 10

The next morning, Jake awoke with a start. He was floating only inches beneath the ceiling fan, his sheet and blanket draped over him, his pillow clutched to his chest. The blades of the ceiling fan whizzed past him, almost tickling his face with their gusty air currents.

"What the--?" he said as he dropped his pillow to the ground. Holding his blanket, he descended from his high slumber perch. He gently touched his feet down on the soft carpet of his bedroom floor and sat sleepily on his bed. Rubbing the sleep from his eyes, he stood back to his feet and ambled over to the mirror where he caught a glimpse of an unfamiliar reflection. Gone was the lankly-lean six-year-old kid. Standing in his place was this unbelievably muscled boy-man, chiseled like a young Greek god.

Jake haphazardly made his way across the room to his dresser and pulled some clothes out of the drawer to wear to school. He selected a loose fitting sweat shirt and a pair of stylishly baggy jeans to conceal both his abnormally muscular physique and his Titan uniform.

He strolled down the hall to the bathroom to shower and brush his teeth; returning to his room to don his uniform and his school clothes. He slipped his boots carefully into his backpack and put his sneakers on.

He made his way downstairs and into the kitchen where Nancy had his breakfast waiting.

"Jake, honey, did you sleep OK?" Nancy asked her son.

"Yeah mom, I slept OK. But when I woke up, I was floating almost clear up to the ceiling. I gotta figure out a way to get that under control." he giggled. "Maybe a boat anchor tied to my ankle."

Nancy laughed along with her son. "I'm sure it won't come to that. Hey, maybe we could tie a rope to your feet"

When he sat down at the table, Charles placed the morning's newspaper before him. Jake glanced at the headlines. He glanced over at Jake as he watched him scanning the articles.

"Two bank robberies were foiled by flying boy calling himself 'Titan'", the caption read. And, further down, it read: "Titan prevents twin engine Cessna from crashing into Capitol."

"Well, looks like I made the news..." Jake said, blushing as he read the headlines.

"Yes, it appears that you have, son..." Charles responded. "Are you ready to go to school?"

"Yes sir. I'm good to go. I got my uniform on under this."

"Remember that with your super powers you have to be extra careful!" Charles added. Jake just nodded. He had resolved to be cautious and not to give away his secret to his classmates. It would be a new challenge for him. Challenges, however, were becoming a daily thing for the new super-hero.

When Jake arrived at school, all of his classmates were talking about the boy of the hour, Titan. They were completely in awe of the newly emerging super-hero's strength and power. They were chattering excitedly about how this boy just popped on the scene, and doing so many amazing things. One boy exclaimed, "Can you believe it? He rescued that plane before it could crash into the Capitol building!"

During lunch, several of the students had managed to find copies of the morning "Washington Post." Several students gathered together and read the articles repeatedly, in the attempt to learn more about the cities new hero. Thoughts were running rampant throughout the school as they read the supposed age of the amazing hero. They wondered if he could be standing among them right now.

Little did they know, and much to Jake's amusement, Titan was closer than they could have imagined. Sitting almost alone at a table in the cafeteria, Jake listened intently to his classmates' kind words. He fought back a smile for fear that someone may think that he was in fact Titan. Jake knew that he was going to have to visit the school one day, not as the brainy student that he was, but as Titan, Washington DC's very own protector.

After school, Jake made his way to the locker room of the school's gymnasium. He knew that there would not be anyone still in the gym this late, so the chances of being spotted changing were slim. Jake did not want his first day back at school to end with the discovery of his secret identity.

No sooner had he left for home, he spotted a school bus packed with kids. The solitary yellow vehicle was stranded alongside the road, with its hazard lights flashing. Titan noticed that the hood had been propped open, and judging from the visible-only-to-him heat signature, the bus' engine was overheated. He slowly landed in front door of the bus. Startled, the driver opened the door.

"What's the matter, sir?" Titan asked him.

"We are having engine trouble, and this darned cell phone is not working, I can't get a hold of anyone at the station to get a replacement bus sent out. I wish that I could just get these kids back to school so they could call their parents to come pick them up" explained the frustrated bus driver.

"Well, maybe I can help!" Titan chuckled. "First off, you need to get one of these" Titan said as he pulled out his Call-Tel cell phone. "You get service everywhere!"

"What?"

"I was just kidding" Titan chuckled. "What school do you need to get to?" asked Titan.

"Oh, Dalton Middle School, it's not too far from here, but it is too far for me to try and walk twenty plus kids back there safely" replied the driver with a half hearted grin.

"That's easy, I can get you there!" Titan cheered.

"How are you gonna do that, you are just a kid?" asked the confused man.

Titan puffed out his chest, and curled his arm up into a massively monstrous bicep flex. "Just close the door and tell the students to hold on tight! I am no ordinary kid!" smiled Titan as he readied himself for his job at hand.

Titan crawled under the school bus, grabbed hold of the frame and gently lifted the school bus off the ground. He then took off and rose to an altitude of about thirty feet above ground and, at a safe speed, flew the bus back to the schoolyard. During the brief but amazing journey his passengers were all squealing with delight. Bystanders on the ground stopped and stared up into the sky with sheer amazement, as they watched a flying bus pass them by.

Ten minutes later, Titan gently slowed to a hover above the parking lot in front of his destination and descended to the pavement. As he crawled out from under the bus, the children were already emerging, babbling excitedly about their amazing school bus flight. When they spied their hero, they greeted him with a rousing cheer.

They gathered around him asking him to autograph their notebooks while they waited for their parents to come and pick them up. One girl pulled a camera out of her backpack and began snapping pictures. She enthusiastically took many pictures of Titan posing with several of the students.

Word of Titan's bus rescue quickly reached the media. One of the local newspapers managed to locate some of the photos that were taken. Titan's face had been plastered all over computer screens, and televisions everywhere. Instantly, Titan had become a hero to young and old people everywhere.

Titan had been in route home to visit with his parents, when he was stopped in mid air by the familiar sound of gunfire. He quickly scanned the area, attempting to locate the source of the terrifying sound. Just then, his super sensitive hearing picked up the faint buzz of a silent alarm. He hovered around, turning himself towards the sound. He spun and flew toward a convenience store, when he spotted a man running out, carrying a plastic bag filled with cash in one hand and a hand gun in the other.

The young super-hero quickly landed right in front of the fleeing man, blocking his path. Titan folded his arms and confronted the man with a hard, menacing look.

"Excuse me, but did you just rob that store?" Titan asked the startled delinquent. "You need to take that back! Didn't anyone ever tell you that it is not nice to take what doesn't belong to you?"

The man stopped and gawked at the muscular kid in disbelief. He had heard the accounts of a young, flying muscle-bound kid who had stopped other robberies, but really did not believe them. He wondered if this was the kid they were talking about in the news.

The robber tried to dart around the young hero but at blinding speed, Titan appeared directly in the robber's path blocking his escape.

"What? Who the heck are you?" the robber demanded.

"Look mister, you are not going anywhere with that! Now, take that money back to the store!" Titan ordered as he pointed to the bag containing the cash.

"Fat chance kid! Get out of my way, or I'll blow yer head off!" the robber threatened as he brandished his pistol at the boy.

"I'm not moving…" Titan answered defiantly, as he closed in on the robber.

"You asked for it, you little punk," the man snarled, as he squeezed off a round, aiming for Titan's chest.

"POW!" the shot rang out.

Titan was briefly overcome with the same fear as before. It was still very scary, to have a weapon pointed at him. He struggled to muster his faith in Zhango-Rhe's promise of invulnerability. He still was struggling with his faith that bullets couldn't hurt him at all. Titan swallowed hard but the boy bravely stood his ground, facing down both this robber and his own momentary terror.

Putting his initial contact with a gun aside, Titan reached out, and snatched the bullet with his right hand. He was much better prepared to face someone with a gun after already facing it once.

"Holy smoke! I thought I hit him…" the man said to himself. Then he aimed his gun again and pulled the trigger.

He fired two deafening rounds at the boy. Titan moved at super speed and caught both bullets with his right hand, quickly dropping them into his left hand.

"I've gotta be trippin'" the man exclaimed.

He glanced at his gun, bewildered. The vile criminal then emptied the rest of the pistol's clip as he pulled the trigger repeatedly. He had hoped that this would finally finish off the one thing that stood in his way to freedom.

Titan easily caught all three of the remaining bullets in his right hand. Titan opened the palms of both hands, revealing five bullets three in his right hand and two in his left. He dropped them to the pavement. He dropped his gaze at his assailant and glared with intent as the boy started to close in on the man.

"You just wasted five bullets on me! You just shot at me! You were willing to kill a CHILD!" Titan growled.

Realizing his weapon had no effect on the boy, he dropped his weapon to the street.

"Hey! You dropped your gun" Titan said. "I have guns too. But I guarantee that mine work much better that yours!"

Titan concentrated and aimed his bawled up fist at the fallen firearm. Suddenly and amazingly an intense burst of plasmoidal energy shot from Titan's hand. The super heated and concentrated blast of energy effortlessly melted the gun into a pool of useless metal.

"Who... WHAT ARE YOU!" the man shouted.

With an ironic grin, Jake answered "The name's Titan, I am here to clean up the trash!"

A police car raced down the street with siren blaring and lights flashing. It came to a screeching halt right in front of them. The officers leapt out with their weapons drawn.

"OK NOBODY MOVE! HANDS WHERE I CAN SEE THEM!" bellowed the police officer.

"Officer, this man just robbed the Qwik Stop. You will find the cash over there" Titan said as he pointed to the bag that was laying a few feet from the criminal.

The officer quickly arrested the robber and placed him in the back seat of the patrol car. Then he returned to speak with Titan.

"Hey wait, kid... You're Titan right?" the officer asked him.

"Yes, sir, that's me" the boy answered honestly.

"I have a letter for you. It's from the Police Commissioner," the officer said, before returning to his patrol car. "He's given every patrol officer a letter like this, in hopes that we would run into you."

Titan opened the envelope and read the letter. It was an invitation to visit the police station the following afternoon and meet with Commissioner Wilson. Titan folded the letter and stashed it in his pocket. He thought that it would be wise, and the right thing to do, so he made up his mind to take the Police Commissioner up on his invitation to hear what he had to say.

Titan walked away from the scene, playing the events over in his mind. While he was strolling away, lost in thought he walked right past a tall man wearing a black suit, and dark sunglasses. The moment Titan leaped in the air and took off flying, the sinister man reached for a cell phone and dialed a number. Methodically he raised the phone to his ear and in a monotone voice, spoke into the receiver.

"Target: Titan.....Acquired!"

Chapter 11

The next morning, back at school, it was business as usual. All the kids were all singing their praises of the new hero. They recounted to each other the news reports from the night before. Jake listened, for the first time, a boy telling his friend how he would love to be like Titan. Jake's heart and soul stirred at that very moment. He smiled at the fact that he had, in a few short days, impacted so many people's lives for the better.

When school was over, Jake went to the locker room in the school gym and changed into his Titan uniform. He took off and flew home to drop his street clothes and his backpack off before flying on a late afternoon patrol. Luckily, there wasn't much going on, so he just enjoyed being in his favorite new place, the skies. He flew aimlessly all over DC. Glancing down at the time piece his father installed in his gauntlet, he realized that he had an hour to kill before his appointment with the police Commissioner.

When it was almost time for his appointment, Titan flew to the police station and landed in the parking lot near the rear entrance. There were two patrolmen standing near the rear entrance, inspecting their patrol cars. Titan approached them and said, "Excuse me, sir" Titan said politely. "Hi I'm Titan; Police Commissioner Wilson wanted to see me."

"You, You're Titan? I was expecting a little…well a little more! I thought you would be bigger" the other officer responded. "You're just a little kid!"

A little self consciously, Titan laughed. "Yeah I seem to get that a lot!"

"Frank, he ain't that little! Get a load of his guns!" interjected the other officer.

"Guns? What guns? I don't carry any weapons officer…" Titan responded innocently.

"Not GUNS…Your guns, your arms!" the officer explained.

"Oh! These?" Titan asked as he flexed his mighty arms for the officers to see.

"Okay, I take that back! Maybe you are not that small after all" Officer Franklin said apologetically.

The officers both nodded to one another and escorted the young boy into the building, to the elevator, leading him to Commissioner Wilson's office, up on the third floor. They introduced Titan to Commissioner Wilson's receptionist who had been expecting young hero arrival.

"Well, hello young man. Commissioner Wilson is expecting you." She opened the door to Commissioner Wilson's office and gestured Titan to enter.

"Commissioner, you have a visitor" she announced as Titan walked past her into the office.

Commissioner Wilson was a short, stocky man with black hair and a mustache. He was very surprised when Titan walked in. He had expected the young hero to be older and larger. The Commissioner rose from his chair to meet Titan as he stepped into the office.

"Good afternoon, young man. You must be the mighty Titan!" the man said, as he shook his hand.

"Yes sir, that's me!"

"I've heard so much about you!" the Commissioner said. "Here, please take a seat. Could I get you anything to drink?"

"Oh, a glass of water would be fine…" the boy replied shyly.

The Commissioner poured a glass of water for Titan and handed the glass to the boy, as he sat down. Commissioner returned to his seat behind his oversized oak desk.

"I want to thank you for helping us out as of late. You've been a tremendous help, tracking down and stopping several of the city's repeat offenders, to say nothing of your fantastic save you made with that plane. That was the most spectacular thing I have ever seen! I very much appreciate everything you've done for us. All of us on the force are hoping we can count on more of your help in the future!"

"Umm, sure, I would be more than happy to help..." Titan replied.

"Is there any way for my officers to get a hold of you, in case we need you?"

Titan pondered his question for a moment and realized that there was no way for the police officers to get in touch with him. He did have his cell phone, but he did not want to have the police calling him on that one, for fear that they may learn who he really is, or who his parents were.

"Not really. I just fly around over the city in the afternoon and sometimes in the evenings..."

"That's fine, but I think we can do better. We'd like to be able to get a hold of you. I have an idea. Would you be willing to carry a cell phone with you? The police department would provide the phone and pay the monthly charges."

Titan thought about that for a moment. He already did carry one, and did not see the harm in another one.

"Sure. I don't see why not." he answered.

"Good. I'll arrange to get you that cell phone. The dispatchers will have your number and they would only call you in case we need your assistance. We wouldn't ask you to do anything for us that we could just as easily handle ourselves. Are you alright with that?" the Commissioner asked him.

"I understand, and that is fine with me, Commissioner!"

The Commissioner placed an immediate order for a cell phone to be issued from the equipment storage. Ten minutes later the receptionist buzzed the intercom within the office to alert her boss that the phone order was complete and at her desk. Commissioner Wilson thanked her and asked his devoted assistant to bring the item to him. The young lady concurred and politely let herself into the office, handing her supervisor the phone.

The portly head of the police department inspected the phone, to make sure that it worked properly. He tested all the buttons and lights. Once he was satisfied that it would work well enough, he handed over to the young hero, who received it with a smile.

"Here is your cell phone. Let me make sure it's working properly."

He dialed the number. The cell phone chirped, Titan flipped it open and answered it. After a brief sound check, both the Commissioner and Titan were satisfied.

Commissioner Wilson smiled, "Remember, son. That phone works both ways. If you are ever faced with a situation where you need our help don't hesitate to call on us! Just press and Hold the one-button, NOT 911. We replaced the voicemail speed dial with a direct hotline to the dispatch center, if you ever need us, just press it. If you ever lose the phone and need to contact us as well, just dial 9999, it is a quick dial that we set up for off duty officials in times of need. I would appreciate it if you wouldn't let that information out. We keep that in the 'family.'"

"Thank you, Commissioner! I'll keep that to myself."

Titan and the Commissioner shook hands and the boy left the office and walked out of the station. He stowed the cell phone in his pocket.

He decided to keep the cell phone set to vibrate. He would know when he was receiving a call, but no one else would. In case of an emergency call during one of his classes, he would ask for a hall pass, make his way to the boys' restroom, and change into his Titan persona and slip away to handle the problem as quickly as he could before returning to class.

The first call came barely a week later. Jake was in math class when he felt his cell phone vibrate. He raised his hand and requested a hall pass for the restroom. At blinding speed, he dashed to the locker room. He executed a quick change into his Titan uniform before running outside to leap into the sky. During his ascent, he keyed his cell phone to retrieve his voice mail.

The message was from police dispatch who said that a bridge had collapsed north of the city. Titan made a quick decision to change his direction and fly to the scene as quickly as he could.

As soon as he arrived on scene, he began pulling cars out of the river. He worked as quickly as he could, determined to save as many lives as possible!

Titan retrieved all of the cars that had fallen into the river and had flown them to the southern end of the bridge where police and rescue units were waiting.

Titan made his way through the air back to the scene of the massive accident, his heart nearly stopped when he noticed a small bus carrying elderly residents of a retirement community teetering precariously over the edge of the bridge. The young hero flashed to the rescue. He lifted the front of the vehicle that had been dangling over the edge of the gap left by the bridge collapse. He shoved the vehicle back onto the only remaining solid decking. He then positioned himself under the vehicle so that he could fly it to the opposite end of the bridge, and to safety. After setting the mini bus down on the pavement, he stepped up to the door which the driver opened. "Is everyone OK in here?" Titan asked.

"Yes!" answered the driver, a young lady no more than twenty years old. "Thanks to you, we're all just fine! Thank you for saving our lives!"

Titan nodded gravely. "Yes ma'am. I'm just glad everyone is OK."

Titan lifted back into the air conducted a thorough examination of the structure, satisfying himself that no one had been left in danger and that there was no danger of further collapse of what remained of the structure. Once he was certain that no one was left in harm's way, he waved to the crowd and took off.

Chapter 12

Early the following Sunday morning, Jake, who was a light sleeper, heard his cell phone vibrating. As he answered it, a kind, yet frantic voice told him that a luxury cruise ship had struck and iceberg, just off the coast of Antarctica. The dispatcher also informed the young hero that rescue vessels were on the way; however they would not reach the condemned ship before its imminent submersion. Within seconds Jake had taken to the air as Titan.

After flying due south at top speed for no more than ten minutes, Titan looked down and saw the large icebergs floating on the surface. From the briefing he had received, he knew he must have been in the right general area; he just needed to locate the disabled ship. A few minutes of searching the area, he spotted the cruise ship. She was 848 feet long, 108 feet wide at the center beam. Using his preternatural sight, Titan had accounted for over two-thousand people onboard. He noticed that the ship had little time before her and the compliment occupants would meet certain doom.

Titan landed on the bridge and asked for the Captain. The Captain was on the boat deck directing the loading of passengers into the life boats. The boy quickly made his way to the boat deck and introduced himself. "Hello, Captain! My name is Titan! I'm here to help!"

"Thanks for coming, I have heard and read a lot about you, my young friend! See if you can push or tow us to the nearest port!"

"Fine… Where is the nearest port?" Titan asked him.

The Captain replied, "The closest port would be Puerto Williams on Tierra del Fuego, Argentina. Follow me, I will show you in the mapping room. Better to show you than trying to explain."

When they arrived in the chart room, the Captain explained, "This is our position, here, and here is Puerto Williams on Tierra del Fuego. We could never make it there on our own. We won't even manage to remain afloat for much more than an hour or so."

"Oh, so we need to go north! I can do that!" Titan cheered. "I'll dive under the keel and right the ship. Then I'll propel you to port."

The captain was skeptical. "Son, you cannot possibly remain under water for that long. Even if you could breathe under water, you'd die from hypothermia. We'll have to try something else that is not so dangerous for you."

Titan explained, "Trust me Captain, I can hold my breath a really long time! Don't worry about it; just leave this all up to me. You will be safely to port before you know it!"

Before the captain could object, Titan had leapt over the rail, diving head-first into the sea. While underwater, he swam under the hull observing the big gash running aft from bow to mid ship just below the waterline. He dove under the keel and righted the ship, correcting the forty-five degree list. He considered lifting the ship completely out of the water but rejected that idea.

"I better not do that, if I lift it outta the water, the ship might break in half, and that would be bad! A lot of people could die! I need something to make that more stable so that I can get this thing to port faster…"

Then it hit him! "Ice, I just need to snag one of those icebergs! I'll need a really big one!"

He released his hold on the hull and rocketed out of the sea and into the sky, searching for a suitable block of ice. He spied a massive iceberg no more than a dozen miles away and flew straight for it. It had a jagged peak and no flat horizontal surface suitable for supporting the ship.

"No problem," Titan chuckled. "I'll fix that!"

He dove for the iceberg, aiming his first, and unleashed a plasma beam blasting off the peak and then with his bare hands carved out a flat surface with an indentation approximately the same size and shape as the ship's hull suitable for cradling its mass.

Titan pushed the iceberg a dozen or so miles back to the ship. Arriving alongside, Titan flew himself into position dead center above the berg and gently lowered himself onto it. Then he forced the berg to submerge and positioned it under the ship's hull, allowing it to rise gradually until it surfaced under the stricken vessel. Amazingly, the iceberg lifted the ship completely out of the water as the hull settled neatly into the indentation prepared for it by Titan moments before. Titan found himself trapped between the keel and the ice. He easily drilled himself a small exit tunnel through the ice and flew back to the bridge.

To say the Captain had been impressed both by Titan's demonstration of raw power and his ingenuity, would be the understatement of the year!

The boy beamed with pride under the Captain's praise.

With his amazing power, Titan propelled the ship-laden iceberg to Puerto Williams. Upon arrival, he forcibly submerged the iceberg and maneuvered it clear of the ship's hull. Then, he maneuvered the ship into a floating dry dock that had been arranged beforehand by radio contact with the shipyard from the Captain.

As the passengers began to disembark, the Captain thanked Titan for his rescue of the passengers and crew and for preventing the loss of the cruise ship in the cold waters of the Antarctic!

While Titan was standing at the dock, talking to the Captain of the ship, an unknown man wearing a dark suit quickly and quietly dialed his cell phone. He covertly spoke in a low baritone voice.

"Target: Titan.....Acquired!"

One morning, a few weeks later, Jake was about to leave for school, when his cell phone rang again. He answered and heard over the phone, that a large retail store had caught fire in the downtown area.

Jake immediately raced back into the house and changed into his Titan uniform. Then he leapt into the sky and flew over to the downtown area of DC, where he spotted a large cloud of smoke. He flew toward the smoke. As he approached the site, the flames had engulfed the building, which was situated next to a small strip mall.

Titan realized that he needed to quickly extinguish the fire which was threatening to spread to a neighboring strip mall. He pondered, how could he get a large quantity of water to the building?

Then he remembered flying over a large scrap yard on his way over to the fire. He doubled back and returned to it. As he arrived over the junkyard, he searched the site, spotting the carcass of an abandoned dump truck. He floated above the dump truck and, using his beams, he blasted the large, rear bed loose from its steel hinges. Then he lifted the large, metal box up over his head and headed straight for the river, where he used the box as a giant bucket, filling it with water.

Titan returned to the site of the fire and dumped the water directly onto the flaming building just as units of the Metro DC Fire Department were arriving on scene. As the firemen hooked their hoses to nearby hydrants and began to combat the flames, Titan left with his makeshift "bucket," returning to the river for another load of water.

Once the fire had been extinguished, he discarded his "bucket" and returned to the scene. He needed to fly back to the burned building, just to see if he might be needed. Luckily the firemen had gotten everyone out of the burning retail outlet, as well as from the neighboring strip mall. Titan decided to do a fly-by of the strip mall; luckily none of the shops had been damaged.

Titan landed and began a conversation with the local fire chief. The man shook his hand and thanked him for the assistance. Titan was just about to take to the skies, when suddenly a large portly man came running up to stop him.

"Hey kid," he called. "Titan!"

"Yes, Sir!" the boy answered shyly.

"Hello! I'm Mark! I'm the owner of the Icetown, the ice cream shop in the strip mall next door. We almost got burned out today. Probably would've if it wasn't for you…"

"Oh it was nothing…" Titan said. "Did you say ice cream?"

"I'd like to offer you a free cone! But, hey, you do like ice cream, right?" Mark asked the young super-hero.

Titan flashed Mark an all-boy grin. "Yes sir! I love ice cream!"

"Great! Whatever flavor you want… It's on the house!" Mark added, as he opened the door for Titan.

Titan followed Mark into the small ice cream parlor. It was decorated from top to bottom with old soda fountain merchandise, giving the building a more laid back atmosphere of the past. Mark quickly stepped behind the counter and asked the boy what flavor he wanted.

"I like the one with chocolate, almonds and marshmallows!" Titan pointed out.

"Ahh yes, that's 'Rocky Road'! One of our more popular flavors, good choice!" Mark grinned. "Two big scoops of Rocky Road, comin' right up!"

Mark scooped two generous sized dollops of ice cream and dropped them into an over sized stainless steel dish. Then he sprinkled some pecans over the ice cream and placed a bright red cheery on top. He passed the concoction to Titan who accepted with a smile and profuse thanks!

"Sure, Kid! It's the least I can do. You come here anytime you want and it's on the house each and every time. Your money's no good in here."

Mark pulled out a digital camera and took photos of Titan as he was eating his ice cream. After he had finished, Titan posed for photos with Mark and with each member of his staff as well as all of the customers that happened to come in.

When Titan was ready to leave, Mark thanked him again, reminding him that he had a lifetime "free membership" at his ice cream store. Titan could always enjoy his ice cream there for free!

As Titan walked out of the ice cream store, he bumped into a tall man who was wearing a black suit and who was wearing dark sunglasses.

"Excuse me, sir…" Titan said politely, as he walked onto the open street before he leaped in the air. Unknown to the flying boy, the strange man in the dark suit was watching every move he made, until he flew away. Then he took his cell phone out of his pocket and dialed a number, before he spoke just three words into the small device.

"Target: Titan…..Acquired!"

The following morning, a large ad appeared in the newspaper for the "Icetown" ice cream store, with a picture of Titan eating a bowl of ice cream, with a large smile on his face.

Chapter 13

The Secretary of Defense contacted Police Commissioner personally. He explained in their conversation that there was a meteor on a collision course with Earth. He continued by explaining that they could not predict the precise point of impact with one hundred percent accuracy, but astronomers from observatories around the world have reached a consensus that there is a better than even chance that the meteor will strike in the vicinity of the Washington, DC.

"Commissioner I need to know if Titan can help with this thing" requested the Secretary of Defense.

At first, Commissioner Wilson balked. "Mr. Secretary! I can't ask him to try that! He's an amazing kid, but there's no way! No sir. Not that. That's way too much to ask."

The Secretary of Defense pressed. "Commissioner Wilson, I don't like having to ask him to try this any better than you do. But if we don't do something, thousands of people could die. If you want, I'll ask him myself and I'll make it very clear to him what's at stake."

Commissioner Wilson clearly understood the Defense Secretary's veiled threat, that HE would ask Titan to do this if he, himself would not. Wilson resolved to frame his request in such a way as to give Titan the option of refusing if he felt he couldn't handle an attempt to deflect the meteor from its collision course with Earth.

Titan did not show an ounce of hesitation. He would face the meteor with all the confidence of David, the Israelite shepherd boy as he had faced down the Philistine giant, Goliath, so many centuries ago. He saw the worry in Commissioner Wilson's eyes and hastened to reassure him. With a grin, Titan said to him, "Please don't worry Sir. Everything is gonna be OK. I promise!"

Wilson murmured to himself, "If that boy gets hurt or killed, I'll never forgive myself. God help him!"

Meanwhile, dozens of telescopes and cameras were aimed at the planet threatening meteor. All the major news networks and wire services were covering Titan's attempt to deflect the meteor from its collision course with Earth. Many were feeding images from the Palmer Observatory in Texas to their TV audiences as the boy-hero ascended to meet the oncoming threat.

As soon as Titan spotted the approaching meteor, he flew straight toward it and bracing his shoulder against it with every ounce of strength that he could muster. He understood full well that if the meteor were to crash into the city below, it would mean certain disaster. Thousands of people, if not millions, would die. He could not let that happen.

After twenty strenuous minutes, Titan had managed to deflect the meteor from its murderous course. It was clearly headed away from Earth on a direct collision course with the sun. It would never again pose a threat to anyone on Earth.

Titan, exhausted, returned to Police headquarters where he was greeted as the hero he was. The Commissioner was clearly relieved not only that disaster had been averted, but that Titan had returned alive and unharmed. The boy sensed Commissioner Wilson's concern, as well as his relief, and it touched him deeply. He felt honored to be counted among the friends of this grizzled old police veteran. As humble and self-effacing as Titan by nature was, he would've been surprised to know that the feeling was entirely mutual. In anticipation of Titan's success, the Commissioner had ordered a huge chocolate cake, snacks and soft drinks for a little celebration. Titan pleaded with the Commissioner not to throw accolades like that upon him, however the officers and the Commissioner insisted that their hero be honored. As they enjoyed cake and refreshments, the staff at police HQ had plied Titan with questions about his bout with the meteor, to say nothing of the press who had converged on the scene to get photos and quotes from the young hero.

The next morning, Titan was featured on the front page, both of the Washington Post and the Washington Times, his photo prominently displayed just under the mast heads of both news papers. And all the local TV stations did news segments on Titan's heroic rescue of the city from annihilation.

Titan had made the headlines not only in Washington DC, but in every major news and feature publication all over the world. A banner headline in "The New York Times" read "Boy Hero Saves Nation's Capital and Millions of Lives at Great Risk of His Own Says DC Police Commissioner Wilson."

Several weeks later, a Russian Soyuz spacecraft was launched from the Baikonur Kosmodrome near the village of Tyratam in Kazakhstan. Without warning, the Soyuz main booster rocket experienced a catastrophic failure. The main engine burn had simply ceased to function before the spacecraft had achieved escape velocity. Instead of attaining low Earth orbit, the spacecraft was plummeting earthward. The crew, which consisted of two Russian Cosmonauts and one US Astronaut, was bound for the International Space Station. The crew attempted to detonate the emergency separation flares. After separation, the Soyuz crew capsule would deploy an emergency descent chute. However, the explosive charges that would have separated the Soyuz capsule from the ascent rocket had failed. Backup protocols had been executed repeatedly, all to no avail. "Отрицательная функция!" ("*Otritsatyelnaya funktsiya*"/ "negative function!") The Soyuz crew had reported to the Russian Space Agency's main control room at Star City outside Moscow.

The quick-thinking senior controller, Akademik Yevgenii Sokolowski, picked up his telephone and punched in the number of the direct line to the office of President of the Russian Federation. When the Russian President answered, Sokolowski explained the nature of his emergency and demanded that he be placed in immediate contact with the Russian Embassy in Washington, DC. The President, without need of explanation, immediately understood exactly what Sokolowski wanted. Within minutes, the President had been patched through to the Russian Ambassador who had personally patched through to Police Commissioner Wilson at Metro DC Police HQ. Sokolowski had recruited his American NASA liaison to explain the emergency to Wilson. Wilson in turned dialed Titan's cell number and patched the NASA liaison officer through to the young hero.

Jake had been in his room, doing his homework. He dropped his school book, pulled off his street clothes, revealing his Titan costume and leapt out of his bedroom window and into the sky before his homework had had time to fall to the floor.

At hypersonic speed, Titan flashed over the horizon headed for the skies of Kazakhstan. With his ultra keen eyesight, he easily spotted the stricken space craft and quickly maneuvered himself alongside. He adjusted his position relative to the plummeting Soyuz rocket and space capsule, bringing himself even with the seal between the crew capsule and rocket. He pressed his fingers into the seal, forcing a gap between the docking collars of the rocket and crew capsule. He worked his way around the circumference of the space craft, with both hands, prying apart the docking collars, with brute strength shearing the explosive bolts one by one. Finally, the Soyuz capsule was free of the rocket. Titan maneuvered the rocket away from the crew capsule and hurled it into space, making sure that it would not collide with anything in Earth orbit. Then he turned his attention to the still plummeting Soyuz capsule. He flew after the capsule drawing alongside, then adjusting his velocity to match that of the capsule. He grasped the docking collar of the capsule and gradually slowed its descent, bringing the spacecraft to a dead stop five thousand meters above the ground. Then, balancing the space craft on his back, he reached into his pocket and drew out his cell phone. He dialed 9999 and within less than a minute had been patched through to Commissioner Wilson. "Sir, I have the space capsule. Soooo… Now what do I do? Do I take the space capsule back to Russia or do I take it out into space and dock it up with the International Space Station?"

Wilson tried his best not to laugh but it was a lost cause. Finally after getting his laughter under control, he contacted the Russian Embassy who re-established his patch through to the control room at Star City in Russia. The answer came back almost at once, thanking Titan for his offer to save the mission but requesting that the Soyuz crew capsule be returned immediately to Baikonur Kosmodrome. With two system failures, both the ascent rocket and the emergency escape system, reliability of the remaining systems onboard the Soyuz capsule was suspect. In the interest of crew safety it was decided it would be best simply to call a "Mission Abort." Titan obligingly flew the crew capsule to Baikonur where the relieved Cosmonauts and Astronaut emerged to give the boy their thanks for saving their lives.

Titan was asked to accompany the director of the Baikonur Kosmodrome to the main headquarters building where he was placed in telephone contact with the President of the Russian Federation. In passable English the Russian President expressed his heartfelt thanks to Titan, also passing along thanks from the President of the United States with whom he and been in continuous telephone contact throughout the duration of the emergency.

Within only a few short weeks of his meeting with Zhango-Rhe, Titan had become the greatest hero on Earth. No longer was he a hero just in Metro DC or even in the US. From now on, he belonged to the entire world. He had truly become, exactly as Zhango-Rhe had intended, "Guardian of Earth."

Titan's cell phone rang. It was Commissioner Wilson. Without preamble he spoke, "Titan, there's been a midair collision of two commercial aircraft just north of BWI (Baltimore/Washington International Airport). A Southwest Airlines 727 jet. They're on final approach right now for emergency landing at Baltimore. Pilot says they've sustained damage to their port wing and they're leaking fuel but there's no question they'll make it just fine. Crash crews are standing by in case of fire. But the American Airlines 767 has a bad hydraulic leak. Controls are very sluggish. The pilot and co-pilot are having difficulty maintaining control. There's no way they can land safely. The pilot and his co-pilot are barely able to maintain straight and level flight."

Titan answered tersely, "OK Commissioner, I'm on it!"

Titan pocketed his cell phone, dashed out of a local photographer's studio, where he had been shooting pictures for charitable poster sales, and leapt into the sky. He flashed northward toward BWI. He spied the airport just as the crippled Southwest 737 touched down. Crash trucks were waiting at the end of the runway and fell in behind the jet as it executed its landing rollout. "They'll be just fine," Titan murmured.

The pilots of the American Airlines 767 had managed to wrestle their aircraft onto an easterly heading, in straight and level flight at 19,000 feet above sea level. The aircraft was just crossing the coastline as Titan drew alongside the pilot's side cockpit window on the port side. Without hydraulic assist, pilot and copilot were obliged to struggle with their controls, barely managing to maintain aircraft attitude, altitude and heading. Titan tapped on the pilot's side window. After the third try, the copilot, seated on the opposite side of the cockpit caught sight of Titan out of the corner of his eye.

"Brad!" He said to his pilot-in-command, "That kid-hero, Titan..."

"Yeah," the pilot answered without look up from his exertions, "We sure could use his help about now."

"Well it looks like we've got it. He's right outside your window!"

The pilot looked to his left and was momentarily startled, so absorbed had he been in his struggle to keep the aircraft under control.

Using improvised hand signals, Titan indicated he wanted the pilot and co-pilot to release their hold on the aircraft controls. He motioned with his hands, mimicking the pilots' hold on the control yoke; then folding his arms across his chest. He repeated this motion, keeping eye contact with the pilot until he saw the pilot and co-pilot remove their hands from the controls. He nodded vigorously and gave the pilots a thumbs-up. The pilot also responded with a thumbs-up.

Satisfied that he had communicated effectively with the flight crew, Titan dove underneath the aircraft and positioned his body under the belly at the center of gravity. He ascended about 500 feet easily lifting the aircraft resting on his back as he gained altitude. He spread his arms to the side to enhance his control of aircraft roll (dipping or raising right or left wing). By reorienting his body, raising his head and shoulders or his legs, he adjusted the pitch (up or down attitude) of the aircraft nose. By planting his heels firmly into the belly of the aircraft and shifting his hips, he controlled the aircraft yaw (orientation of the aircraft's nose to the right or left). The boy initiated a gentle descending left turn. As he did so, he heard a reduction in the howling whine of the jet engines. Titan smiled to himself.

"Good! The pilot has throttled back to flight idle! Awesome!" Titan cheered. "That gives me a lot more control!"

The boy made a mental note to compliment the pilot on his decision and to thank him for trusting him to guide the aircraft to a safe landing. Titan well understood the reluctance of a command pilot to relinquish control of his aircraft to a youngster, even a super-powered youngster like him. The pilot might have relinquished control, but he could not relinquish his responsibility for the safety of his passengers and crew.

The boy managed to turn the aircraft around, aligning his heading for a straight-in approach into BWI, arriving from the east for landing on the major east-west runway. About a mile from the runway threshold, the landing gear came down. The hydraulic system had failed, but the emergency gravity-fall backup had operated perfectly. Titan grinned as he heard the satisfying "Ker-THUNK" as the landing gear locked in place.

"Good to go!" he cheered. "Gear down and locked."

He spied a green light being flashed at him from the control tower and then glanced at the intersection of the taxiway at the runway threshold. Crash trucks, their emergency lights flashing were waiting.

"Cleared to land! Emergency crews are ready."

Titan lowered the aircraft onto the runway and as the aircraft rolled out; he lowered his body from the belly of the aircraft and flew up to the top of the tail. He grasped the tail and guided the aircraft to a waiting passenger jet-way at the main terminal building, following a guide truck with a flashing amber light and a large billboard sign labeled "FOLLOW ME." Titan slowed the aircraft to a stop as the jet way moved up to the front passenger door. Titan floated from the tail down to the ramp and climbed the air stair-access from the ramp up to the jet-way, arriving at the door of the aircraft just as it was opened from the inside by a male flight attendant. The boy entered the aircraft and asked is "Is everyone OK in here?"

The male flight attendant assured him that everyone was just fine. He led Titan into the passenger compartment where he was greeted with wildly enthusiastic cheers. Titan grinned at the passengers, as relieved as they were that this near catastrophe had been narrowly averted. The pilot and co-pilot stepped up behind him. With a flourish, the Captain removed his pilot wings from his uniform and stooped over and pinned them onto Titan's chest, just as a passenger snapped a photograph with his cell phone. That photograph was flashed round the world and by the following morning it had been splashed across the front pages of every major newspaper on the planet, as well as on all the major television news networks around the world.

Titan grinned at the command pilot, basking under his copious praise. "Son, if you ever want a job with this airline as a pilot, just let me know. I'll be the first to sign a letter of recommendation."

Titan momentarily became very grave as he looked the pilot in the eye.

"Sir, I know what you did when you throttled back to flight idle. It made what I was trying to do, about one-thousand-percent easier. But I want you to know that I realize how hard it must have been for you to do that. Thank you for trusting me!"

The pilot was very impressed with Titan's empathy. He looked the boy in the eye.

"Frankly, son, I'm as impressed that you picked up on that as I am with this fantastic rescue you just pulled off! I don't really understand where you come from. But the world is a lot better off for you being here. Thank you for this rescue. Thank you for these people who are going home to their loved ones tonight, instead of to a slab in some morgue. From the empathy you just showed me, I think, young as you are, you know very well what you've done here today."

Titan blushed shyly. "I'm just glad I was able to help. And, Sir, I really hope you understand how much you helped when you and your co-pilot released your hold on the flight controls and throttled back your engines to flight idle. That was titanic!"

Man and boy shook hands as a bevy of passenger snapped photos with their cell phones; more dramatic images for the newspapers around the world as well as for the wire services and televisions news networks.

Afterwards, Titan walked back through the airport terminal, where he passed a man wearing a dark suit and sunglasses. Several teens that were traveling with their parents, had come up to the young super-hero, and asked him for his autograph. While Titan was busy signing his autograph on copies of his photo for the teens, the sinister man placed a call on his cell phone, while he continued to watch Titan from a distance. His message was very short and to the point.

"Target: Titan.....Acquired!"

Chapter 14

Within six months of Titan's first introduction to the world, he had become a household name. News coverage of all his exploits was featured in the media daily. Images of Titan were everywhere, appearing on teen fan websites, posters, stickers, notebooks and numerous novelty items. Since the "Icetown" ice cream parlor had posted that large ad in the newspaper, with a photo of Titan enjoying a bowl of ice cream, other companies had requested access to Titan's image for their advertising and promotion as well. Titan agreed with the stipulation that royalties for rights to his image be paid to charity.

Over the past few months Jake paid occasional visits back to the dig site to confer with Zhango-Rhe. He felt it was time to talk with him again. Jake's two most important confidants were his dad and Zhango-Rhe. They knew all of Jake's innermost workings, so it helped to have someone to talk to in times of need.

As Titan, Jake landed at the archaeological site. He entered the cavern, oblivious of the fact that it was being watched by some sinister being from nearby.

Inside, Jake aided by his superb night vision, made his way through the dark subterranean corridor into the chamber where the alien spacecraft rested. As he approached the spacecraft, blue light, matching the blue image on Titan's uniform, illuminated the darkened cavern.

Zhango-Rhe spoke. "Greetings, young Titan. Welcome!"

Jake bowed his head. "Greetings to you, Zhango-Rhe! I've come to report to you my activities as Titan."

"Thank you for coming, Jake. I regret to inform you but my power source is nearly depleted. Soon this ship and my avatar will power down for the last time. However you will still have your father. I have given him everything I know, and everything he needs to council you. Heed his words, young Jacob. He is wise and knowledgeable. He is your father, and he has your best interests at heart."

Jake nodded emphatically. "Yes sir! I will!"

Zhango-Rhe smiled. "Good! So, tell me, how have things been going for you?"

"Oh, it's been great! I helped the police and I stopped a bunch of criminals and prevented a couple of plane crashes. I rescued a man from drowning and now people know about me everywhere I go..." Titan said excitedly.

"So, the news media here on Earth has made you famous?" Zhango-Rhe asked.

"Yes, the news media and they're selling notebooks, t-shirts, posters and all sorts of stuff with my picture on it..." Titan answered.

"That is not appropriate." Zhango-Rhe sternly replied.

"Oh?" Titan responded, with his face downcast.

"You are a super-hero, not a rock star, Titan..." Zhango-Rhe explained. "Fame and fortune are not your purpose. Your purpose is to help people. You're mission is to serve all the people of the earth, and nothing else! You must not use your notoriety for personal gain, is that clear?"

"But I don't get any of that money. It goes to the schools, hospitals and dozens of other worthy causes. I thought if Titan's name and picture could help raise money for charity that would be just another way of helping people. I thought you would be all for that." the boy protested.

Zhango-Rhe nodded. "I should have realized you would not use your name or image for profit. I am sorry for jumping to the wrong conclusion and for correcting you unjustly. Just remember, you must guard your name and image jealously. An important part of your mission to help the people of your world is trust. And there are those who will try to exploit you and your good name. And if people are hurt in connection with that, even if you haven't done anything wrong, that trust could be eroded. Please pass my warning along to your father. The responsibility to monitor this will fall to him, even though he must operate from the shadows."

Jake nodded gravely. "Yes Sir, I understand. And I will talk with my dad about this. He'll know what to do."

"Never lose sight of your purpose and your powers, Titan… Right now, things may seem simple and easy, but the day will come when you will be faced with a worthy adversary who will use very destructive weapons to destroy all people on earth. He has tried to kill me, and he will find you and he will try to kill you, too. You must be ready!" Zhango-Rhe warned him.

"What? Who? Who wants to kill me? Why?" the boy wondered.

"There is no need to worry about that now. For now, just be on your guard and focus on your purpose. I will tell you more during your next visit. Your adversary will come. His time is not yet ripe. But, it will not be long before he comes and when he does, he will find you, Titan…"

"So, for now, I should just keep doing what I've been doing?"

"Yes… Focus on your purpose and use your strength and your powers to help the people around you. Never forget who you are and where you came from and who you were before you became Titan. You were just an ordinary boy, just like the people you're trying to help now. Treat everyone with dignity and respect. Unfortunately, all the press and publicity and commercialism will only make it easier for your adversary to find you. But what is done is done. You meant well and I cannot believe, that, in the end, your charitable impulse will work to your detriment. Though your enemy will try his best to exploit your notoriety to his advantage as he tries to hunt you down in order to destroy you, do not lose heart my young friend."

Jake set his jaw and faced Zhango-Rhe grimly. He growled. "Whoever it is won't have any trouble finding me. If he tries to harm anyone, I'll know. And then I will be the one hunting him."

"Your bravado is praise-worthy, young Jacob. But it is also fool-hardy. Your strength and speed and physical resilience will not be enough to save you and your people. You will need stealth and cunning. And you will need help, not only from your father but also from your friends, some of whom you do not yet even know. Do not make the mistake of trying to face this adversary on your own. You will need help. Do not let false pride keep you from asking for it when the time comes."

"I-I'll remember, Zhango-Rhe… I promise!" the boy assured the disembodied voice from the small spacecraft.

"Very well, young hero. Now I must shut down… It will go well with you, Titan… I will see you again soon…"

The blue light gradually dimmed finally, leaving Jake in total darkness. He turned around and slowly made his way to the entrance of the cavern. He left the cavern, still pondering Zhango-Rhe's words, slowly stumbling across the sandy desert. Then he stopped to look up at the starry sky, before extending his arms and leaping into the air. Jake didn't realize that, behind one of the larger rocks, was a strange, sinister being, who watched as he took to the sky.

M.A.C.H. (Mobile Armored Chameleon Humanoid) watched as Titan took to the sky. His master had sent him to find the space craft of his lifelong nemesis. He had not counted on the fact that Zhango-Rhe's powers had transcended time and space.

MACH scanned the figure as he streaked away from the dig site. What he recorded was far beyond any conceivable notion of power. MACH himself was in awe of the power that was at the young super-hero's command.

He stepped out from behind the rock formation that had concealed his presence from Jake, and negotiated the pathway leading to the archeological dig site. As MACH approached the entrance an audible beep sounded on his communication transceiver.

MACH tapped a button on his wrist. "Yes Sir? How can I serve?" asked MACH in a very monotone mechanical voice.

"REPORT MACH! What have you found?" asked the raspy voice at the other end of the communication link.

"Sir, it would appear that your nemesis has found a successor to infuse with his powers."

"How so, you worthless excuse for an android? Tell me what I need to know or I will deactivate you!" rasped the voice.

"How accomplished: UNKNOWN. From direct observation, I conclude the replacement has at least two of the abilities for the enemy, including flight and speed. He might possess other powers as well but thus far no other powers directly observed. As far as I have gathered. This is the same target your human agents are tracking."

"Shall I proceed to the target?" asked MACH.

"Negative, MACH! Maintain surveillance of Zhango-Rhe's vessel" the voice replied.

"By Your Command!" MACH said as he broke the communication link.

MACH returned to his well concealed observation post hidden from prying eyes by a jagged rock formation. He had not shared all of the intelligence with his master; his most notable omission was the tender age of the target. A continuous direct data link between MACH and his master had proven infeasible given the changing aspect of earth due to rotation on its axis, affording a relatively small time window for communication, plus interference by Earth's magnetic field with MACH's ultra sensitive, ultra high bandwidth, ultra high speed data link. MACH's software had not been programmed to allow for a step down in data rate. It was all or nothing, save the incredibly low data rate of voice communication. MACH's master had cursed his lack of foresight in allowing this limitation into the cyborg's design. And he had rejected the possibility of flashing a software upgrade for fear of corruption in transmission. Better live with the limitations at hand than introduce a software glitch that could sever the communication link altogether.

Chapter 15

One afternoon Jake had to meet with Cathy, who was another girl from his class. They had to work on a school project, so he had his mother drop him off at the public library to meet her. When he found the girl sitting at one of the tables in the study hall at the library, he noticed a large poster of Titan hanging on the wall. It made him feel a little uneasy at first, although he did feel proud of the fact that the poster was hanging there and that it was serving a good purpose.

"Wow... I've never been in this part of the library before..." Jake said to Cathy.

"I like this place, because it's nice and quiet..." Cathy said, as she laid her books on the table.

"Umm... Can we sit somewhere else?" Jake asked her.

"Why?" Cathy wondered. "This place is perfect! Nobody's going to bother us!"

"Yeah but..." Jake said, as he looked up at the poster. "We have this big poster of Titan looking down at us..."

"So?" Cathy chuckled.

Then Cathy took her binder out of her backpack and put it on the table. There was a picture of Titan on the front cover of that, too!

"I like Titan!" she whispered to Jake. "I think he's the coolest kid on earth!"

"Oh... Oh yeah?" Jake chuckled.

"He's cute; he's strong; he's handsome; he's fast; he can fly..." Cathy mentioned. "I don't know who this kid is, or where he came from, but he can do anything... I think he's very, very cool, if you ask me!"

Jake grinned.

"Maybe you should tell Titan that if you ever meet him in person."

"OH Yeah! I'd love to meet him! Trouble is, how do you get a hold of him? I mean, the guy can FLY! So, if he's flying around way up there and I'm down here, how do I get his attention?" Cathy asked rhetorically.

"Shout his name when you see Titan flying overhead…" Jake suggested. "Or, wave a flag or a banner with his name on it. He'll land to talk to you!"

"No way, Jake! He's way too busy and way too important to stop and talk to a kid like me."

"Gosh, Cathy, from what I can tell, hey, he's a kid like us." Jake shrugged. "You'll never know if you don't try! He seems like a really cool guy. You might be surprised."

"I mean… Does a guy like Titan ever hang out with normal kids, like us?" Cathy wondered.

"Well, I heard that he spent almost an hour with a bunch of guys at the mall the other day!" Jake answered. "Several kids supposedly saw Titan there!"

"Well, Jake… Can you do me a big favor?"

"Sure, Cathy!"

"If you ever get to meet Titan, please put in a good word for me. I would love to meet him in person!"

"Sure… It can't be that hard to talk to him." Jake grinned.

"You make it sound so easy."

Jake just smiled at her in silence.

"Do you know him? Have you ever met him before?" Cathy pressed.

"Well… I… Umm…" he mumbled.

"Please, Jake! Tell me!" Cathy insisted.

"Yeah, you could say I know him" Jake admitted. "And I think you'd like him, Cathy." Jake gave Cathy a half smile as he added, "And I think he'd like you too."

"Ask him, for me, okay?" Cathy repeated. "Don't forget!"

"I won't." Jake replied. "I promise."

Jake and Cathy continued to work on their project for school. They finished in about an hour. Then they left the library and walked home. Cathy reminded Jake of his promise, and waved to him as she watched him round the corner.

One Sunday afternoon, as Jake was having breakfast with his mother in a small bagel shop in the downtown area, they were startled to hear sirens as a column of police cars raced past the shop. This would not necessarily have been an emergency for Titan, but then his cell phone began to chirp.

He answered. It was Deputy Police Commissioner Rob O'Brien.

"Hello? Yes Sir. What? A jewelry store? Sure, I'll be right there!" He said before he hung up his cell phone.

"Excuse me, mom." Jake whispered to his mother. "It's a jewelry store robbery. I hafta go."

"That's OK. I'll just wait right here. But if you get tied up for awhile, I'll just see you later back at home." she replied.

Jake then walked out the store, slipped into a secluded alley, hid behind a large trash dumpster and quickly changed into his Titan persona. He took off and flew after the police cars in hot pursuit of the jewel thief.

The jewel thief's small sports car came to a dead end. The robber opened the car door and ran. Titan swooped down from the sky and snatched the thief by sides of his leather jacket, lifting him off the ground!

The thief had not seen Titan's approach from above. He felt himself from his feet by a set of powerful fists as Titan flew the thief to a deserted alley just a few feet away and set him back down. When the thief turned around, he gasped, when he saw how young Titan appeared. He had heard about Titan from the news paper and televisions reports. But somehow, the boy's extreme youth had not sunk in.

"HEY! You are just a kid!" The thug gasped, after he had taken a good look at the short, muscular boy in the space-aged red costume.

Titan bristled. He folded his arms and stood as tall as his height allowed.

"I may be a kid, but I'm big enough and strong enough and MAN enough to stop your little stunt in its tracks! We're just gonna wait right here till the police arrive to arrest you!"

"Forget that, you little punk!" the thief said, as he turned and ran.

Hearing the term "punk" used to describe him angered Titan beyond recognition. He flashed out of sight only to reappear in direct line of the criminal's escape route. Desperately the thief brandished a knife at Titan waving it threateningly at the outraged hero.

"Don't come any closer, or I'll slice your throat, punk!" the thief snarled.

Upon hearing the word "punk" again, Titan cracked his neck and doubled his fist with his right hand, aiming his knuckles at the blade.

"I don't think so…" he said calmly. "DON'T EVER CALL ME PUNK AGAIN!" he bellowed.

A red beam of energy flashed from Titan's fist, striking the blade, instantly heating the knife red hot. The thief howled as he dropped his weapon to the ground.

"YEEEEEOOOOOOOWWWWWWW!" the man screamed.

In shock and horror, the thief gazed at his scaled hand.

Titan aimed his fist at the man.

"OK, you saw what I did to your knife. Call me "punk" again, and the next blast is for you! I'm not so sure what it'll do to you. I haven't quite got the hang of controlling these energy beams yet, so no guarantees!" Titan snarled.

"Hey, k-k-kid. P-P-Please don't kill me…" the man begged.

"Well that is totally up to you. Stay put and let's not let this get outta hand" bluffed Titan. He knew that he could not pull himself to kill another living being.

Ironically and much to the relief of the would-be thief, three police officers arrived on the scene. They handcuffed the perpetrator and led him away. The criminal kept babbling incoherently about laser beams and other non-comprehendible phrases.

Titan was about to fly away, when a TV news reporter came running up to him.

"Titan! Excuse me, Titan," he said, panting and out of breath.

"Yes, Sir! Can I help you?" asked the ever polite super-hero.

"I'm from Channel 6 News. We would like to feature you on our morning news program. We would love to have you on the show to demonstrate your strength and some of the other powers that you posses. We are scheduled to have four world-class bodybuilders on the program, we would love to see how you measure up to them" the man said, as he handed Titan a business card.

"Oh, I don't know." Titan sighed at first.

"Please, Titan! It would be an excellent opportunity for the people of DC to get to know their hero. Learn a little about what makes you tick as a person! It will give you the opportunity to let the people know more about you and what you stand for" the news caster added.

"Alright, seeing as though you put it that way, I'll see if I can make it! As long as some kind of emergency doesn't come up, I'll do it." Titan agreed.

The man passed a business card to Titan. "Just come to this address on the day and time listed on the back of this card, okay?" the man pointed out. "We'll take care of the rest!"

After the reporter left, Titan flew back to the dark alley next to the bagel shop, where he changed back into his street clothes. He rejoined his mom. A little tentatively, he handed her the business card that was given to him by the channel-six reporter.

He explained, "They want me to make an appearance as Titan on their morning news show. They want me to kind of show off a little and tell the people of Washington a little about myself."

His mom was supportive but insisted they check with Jake's dad which they did that evening. Charles was slightly hesitant but was willing for Titan to go forward with the television appearance. He did, however, insist to Jake, that if they attempted to make him look like the proverbial circus freak, he was to politely bow out and excuse himself.

Chapter 16

On the requested morning, Titan landed at the TV station. He gingerly walked into the building. Just inside the entrance, the receptionist smiled, warmly greeting the young super-hero. She took a moment to enter his name into her visitor log and escorted him to the studio where feature segments for the morning news and variety program were being videotaped. The receptionist introduced him to Gary Whitmire, the interviewer.

Titan sat down in a big overstuffed chair across from Gary who dressed in a blue three-piece suit with a maroon and gray regimental tie.

"Good morning, Titan. Welcome to the morning show. On behalf of our viewing audience, I'd like to thank you for appearing on our program!"

Titan smiled as he replied. "Yes, sir, it is awesome that you would invite me!"

Gary began. "Titan, your exploits these past several weeks since you revealed yourself to the world have been among the most amazing as any in human history! And yet, you are so young! Just how old are you right now, Titan?" Gary asked the super-kid.

"I just turned six a few months ago..." Titan replied.

"Six years old, Wow! How long have you had these amazing abilities?"

"I think it's been nine or ten months now..." Titan answered.

"Can you tell us how you got your powers?" Gary added.

"Umm... Well that is something that I can't go into, sir..." he apologized. "I'm sorry..."

"Now, it says here..." Gary said, as he read from his research notes, "You can fly; you are very strong; very fast; you can see in the dark; and you can fire bursts of energy from your finger tips!"

"Actually," Titan smiled, "the energy beams are directed by my hands, they can be fired from either my fists or my fingertips. But, yes, the rest of it is true."

"Wow. That is amazing!" Gary said, "So young yet so powerful!"

Titan half smiled. "I guess so" he said humbly.

"I bet nobody bullies you in school!"

The studio audience burst into laughter as Titan blushed.

"It says here that you possess unlimited strength?"

Titan objected right away. "Well that may not be totally true sir. I have my limits." he said as he cracked his knuckles. "I just haven't found out what my limits are yet."

"So, you're saying you haven't come across anything too heavy for you to lift?"

There was a slight buzz from the studio audience.

Titan faced the camera and with a grave expression responded, "Mister Whitmire, I'm just grateful that, so far, I've had all the strength I've needed to help out when I'm needed. I hope that I never let anyone down."

Gary nodded. "Well, of course we all join you in that hope."

He then faced the television camera. "After the commercial break, we'll get to see a demonstration of Titan's strength." Gary said. "But before we go to commercial, it says here that you can fly. Now, can you show us?"

Titan stood up from the chair with a wide grin on his face. He loved to fly, and it showed. Then he slowly began to rise off the stage, allowing his body to hover about three feet above the floor. The moment he levitated off the ground, gasps and sighs erupted from the audience. After a few moments, the audience started to applaud Titan's feat.

"There you have it, ladies and gentlemen... This young man really can fly!" Gary exclaimed. "Amazing!"

Titan then flew over the seated audience, slowly and just a few feet above the guests, making wide circles in the auditorium before he turned around and made his way back towards the stage. There, he remained floating at eye-level right next to Gary, with his white boots more hovering than a foot above the stage floor. The red light on the camera faded off signaling that they went to commercial.

The stage director counted in as the show came back on the air. "Welcome back ladies and gentlemen. Now, Titan… We would like to see how strong you are. Do you mind giving us a demonstration?" Gary asked the young hero.

The young pre-teen hero was still hovering before Gary at his eye level.

"Sure!" the boy smiled shyly.

"I'm going to have four finalists of last year's Mister Olympia pro bodybuilding competition come out. These four incredibly powerful muscle-men, some of the strongest men in the world, will bring out a twelve hundred pound concrete block and set it before us. Do you think you could lift that for our audience?"

Titan shrugged. "We'll I'll sure try. Guess we'll find out."

Gary called the four amazing bodybuilders onto the studio set. They hefted the massive concrete by two long steel poles attached to the cement block by four rings, one at each corner, two men in front and two behind. It was a struggle, but they managed to maneuver the cement block into position where they set it down on the floor. There was a heavy duty D-Ring fastened to the center of the block.

Gary turned to Titan and said, "Titan, you saw these phenomenally powerful men move that block into position. They managed, but as you saw, it was a challenge even for them. Now it's your turn."

Titan drifted over to the cement block, reoriented his body to parallel to the floor, maneuvered himself into position, reached down and grasped the D-Ring and began to rise three feet off the floor. Then, with his right hand, he began to do one arm bicep curls. After 5 reps, he changed hands and easily pumped out another 5 reps. Then he looked up at Gary and asked. "Where should I set this down?"

Gary was speechless, as was everyone else in the studio. Titan asked again. "Hello! Sir, where would you like me to set this down?"

Gary managed to collect his wits as he stammered. "Right there will be fine. We'll get a crew to move it out after the show."

"Oh, no need for that," Titan answered. I'll just get this thing out of the way. No need to make somebody else struggle when I can just as easily get it out of here."

A stage hand motioned for Titan to follow him offstage. As the young hero floated after him, still hefting the 1,200 pound cement block he called over his shoulder "I'll be right back." He was back onstage settling down to the floor in front of Gary inside of one minute.

"We have one last request for Titan…" he said, as he pointed to steel tub, fashioned out of a fifty-five gallon oil drum, cut down the middle from top to bottom, set sideways onto four angle iron legs, each leg fitted at the bottom with rolling castors. The makeshift tub had been filled with cold water.

Gary asked, "Titan, can you use your energy beams to boil the water in that steel tub?"

Titan nodded as he obliged, pointing his right index finger at the center of the tub. As the energy beam fired into the cold water, within seconds, it began to boil. A little shyly, Titan said, "I guess I'd better stop before this whole place turns into a steam bath." He shut down his energy beam as the cauldron continued to boil furiously for a few moments before it began to cool, steam still vaporizing from the scalding hot water.

"Wow! There you have it, ladies and gentlemen… Thank you, Titan!" Gary cheered. "This kid is armed and dangerous. He can do it all!"

Titan interrupted. "Well, armed. I guess you could call it that. I have the strength, the speed and the energy beams, but I am NOT dangerous. If you do not mind Sir, I would like to take a minute and let you all know a little about ME, Titan, the person. I was given these powers as a gift. A gift, given to be used for truth and justice. I was normal just like all of you, and I was chosen to be your hero. I am not here to scare anyone, I am here to help. Commissioner Wilson of the Washington Police Department will tell you, I am just another one of the boys in blue, I just happen to wear red, and be six years old. I may be able to do all these amazing things, but I am just like each and every one of you folks. I am here to protect and serve, not to rule or lead!"

The audience rose to their feet, giving Titan a standing ovation as Gary thanked him for appearing as a guest on the program.

The bodybuilders came and took turns shaking Titan's hand. One of them, Jay Cutler, the reigning Mister Olympia, squatted down, inviting Titan to climb onto his shoulder. He stood back up with Titan sitting on his shoulders.

After the show, Titan mingled with members of the program crew and studio audience signing autographs, and posing for pictures. Afterwards leisurely strolled outside the studio and flew home.

Chapter 17

A few evenings later, as Jake was getting ready to go on patrol as Titan, his father came into his room and stopped him. Charles said that he needed to talk to him and that it was important.

"Son, Tim just called."

"Tim! I haven't seen Tim since last year at the dig site!" the boy exclaimed, his face lighting up at the mention of Tim's name.

"He's on his way over here. He'll be here any minute. Do you think you could hold off on your patrol? Tim would really like to see you."

"Sure dad," Jake said, as he raced to the bathroom, quickly changing clothes. No sooner had he slipped into his pajamas than the doorbell rang.

Charles answered the door and invited Tim inside. Tim walked in and greeted Charles and Nancy. Nancy offered Tim a seat and as they all sat down, they immediately began talking business. Presently, Tim felt a gentle tug on his shirt sleeve. He turned around, and was Jake on his knees, hiding behind the sofa. Jake had always loved to sneak up on Tim, even as a little kid.

"You snuck up on me again tiger!" Tim said, as he leaped out of his chair and grabbed Jake from behind. Then he lifted Jake up, and he immediately noticed a difference in the boy.

"Oooh man! You've gotten heavy, kiddo!" Tim said, as he immediately set the boy back on the floor. "What happened to you? What have your folks been feeding you?"

Jake just stood before him with a wide grin on his face, while Tim examined the boy from head to toe. Suddenly, Tim caught Jake by surprise, and reached out with his arm and pulled on his pajama top, raising it almost over his head. "I gotta see this."

"Hey! Quit pulling on my shirt!" Jake protested, as he pulled his shirt back down with a giggle. But it was too late. Tim had already seen some of his abdominals and his pectorals.

"What on Earth! Where did all those muscles come from?" Tim gasped, before he turned towards Charles. "He's gotten huge!"

"Jake's had a remarkable growth spurt!" Charles answered.

"I'll say!" Tim said in disbelief. "What happened to that skinny little kid who I used to be able to lift up with just one arm? My goodness! He must have gained thirty pounds, all of it muscle, since last time I saw him in the Nevada desert!"

Jake hung out with Tim for a few minutes. Then, at his mother's urging, he excused himself to bed, wishing everyone a good evening. As he was leaving the room, he walked over to Tim and wrapped him in a friendly hug. "It was good to see you, Tim. I hope I won't hafta wait a whole year next time!"

Tim laughed, "I'll try to get by here more often. I know if I wait too long, not only will you be too big for me to pick up, you'll be the one picking ME up!"

Jake smiled shyly as he mused. "Little does Tim know…"

Jake actually fell asleep for a few short hours, until just past midnight, when he woke up and donned his Titan costume. He went outside and made his way into the nighttime sky to spend a few hours on his evening patrol.

It was on a cold, Friday afternoon when Titan was flying above the university area when he spotted what appeared to be a teenager sprawled unconscious in the snow. Surveying the area, Titan concluded he had fallen off his motorcycle, since the motorcycle was lying on its side just a few feet away on the street.

"Oh, he looks like he needs some help," Jake thought, as he swooped down and landed right alongside the teen. Jake knelt beside him and attempted to rouse him. Gently he touched the boy's shoulder, careful not to move him. Groggily, the boy came to.

"Hey, are you alright?" Titan asked softly.

"Uhhh... I think I must've hit a patch of ice and lost control of my bike," the teenager answered, as he shook his head, trying to clear away the cobwebs.

"Easy, don't move too much or too fast. Here, let me help you up..." Titan said, as he reached down with his hands and gently lifted the teenager up under his arms. The tall boy finally got back on his feet and brushed the snow off of his black leather jacket, his jeans, his boots, and his scarf. Luckily, he had been wearing a helmet. If he had not been, the outcome could have proved fatally worse than a few scrapes.

"Thanks..." the teen said, as he turned and looked at his rescuer. "Oh wow! You're that Titan-kid?"

"Yep!" Titan grinned. He noted that his new friend had a slight British accent and wondered exactly where he was from.

"Thank you so much for helping me out. I guess I suffered a nasty spill on that patch of black ice in the road," the teen said, as he looked back over the road where he just came from. He tried to lift the motorcycle upright. He drew his left hand back, guarding it in pain.

"Hey, are you ok? I saw you flinch. I really don't think you need to be riding this thing. You may want to let a doctor x-ray that arm" Titan suggested.

"I guess so..." the teen responded.

"I can fly you to the nearest hospital!" Titan smiled. "There's one right down the road!"

"Well, I'd really appreciate that, mate! But, I can't just leave my bike here by the road." the teen replied, as he gingerly swung his leg over the seat on the motorcycle; as he prepared to kick start the engine before continuing on his way.

Titan stopped him, "Well, how about I just fly you on your bike, then?" Titan said, unwilling to give up. "If I was gonna lift your bike, then where would I hold on to it?"

"Lift my bike?" the teen wondered. "It's very heavy, you know!"

"I got this, don't worry..." he assured him.

"You could lift the motorcycle anywhere by that metal bar there, the frame..." the teen said, as he pointed at a thick, metal bar with his right index finger.

"Alright!" Titan cheered. "Hold on tight!"

Titan grasped the metal bar with both hands, lifting the entire motorcycle, with the teenager sitting on it, off the ground! Then, he slowly took off with the bike, and flew motorcycle and rider to the nearby hospital.

Five minutes later, Titan gently set the motorcycle down on the parking lot, near the entrance of the Emergency Department. The teen then took his key, and stepped off the bike.

"Wow! That was amazing!" exclaimed the awe-struck teen. "I fly on my bike, but never like that!"

"By the way, my name is Thomas O'Donnell. But you can call me Tom. I really appreciate all your help..." he said, as he extended his right hand to Titan for the handshake.

"Name's Titan, but you can call me, uhhh, well, Titan!" Titan chuckled.

The two walked into the emergency room and Tom filled out a registration card with the attendant. They sat down in the waiting area, where three other people were seated. There was a TV set and a magazine rack filled with magazines and newspapers. The room was quiet, dull, and boring for the most part. An occasional cough broke the monotony of the silence.

Tom got up and pulled a magazine from the rack and sat down again, next to Titan. As he flipped through the pages, he stopped when he suddenly came across an article about his new friend, Titan. He glanced over the article with amazement.

"Hey... This article's about you!" Tom exclaimed, as he displayed the magazine to the boy hero.

"Awww..." Titan grinned, as he covered his face with his hands. "Those things are everywhere now!"

"It says here you can fly... I know that much. It's how you got us here. You can fire bursts of energy with your fists... - I'd love to see that. - You can see in the dark... Wow! And, you're super strong! Well yeah, I saw that, too, by the way you handled my bike with me on it."

"Don't believe everything you read..." Titan laughed.

Tom answered, "If I hadn't seen it with my own eyes, I wouldn't have believed any of it. I'd heard things about you on the news but never saw anything. But nothing they ever showed on the news prepared me for an up close encounter with the great Titan himself."

Titan just smiled at Tom's kind words. Just then the nurse came and called Tom's name. He was lead into one of the exam rooms, so the doctor could look at his hand, while Titan waited for him. Fifteen minutes later, Tom came out, with his left hand bandaged.

"There! Aren't you glad I talked you into coming here?" Titan said to him, as they walked out of the ER.

Tom, very surprised that Titan had waited for him, exclaimed, "You're still here? You didn't have to wait on me, mate."

Jake smiled. "Well, of course I waited. I wanted to make sure you were OK. You are OK, aren't you?"

"Yes, thanks, but I'm really not supposed to ride my bike for the next few days, until my hand gets better..." Tom answered morosely

"Well, see, it was a good thing that I waited for you!" Titan answered. "I'll fly you home."

"Are... Are you sure?"

"Just tell me where you live! I'll fly you and the bike home!" Titan offered him.

Tom gave Titan the address of his apartment before he climbed aboard his motorcycle. Then Titan flew him to his apartment that he shared with his mother. Tom parked his bike in the small garage where it was safely locked up, before he opened the front door to the apartment and let Titan in through the entrance.

"Hey, cool place..." Titan said, as he looked around the small living room. Tom then showed him to his bedroom, where he had a laptop, a stereo, a video game console, and a large rack containing hundreds of CD's, DVD's and video games. His collection was staggering!

"Dude! You got a ton of games!" Titan said. Like any other kid of his age, Titan loved video games, and he was very impressed with Tom's extensive collection.

"My uncle works in the video game industry, so he sends me all the newest games the moment they come out!" Tom explained. "I get all the latest games for free, so I can play them on my video consoles.

Sometimes I get to test them before they hit the market, rate them and write a report about how I liked them or disliked them…"

"You're kidding!" Titan gasped. This time, it was the young superhero's turn to be impressed. Titan just stared at him with his mouth wide open.

"Wow…"

"You can come over now and then, if you like" Tom offered Titan. "Weekends are better for me, because then I don't have classes. You're always welcome to come over and play games, or just hang out if you like!"

Titan flew over to Tom and hovered just high enough, so that he saw him at the same level.

"Tom, I promise you this, you can always count on me as a friend" Titan said.

The two talked a little longer that evening. Titan learned that Tom was finishing his last year of high school, and taking some college courses on the side. Tom told Titan that his schedule was rough, but he would make the time to hang out whenever he could.

The two quickly became great friends and shook hands again. Titan already looked at Tom as a big brother, and promised that he would come over to visit him from time to time. Tom also promised Titan that he would call him on his cell phone if he ever heard of any emergencies at his high school or on the university campus.

Titan needed to leave, and they said their farewells to one another. Titan made his way back outside into the crisp winter Washington air. He turned and waved one last time as he took to the skies.

Unknown to Tom and Titan, a tall man wearing a black three-piece suit was standing across the street from Tom's house. As soon as Titan had walked out the front door and had taken off, the man reached into his pocket and retrieved his cell phone. He dialed a number before he placed the phone before his lips.

"Target: Titan…..Acquired!"

Chapter 18

One Monday afternoon, as soon as school was over, Jake saw something unusual when he changed into his Titan suit and took off from the deserted locker room in the gymnasium. He flew over the school yard; a familiar girl was waving a large white flag with his name blazoned across it.

"Titan!" she shouted at him. "Please land!"

"That's Cathy..." Titan whispered to himself. Of course, he decided to act like he didn't know her, since that could possibly give away his true identity. He could not let her learn that he was in fact, Jake Knight, her classmate.

Titan circled around and landed a few feet from where she was standing. She, being very happy that he actually noticed her, tossed the handmade flag on the grass and ran towards Titan. Alternately, Titan, being impressed at the flag, dashed over and picked it up off the ground.

"Wow... Did you make this?" Titan said, as he lifted the pole and admired the flag.

Cathy turned back and walked back to where Titan was standing.

"Yes, that's mine. I made that because I figured that was the only way I could get your attention, Titan..." Cathy said to him.

"WOW! That's awesome..." he said, as he admired the flag. Then he looked up at the girl, who was standing right in front of him. He set the flag back down and extended his hand. "Nice to meet you, what's your name?" he asked.

"Oh, I'm Cathy. Nice to meet you too..."

"So… How are you?" Titan asked shyly.

Cathy blushed a little bit, now that she was standing face-to-face before her hero. She examined him from head to toe with a wide grin on her face. Titan realized that as he patiently waited for her answer.

"I-I'm sorry… I'm just so excited to finally meet you in person…" Cathy said excitedly. "I wanted to ask you a small favor…"

Cathy then reached into her backpack and pulled out an invitation card, which she handed over to Titan.

"I have a small birthday party at my house next week Saturday. I'll have about six friends over. There will be all girls and just one other boy besides you, so it'll be a small group. I'd love for you to come to my party, Titan… I think that would be so very cool if you could make it…" she said to him, while he looked over the card.

"Gosh… I-I don't know what to say…" Titan replied. "I've never been invited to a party before…"

"Are you serious?"

"Yeah… With the whole super-hero thing I really don't get the chance to make too many parties…" Titan continued.

"Oh…" Cathy said dejectedly. "I really hope you can make it… Even if you can come for just a few minutes…"

"I'll do my best to show up! I promise!" Titan said, as he placed the card back into the envelope. "I'll be there!"

"Thank you, Titan! My address is on the card! I really appreciate it!" Cathy grinned. "Thank you so much…"

"Well I have to get going" Titan said as he took to the skies. "I will see you soon, and I promise to try and make it to the party" he continued as he flew overhead and out of sight.

Later that afternoon, he landed back at home. He recounted what happened right after school, and asked if he could borrow ten Dollars from his mother. He thought of what his friend may like for her birthday. After much deliberation he opted to go to the bookstore down the street from his house, where he purchased a small birthday gift, and took it home to gift wrap it.

When Saturday afternoon finally arrived, Jake first got up and took care of any chores that he had around the house. He helped Nancy with the dishes and the laundry, and he finished all the reading he had to do for the following week. Then, donning his Titan costume he took off, and patrolled the downtown area for a few hours before the party. When the time came to go to the party, he flew back home and retrieved the invitation card and the gift, so that he knew exactly where to find her house.

Titan flew around for about ten minutes, attempting to find her house. Finally he landed by the front door, where he rang the door bell. A friendly lady opened, who immediately recognized Titan. As she let him in, Cathy came walking up to him with a wide grin on her face.

"I'm so glad you made it, Titan!" Cathy said, as she accepted the present from the young hero.

"Well, thanks for inviting me…. happy birthday!"

Cathy showed Titan to where the other kids had gathered around the food and present table. There was a large cake with seven candles atop its sugary surface. Presents were all around, and kids standing in awe as the hero made his way into the circle of friends.

They all laughed and carried on, playing games and talking. For the first time since his meeting with Zhango-Rhe, Titan felt like a "normal" kid again. He soaked up the feeling, knowing that would be few and far between for him now. They all continued playing party games until one kid asked if Titan would take him flying.

Being the good sport that he was, Titan agreed and took turns taking each and every one of them up into the sky. He flew each kid around the yard, before setting them down and then taking the next person in line. The kids loved it, and Titan became an instant hit.

Cathy's dad loved making model trains for kids, and since he had built a locomotive that was big enough for five kids to sit in, Titan asked for all five of them to climb on board of the wooden locomotive. The locomotive was sitting in the back yard of Cathy's house, and Titan made sure it was sturdy enough for him to be able to lift it up and over the ground before he tried to fly it first. Titan gently lifted the locomotive without the kids, and he flew it high above the air. When he saw that it held up okay, he came back and allowed for the kids to get in.

Once the kids had climbed aboard, Titan lifted the locomotive again, and he positioned the wooden vehicle on his back. Then, he slowly took off and flew over the house, carrying the locomotive and the kids on his back with him. The kids cheered and shouted and Titan flew them on a tour over the neighborhood, as he slowly flew over the streets and the surrounding areas. After about thirty minutes of flying around, he returned to Cathy's backyard and set the wooden locomotive back on the grass again, so the kids could get out safely.

Everyone there had a great time and they all thanked Titan for coming to the party. As they left, Titan realized that this would probably be the first and definitely not the last time that he would be invited to come to a party, once word got out about how much fun the kids had with him.

Chapter 19

Charles had taken Nancy to the doctor's office early one Monday morning. They had wanted to have a second child for a long time already, but they were unable to conceive. A visit to the doctor's office had confirmed their worst fears, that the difficult pregnancy Nancy had with Jake had left her in a state where she could no longer bear children.

While they were driving home, as devastated as they felt, Nancy and Charles began discussing the idea of adopting a second child. They wanted to surprise Jake with a little brother or sister, but they felt that if they kept it a secret, even Jake may come to resent the child.

Charles and Nancy informed Jake that they would be visiting with a representative of an adoption agency while Jake was in school. Jake had a ton of questions, which his parents did well in easing. Charles told Jake that he and his mother would be making multiple visits to the adoption agency. Jake talked to them about the reasons. Nancy, in the most heartfelt way, told her only biological son, that they had wanted to provide for him a brother or sister to look after. Jake sensed his mother's emotions, accepted what she was saying.

The Knight's met with the agency, filling out a mountain of paperwork, and selecting a boy as their choice for adoption. The representative began an extensive search and located a boy who fit the Knight's profile perfectly. The boy had been orphaned at an early age, and his guardian, who was his grandmother, had major health issues. She was unable to continue caring for the young child. The boy was shy and lonely, and longed for an older brother. Charles and

Nancy finally got the opportunity to meet the grandmother, and they were introduced to the boy, whose name was Madison.

Jake knew that they were going to adopt a child, but whom and when a mystery to him remained. His heart would flutter every time his parents would mention it over dinner. Jake was getting excited, but nervous at the prospect of being an older brother. He was scared that the child would not like him.

Two weeks prior to Jake's seventh birthday, the final meeting between the Knight's, the agency and Madison took place. Madison was only five years old now, and he was quiet and lonely, although he was known to be friendly and outgoing when he was surrounded by other kids. He was a few inches shorter than Jake but still very athletic; he had long, jet-black hair and brown eyes, and he was extremely bright for his age. Lastly, he had a keen interest in computers and anything electronic. He also longed to be with other kids, and he always expressed a strong desire to have an older brother whom he could look up to.

When Charles and Nancy heard that, they were confident that Jake would be a perfect "older brother" for little Madison. They signed the paperwork and they arranged for Madison Jacob Wayne Knight to become Jake's adopted little brother on the morning of Jake's seventh birthday.

During the evening before Jake's seventh birthday, Jake was flying around the Capitol area, where there was a serious traffic accident. Two cars had crashed earlier, and Jake helped flying the passengers to the hospital. He also helped move the cars out of the way, so that the traffic wasn't blocked any longer.

When he was done, Jake continued his night patrol as his Titan persona. He stopped on several rooftops and paused for a few moments, when he realized that everything was quiet. Then he leaped into the air and flew to the park, which was located down the street from his school. He walked around there for a few minutes and decided it was time to fly back home, when he became bored.

When Jake landed on the balcony of his house, it was almost midnight. It had just occurred to him, that it was his birthday. He decided to be as quiet as he possibly could, since he expected everyone to be asleep by now. By the time he came down the stairs, he was startled to see his parents sitting quietly on the couch in the living room, along with one other boy, who was seated next to Charles on the couch.

"Hey... Mom and dad... You're still awake?" Jake asked surprisingly, as he came down the stairs.

"Oooh cool!" Madison whispered to Charles. "That's Titan!"

Jake then walked a little closer.

"Who... Who's that?" Jake wondered, as he pointed to Madison.

"Jake, this is Madison!" Charles explained. "He's your adopted little brother, as of today..."

Jake just froze in his tracks, with his mouth dropped wide open.

"What? Little brother? This is my little brother? You guys did it!" Jake stuttered.

Madison then got off the couch and slowly started walking towards Jake, with a big smile on his face.

"Happy birthday, Titan..." he said, as he extended his arms so he could hug Jake for the first time as his big brother.

"DUDE..." Jake said, as he gently embraced Madison for the first time, with tears rolling down his cheeks. "You're my little brother! This is....well....AWESOME!"

Both Charles and Nancy held on to one another as they watched the boys embrace for the first time. They couldn't help but break down in tears as well.

Finally Jake pulled back and looked down at Madison, who was only a few inches shorter than him.

"I don't know what to say...." Jake sobbed. "This is the most amazing birthday present ever... I must be dreaming... To have a little brother, is just awesome!"

"Look who's talking!" Madison laughed. "I must be living in a dream right now! My big brother is none other than TITAN!"

Jake couldn't help but smile as he looked down at the boy. He was still fighting back the tears.

"Hey, Madison..." Jake whispered to him. "When we're at home... You don't need to call me 'Titan'. You can always call me 'Jake', okay?"

Madison looked up at Jake with his innocent, brown eyes.

"Sure... And when we're here at home, you can always call me 'Maddie'" Madison replied. "But, please don't get mad at me if I call you 'Titan' now and then, okay?"

"No problem, little bro..." Jake replied. "Just remember to keep it a secret, okay?"

"I will..." Madison whispered back. "I won't tell anyone who you are, Jake!"

"Good..."

"Jake, we are going to let Madison sleep in your room for a few days. Just let him use the extra bed until we finish converting the guest room into a separate bedroom for him. Then we can have him move into his room over the weekend." Charles suggested to him. "I already put his suitcase in your room upstairs."

"Great!" Jake said, as he turned towards Madison. "Let's go upstairs, Maddie!"

Jake turned around and ran up the stairs, with Madison following close behind. They quickly dashed in the room, and Jake sat down on the edge of his bed. Madison sat down right next to him, and opened his suitcase, which lay on the floor by his feet.

"I got something to show you" he said, as he reached down and pulled out a small poster that was folded up in fours. Madison removed the poster from the suitcase and completely unfolded it, revealing a small, and full-color poster of Titan. "I hope you don't mind me hanging this on your wall..."

Jake just stared at the poster with a chuckle.

"Maddie... Why would you want to hang that in here, when you have the real thing?" he asked his little brother.

"Well... You won't always be home..." Madison replied. "Besides, you're still my hero! Can I hang it on the wall? Can I?"

Jake stared at the poster of him and pondered what to say. He felt a little awkward having a poster of him hanging in his own room, but he understood that it would make Madison feel better.

"Please?" Madison asked him again.

"Alright, but one of these days, we'll ask dad to take a REAL photo of the two of us, okay? Then we'll hang that on the wall, somewhere..."

"A picture of me and Titan!" Madison cheered. "That's awesome!"

"Well, it'll be a picture of you and your brother, who just happens to be Titan..." Jake corrected him. "But nobody else needs to know that, right?"

"You got it!" Madison laughed.

"Well, let's get ready for bed, okay?" Jake suggested.

"Sure! I already took a shower this evening... So, I'm ready for bed..." Madison explained.

Jake then walked up to his dresser and got his pajamas, before he headed to the bathroom. He took a quick shower and dried off, before he put on his pajamas and walked back into the bedroom where he found Madison working on his laptop, while he was sitting at his desk.

"Ahh, you found my laptop, huh?" Jake asked him.

"Yeah, well you'll be happy to know that I'm really good with computers!" Madison pointed out. "I can take them apart, put them together, and fix them in no time at all!"

"Really?" Jake wondered, as he walked up to his desk, where Madison was sitting.

Madison had already altered the configuration of the laptop so that it ran much faster than before and the laptop didn't crash that many times, as it used to do earlier.

"Wow... You really did fix it up a lot! It's running a lot better now!" Jake noticed. "Thanks a ton, little bro!"

"I'm good at working with anything that has to do with computers or electronics" Madison explained. "I love working with these things...Just call it a gift....I don't know how I know it, I just do."

"Wow... That will definitely come in handy..." Jake wondered out loud.

The two boys just chatted about computers for a bit before they each crawled into their own bed. Jake's bed was on one side of the room, while Madison's bed was on the other. Jake had always had a large room, so that he could house all of his toys and books, so an extra bed was no problem.

As soon as Jake's head hit the pillow, he passed out into a deep sleep. Madison still had a hard time falling asleep, since it was his very first night at the Knight's house, and he was still very excited about all the changes.

Madison finally dozed off into a light sleep for awhile, until he woke up again about two hours later. When he looked around the room, he noticed that Jake wasn't lying in the same position as before.

In fact, it almost appeared as if Jake's bed was raised up slightly higher than before. Madison thought it was really odd, for he could have sworn that Jake's bed was at the same level as his own. He closed his eyes and turned around again, and tried to fall asleep.

A few moments later, Madison heard a light moan coming from Jake's side of the room. He turned his head, and realized that Jake had moved. Then, Madison looked up and was startled when he realized that Jake appeared to be almost two feet over his mattress, with his sheet and blanked draped over his body.

Madison blinked and rubbed his eyes, trying to get adjusted to the darkness. He strained attempting to see Jake's peculiar sleeping position. He tried squinting his eyes to make out Jake's floating form in the darkness.

Madison then heard Jake turn around, which made his sheet and his blanket fall off the left side of his body and tumble to the empty mattress, which was about three feet below him. This exposed Jake's body, showing him floating in mid-air, while the sleeping boy was holding on to a pillow with both hands.

Madison couldn't believe it! His mouth dropped wide open in utter amazement when he saw his adopted big brother hover above his bed while he was sound asleep. He wasn't sure of what to do, since this was his very first night. He knew his big brother was special and has these unusual abilities, but he hadn't expected this.

Madison quietly climbed out of his bed and walked over to Jake's bed, where he stopped right before the empty bed where Jake was still floating above the mattress. He extended his arm and placed it just under Jake's body, about a foot above the surface of the mattress, where the sheets were laying.

"Wow… This is too weird…" he thought to himself, as he verified the fact that his big brother was indeed flying in his sleep. "It's weird, but cool!"

Then he decided to gently wake him up. "Titan! I mean, Jake!" he whispered to his brother. "Wake up!"

Madison reached out and tugged on Jake's pajama shirt, and slowly pulled Jake towards him. This caused Jake's body to slowly hover closer to where Madison was standing.

"He's like a human balloon!" Madison whispered.

Then he tried to wake him up one more time.

"Jake! You're floating above your bed!"

"Hmmmm?" Jake groaned, as he slowly turned his body around, so that he now lay on his stomach. He was now facing Madison.

"I'm sorry if I scared you, Maddie…" Jake said groggily. "I always float in my sleep…"

"Really?" Madison replied. "Oh wow! That is so cool!"

"If you wake up in the middle of the night and you see that I have drifted off to the other end of the room, just pull me back to my side of the room, okay?" Jake said to him, while he still had his eyes closed.

"Sure, bro… Now that I know that you sleep like this, I won't be so freaked out!" Madison chuckled.

"I'm sorry, Maddie. I guess I should have told you, but I was too excited last night when I met you…" Jake said when he finally opened his eyes and looked up at his brother. "My flying-power takes over as soon as I fall asleep. I guess it's one of the side effects of having super-powers…"

"Ooh I think it's very cool, just being able to share a room with Titan…" Madison chuckled, as he looked up at Jake, who was still hovering above his bed.

"Hey, you're the coolest brother I can ask for…" Jake said, as he reached out and ran his hand over the top of Madison's head.

Madison quickly reached down and grabbed the end of the blanket, and pulled it up and over Jake's back. He kept on pulling until Jake was completely covered.

"Thanks little bro…" Jake said, while he let out a yawn. "I'm really tired… I only need a few hours' worth of sleep but when I'm tired, I'm really drained…"

"Good night, Titan…" Madison said, as he turned around and walked back towards his bed. He got back on his mattress and looked back at his big brother, who was still floating three feet above his bed.

"Wow... I have the coolest brother in the whole wide world..." Madison thought.

Both boys finally fell asleep again and they slept until the next morning.

Chapter 20

Jake was usually the first person to wake up in the morning. He routinely got up very early and donned his Titan suit so he could fly around the area before he would go to school. He would check the neighborhood and the residential areas, which was easy for him to do since it never took long for him to shower and get ready for school. Once he was finished, he would meet in the kitchen and join the family for breakfast. Now that Madison had joined the family, they would have breakfast with the four of them, before the boys would leave for school.

Jake would normally fly to school as Titan, but now that they had Madison with them, Jake and Madison would ride the bus together for the time being. Eventually, Jake would go back to flying to school, once Madison was settled and had gotten used to his new classmates and school surroundings.

Since it was the morning of Jake's birthday, Madison and Jake still had a few minutes in their bedroom upstairs, after Jake had returned from his early morning patrol. Madison had already showered and had gotten dressed. He was sitting on his bed when Jake walked in, while still wearing his Titan uniform.

"Happy birthday, big bro!" Madison said to him again, as Jake sat down next to him. Jake reached out with his arm, and gently embraced his younger brother, while pulling him closer towards him with a gentle squeeze.

"I'm so excited I have you as my little brother..." Jake smiled. "What an incredible birthday present..."

"Well, I've always wanted a big brother who was cool," Madison said with a grin. "But I had never counted on getting Titan as my big brother! That is just the ultimate dream-come-true!!"

"Thank you, Maddie…"

"Now, I didn't get you a present… Is there anything you'd like for your birthday?" Madison asked him sadly.

"Don't be silly! You are my birthday present!" Jake replied. "You don't need to get me anything!"

"Alright…fair enough" Madison replied, after he had given that some thought.

He pondered that a moment longer, before he asked his next question.

"Is there anything you'd wish for?" he asked Jake.

"Well…" Jake thought out loud. "I sometimes wish I could get to places faster… I often find out about emergencies or crimes at the last minute, and it takes me a few minutes to fly to places before I can help those in need. I can't be everywhere and I can't be two places at once. I just wish someone could tell me when there was a problem or an emergency, and I wish there was a way I could get there instantly…"

"You mean you wish you could teleport?" Madison wondered.

"Something like that…" Jake answered. "I think it would definitely help…"

"Maybe someone could invent a teleportation machine and you could use it to teleport to different places!" Madison said excitedly. "When a news bulletin comes on, they get the coordinates and the location of the problem, and you step into the machine and it teleports you there instantly!"

"Yeah…" Jake sighed. "We just need someone who can build us a teleportation machine…"

"Well, are there any super-heroes who have teleportation-powers?"

"I don't know of any" Jake shrugged. "When I meet someone who does, you'll be the first to know!"

"It'll be great if you could make friends with someone who had teleportation-powers! He could teleport you to places where there is an emergency!" Madison suggested. "You'd be able to help so many people then!"

"Not only that..." Jake chuckled. "I'd ask him to teleport me to school every day!"

"That's not fair!" Madison said angrily. "You can fly! You should fly to school! If you meet a friend who has teleportation-powers, then I'll ask him to teleport me to school instead!"

"What if this person were a girl?"

Madison gave Jake a horrified look on his face.

"Then she can teleport you. I'll take the bus to school!" Madison responded.

"Jake! Madison! BREAKFAST!" Nancy yelled from the kitchen below.

"Let's go!" Jake said, as he got up and ran down the stairs, with Madison following right behind him. It was almost time to go to school, and it seemed that Jake and Madison had enjoyed their first early-morning brainstorming session together.

Luckily for Jake, his day at school went by rather quickly. Jake was one of the best students in his class, thanks to his powers. He had no trouble studying for any of the tests, and he always completed all his assignments much quicker than most other students. Jake never spent more than five minutes doing all his homework, and he always got very high grades on all his tests, quizzes and assignments. He studied faster, better, and remembered more than everyone else.

Once school was over, he was supposed to meet Madison by the main gate of the school. He stood there and waited patiently for his little brother, so that they could board the bus together. Normally, Jake never took the bus home from school, but he started doing that, now that Madison was living with him.

As soon as Madison got out of the classroom, he came running towards Jake, who was patiently waiting by the front gate.

"Maddie!" Jake shouted, so his brother could see him. "Over here!"

Madison came running and stopped right in front of him. Then, the two walked up to the school bus, which pulled up a few feet in front of them. The two boys got on, and sat near the back of the bus.

"I bet this is different from flying home, huh?" Madison whispered to Jake.

"Yeah... No kidding... I can run faster than this..." Jake replied. "I'm still gonna go flying this afternoon, though..."

"What?" Madison shot back in surprise. "You're going flying? What about me?"

"Sssshhhhh" Jake whispered to his little brother. "Don't tell everybody on the bus..."

"Oh...sorry, Jake..."

"Tell you what" Jake continued. "How about I take you with me? Would you like to go for a ride?"

Madison stared at him with a huge grin on his face.

"Let's not talk about it now. Wait till we get home, okay?" Jake said to his little brother.

"Okay, big bro..."

The two brothers just continued to talk about school until the bus came close to their house. Then they got off the bus and walked to their house. Jake unlocked the front door and let Madison in, and both boys went up to their rooms so they could do their homework. Jake quickly changed into his Titan uniform and he turned on his laptop so he could check his e-mails.

After about twenty minutes, Madison walked in and smiled when he saw Titan standing before him.

"Wow! You're dressed up as Titan already!" Madison noticed.

"Oh yeah!" Jake replied. He was sitting at his desk while reading a magazine. "As soon as I get home, I change into my uniform!"

Madison sat down on the bed and stared at his big brother. He was completely in awe of his super-hero brother. "Do you also do your homework while you're wearing your Titan costume?" he asked.

"Absolutely! I spend more time in this than I do in my normal clothes..." his big brother replied, pointing down at his uniform.

"So, what do you do now? Do you just wait for the police to call you?"

"Yeah, unless I just go out on patrol. Speaking of which..." Jake pondered. "I'm just itching to go flying. I've been on the ground all day, so I'm ready to get my hair in the wind. Do you want to go for a ride with me?"

"Yeah...Of course!" Madison said, as he stood up and walked right up to his big brother.

"Now, you might want to wear a jacket so you don't catch cold..." Jake suggested. "I can take the cold, but I don't want mom to get mad at me for taking you flying and for allowing you to get sick!"

"Okay, I'll grab my jacket!"

Madison went into his room and put on a jacket, before he returned to Jake's bedroom. Then the two boys walked out to the balcony from there, and Jake grabbed hold of Madison by his torso before he slowly lifted off.

"Hold on, Maddie! We're off!" he announced.

"Come on, Titan!" Madison cheered. "Let's go!"

Jake slowly ascended into the sky while holding Madison against his chest, as he flew over the neighborhood. Madison got his first bird's eye view of the city, and was just in awe. They flew over their street, and then passed over the park and over the school, which were several blocks away. From there, they then flew over the business part of the city, before they came nearer to the downtown area and then the part where the government buildings were.

They saw several historic landmarks and national monuments from the sky, including national parks and several large museums and large, federal buildings. They even saw the Capitol and the White House from a distance! Jake then looped back and took Madison around to other parts of the city, before landing on the rooftop of one of the skyscrapers so they could take a break.

"What a nice view!" Madison described, as he looked down from the edge of the wall that surrounded the rooftop. The two boys just leaned up against the wall, which was only four feet tall.

"You're not cold, are you?" Jake asked him again. He wanted to be absolutely sure his little brother was feeling okay.

"I'm fine now but it's starting to get a little cold..."

"Well, how about we make our way back home before it gets dark?" Jake asked him.

"Sure..." Maddie replied, as he looked over across the sky. "Look! You can see the sunset!"

"Yeah... Isn't that beautiful?"

"Man… I am the luckiest brother in the world…" Madison sighed.

"Why is that?"

"Because I'm living here, I have such cool parents now, and I have you as my big brother!"

"Well, you know what, Maddie?" Jake added. "I don't think I've ever taken anyone flying like this before. I've always had to go out on rescues or stop bad guys or help people in need… But this is the first time I've ever had the chance to take someone flying… Just for fun…"

"Really?" the younger brother wondered.

"Yes, really… Being 'Titan' has become a little bit of a job for me… But now that you're here, I actually have someone I can share my experiences with…To share in the lighter side of my powers… You know what I mean?"

"Can't you share with mom and dad?"

"Yes, but to a degree…" Jake replied. "But it's not the same as sharing with a brother…someone close to my age….someone who shares in the awesomeness of it."

"Well, I would love to hear all of your stories and adventures!" Madison announced.

"Alright, then… We'll make a deal! When I come home from my patrol, I'll tell you all about what I did that day, okay?" Jake said to his little brother.

"Cool! So, I don't have to read it in the newspaper or wait to watch it on TV?"

"Nope, you'll hear it straight from source!"

"Alright, that sounds like a good deal, big bro!" Maddie said, as the two boys shook hands on it. Just then, they turned and realized that it had already started to get dark outside.

"Oooh look! That stars are coming out!"

"I'd better get you home… I think we're going to have supper pretty soon, and mom and dad should be coming home any minute now anyway! They'll probably wonder why you're not home…" Jake said.

"Well, they're probably used to you not being home…" Madison pointed out.

"Yeah, but you not being there, will probably have them worried…. So, are you ready?"

"Yes, let's go, Titan!"

Jake gently wrapped his arms around Madison's torso before he lifted off. Then he flew back to their house in one straight shot, landing on their balcony on the second floor of the house. They landed right on time, for Charles and Nancy arrived home from work about ten minutes later.

For Madison it was the most unforgettable first full day at the Knight's house. He loved going flying with Jake, and he hoped that this was just the first of many times he would have the opportunity to go flying with his famous big brother.

Chapter 21

Several months after Jake's seventh birthday, the Knight family had decided to have dinner at a steakhouse near the downtown area of Washington. Jake, Madison, Nancy and Charles had dressed up in nice dress clothes.

Once they arrived, they were seated at their table, which was by the window overlooking the city. Both Jake and Madison were enjoying the view from there and were looking at the traffic from where they were seated.

"Wow, you can see everything from here; you see the planes flying in the sky above us; you see the cars in front of us, and you can even see the railroad over in the distance!" Madison pointed out.

"I think there's a freight train leaving right there…" Jake noted, as he saw a freight train move across the tracks.

The train wasn't very long. It consisted of the locomotive and about fifteen container cars behind it. The boys gazed out the large glass window as the train slowly moved out of the city.

They finally ordered their drinks and their food, which arrived about fifteen minutes later. The family had just started eating their dinner when Jake's cell phone started buzzing in his pocket. Jake immediately stopped eating and answered it.

"Hello? Yes, officer! A freight train? It's where? Near Highlands and Water Street? It's stuck on a what? At a crossing? There's a passenger train coming on the other track? Gotcha! I'll be right there! Yes sir! Bye!" Jake said over the cell phone.

"Mom, Dad, Madison, I am sorry, I have to go! I need to handle this. I am so sorry that something came up.…"

"Jake we understand sweetheart.....GO......Do what you need to.... We will pack all your food up and take it home if you are not done when we finish here....Be careful son!" Nancy urged her son.

Jake quickly walked over to the restroom and changed into his Titan costume. Then, he flew out of the restaurant at super speed, so that nobody saw him.

Titan took to the air and soared to the location at top speed. Apparently, it was the train that he had spotted several minutes earlier, as it had rolled by the restaurant from a distance. He spotted the freight train, which had suddenly gotten a serious mechanical failure, which prevented it from moving any further down the track. Unfortunately, the train had stopped right where the fourth car was left blocking an intersection of another track. To make matters worse, a passenger train was scheduled to pass through that intersection in less than ten minutes!

"I've got to move the train out of the way!" Titan said, as he surveyed the situation from the air. He saw the stranded freight train, and he spotted the tracks coming from the other side, which intersected the tracks that the stranded train was on. In any case, the freight train was blocking the passenger train's way!

Titan flew over to the locomotive and landed right in front of it, while walking with his white boots over the wooden pillars that the train tracks were bolted on to.

"I need to push the train out of the way..." he said, as Titan spit in his hands and rubbed them together. "Time to get to work..."

The mighty boy them rested his hands on the front of the locomotive and gently applied some pressure. Then, using his titanic strength, he slowly started to walk forward, while pushing the locomotive, and all fifteen cars behind it, backwards.

Several representatives from the railroad company arrived and got out and watched. They were completely amazed by the sheer strength of the boy, who slowly brought the entire train into motion and was able to push it back, step by step.

"Look! It's moving! Look how that kid is pushing the entire train back with his bare hands!" one of the men said, who worked for the company who ran the railroad.

As Titan pushed, the train continued to roll backwards, thanks to the boy's superhuman strength. It was an amazing feat.

"Come on…" Titan said to himself. "Just three more cars…"

The train was heavy, even for him. He wanted to get the train past the intersection so that the other train could cross, and prevent a major catastrophe from happening.

"The other train will be here in two minutes!" the representative said. "Please hurry!"

The pressure was on, and Titan was feeling it.

"Faster… Come on…" he said, as he gritted his teeth. Titan wished that he was bigger and stronger now. He knew that he would eventually grow even stronger than he was now, but he needed to muster every ounce of strength he could come up with now, in order to get the train out of the way as quickly as possible. He reached deep down within his innermost being, and pulled up the amazing strength he needed to push the train.

"A little more… Just a little more…"

"The train will be here in about one minute, Titan!" he heard someone yell.

Titan took a deep breath and closed his eyes. He grinded his teeth and gave it his all. He poured on every ounce of power he had inside his compact form.

"Rrrraaaaaaaaahhhhhh!!!" Titan shouted, as he pushed the train back with an incredible burst of energy.

The oncoming train's whistle bellowed out its warning. Titan knew that he had to move faster if he were to avert disaster. He dug his heels into the ground and pushed with everything he had.

Titan got the freight train past the crossing, so that it had just cleared the intersection, when the passenger train came and passed through at high speed! He had pushed the freight train out of the way in the nick of time!

The representative from the railroad company walked up to Titan and shook his hand, thanking him for saving the day and for coming out and preventing this major disaster from happening.

Titan then said goodbye to him and took off. He then flew back to the restaurant, where he quickly changed back into his normal clothes so he could rejoin the rest of the family for dinner at the steakhouse.

"Good job, son!" Charles whispered to Jake, as he sat down in his chair. "We just saw it in the news on the TV that was hanging on the wall…"

"Yeah… but now my ribs have gotten cold…" Jake sighed.

The waiter came and took Jake's plate and promised to heat up his food for him. A few minutes later, he returned with a hot plate with BBQ Ribs.

"Dig in, son! You deserve it, after that workout!" Nancy chuckled.

"Yeah! You don't get to push a train every day, huh, Jake?" Madison laughed.

"No, ya sure don't!" Jake said, as he started to pour sauce all over his ribs. As soon as he started to eat his first rib, he spilled sauce on his shirt, not to mention the sauce that was now adorning his face and hands.

"Jake! You're making a mess!" Nancy said.

"Leave him, honey! He worked hard today. Let him enjoy his food…Not to mention…. ribs aren't good unless you are wearing them!" Charles said calmly.

At long last, the Knight family got to enjoy a meal together as a whole. This was the first time since Jake had gained his Titan powers that they had been able to share a family meal out together, and the first time with Madison as part of the family.

Chapter 22

Jake experienced one of the scariest moments in his brief heroic career shortly after his eighth birthday. One morning, while Jake was in class, the Commissioner phoned him and left a voice mail. Excusing himself from class, he dashed to the gymnasium to listen to his message. What he heard chilled him to the bone. A lunatic gunman had entered Roosevelt Middle School and taken a classroom full of students hostage.

Fearing the worst, Jake immediately changed into his Titan uniform and flew off to the school, which was blocked off to traffic and which was surrounded by police officers and members of the SWAT team.

The Commissioner came up to him with the tactical commander of the SWAT team and pointed out the classroom, where the gunman was. The Tac-Commander revealed that there were estimated to be about twenty students in the classroom, one teacher, presumably either dead or wounded, and the door to the classroom was closed and locked. There was no other way to get into the room.

Jake realized he needed to take a big risk, either by smashing through the window or by breaking through the wall in order to get in. Either way, he needed the gunman to know that he was going to be cornered. He flew over to the classroom, and peered through one of the windows. He saw that all the students were kneeling on the floor, and the gunman was standing near the front of the room, holding an automatic rifle in his hand. Titan knew that he had to act quickly in order to get the students out. He needed to use the element of surprise.

He got up and used his mighty shoulder to break a hole through the brick wall, causing the entire wall to cave in. Suddenly, there was an opening into the classroom, and when all the bricks had fallen and the dust had settled, Titan stepped into the room. Obviously, the students, and the gunman were startled when Titan suddenly burst through the brick wall at the back of the classroom!

"Drop your gun, you creep!" Titan said to the gunman, as he slowly walked towards the front of the classroom.

The gunman quickly grabbed the girl, who was lying on the floor nearest to him, and he pressed her against him, dropping his rifle and grabbing his pistol, he pressed the barrel to the side of her head.

"One step closer and this pretty little girl's brains will become part of the wallpaper…" the gunman said in a threatening tone.

The girl was scared to death, she was trembling with fear.

"Let her go!" Titan ordered him.

"Don't you dare come any closer, I swear I will kill this little brat!" the gunman said to him.

"You're not going to get away with this…" Titan said angrily.

Titan knew that, while he had the girl in his arms and the gun against her skull, he couldn't do anything. He wished for some distraction. He was hoping for anything that would distract the gunman.

"OK so what now? What are you gonna do, just stand there all day with that kid?" Titan said, as he folded his arms in defiance. "I case you haven't noticed, the SWAT team is all over the place!"

The gunman knew it was hopeless. He had nowhere to go. What could he do?

Suddenly, the bell rang! There was a loud ringing noise, which sounded throughout the entire school!

"What was that?" the gunman wondered.

"That was the bell, indicating that the class period is over…" one of the students said, who was lying on the ground in the corner of the classroom.

The gunman looked over to see who spoke up.

That was Jake's chance! That was the distraction he was hoping for!

Jake ran over to the gunman at super speed and grabbed his right arm, which was holding the gun, and pressed it pointing straight up, towards the ceiling, and away from the girl.

This startled the gunman, who immediately pulled the trigger, and started shooting at the ceiling, knocking several tiles loose in the process. Several people in the classroom started to scream out of fear.

"Everybody out of the classroom, NOW!" Titan shouted at them, as he held the gunman pinned against the wall.

Immediately, all the students got up and ran out of the classroom and raced down the hallway towards the exit, so that they were free and out of the building where they could be received by the police officers.

The gunman fired off the gun until all the bullets were gone and the gun was empty, leaving just him and Titan in the empty classroom. Titan looked up at the man, who was naturally taller than he was, with an almost angry smirk.

"Let me go…" the gunman pleaded with the super-powered boy. "Please…"

"Oh, now you want to leave…" Titan said angrily. "Thought you wanted to stay a while, pal. You think that you can just come in here and hold up a classroom of kids and expect to just walk away…NOT A CHANCE, CREEP!"

Just then several police officers stormed the classroom and pointed their guns at the gunman, who was being held by Titan against the front wall of the classroom.

"FREEZE!" they shouted. "DOWN ON THE GROUND….. HANDS BEHIND YOUR HEAD….NOW!"

Titan finally let go of the gunman and stepped back. It was time for the cops to take over. Titan was actually breaking out in a sweat himself, for he felt very scared for a moment, especially for the students. He was just glad that it all ended well and without anyone getting hurt or worse.

As the police took the gunman into custody, Titan was standing at a distance, watching them do their jobs. He wasn't paying any attention to the man in the dark three-piece suit, standing just a few feet away from him, who was making a call on his cell phone.

"Target: Titan.....Acquired!"

As Jake celebrated his ninth birthday, he had become an international celebrity. He performed countless rescues not only in the Washington DC area, but also in several other cities around the United States, and overseas. Commissioner Wilson had actually become Titan's unofficial global ambassador. When there was a need for the young hero, Wilson was the first to be alerted.

By this time in his life, Jake had gained over three years' experience as a super hero and a star in the media. Titan had become a household name, uttered on the lips of the young and old alike. His face was plastered on posters, billboards, notebooks, comic books, and even a line of kids' action figures. One even had a light up fist that was supposed to be his plasma blast action. People were permitted to sell these items, only if the proceeds went to some honest charitable organization.

There were certain bookstores that sold a few posters and books about Titan, with stories about his adventures and exploits from the past four years. These quickly sold, since they were all bestsellers and actually authorized by Titan himself, as authentic accounts.

Up till now, Jake has done all his crime-fighting alone as Titan, and he often wished that he had someone else to help him. He spoke about it often with both his father and little brother. Even with his fantastic powers and abilities, Jake often struggled with the loneliness that came along with all his amazing gifts. He would often have to hide away from his friends when he was in school because of the fear of discovery. He often wished that he could meet someone else, who was just like him, who also had these unusual abilities, so that he could relate to him. He longed to meet someone that he could open up to, other than his family. Someone that felt the way he did about using the powers that he was granted. He had heard stories of mutants, and he knew that there were, in fact, people out there who had special talents and abilities, but he figured that he just hadn't met any of them yet because they were probably – just like him – scared to show their abilities to anyone in the real world.

Still, deep down, Jake hoped that some day, he would meet others who were just like him...

Chapter 23

The rest of the summer was a blur to young Robby McCloud. He spent his mornings in his room reading his comics, to extract the knowledge on how to utilize his powers to the fullest. His afternoons were spent working out with his baseball team, and lifting weights secretly with his "big brother" Brandon.

One afternoon after practice he was sitting in his room doing pushups when he decided to hone his skills at scanning thoughts of others and his teleportation abilities. He decided to practice as hard to perfect the use of these powers as he did honing his skill for baseball and soccer. However, he would make sure no one in his family would ever catch him in the act. He promised himself, that if the need ever arose for him to use his powers, he would be ready.

Summer came to an end much too soon for Robby's liking. Robby enjoyed school, but the absence of his favorite sport saddened the red-headed youth. He felt as if he lost his best friend at the end of every summer. There was nothing like the feeling that he had gotten from his team and the game itself.

One afternoon Robby was at recess with his best friend Travis just playing around like all boys do. They started to play a game of tag. Robby being extremely fast was able to out run Travis with ease.

"Tag! You're it, Red!!!!" Yelled Travis, as he ran off.

Travis ran as fast as he could towards the far side of the playground and climbed up the gym set. He began to cross the monkey bars with Robby in hot pursuit of him, when suddenly he lost his grip. Travis plummeted to the ground with such force it rendered the boy unconscious.

"Travis!" screamed Robby as he jumped off the monkey bars and dashed to his best friend's side.

He bent down and took his pal in his arms. His hand ran over the back of his head and he felt a huge gash where he hit his head on the cross tie after he fell.

"Oh no, Travis, please wake up!" Robby pleaded in anguish.

As he held him, he attempted to scan his mind. He felt Travis' mind wandering as if he were lost. He felt a slight tugging in his stomach as he held his friend. He panicked and tried to gently set his friend down.

Robby was amazed at what he was beginning to see. He had instinctively pressed his hands over his friend's injury, when all of a sudden; he felt a tingling sensation much like those he had experienced during his self-teleportation incidents. He began to panic.

"What's happening to me? What happens if I hurt Travis?" Robby worried.

Almost of their own accord, his hands began to transmit this tingle of energy into Travis' body at the site of the wound, closing it, and healing it before Robby's eyes.

As Travis began to come around, Robby, relieved that his friend would be OK, quickly scanned the vicinity. Good! No one had seen anything.

As Travis came to, he found Robby hovering over him. He asked Robby. "What happened?"

Robby answered, "We were playing tag. You were on the jungle gym. You fell and bumped your head. It cold cocked you. Are you OK?"

As Travis pulled himself to his feet, he rubbed the back of his head with the palm of his hand.

"Yeah, Robby, I think so! Except for this funny tingling at the back of my head but it's going away now. And, the funny thing is. It doesn't hurt. It actually feels good in a weird kinda way."

Robby, feeling a bit drained from this new experience but trying his best to hide it smiled at his friend. "Well, Travis, don't go banging your head like that just to get that feeling. You might not be so lucky next time."

Travis laughed. "Don't worry bro. Hey, I said it felt good, you know, like how good it feels when you stop banging your head against a brick wall, or the ground." They both laughed.

The rest of the day, Robby was in turmoil. Mixed emotions warred inside him. On one hand, he was glad he had been able to heal his best friend's head wound, and possibly a concussion. What if he had been caught? He considered giving up on his power. Sure it would make his life a lot simpler. However, deep inside, Robby knew that was impossible. He could never look past someone in trouble and pretend he could do nothing when he had the power to help. He faced the overwhelming irony that, on one hand, his father, his hero, would expect him to help if it were in his power to do so. Yet, on the other hand, he believed that he knew how utterly his father detested mutants and aliens.

Dejectedly, little Robby shook his head. "Stuck between a rock and a hard place! Oh well, I'm just gonna hafta make the best of it and do what I can from the shadows."

One afternoon after school, Robby called home and asked his mother if he could stop in to the comic store on his way home. The McCloud's did not live to far away from either the school or the strip mall that housed the comic shop, so Susan agreed.

As he strolled towards the comic book store, Robby McCloud's thoughts were plagued with the events of the day. He couldn't help wishing these powers hadn't come onto him as they had so suddenly. "Why me?" Robby pondered. Everything was going just great for him until this happened. I can't use my powers without making my dad hate me. If I don't, and someone I could've helped dies or gets hurt, he'd be so disappointed in me. What am I supposed to do?"

Absorbed in thought, he never saw the car careening toward him, out of control. Little Robby McCloud's "problem" was about to be resolved, but not in a way he would've chosen. Without knowing it, he was at the brink of death.

Suddenly a red, white, and blue blur swooped out of the sky and snatched Robby out of the path of the oncoming four-wheeled killing machine. Robby clutched his arms around the neck of his rescuer. He looked at the hero in the face and realized that he had to be the same age as he was.

The young hero gently landed with his cargo. He gracefully set Robby down and went to take off. Robby reached up and grabbed his ankle.

"Wait dude. What is your name?" asked an amazed Robby McCloud.

"You can call me Titan!" replied the muscular youth.

"Thank you for saving my life. My name is Robby McCloud" stated the extremely startled youth.

Robby watched as Titan settled onto the ground in front of him again. Robby extended his hand to the super-powered muscle kid. Titan reached out and gently grasped the red-headed youth's hand in friendship. When the two kids touched, Robby suddenly got a psychic flash off of the amazingly powerful youth. A bright smile lit up Robby's face for the first time in days. He was overcome with curiosity. Here was another boy with strange powers. He'd heard about the super-kid from Washington, DC. He hadn't really known whether to believe the stories about him or not. He got his answer in that very moment. Could this boy be another mutant like him? Even more amazing, Could he be an alien? The psychic flash that he had gotten told him that neither was a totally accurate assumption. He wanted to get to know this young hero, but he did not know how. Then it hit him like a ton of bricks.

"Hey Titan, you wanna come to comic book store with me?" asked Robby.

"Sure man, I guess I could hang out for a while. Seems all is quiet for the moment anyway" replied Titan.

"COOL!" cheered Robby.

The two walked into the comic store, and were met with a friendly greeting by the store-owner. He looked at Robby's friend all dressed in a super-hero costume and muscles bulging everywhere on his small youthful frame. His jaw fell agape at the sight. He instantly recognized the super-youth.

"Great Scott! You!!! You're that super-kid from DC. YOU are Titan!!" yelped the store owner.

"Ha Ha! Guilty as charged!" Titan laughed.

"Wow! I have a real-deal in-the-flesh super-hero in my store and he is a not-so-little boy!" marveled the Comic store owner.

"Yeah, I am here with my buddy over there" he stated, pointing at Robby. "Mind if we have a look around?" he asked politely.

"Sure thing, anything you need, Titan, just ask. I will be right here" stated that still shocked shop owner.

Robby stood there and watched as Titan just took it all in stride. Titan finished his conversation with the guy and made his way over to where his new friend was standing. He put his arm around his shoulder and looked down at what he was reading.

"Man that never gets old! Whatcha readin', bro?" asked Titan.

"Mr. Amazing # 3, it's where he gets total control over his mental powers." answered Robby.

"WOW! I love that comic! Mr. Amazing is my favorite," Titan replied, as he grabbed up his own copy of that issue.

"Cool, it's my favorite too" Robby grinned.

The two kids stood there and looked through comics for at least a half an hour. Robby made his selection and walked with Titan to the check out. He smiled a huge grin as he handed two comics to the clerk to check out. Titan placed his comic on the counter as well, and put his hand on top of Robby's.

"I got this, man. It's the least I can do for a fellow Mr. Amazing-fan" said Titan with an honest and sincere smile.

"Thanks, Titan, you really don't have to do that!" admitted Robby.

"No, it's nothing, bro. Hey man, I hate to admit this, but I am really bad with names. What was your name again?" said Titan.

"Oh, I am sorry. My name is Robby, Robby McCloud. I guess I was too shook up!" laughed Robby.

"It is OK, man. I understand" answered Titan. "It took everything I had to get to you in time. I was pretty shook up myself!"

"Well, thank goodness you made it!" Robby replied gravely. "And thank YOU for saving my life!"

Titan looked Robby in the eye. "Don't ask me how I know this. I just do. But I know you'd do the same for me! Or for anybody else, for that matter. Just call it a hunch…"

Robby blushed at this word of encouragement from Titan even as he wondered, "Wow! Where did THAT come from?" But even as he wondered, he resolved, "If I ever get the chance to help someone or save them like Titan did for me, I will! There is a REASON my life was saved today, so I've gotta live up to that! Just gonna hafta make sure I don't ever get caught!"

"Hey, let me repay you for the comics. Come grab a pizza across the street. I would like to personally thank you for being so cool" pleaded an insistent Robby.

"Well, I am sort of hungry after a long flight from Rhode Island" Titan chuckled.

"Rhode Island? What were you doing in Rhode Island?" asked an amazed Robby.

"Oh, I don't wanna bore you with that..." Titan replied shyly.

"Try me!" urged Robby.

Titan reached over and grabbed his new friend by the waist. He lifted off, flew straight up about thirty feet or more, and then propelled the two of them across the six busy lanes of traffic below. He then gently lowered them both back onto the sidewalk, across the street from where they had started.

"Dude that was totally wicked!" giggled Robby.

"Glad you liked it" said Titan. "So is this place any good?" he asked.

"Best pizza in Boston. Well at least, in my opinion" smiled Robby as he opened the door for his hero.

The two sat down and ordered a large pepperoni pizza, with two large sodas. They began talking about comics. Robby intently listened and hung on every single word that this world renowned hero had to say. He was amazed that the incredible Titan was so humble and friendly. He almost expected someone like him to be more stand-offish. The contrary was evident, much to Robby's surprise.

The boys chatted about everything from Titan's powers, to the design of his costume, to the top speed of his flight. Robby soaked up all the information that he was getting like a sponge. Titan too was interested in this young kid himself. For the simple reason, that he found someone his own age that he felt like he could relate to on some level.

"So what do you like to do for fun, other than comics, Robby?" asked the hero, between bites.

"Well I love to play baseball; I work out all the time with my bro, Brandon. I hang out with him, my cousin Petey, and my two best friends Travis and Derrick" explained Robby.

An almost depressed look slowly emerged on Titan's normally happy face. "I wish I could play sports. I am too strong to do that, I would probably hurt someone if I tried" said the dejected hero.

Robby saw the look in his new friend's eye, and for the first time, his empathy took over. The depressed feeling that Titan was having, is one that has been deep rooted within the young hero for some time. Robby actually felt a twinge of sympathy for him. He knew that this kid was in fact, the person that would most likely understand him, and his powers. He knew that Titan would never pass judgment on him.

Robby reached over and placed his hand on Titans massive shoulder. "Bro, just because you can't play sports does not mean anything. You can do all those other things. Things that I wish I could do."

"Thanks" Titan uttered as he swallowed his pizza. "You know, I think you are the only person I have ever told that to. Think that we can keep that just between us?" asked the young hero.

"I won't tell if you won't" giggled Robby.

Titan smiled. Suddenly his cell phone buzzed in his pocket. He pulled it out to answer it. After a brief conversation, he hung the phone up, and placed it back in his uniform's pocket.

"That was my little brother, he was wondering when I was coming home. I guess we lost track of time" stated Titan.

"OH shoot, my mom is gonna kill me!" yelped Robby. "Wait, you have a little brother?"

"Yeah. I do have a normal life outside of the tights and boots, bro" laughed Titan. "Look seeing as though you may get in trouble trying to make it home, let me fly you home."

"That would be awesome. Thanks!"

They made their way outside where Titan once again grabbed his friend by the waist. This time he asked Robby for directions as they took to the sky. Titan propelled both of them towards the McCloud's residence. Robby, thinking ahead, and to protect Titan, told him to land in Brandon's back yard.

Titan set down stealthily in the neighboring yard. He released his grasp on his new confidant and bid him farewell.

"Well bro, I gotta fly outta here. Just make sure you watch where you are going from now on..." laughed Titan.

"Thanks Titan. You are the best" replied the red head.

Titan took to the sky with a mighty leap. He looked back and waved at his new friend as he pointed himself towards the direction of his home. Robby was left standing in his best friend's back yard with a look of total amazement, and a content heart.

"Wow! He is AWESOME!" Robby thought to himself. "I can't wait to tell Brandon and Derrick about this!"

The next afternoon, Robby again phoned his mother, this time asking if she would not mind picking him up from the news stand down the street from the school. He walked in and asked the owner if there were any magazines that had articles with information on Titan. The owner handed him a "Daily Globe," an "Info Week," and a "Teen Street Scene" poster magazine. Robby proffered payment; tore the magazines open and pored over them for information about his new hero.

"Wow, this kid is only nine years old. He was so big, though..." Robby said to himself.

He continued to excitedly read everything about Titan. Robby learned about the extent of his powers. The boy stood there amazed at what his hero was capable of. Never had he heard of any being with that much power, not even in his favorite comics.

"Gosh, it says here that he has unlimited strength, he can fly, he is invulnerable, can see great distances, and in total darkness, and he can project some form of weird plasmoidal energy from his hands. Man this kid can do it all!" thought Robby.

Once he finished, Robby called his mom to come and pick him up. He sat on a nearby park bench and got totally lost in thought, for the second time. He pondered how he could use his power for good the way Titan was doing but still not get caught doing it.

Robby resolved, "Man, if this kid is making this big of a difference to the world out in the open, I think I should be able find a way to do it from the background."

Eight-year-old Robby McCloud was standing at a cross road in his life. He was so young and so full of energy, yet as perplexed as to what to do and where to go with his gifts. He sat on that park bench, pining over the "Info Week" article, totally entranced in the thought of helping others with his gift.

As his mother pulled up to pick him up, he slowly approached the car, nose still buried in the magazine. He slowly opened the door and climbed into his mother's minivan. Still reading he did not look up until his mother spoke.

"Son is there something wrong?" she asked with concern in her voice.

Robby looked up startled for the second time today. He shook his head with an emphatic "no", and went back to reading. Robby was completely silent, and entranced for the remainder of the trip home. Occasionally he rustled the pages of his magazine.

As the two of them reached their home, Robby slowly opened his door and slid out onto the driveway. He and his mother walked to the front door. Robby began fidgeting nervously as he awaited his mother to open the front door.

When the door swung open, Robby made his way to the curio stand in the foyer of their home. He opened the drawer and pulled out the tape and a pair of scissors and headed for the stairs. He bounded up the stairs and was completely out of sight before his mother could say a single word.

Robby dashed into his room, and closed the door behind him. He made his way over to his bed and spread all his comics and magazines out all over his bed spread. He moved his comics over to a safe section of his bed so that nothing could bend or damage them.

He looked up at his "Wall of Heroes" that he had been constructing out of newspaper and magazine articles of his favorite baseball players. He now had someone his own age who would adorn the wall along side Derrick Jeter, Greg Maddox, and his big brother Brandon. A bright smile crept across his face as he opened the Info Week magazine to the pages that contained the article on the young hero named Titan.

After reading the article, Robby carefully cut it out of the magazine. Then he sealed it in a plastic comic book cover and taped it to the wall. He then pulled out the Teen Street Scene picture magazine and began cutting out the pictures that were snapped of the youthful hero in there and fastened them alongside all the other heroes that made up his shrine of heroes.

"I wonder if he is like me, scared at times to be who he is?" pondered the young mutant.

"How could he be scared? Everyone loves him, heck I look up to him." continued Robby.

Robby continued to attach photos and articles about his new hero to the wall. All the while thinking of what it would be like to be a hero like that. To be able to use his gifts out in the open; admired by one and all. He wanted so much to be revered like that. But that life was not for him. Grimly, he faced the hard cold truth; that he would have to hide who and what he was from everyone.

Robby sat there and was almost reduced to tears when he contemplated what he had gleaned from his father's mind. How what he thought he felt from his father was hatred for mutants and aliens alike. He wanted to exterminate them.

"Would he exterminate me?" he wondered.

That was a chance that Robby was not prepared to take. He knew that with his gifts he could remain in the shadows and help when he could. He could not help yearning to be right beside Titan, helping him. He dreamed of being his partner. Robby felt sure he could be a big help to the muscle-bound mountain of super-human youth.

Chapter 24

It was about three months or so, after Jake's ninth birthday had passed, when Jake met someone who had struck him as having the possibility of being a mutant. It happened while he was flying back home from Rhode Island as Titan, he passed over Boston. He had met a boy who almost got run over by a drunk driver on the parking lot of a large shopping mall, and he performed a quick save right before the boy got struck by the oncoming car.

As soon as Jake had returned from Boston, he sat on the edge of his bed in his bedroom and pondered the encounter, which had just happened, which was something very unusual for him, since he normally would go up to Madison and let him now that he was home and what he had just done. He just sat there thinking about how he had totally opened up to this kid about his hopes and fears. How he had felt so totally welcomed by this complete stranger, and not just because he was Titan. On the contrary, it was because he was a genuine person.

Madison was in his room doing his homework when he heard the door to the balcony slide open and shut. He knew it had to be Jake, but he was curious why his big brother didn't come right in to his room to tell him that he had arrived, seeing as though he had called him to check in on him.

Maddie got up and walked down the hall to Jake's room. Indeed, there was Jake, still wearing his Titan costume, but he was lying on his bed and staring at the ceiling, deep in his thoughts.

"Hey bro!" Maddie cheered. "I heard you come home!"

"Yeah…" Jake replied, in a serious tone of voice.

"What... What's the matter?" Madison wondered. Right away, he noted that Jake wasn't his cheerful self.

Madison sat down on Jake's chair and rolled it closer to his bed.

"I'm just thinking..." Jake spoke. "I just met an unusual kid, bro... I'm just wondering if he could be some sort of mutant. Or maybe, he had some special powers or something?"

"What are you talking about?" Maddie wondered. "What kid?"

"Well, I was helping the Coast Guard rescue a sinking ship off the coast of Rhode Island, a few miles at sea just now. When I was done, I was on my way home, and flew over Boston. I had some time to kill, so I decided to take it slow, since I really wasn't in much of a hurry at first to get home. Plus, I've never been to Boston before, so I figured I'd take my time and fly nice and slow, so I could check out the city!" Jake explained to his little brother. "So, while I was flying over the business section of the city, I was going over a shopping center at one point. Well, I didn't see anything unusual at first, until I spotted a car that was speeding out of control down the street..."

"So? Some guys can't drive! You know that..." Madison noted.

"Yeah, but this guy was swerving from one side of the lane to the other, and I saw this kid with red hair walking really close to the road..."

"Oh no!" Madison gasped. "What did you do?"

"Well, I realized that if I didn't do something, this car was going to hit this kid! So I made a dive for the kid and grabbed him from behind and I lifted him off his feet before the car was going to hit him!" Titan explained. "He was going to be killed for sure!"

"Oh, man! Good thing you were there, bro!"

"Yeah! Well I flew him over to a safer spot. He stopped me before I could take off and fly home."

"Really?" Madison asked him. "What did he say to you?"

"Well he grabbed my ankle and asked me to just hang out. Not sign autographs or anything like that. Just hang out. When I shook his hand, something weird happened. It was like my mind was opening to him. I felt comfortable talking to someone other than you, mom or dad, for the first time."

"So, what happened then?"

"Well, he asked me if I wanted to go to the comic bookstore with him." Jake explained. "We just hung out. I even bought his comics for him. I dunno bro; there is something about him…"

"Oh… Well, at least you weren't here in DC. Nobody knows you in Boston, right?"

"Wrong, little bro!" Jake chuckled. "The store owner recognized me right away!"

"Oh wow! You're more famous that you thought you were!" Madison laughed.

"Yeah… It was cool. I talked to the owner of the store for a few minutes before I joined Robby looking over the Mr. Amazing comics!"

"Oh wow… So what happened next?" Madison wondered.

"Well we both were hungry so we went for pizza at this place across from the comic book store. We talked about everything from him playing baseball, to what my powers are. I was just totally honest with him for some reason. Then I noticed a faint aura about him, Maddie. I think there is something about him, little bro…"

"Maybe Robby has powers just like you?" Madison asked him.

"I don't know. I saw it really briefly. Who knows, if I'll ever see Robby again…" Jake wondered out loud. "Only time will tell…"

Madison stared at Jake and realized that Jake started to tear up.

"Hey… It's alright, bro…" he whispered to his big brother.

"I know, Maddie…" Jake sobbed, trying his hardest to fight back the tears. "It just makes me so happy, just knowing that there are others out there, who are like me, you know?"

Maddie got off the chair and walked up to Jake, who was now sitting up on his bed. The two brothers embraced, with tears rolling from Jake's eyes.

"They're out there, big bro…" Maddie assured him. "I know they are. They may not have the same abilities as you do, but there are other people out there, who have special abilities. I know you'll get to meet them some day… Just be patient…"

"Thanks, Maddie… You're the best…" Jake replied, as he gently hugged his brother back. It was an endearing moment, and an emotional one for him. But this was a time when he needed Madison, and he was there to lend his emotional support.

Chapter 25

The days, weeks, months and years seemed to fly by. Robby McCloud had decided that fateful September evening to become a hero. He dedicated himself to improving control of his abilities. He trained his body to the height of physical perfection, or at least as close perfect as any kid could achieve.

When he turned nine years old, Robby begged his father to buy him a weight set. He told him that he wanted to get stronger for baseball, in which he had been league MVP for the past three years running. He trained almost every day and pushed his body to the point of his human limitations and a little further. He knew that if the dream of becoming Titan's partner was going to come true one day, he would have to push himself harder than any soccer or baseball coach ever would.

Brandon would come over every day and help young Robby train his physical prowess to its limits. Brandon knew that Robby was pushing himself hard, but the reason for the dedication was totally unknown to him. Every day Robby would sprint the neighborhood, and as he would pass Brandon's house, they would meet up and make their way to his garage. There the weight training and other exercises began. Brandon would crawl inside Robby's mind and push him harder than he even thought possible. Robby was grateful for Brandon's help, but secretly he had appreciated it more deeply than he let on.

While in secret, he trained his powers along with his body. His teleportation jumps were getting longer and longer with greater accuracy. He practiced reading thoughts and emotions as well as putting up mental barriers to keep the multitude of voices down. The months flew by, as Robby would train daily with Brandon, and secretly on his own. Robby had grown into a well rounded and gifted athlete, with a physical prowess much more advanced than his almost twelve years would lead people to believe.

One afternoon he was out with his best friend from baseball, Derrick Malone. They were out at the walking track next to the hospital. Robby and Derrick loved coming here during the off-season to stay in shape. The track had many pull up bars, dip bars, sit up bars, and stretching posts available.

"Hey Red, watch this" challenged Robby's best friend.

With that Derrick strutted over to a pull up bar. He grabbed the bar and flipped upside down on it. When he completed the flip, Robby heard an awful crack and Derrick fell to the ground with a blood curdling scream.

"AAAAARRRRGGGGGG!!!! My Shoulder......it just broke Robby, get help!" howled the tough baseball star.

Robby raced over to where his friend lay writhing in agony. He knew that he could help him. The only thing was Derrick was still conscious. Robby just had to help him without betraying his secret, but how?

Then an idea from a Mr. Amazing comic book popped into his head. He thought maybe if he could read minds, he could project different memories, perhaps erasing the real memory and replacing it with an "artificial" memory from his own imagination. There was only one way to find out. He just had to try it. There was no other way. No way could Robby leave his friend like this. He would heal him at whatever cost.

"Derrick! Calm down. Lay back, dude..." exclaimed the red-headed young hero.

Robby concentrated as his eyes shifted from bright emerald green to coal black. First, Robby focused on easing Derrick's pain. Then he set about blanking out Derrick's mind so that he would not remember anything of what was about to happen. "Derrick!" Robby commanded. "You will forget what is about to happen. You will have no memory of the past few minutes. Your fall and injury never happened. Instead, you will remember spotting me with my pull ups!"

As Derrick lay motionless, completely under control of Robby's powerful mutant mind, he shifted his attention to Derrick's wounds. He laid his hands on the affected shoulder and closed his eyes. In his mind's eye, he could clearly "see" the fracture beneath the skin.

He opened his eyes and began concentrating on activating his healing factor. His eyes shifted from black to bright golden yellow, with a matching aura surrounding the two of them. He focused his power on the shoulder and felt it slowly healing, as bone and sinew knitted back together.

When the healing was completed, young Robby McCloud collapsed next to his friend. He was glad that he implanted the fake memory of Derrick helping him complete his pull-ups, a perfectly plausible explanation of his total exhaustion.

"Man, Robby, you really pushed yourself hard." said Derrick as he sat up next to his friend.

"Yeah bro, I would not have been able to do it without ya!" Robby grinned.

Derrick was none the wiser for what had taken place, just as Robby had hoped. Even though he did feel a slight twinge of guilt at having to dupe his friend, he reasoned that it had been justified to hide his secret.

Later that night Robby was lying in his room thinking over the day that had just transpired. Suddenly a knock came at his bedroom door, as his mother let herself in.

"Hi sweetheart did you and Derrick have fun at the walking track today?" she inquired of her son.

"Yes mom, we sure did" he replied with a puzzled look on his face.

Robby had always been able to sense when someone was approaching him. However his mother was different. Even when he tried to scan for her, there was a vague sense of her presence, but no definitive thoughts or emotions. What mystified him was why he could penetrate his father's thoughts but not his mother's.

"Honey we have to talk to you, can you come downstairs?" she requested.

"Sure mom, what's up?" asked Robby.

"Well, your father and I need to discuss something that is very important and we need to let you in on it" she replied honestly.

Robby could still tell if his mom was hiding something from him. But he could not discern what it was. He stood up, laying aside his baseball and glove down and went downstairs with his mother.

They entered the den where Bob was sitting with a bunch of paperwork. He sat across the room from his father, sensing his uneasy emotional state. He decided to not scan him. He would just wait and see what was up. Robby hoped for the best and prepared for the worst. What if his father had somehow found out that he was a mutant? What would he do?

"Son, what I am about to tell you is going to be kind of rough to handle." Bob started explaining.

Robby looked at him with a worried expression on his face. Now he really wanted to use his powers to find out what was going on. He thought to himself, that if he did, his father would notice the change in his eye color and that would give him away.

"What is it dad? Robby asked.

"Well son, to put it bluntly, I am being transferred." his father replied.

"What!!! Where???? Where are we going and when dad?" stammered Robby nervously.

"Well son, we are moving to DC. I will be leaving next week. You and your mother won't be joining me until after baseball season" answered Bob.

When Robby heard that they were moving to Washington DC, he felt a little bit easier. After all his hero of heroes, Titan hailed from DC. He still had a wave of sadness wash over him. What about Derrick? What about Travis? What about his baseball team here?

All these questions were going to be addressed by his father. Robby had mixed emotions about the move. He wanted to meet Titan again, and soon. But he did not want to sacrifice his close friendships. What twelve-year-old wants to be uprooted from his friends?

"Well at least I get to stay for all of baseball season," said Robby.

"That is the spirit, champ" stated Bob.

"You are OK with this, right son?" asked Susan.

"I guess mom, I am just going to miss Brandon, Derrick, Travis, and Petey that's all" responded Robby.

"Well son, I am still going to be coming home to Boston from time to time wrapping things up at the office here" Bob said reassuringly.

"And not to mention Nanna and Poppa McCloud, and Nanna and Poppa Taylor are here, and you know that we will be back to see them. AND....They absolutely love Derrick and Travis, not to mention how they adore Brandon, so I know they can stay the night with you when you come up to visit." added Susan.

"OK, I agree, not that you were asking my permission, but I am OK with it" said Robby.

Robby got up and hugged his father and mother and excused himself from the living room to his bedroom. The once tense atmosphere had all but disappeared, leaving a sense of calm over the whole family.

"That went well honey" uttered Bob.

"Yes darling it did, I am glad he took it so well," Susan replied.

Robby walked back into his room and grabbed his glove and ball. He jumped onto his bed, laid back and began tossing the ball towards the ceiling. He became lost in thought and dreams.

The family was moving to Washington DC. Robby wondered what would it be like in DC, having to start over, making new friends, and maybe meeting up with Titan again. Robby's super abilities were very different from Titan's but every bit as powerful in their own way.

Chapter 26

The dog days of summer were upon the people of Boston once again. Baseball season had been in full swing for a few months, and the Bobcats were doing well as usual, thanks to its two stars Derrick Malone and Robby McCloud.

The years of training had really paid off for these two stars. Robby had kept a lean muscular physique that was typically associated with a high caliber teen athlete. Derrick was a bit stockier than Robby. He carried about fifteen pounds more muscle than Robby, and it showed. His Baseball uniform was stretched to the max in his legs and chest. Derrick, unlike Robby, played football in the fall, while Robby played soccer.

Derrick sauntered out to the plate with his batting gear on. He stepped up to the plate and eyed Sean O'Hannon, the Lion's pitcher. These two kids hated each other. After all they were bitter rivals. Derrick was a pitcher as well. Both boys were fiercely competitive; each determined to prove once and for all who between them was top dog on the pitcher's mound and at bat.

Derrick ground his cleats into the clay at home plate. He twisted his grip around the bat. The fans were all on their feet. This would be the tying run of the last inning. If Derrick used all his power he could tie it up and bring Robby up to bat for the win.

"COME ON DERRICK!!!! YOU CAN DO IT BROTHER!!! Robby screamed.

"YAY!! DERRICK!!!COME ON BIG BRO!!!" yelled Petey.

"COME ON MALONE!! DO IT LIKE WE PRACTICED!" bellowed Brandon from the stands.

Peter McCloud was always at the games with Robby, Derrick, and Brandon. Petey acted as their cheering squad. He loved his cousin and looked up to Derrick. Robby had always been really close to him, being his cousin, Derrick was like his big brother, and Brandon would watch all three of them like a hawk, trying to keep them all safe and sound. Knowing that this was the last game that he was going to get to see Robby play regularly, he was going to go all out. Even at the expense of his voice.

Robby scanned Sean's mind. He read that he intended to throw a curve ball to break just a bit on the outside. If he Derrick knew what was coming he would destroy that curve ball with his powerful swing.

"Watch that breaking curve, Derrick!" encouraged Robby.

Derrick looked back and nodded in understanding to his best friend. He returned his gaze towards a belligerent, glowering Sean. Derrick gritted his teeth and tensed his muscles like a cobra prepared to strike. His well trained body swelled with power, in preparation for the incoming pitch.

The pitch was thrown and, just as predicted by Robby, it was an outside breaking curve ball. Derrick swung the bat and smashed the ball with every ounce of power he had. His efforts did not go unrewarded. It earned him a home run.

"HOME RUN...HOME RUN MALONE # 15...That ties the ball game at the bottom of the Ninth with 2 outs and none on Base....#18 Robby McCloud is next up to bat for the Bobcats" bellowed the announcer.

"ALL RIGHT DERRICK!" yelled Brandon and Petey in unison.

"Ladies and gentlemen. This will be the last at bat for #18 here in Boston. Next season he will be with the Washington DC Wildcats. Maybe we will see him in the Little League World Series!" boomed the announcer.

The entire stadium rose to their feet in appreciation of Robby McCloud and his accomplishments as a member of the Bobcats. Even the Ludlow Lions fans were paying tribute to the young prodigy of America's favorite past time. Brandon lead the cheer in the stands, he stood side by side with Robby's parents as they cheered the final at bat for this hometown hero.

Robby grabbed his bat, and batting helmet, and swaggered out of the dugout. He faced the crowd, set his equipment on the ground and applauded the spectators out of respect for them. He pointed to the crowd and bowed to them out of honest gratitude. Robby McCloud was a really classy kind of kid. He put on his helmet, and saluted his coaches and team. Robby then took a few warm up swings as he picked the brain of the pitcher.

Robby peeled Sean's mind open like a comic book. He was going to try his new fastball. The kid could throw, but there was no way that he was going to strike Robby out this time.

"Not today, pal" thought Robby as he smirked at Sean.

Sean wound up and hurled the ball with all the power his superbly honed twelve-year-old body could muster. Fast and tight to the plate was his aim. He was attempting to intimidate Robby. He would not succeed in that futile effort.

Robby gnashed his teeth and with a fierce yell, he swung the bat with all he had. Long and clean, right over the center field wall, sailed the ball that rocketed from Robby's bat. Robby began trotting the bases.

"AMAZING FOLKS!!!! #18 HAS GIVEN YOU, THE FANS JUST ONE MORE TO REMEMBER HIM BY!!!HOME RUN # 18 ROBBY MCCLOUD!!" bellowed the announcer with excitement.

"That's my boy right there, folks!" cheered Brandon.

Waving to the crowd as he rounded the bases, he looked over at home plate and there stood his cousin and his best friend. Derrick was squatting with his hands resting on his thighs, in a happily aggressive stance. Robby knew the second he hit home plate, "Bull Derrick" was gonna bear hug the life out of him!

"RED, YOU DID IT AGAIN!!!" exclaimed Derrick as he grabbed his best friend up in a mighty bear hug.

Derrick hoisted his friend up onto his shoulders with Petey and Brandon tagging alongside. Robby McCloud and Derrick Malone had won this game against the Ludlow Lions. The two best friends had won their last game just as it should be, as teammates.

The team celebrated at the park for over an hour. All of Robby's teammates signed his bat for him to keep as a memento of his last game. His coaches gave him the game ball. He also had the kids pose for one last team photo. Everyone was celebrating the win, everyone except Derrick. The finality of the moment had settled onto his young shoulders like a funeral pall.

Robby walked over to where his best friend was sitting and laid his arm around his shoulder. He shook him a little bit trying to get some response out of him. He even scanned him, finding what he had expected. Derrick was devastated that his best friend since pre-school was leaving.

"What's the matter Derrick?" asked Robby.

"Dude, you are moving in the morning, what am I gonna do without my red-headed brother?" Derrick answered as tears began to flow.

"Aww Bro! Man, I am not gonna be gone forever, besides, mom said you can come stay weekends with me in DC, and your parents are all for that" responded Robby, attempting to comfort his best friend.

"Man, I can't play baseball without you!" Derrick said.

When those words had parted his lips, he pulled his Bobcats jersey off and tearfully handed it to Robby. Derrick began to cry harder. He knew that this was his last game of his baseball career too.

"What are you doing D?" asked Robby.

"I am giving up baseball to concentrate on football, man. Baseball won't be the same without you. We've been teammates since we were five." Derrick explained.

"But you are so good at it D!" Robby objected.

"No, Red.... You are great at baseball. We were great together, but I am not playing without my bro on the team, and not to mention I am a heckuva lot better at football than I am at baseball," he continued emotionally.

"Well when we visit each other, we play baseball, agreed?" Robby asked as he slugged his best friend in the shoulder.

"Of course, Red!" giggled Derrick as he grabbed Robby in a head lock, tussling his hair.

The two laughed together and returned to the party. Robby could not help but feel a sense of loss about the whole moving issue now. He gripped Derrick's jersey with every ounce of strength he had, fighting back tears. He held his best friends jersey to his chest for the rest of the party, not letting go of the symbol of unity that Derrick passed onto him.

The party ended as Susan returned to pick up Robby, Derrick, Brandon and Petey. She had arranged that the four boys could stay the night with one another at the house one last time before the move in the morning. Robby was so very thankful for that.

The night carried on like there was no end in sight. The boys stayed up all night playing video games and reading comics. They wrestled around in the empty basement for a few hours. Somewhere about three in the morning Petey passed out on the couch, Brandon had passed out in the old tattered recliner shortly after, and that left Derrick and Robby awake talking.

"Dude, can I tell you something that will not freak you out, or make you mad at me?" asked Derrick.

"Sure D, What's up?" responded Robby.

"Red, I know you are different somehow. You have like this ESP thing going on. Not to freak you out that I know. I just wanted you to know that I think it is pretty awesome that you have that, uh…gift" said Derrick honestly.

"What are you talking about D?" inquired Robby nervously.

"Look bro, I know what you are dude, and don't worry man, I am not gonna tell a soul about it" answered Derrick.

Robby began to cry. The pent up emotions from his last ballgame, and now with his best friend's admission that he knew about his powers, was more than he could take. He was so confused at what to do or say at this moment. Even without ESP, his best friend had "read" him like a book. He reassured him that, just because he was different, it wouldn't matter to him in the least. However, he'd hidden who and what he was so carefully, even from Derrick. No mind read had been needed so Robby didn't even bother to probe Derrick for confirmation. What his best friend had said was so obviously from the heart there had been no need for intrusion. Just as Derrick had been able to read Robby without ESP, so Robby could read Derrick.

"D, I am so sorry I haven't told you, I haven't told anyone about it" said Robby through the tears.

"Red, I think it's cool! I envy you. You have that super power and you are an awesome athlete too" comforted Derrick.

"You are jealous of me? Look at you. You're built like a tank. You're as strong as and as tough as an ox. I think I should envy you" squeaked Robby.

"Well then we are even" giggled Derrick. "You have the powers, and I am tough. We have always made a great team."

Robby stood up and walked over to his best friend and hugged him. He thought for a moment that he needed to totally share with him everything.

"Look man I am going to show you something. Please, don't make a sound" demanded Robby.

With that, he placed his hand on his friend's broad shoulders and began to concentrate. His eyes shifted from bright green to coal black in a millisecond. The Two disappeared in a cloud of mist, and reappeared outside in the back yard.

"Dude that was totally WICKED!" stated Derrick.

"Thanks" said Robby.

"Robby, you are the coolest person I know, I promise that I will keep this between you and me" promised Derrick solemnly.

"Thanks, I feel better now that SOMEONE knows" Robby sighed.

"Answer me one question though, Red?" asked Derrick.

"Sure" Robby said.

"Does Petey or anyone in your family know what you can do?" asked Derrick. "Have you told Brandon anything about this?"

"D, no one knows but you. Dad hates mutants, which is what I am, and I am not telling anyone else" responded Robby.

"Probably best, Red" uttered Derrick. "In a way, I think you should tell Petey. But I don't think he's quite ready yet. But, dude, he really looks up to you, yah know. And now, with these powers you've got, you'd be all that much more of a hero to him. Like you are to me!"

"D, I also have to tell you something," Began Robby intrepidly. "Remember that day when we were out at the walking track?" he asked.

"Yeah what about it?" Derrick responded inquisitively.

"Well you broke your shoulder" Robby stated bluntly.

"No I didn't dude, I would still be in a sling if I had bro" Derrick corrected his best friend.

"No, you broke it, I wiped your memory and blocked the pain with my power, and then I healed you" said Robby as he glanced at the floor in abject embarrassment.

"What!?! You healed me, wiped my memory? What are you talking about?" Derrick inquired.

"D you have to promise to not get mad at me" said Robby.

"OK I promise, now spill it before I pounce on ya and give you a wedgie!" giggled Derrick.

Robby began recounting the tale of what had happened last year in the fall. He told him that he was trying to do a trick and his shoulder just snapped. Robby told him how he fell and the scream he let out. Derrick listened as Robby told him how terrified he was at the fact that his best friend was laying there in severe pain. He continued by telling him of the mental imagery that he had implanted as to allow him to heal him. Robby told him that he could not just let his own best friend suffer, so he did what he had to do to fix the problem.

"See, I knew that there was something about you, Red" said Derrick through a genuine smile.

"What do you mean?" asked Robby out of worry.

"See I vaguely remember this dream about a guardian angel that helped me out. That angel looked just like you, Red" replied Derrick as he hugged his best friend.

"You are not mad at me?" inquired Robby.

"Not at all, I have my very own guardian angel, how cool is that?" stated Derrick.

Derrick reached over and ruffled his best friend's hair. Secretly Derrick may have harbored some hidden jealousy of the abilities that Robby had been blessed with. He quickly stifled those feelings as he thought about how close the two of them were. Another thought bounded into his skull. The thought of why Robby chose him and not Brandon to bear the burden of his amazing secret.

"Why haven't you told Brandon though, man?" inquired Derrick.

"I look up to him. I look up to him a lot, and I am not sure how he would take it" answered Robby.

"Well I suggest that you tell him, but only when you are ready, bro" smiled Derrick.

The rest of the morning Derrick and Robby hung out as they talked about Robby's gifts. Derrick hugged his best friend and reassured him, "I'll guard this secret with my life. And, if you ever need me, I'll be there for you."

Robby assured Derrick, "Same here, bro. And if you ever need me, well, now you know I can be at your side in a flash."

The two finally fell asleep at five in the morning, only to be roused awake at nine. Robby opened his bright green eyes and looked up at his mother with sheepish smile.

"Hi Mom" groaned Robby.

"Hi yourself, sleepy head. You need to get up and wake up Petey, Brandon and Derrick," said Susan.

"Are we leaving soon mom?" asked Robby as he rubbed his eyes.

"Yes son, we have everything already loaded up stairs, all we need is to load the air beds from down here and your clothes" replied Susan.

"Gosh does this mean I am saying goodbye to Derrick and Brandon now?" he asked.

"Red, you ain't ever sayin' goodbye to ya old buddy D here!" Derrick said as he bolted straight up.

"You were listening Mr. Malone?" inquired Susan.

"I sure was, sorry" he chuckled

"Not a problem, you guys gently wake up Petey, Aunt Beth and Uncle Richie will be here in ten minutes to get him, and they are taking you home too Derrick."

"Aww Mrs. McCloud I wanted to stay until you guys left" pleaded Derrick.

"You are D, Richie and Beth will not be leaving until we have to pull out" replied Susan as she smoothed Derrick's wildly messy dark brown hair.

"YAY! I was worried that I was gonna be sitting home and not able to say bye to you guys" Derrick exclaimed.

"I would never let that happen, kiddo" said Susan with a warm smile.

Derrick walked up to her and hugged her tightly. He had always thought of the McClouds as family. They had always watched over him when his parents were away on trips. Derrick loved the whole family as much as he did his own, and it showed.

"Thanks, Mrs. McCloud" he replied.

"Oh and you two wake Brandon up, his parents called and they want to have him home the minute we pull out of the driveway" requested Susan

When the last bit of furniture and personal belongings were loaded into the moving truck, the mood seemed to shift. The boys had stopped playing around as much and came over to where the truck was. Derrick put his arm around his best friend. He pulled Robby close to him as if to say that everything was going to be OK. Brandon stood there with his head hanging low. He was fighting with everything that he had not to start crying in front of his young friends.

Susan slowly approached the trio and watched the mood become even more somber. It was almost like she was watching the funeral of a close friend. The feeling was very similar to that. She walked up and put her arm around Petey and Derrick. As she did this they both started to cry.

"Aunt Susan, I don't want you to go" whimpered Petey.

"I know, Pete, I know" she replied soothingly.

"Momma Susan, why did Mr. McCloud have to take a job so far away?" asked Derrick.

"D it is one of the great mysteries of the world what that man does" she retorted with a smile.

The five of them actually shared a laugh amidst the tears. She knew that her young men would be just fine. Susan looked upon her three guys and smiled. She hugged them close with reassurance.

"Mr. Rathbone, I expect that you will watch after Derrick and my nephew?" inquired Susan.

"Momma Susan, you do not have to worry about that. I will watch them like a hawk" said Brandon as he cleared his throat, stood tall and proud at the request.

Susan embraced the young man that had been so instrumental in shaping the athletic lives of her son, nephew, and their close friend. She knew that this amazing boy would live up to his word to always watch over these kids like their guardian angel. She smiled softly as she looked deep into Brandon's dark brown eyes, making the connection that only a mother can.

Just then, Richard and Beth McCloud pulled into the driveway. Beth stepped out of her SUV and walked over to her nephew. She grabbed him up in a warm and loving embrace.

Beth truly loved her nephew with a deep seated love. He was the second son that she had always wanted. He would always avidly look after her son Peter, which she was very proud and pleased of. She was going to miss this young man.

"I am gonna miss you, tiger" said Beth.

"I am gonna miss you too, Aunt Beth" replied Robby.

By then, Richard had reached the family. He walked up to Susan and embraced her. He was, after all her husband's twin brother. He had always thought of his brother's family in the highest regards, and would do anything for them.

"Susan, did you get everything taken care of?" asked Richard

"Yeah Richie, I think I did. Bob left me a list" Susan chortled.

"Bob and his darned lists!" Richard laughed.

Richard walked back to the SUV and pulled out four boxes. He returned to the group. Richard then handed each of the boys a box. He was met with puzzled looks upon their faces.

"Look guys, you know how I work as Area Rep for Call-Tel, the cellular company right?" asked Richard.

"Sure dad" said Petey.

"Yeah Uncle Richie" Robby responded as well.

"Well these are totally unlocked phones, which means you will be able to talk all you want to each other for free guys!" exclaimed Richard.

"WOW! Really?" squealed Petey.

"Man that means I can talk to my boy here about how I am doing in football anytime I want to" stated Derrick.

"Cool" added Brandon.

"That's right. I had to do some string pulling to get this done, but I knew that it would help everyone out in the long run" Richard replied with a grin on his face.

"That was awfully nice of you honey" said Beth as she hugged her husband.

"Yeah Uncle Richie, this is awesome!" screamed Robby as he jumped up into his uncles arms.

"Whoa, Tiger.....you are getting too big to be jumping on your ole uncle here" chuckled Richard through his strain.

Susan corralled Robby and led him toward the van. Brandon, Derrick, Petey, Beth, and Richard all followed them over to beg them a safe journey. The emotions were running so thick you could cut them with a knife. No one wanted to let go, but they all knew that they had to.

It did not help matters that Petey broke down and started bawling like a baby as he was being pulled from Robby and Susan. They all loved each other and that fact was evident here. It was the hardest thing that Robby has had to face, next to his powers emerging.

"Bye, Cuz!" sniffled Petey.

"Bye Petey, be good, Cuz!" Robby said comfortingly.

Derrick came up and gave Robby one last bear hug for the road. He really hated the fact that his best friend and team mate was leaving. He relaxed a little knowing that he could talk to him, but that did not change the fact that he was losing the physical closeness that they shared. These two were inseparable since age five. That is what made saying good bye so hard.

"Later, Red....I ain't too good at sayin' goodbye, bro.....so 'Later' will have to do" Derrick laughed.

"Me neither D....You coming to DC for some holidays, right?" asked Robby.

"You know it, bro!" replied the young linebacker.

Brandon had waited patiently to speak to his protégé. As Derrick finished his goodbyes, he made his way towards the fiery red-headed baseball star. He looked into his adopted little brother's eyes, as tears welled up within his own. He could not hold back the torrent of emotions that had been building up for the past forty eight hours. He let loose as Robby reached out and grabbed him.

"Red! You have been like the little brother that I have always wanted" sobbed Brandon. "It is so hard thinking that you are not going to be here, ya know, right next door" he continued.

"Brandon, I love you man. I think of you as the big brother that I always wanted. You have always helped teach me what to do and when" responded Robby.

"Just remember that I am only a phone call away. You get yourself into anything, you call me. I will come as fast as I can. I have always got your back kiddo" exclaimed Brandon through his tears.

"Thanks big brother" said Robby.

They all said their goodbyes and gave each other hugs. Susan and Robby climbed into their Dodge Grand Caravan, and backed out of the driveway. Susan slowly pulled away, and a tear fell down her cheek. This was all she had known. Her family, her friends, her son's friends, everything that she had ever known, all resided here in Boston.

Robby turned and waved slowly to his family and his best friend. He felt as if someone was stabbing him in the chest. He knew that he would see them again, but that did not change the emotions that he was overwhelmed with.

There were a few things that he was totally sure about at this moment. One being that his secret is totally safe with Derrick. He trusted this boy with everything and this was no exception. The other is that if he is in Washington DC, he would be closer to his all time hero, Titan. That in itself was a comforting thought. Another thought slowly made its way into Robby's mind. He could come home at the blink of an eye, using his teleportation powers, once he mastered them better. A faint smile made its way onto the young man's face as he stared out the window.

Chapter 27

Throughout their seven hour, four hundred plus mile journey, the car was almost annoyingly quiet. Susan turned the radio on to break the monotony of the tires slapping against the asphalt. Robby pulled out some tattered magazines that contained articles on Titan and Washington DC.

The hours seemed to drag on and on to no end. All of a sudden, Robby's new cell phone rang. He glanced at the number and it was his Aunt and Uncle calling him.

"Hello" answered Robby.

"Hey sport. You guys doing alright out there?" asked Richard.

"Sure. We are OK I guess. Mom looks a little tired though." replied Robby.

"I am sure she is kiddo, she has been awake since five this morning and you all have been on the road for three hours now" Richard told him.

"Yeah, I know she's tired" replied Robby.

"Well I was just checking on you guys, I know your dad is at work today that is why I was calling ya" stated Richard.

"Thanks Uncle Richie" said Robby quietly.

"Not a problem kiddo. Keep mom awake and we love you guys" responded Richard.

"Love you too, bye" answered Robby.

Robby hung up his phone and sighed. He already missed home and he had only been gone for three hours. The trip seemed to drag on and on. He put his magazine down and stretched out across the bench seat with his pillow.

He closed his eyes and let his mind wander. He started thinking of Derrick, Petey, his team, Cassandra the girl in his science class that he had a crush on but never really spoke to. Then his heart leaped into his throat. He was, hopefully, going to get to see and talk to his hero, Titan, again. He felt butterflies creep into his stomach at the thought.

Finally the moving van, Susan and Robby made it to their final destination of 3201 Hyperion Way, in the nation's capital of Washington DC. The moving van lurched into the driveway slowly and came to a halt right before the garage of the luxurious home that was now theirs.

Robby's mouth fell agape when he looked at the house that they were going to be living in. It was bigger than big to him. It was a two story mansion like building with a two car garage. Tan paint and dark brown shutters. The garage had a room above it. Robby wondered about that.

"Mom, what's with the room over the garage?" He asked politely.

"Oh that. Well that is your room Robby. It is as big as the garage and about five times the size of your old room" she answered.

"WOW! Really, that is all for me. My little bed is going to get lost in there." he added.

"Not really we have a surprise for you in your room. Your Dad has already taken care of it" Susan replied.

Just then a red, white and blue streak shot across the sky above the McCloud's new house and disappeared, causing Robby to drop the box that he was carrying. He could not believe his eyes or his luck. He was a resident of Washington DC for no more than five minutes and he had already had a 'Titan'-sighting. He knew everything was going to be OK.

He grinned as he picked up the box and headed towards the garage. He walked in and saw part of what he guessed was another surprise for him. There hanging on the wall was a rack of brand new baseball equipment, including, cleats, bats, balls, a batting practice device, bat weights and other assorted baseball equipment he had always wanted.

"Gosh this is amazing, I cannot believe this. All this stuff is so expensive" stated the red-headed baseball fanatic.

"Well, dad did get a major pay increase to be here and the place where he is working paid for the house and the move so he had the cash to make you feel at home, kiddo" his mother replied.

"Wow, this is amazing" yelped Robby.

The pair walked to the stairwell that lead up to his new bedroom. Robby was not sure what to expect. He still could not make heads or tails of what his mother was thinking for some reason. They climbed the spiral staircase that lead to his room. The excitement was steadily escalating with each and every step they took. Finally, they reached the top of the stairs.

"Close your eyes son" whispered Susan.

"Really! Man, this is killin' me, mom! Hurry!" Robby yelled.

Susan slowly turned the knob and opened the door. She escorted her only child through the threshold of the door and into his new bedroom. Susan removed her hands from her son's eyes and stood there to watch her child's wide eyed amazement.

As Robby opened his eyes and looked around, he was totally astonished at what he saw. There was a brand new bed, a large screen LCD television, X Box 360 Elite, a Bose surround sound system and a Bowflex. He looked around and was totally amazed at what he saw. All kinds of state of the art electronics and games, all the stuff that he had always wanted, was now his.

"You have got to be kidding me, this is all mine?" he asked.

"It sure is. I have something to show you" replied Susan.

Susan walked Robby over to the alcove window that overlooked their driveway. Upon the walls that made up the alcove, were all the photos of Titan, all the pictures of his favorite baseball players, and even the picture of him and Brandon, neatly arranged on the wall, almost exactly the way that they had appeared back in Boston.

"WOW! Dad did this?" questioned Robby.

"Yes sir, he did. He wanted you to feel really at home here" answered Susan with a warm embrace.

Robby stood there in utter amazement and wonder. He thought to himself that it was peculiar that his father went to such great lengths to put Titan's pictures up on the wall, knowing the feelings that he had for people with special abilities. Even with those thoughts, he felt that his father really loved him a lot, to go to this kind of expense just to make him feel at home here in Washington DC.

The rest of the afternoon Robby spent setting up all his belongings in his room. He started unpacking his comic books, first. He carefully put his display case that contained Mr. Amazing number one and number two on the wall near his "wall of heroes". He continued to unpack his clothes and video games. He finally got tired and came out of his room, climbed down the spiral stair case to the garage. He let himself into the house and headed for the kitchen.

"What's for dinner mom?" asked Robby.

"I was thinking hamburgers and hot dogs on the grill" replied Susan as she smiled at Robby.

"That is cool with me" stated the red head.

"Hey mom, can we go to the comic book store across town when we get done with dinner?" asked Robby politely.

"Sure, do you have all the stuff in your room unpacked and set up?" inquired Susan.

"Yes Ma'am, I do" he responded.

"So you already scouted out the comic stores?" asked Susan.

"Yes Ma'am, I could not help it. Is there anything that you need me to do before dinner?" asked Robby

"Sure, can you go outside and set up our patio furniture neatly?" Susan said.

Robby nodded and hugged his mother. He walked out on the patio and saw a mess of chairs all sitting in the corner of the screened in patio. He let out an audible sigh and got to work. He centered the table on the patio and placed all the chairs with cushions around it neatly as he was requested.

Robby loved and respected his parents with everything he had in every fiber of his being. He wanted to make them proud. The one thing that crept into his mind was the fact that he had to hide what he was to his parents, due to his father's supposed prejudices. "This is no way to live" he thought to himself. Robby knew that he could not reveal his secret or it would tear the family to shreds.

Dinner began in the McCloud's home, and the head of the household was conspicuous with his absence. Susan and Robby ate dinner and cleaned up. Robby went outside and cleaned off the grill for his mother and brought all the grilling utensils back into the kitchen.

"Mom, can we go to the comic store now?" inquired Robby

"Sure sweetheart, let me grab a few things and we can head out" responded Susan.

Robby ran to his room and grabbed his list of books that he wanted to look for. He knew that his mom would help him get the ones that he needed. He descended the spiral stair case and met his mother in the garage.

"Hey slugger, guess what your father just told me?" asked Susan.

"What mom?" Robby responded.

"We are getting rid of the minivan this weekend; you are gonna be riding in style on the first day of school kiddo!" said Susan.

"Really, what are we getting?" Robby asked.

"Well dad is getting me that black Infiniti G-35 sedan I was looking at last year" replied Susan.

"OH WOW!!!! That is awesome!" Robby yelped. "So I guess you are getting it this weekend? School starts Monday" Robby stated.

"Sure am, getting it this Saturday" said Susan.

Robby could barely contain his excitement. This new job may mean that he may not see his father that often, however it has given his family more options and more things that they want and need. Robby was so happy that his father made this transition.

The pair arrived at the comic book store and found a place to park. Susan eyed a scrap book store off to the left side of the comic place. She informed Robby that she was going to browse in there while Robby shopped in the comic store. He nodded his approval and walked from the van to the store.

Once inside his jaw fell on the floor. He had never seen such a magnificent specimen for a comic book store as this. It had everything imaginable there. Action figures, graphic novels, posters, resource books and anything else related to the chosen literary medium of Robby McCloud.

Robby walked over to the resource wall and found the "All about Mr. Amazing" book. He thumbed through it and saw that it went in depth, or as in depth as fiction can be, about Mr. Amazing's mental and teleportation powers. Robby stood there in sheer awe of this fictional character.

Suddenly an image caught his attention out the corner of his eye. It was a life sized poster of Titan himself, Robby's long time hero. He walked over to it and looked at it with wide eyed wonder. He perused the price and saw that he could not buy both. A feeling of utter disappointment and perplexity crept into his soul.

On one hand he really thought that he needed the Mr. Amazing encyclopedia, and on the other he really wanted to get this poster of Titan. He felt really let down because he wanted both. Robby put both items back upon the shelf and went to sit in the reading area.

The bell jingled at the front door announcing that someone was entering the store. He turned to see a kid about his age, with shaggy dark brown hair and crystal blue eyes walk in. He was wearing a baggy sweatshirt and khaki cargo pants. The young man was followed by a kid that looked to be a year maybe two years younger than he was. This kid had shoulder length dark brown hair, and dark brown eyes. You could tell that this kid had a large amount of energy by the way he was fidgeting all over the place.

Something struck Robby as familiar about the first kid. He was not quite sure what it was. He felt as if he had seen him before. The broad-shouldered kid walked past the Titan display with a slight grin on his face. He and his friend walked straight to the Mr. Amazing stack on the shelves and began thumbing through a few comics.

Robby was perplexed for some reason by this kid. Robby looked at his watch and noticed that it was almost time for the store to close. He did not have time to waste, however, he needed to run and talk to his mother about borrowing seven dollars so that he could get the Titan poster and the Mr. Amazing encyclopedia. He quickly dashed out the door and into the scrap book store.

"Mom...Hey Mom!! Can I borrow seven bucks?" asked the bright eyed kid.

"What for son?" returned his mother.

"Well I have enough cash for the Mr. Amazing book I want, but I found this life size Titan poster that I want really bad too" responded Robby anxiously.

Robby's mother conceded to the request of her son. She knew that he always paid back his debts on time, all the time. She reached into her hand bag and pulled out a ten dollar bill to give to him. She instructed him to return all the change to her whenever he was finished.

"Thanks mom! You are the best" exclaimed Robby.

Susan just smiled as Robby ran off in the opposite direction and headed for the door. Robby quickly made his way back to the comic store and pushed open the door. He glanced around in hopes to see the familiar boy. No such luck. In the few short minutes that he was next door the boy and his buddy were gone.

Disappointed, he walked over to the Mr. Amazing shelf, and retrieved the encyclopedia. He then made his way over to the cardboard Titan display and pulled out the poster that he had wanted. He took all of his items and handed them to the man behind the counter.

The man behind the counter asked Robby if he needed anything else. Robby shook his head no and awaited the store clerk to tell him how much he needed to pay.

"OK sir" began the store clerk. "The total for today will be sixteen dollars and ninety-eight cents please" continued the employee.

"Yes Sir, here ya go" said Robby as he handed the clerk two ten-Dollar bills.

The clerk made change and handed Robby the bag. Robby ran out the door of the store to meet his mother in the parking lot. Susan was loading some merchandise in the back end of her soon to be old van. Robby opened the passenger door and climbed in.

Susan looked with admiration as her son pored over the book that he just bought. Never in his short life had she seen her athletically minded son so interested in reading. Not that Robby was unintelligent, he was very bright, but she had never seen him so engrossed in a literary piece. She knew that he loved comic books, but the fact that he was almost studying this book caught her off guard.

Little did she know, Robby was reading up on how to accurately control his developing powers. Mr. Amazing would recount tales upon tales regarding his control of the mind that he possessed. Robby would put all that knowledge into play and taught himself how to call upon and control his fantastic abilities.

The two of them pulled up into the garage, where they saw Bob's SUV parked there. Robby was ecstatic to see his father. He ran up to his room and put all his stuff away. He then ran back to the house and threw the door open. He ran to his dad and almost jumped into his arms.

"DAD!!! I have missed you!" screamed Robby.

"I have missed you too, sport. I am sorry I had to come ahead of you guys, and I was not here when you guys got here" replied Bob.

"It's OK, dad, this house is amazing" said Robby as he hugged his father.

"Yeah, I got a huge pay raise when the C.I.A acquired my contract" stated Bob.

Robby knew that his father had something to do with policing people with abilities. He opted to not peer into his father's mind after he learned that he had a problem with mutants. He thought that being ignorant to what his father does would probably be safer in the long run.

"Well that is so cool dad, and thanks for all the nice stuff you got me, it means a lot" Robby added politely.

"You are welcome, kiddo, I had to do it so you would feel more at home" explained Bob.

"Well it did the trick, Dad!" said Robby with a grin.

The whole family went in and sat in front of the TV. Bob tuned into the sports channel and found the Boston Red Sox playing. Robby sat up and took notice. He watched intently at his home town team. While he was watching he noticed a fan holding a sign that totally caught him by surprise.

The sign was covering the faces of the people holding it, but it read "Robby #18 we Miss you, Derrick, Brandon, and Petey" Robby was consumed with emotions. He looked at the TV in utter disbelief and amazement. His best friends had said hello to him over the TV.

He got up and ran to his room, and grabbed the cell phone that his uncle had gotten him. He dialed Derrick's number and awaited an answer.

"Hello, Derrick, can you hear me? Man, I can't believe you did that for me" giggled Robby.

"Thought you would like it, Red" screamed the voice on the other end of the phone.

Robby chuckled with his best friend for a few minutes as he walked back into the living room to plop down back in front of the ball game. He was so happy to talk to Derrick and Petey.

"Tell D we said hello, son" requested Susan.

"Hey D! Mom said hello" replied Robby as requested.

The rest of the evening came and went, as the ten o'clock hour quickly approached. Susan was busy setting out Robby's new school supplies for the morning. Bob had closed his laptop and was preparing to watch the news. Robby stood up, stretched, and yawned.

"Well son, it's bed time" instructed Bob.

"Yes sir that was what I was thinking anyway" retorted Robby respectfully.

"Good night, son" said Susan as she hugged her only child.

"Night, mom!" replied Robby, as he returned the hug in kind.

Robby left the room and ascended his stair case to his new room. He changed into his sleep pants and grabbed his Mr. Amazing encyclopedia. He lay back on the bed and began to read all about the powers of his favorite fictional superhero. He was so wrapped up he almost had forgotten about the new poster to add to his wall of heroes.

He jumped out of bed and ran to the desk where he had placed the poster for safe keeping. He unrolled the five and a half foot poster and hung it from baseboard up. He stepped back and realized that he was actually a little bit taller than his hero. Titan, however, made up for that height difference in the amount of muscle that was showing all over his compact frame. Titan almost reminded him of Derrick, by the way they were so well built.

Robby smiled at his handy work and laid back down on his bed to face the poster. He closed his eyes and began to drift in thought about the first time that he had met Titan. How cool he was, and how honest the boy was about being a hero. He thought of the conversations that he had with the young hero, and how he actually envied a normal kid, just because he could play baseball.

"Lord, please let me have the strength and will power to be Titan's partner. Let me meet him again, so that I can show him what I can do" prayed Robby in earnest.

Robby McCloud was one who trusted in what God had in store for him. He knew that Titan saved him for a reason. He also knew that he was granted these amazing powers for a reason as well. Robby did not totally comprehend what those reasons were, but he submitted to the fact that God did it and that was all that mattered to him.

Sleep overtook young Robby McCloud's body, as his mind wandered all throughout the night. He kept having dreams of being a hero alongside Titan. He also had visions of his friends and family back home in Boston. Robby missed them and wanted to share more close times with the people that meant the world to him.

Chapter 28

The clock struck six am. As the alarm clock startled Robby awake, he wondered to himself what the new day would bring him. He heard footsteps on the spiral staircase that led up to his room. Suddenly there came a knock at his door.

"Come in!" shouted Robby.

"Hey good morning sport" said Bob McCloud as he pushed the door open.

"Morning Dad" replied Robby with a smile and a yawn.

Bob walked towards his son's bed with an arm full of clothes for his son. He set them on his bedside table and sat upon his bed. He reached over and rustled his son's bright red hair.

"Son, I know this is all new for you, but I promise you will make good friends here in DC" said his father almost apologetically.

"I know I will Dad! Nothing to worry about, except the occasional girlfriend and baseball practice" giggled Robby.

Bob reached over and embraced his brave son. He always thought that his son was a fighter and a survivor. Little did Bob know that his son possessed great power that would be his calling card in the future. Right now, Robby was his little boy, and he loved him dearly.

Bob got back to his feet, and instructed his son to have a great day at school. He clapped his arm around his son's shoulder and hugged him. Bob made his way to the door and turned back to his son.

"Robby...I love you, son!" Bob said with warmth in his voice.

"I love you too, dad!" returned Robby with matching warmth.

Robby hurriedly ran to his bathroom with his clothing. He showered, brushed his teeth, and dressed in almost record time.

No matter what his nerves were trying to tell him, his excitement outweighed them. He grabbed his book that his mother put together for him the night before and descended his stairs.

Susan was in the kitchen pouring Robby a glass of orange juice and cutting up the regular fruit that Robby usually would eat in the mornings, alongside a piece of whole grain toast. She prepared the plate and set it at the huge kitchen table that the family now owned.

Robby pulled his chair out and sat down. He bowed his head and prayed for God to grant him a good day and to bless the food that he was about to eat. His mother looked upon her son with admiration at his devotions that he had ingrained within his psyche.

"Well, are you ready for your first ride in the Infinite kiddo?" asked Susan.

"Oh, yeah, that's right, you have to take me this morning to get all my registration stuff done, huh?" asked Robby.

"Yeah, I sure do" answered Susan as she stood up to grab her purse and keys.

Robby stood up, and took his plate to the sink. He washed it off and put it away. Then he grabbed his backpack and awaited his mother at the door to the garage. As they walked out to the car, Robby could not help but grin at the sight of the shiny import sedan his mother now possessed.

The car ride was uneventful. Robby reveled in the fact that he was being escorted to his new school, JFK Middle School, in a brand new sports car. He was grinning from ear to ear as his mother parked the highly tuned vehicle and shut it down.

"Son, you are going to be late for your first period class because we have so much to do" stated Susan.

"Mom, that's fine, we can take our time, I would like to get it all done now instead of possibly having to fix something later" replied Robby with a sure grin on his face.

The pair walked into the gates of the school and made their way to the visitor center. Once inside Susan inquired where the attendance coordinator was. The receptionist advised them where to go. Susan and Robby set off on their journey down to the attendance center office.

They arrived at the office and let themselves in. It was not long before Robby's class schedule had been hashed out and his locker assignment was given. Robby was amazed at the efficiency of the people in this office.

His mother handed him the schedule that she was given. Robby looked over it. He asked for directions to his first period class. The counselor handed him a map and pointed him in the right direction. He hugged his mother and headed off down the hallway.

Robby reached room 217. He took a deep breath and opened the door. Everyone in the class looked up from what they were doing to glance over at him. He walked up to the teacher and handed her his information.

"Class, may I have your attention please!" announced Mrs. Wade.

"Class this is Robert McCloud, he comes to us from Boston Massachusetts, Let's all welcome him to JFK Middle School" requested Mrs. Wade.

Robby looked around at the students to locate an empty seat. He found one next to an oddly familiar face. He walked over and sat down.

"Mr. McCloud would you like to tell the class a little about yourself before you get settled in?" asked Mrs. Wade.

"Well," Robby began as he stood back up. "My friends call me Robby; I play baseball, collect comic books, and love video games" he continued.

"Well, Robby, I would like to welcome you to our class" said Mrs. Wade in a friendly tone.

Robby sat back down and got out his note book. He glanced over his shoulder at the familiar form behind him. He noticed that the person was leaning in to talk to him.

"Hi, my name is Jake, Jake Knight, and nice to meet you" said the friendly boy behind Robby.

"Hi Jake, nice to meet you" replied Robby.

"Mr. Knight, do you have anything that you would like to share with the class?" asked Mrs. Wade.

"No, Ma'am" responded Jake with embarrassment in his voice.

"Then, I would suggest that you complete your essay" said Mrs. Wade.

Robby raised his hand politely. "Ma'am what essay were they writing?" inquired Robby.

"They are writing a one-page paper on what they did over summer break" answered Mrs. Wade.

Robby nodded and got out his notebook. He fumbled for his pencil in his bag. When he located it, he opened the notebook and began recounting his last baseball game and subsequent move to the Washington DC area. Robby made sure that in this paper he paid the correct tribute to Derrick, Brandon, Travis and Petey.

Class was drawing to a close, as Jake tapped Robby on the shoulder. Robby leaned in to see what the boy needed.

"Hey man, you want to meet up for lunch? I will introduce you to some friends of mine and my little brother" whispered Jake.

"Sure, man that would be great!" answered Robby.

The bell rang to dismiss the class, and Jake looked at young Robby with a puzzled stare. He saw something in this kid that no one else that he knew of, other than himself or his father possessed. He had, what appeared to be, a faint aura of light surrounding his frame.

Jake just counted it as the lights in the class were exceptionally bright or something. The two kids walked into the hall and made their way to the lockers. Much to each other's surprise, they had lockers next to one another.

Robby grinned as he looked over at the stocky youth. He thought to himself that this kid reminded him of Derrick, and oddly enough he thought the same of Titan and Derrick. Then it dawned on him, he was the kid that was in the comic store, the Friday evening before school started.

"Hey Jake, do you like comics?" Robby asked.

"Yeah, I sure do" stated Jake.

"What is your favorite one?" Robby continued with the interrogation.

"Oh that is easy: Mr. Amazing, he is awesome" Jake replied with a laugh.

"Mine too, so that was you in the store last Friday, then?" pressed Robby.

"Yeah, I went to the comic store with my little brother this past Friday, why?" Jake asked.

"I saw you in there. I was going to say hello, because you reminded me of someone." Robby said.

"I get that all the time" replied Jake.

The two chatted up a storm about comics between classes. Robby was relieved to know that Jake shared all his classes with him. He knew that he would not get lost now that he had his very own tour guide.

Lunch time finally arrived, and to the athletic Robby McCloud, it could not come quick enough. Robby and Jake made their way to the lunch room. Jake kept looking around as if he were looking for something or someone.

"Hey, what you looking for, man?" Robby asked.

"Oh, my little brother, Madison" Jake answered.

Suddenly a long haired bundle of energy came bouncing into the cafeteria. He waved over towards Jake. Jake returned the gesture in kind. He was ecstatic to see his older brother and it was obvious.

"JAKE! Hey!" Madison yelled from across the cafeteria.

"Hey, lil bro! How is your first day going so far?" inquired Jake.

"Great, I already had computers. It was awesome!" exclaimed Madison with enthusiasm.

"Madison, this is my new friend, Robby McCloud, he is from Boston" said Jake.

Madison held out his hand in friendship. "Nice to meet you Robby" he said in a friendly tone of voice.

"Nice to meet you too, Madison" returned Robby in kind.

The trio got their lunch and made their way outside the lunch room to the picnic tables that the kids were allowed to eat at, if they wished to. They found and empty one and sat down. Robby bowed his head before he touched his food.

"Hey wait Robby! We will pray with you dude!" exclaimed Jake as he took his brother's hand and his new friend's hand and bowed his own head.

Robby began blessing the food. He thanked God for the fact that he has his first new friends in Washington DC. He prayed for his family, and his friends back home. He concluded and began to eat.

When the boys began talking, Robby found out how much he and Jake had in common. He also made a strong connection with the fact that Jake reminded him so much of Derrick Malone. Through the thick of the conversations Robby and Jake learned that they were actually next door neighbors.

"You mean to tell me that you live right next door to me?" asked Robby.

"Yup! We live at 3203 Hyperion Way. Our yards are connected by that huge lot" explained Jake.

Something in Robby's soul told him that there was a reason that they were neighbors. He felt so comfortable around Jake, even though he had only known him a grand total of three and a half hours. He could see the similarities between Jake and Derrick were so amazingly close, it almost made him giddy.

The three of them made plans to walk home from school together. They were informed it would be a few minutes longer to wait on Madison, because he was coming from the other side of the school. Jake suggested that they meet at the iron gate that marked the entrance of the school. Madison agreed, as the bell rang indicating that lunch was over.

Madison stood up and hugged his brother, shook Robby's hand and headed off in the opposite direction. Jake and Robby walked together to the lockers. They talked with every free moment they had about what each other were interested in.

Jake had never felt so comfortable with anyone, including his own brother, before. He could not put his mighty finger on what it was; he just knew that there was something really special about this kid. Unlike Robby, who had not put it together that Jake, as Titan, saved his life a few years back. Jake remembered the rescue and how much Robby looked up to him. That still did not settle the feeling that there was something really unique about this boy.

The day crept on slowly as the second hand on the classroom clocks seemed to stand still. Robby was excited about hanging out with his new friends that he had made on the very first day of school. Jake too was beside himself with anticipation of hanging out with the one person that he felt would totally understand him.

Jake sat in the classroom right next to the polite red-headed twelve-year-old. He became lost in thought. What was it about this kid? What was it that made Jake want to let him in on his secret after only knowing him for eight short hours? Why is it that this kid made him feel so at peace with him being a hero? Was it the fact that he knew somehow that Robby loved and respected him as Titan already? All these thoughts rained down on the head of the mighty Jake Knight.

The bell finally rang to signify the end of the day. Jake and Robby grabbed their bags and headed for the door. Carefully they navigated the hallway to the lockers. Each put their books up and made their way to the empty courtyard to await Madison's arrival.

"So Robby, what do you like to do for fun?" asked Jake.

"Well I like to play baseball, it's my favorite sport. Keeps me in great shape" responded Robby.

He glanced over at Jake and noticed what appeared to be the outline of extreme muscle showing through his over sized sweatshirt. He was astonished but kept it to himself. He did not want to embarrass his new friend.

"So do you play any sports?" Robby queried.

"No, I am a little bit too clumsy for that; I work out a little bit with weights, though" disclosed Jake.

"A little? It looks more like a lot, you look like you are SUPER strong" implored Robby has he nudged his friend's muscular arm.

"Huh?" responded Jake.

"What do you got under that sweatshirt? Rocks?" grilled Robby.

Jake got a little bit nervous, for the first time around Robby, and decided that he needed a distraction away from the current conversation. He knew that if this intelligent and resourceful kid kept prodding, he may learn his secret long before he would be prepared to disclose it.

"Hey Robby, I need to run to the rest room" disclosed Jake.

"OK, bro" responded Robby.

Jake made his way towards the restrooms. "Hey, Robby meet me by the Soda..." his voice trailed off when he realized he was the only one in the courtyard. "Machines" he finished quietly.

He was perplexed at what had just happened. He looked around, and caught a glimpse of Robby standing by that wrought iron gate that they were supposed to meet Madison at. Even with his super speed he would have at least made noise. His super acute senses would have picked it up, but alas there was no tell tale sign of movement. Jake just shrugged.

Madison had met up with Robby at the gate, now they were awaiting Jake. When Jake joined them, the trio started their journey home. They walked through Perry Park and made their way over to the walking trail that led to Hyperion Way.

While they walked, Madison jumped all over the place with ecstatic hyperactivity. Jake explained that he was the family's bundle of energy. Jake recounted the fact that Madison was adopted by his mother and father. Madison interjected that Jake was his brother no matter who gave birth to him. Robby found that fact comforting for some reason.

They approached 3201 Hyperion Way and Robby insisted that he get the opportunity to introduce Jake and Madison to his mother. The Knights agreed and accompanied Robby to his door. For some odd reason, Jake felt nervous.

Robby opened the door and called for his mother to come meet his new friends. The trio all waited patiently for Susan to come and greet them. Susan descended the stairs gracefully. She approached the boys with a huge grin plastered across her face.

"Well if this isn't Jake Knight" said Susan as she placed her hand on Jake's massive shoulder.

"You know him, mom?" quizzed Robby.

"Of course I know him, honey" Susan started. "Your father and his father were high school buddies and college roommates" she explained.

"Really?" inquired Robby.

"Yeah! And in fact, we were there to watch Jake's birth, son" stated Susan warmly.

"Then why haven't I ever heard of him?" needled Robby.

"Well with your father's job, it was hard for him to keep in contact with people, not to mention the Knight's moved quite a bit until Charles got the job at DCU" remarked Susan.

Robby and Jake stood there for what seemed to be an eternity. They knew when they first met, that they would have become good friends. With this revelation, it seemed that they were destined to be friends since birth.

"Wow! This is amazing; my new friends from school are my next door neighbors and our families know each other! AWESOME!" Robby exclaimed.

Jake introduced Madison to Susan. She was pleased to meet the newest Knight son. She had this deep seated thought that she wished that they would have kept in closer contact with the Knights.

"So Charles and Nancy adopted you, right Madison?" asked Susan

"That's right Mrs. McCloud" responded the ball of perpetual energy.

"Please call me Mrs. Susan" implored Susan affectionately.

"Yes Ma'am" remarked Madison politely.

"Mom, can the guys stay for dinner?" implored Robby.

"I do not mind at all, we are having pot roast and I know that we have plenty" acknowledged Susan, as she walked towards the kitchen. "But honey, make sure that they call Dr. Knight and see if it is OK for them to stay" she added.

"Yes Ma'am!" All three boys responded in unison.

Jake took out his cell phone and called his house.

"Hi Mom! You will never guess who lives next door to us! YEAH! The McCloud's, how did you know? Oh, he did, that is cool, and I'll tell Robby. Hey I was calling to see if I could stay over here for dinner? Yes Ma' am I was invited by Mrs. Susan. Yes Ma'am I will tell her. Thanks mom, we love you" came the one sided phone conversation.

Jake closed his flip phone and stored it back in his pocket. He came over to the couch in the den and plopped down. Jake felt such a feeling of comfort and relaxation around this family. He felt as if he had known them his entire life, and in essence he sort of did.

"Hey Robby, mom and dad know you live here, because Dad helped your dad get this house." explained Jake.

"Really? Is that what your mom wanted you to tell me?" asked Robby in complete amazement.

"Yeah, man, we were destined to be great friends!" affirmed Jake.

Susan had begun to set the table when Bob McCloud came home from work. He walked in and hugged his son. He sneaked over and kissed his wife warmly. Bob then glanced at a familiar form in his dining area.

"Jake? Little Jake Knight?" asked Bob with a look of astonishment.

"Yes Sir, Mr. McCloud, it's me" replied Jake rather shyly.

Bob looked Jake up and down for a few minutes. Gone was that small, frail child that he had seen in pictures with Dr. Knight. Here stood a rather healthy, stocky young man that bore the striking resemblance to those old photographs.

The family sat down to eat. Robby said grace for the meal. The plates were all passed as the conversation started. Susan asked Jake all about the school that they attended, and what he thought of it.

Susan listened and watched this boy intently. She could not help but draw a resemblance correlation between Jake Knight and Derrick Malone. Their stature, nature, and mannerisms were all so similar. Susan saw why her son gravitated to Jake as fast as he did.

"So Jake do you play any sports?" inquired Susan.

"No Ma'am, I am way too clumsy for that" remarked Jake.

"Really?" pressed Bob.

"No Sir, I just work out a lot with weights, that way if anyone gets hurt, it's only me" retorted Jake with a shy grin.

"Well, I can tell, you look like a little tank. You kind of remind me of Robby's friend, Derrick" said Bob.

"Oh Man dad, you are right, he does look a little bit like Derrick" Robby agreed.

The rest of the meal the boys cracked jokes and things that really showed that they were more alike than one would have thought. The closeness between Robby and Jake was totally apparent. It was as if they had known each other for a lifetime. It could possibly be due to the fact that Jake and Derrick were so similar, that Robby felt at home with him.

Later that evening Jake's cell phone rang. As he answered it, he had a look of concern on his face. He politely got up and excused himself.

"Well guys, it is getting late, and my parents need us home, so we have got to head out" explained Jake.

"Aww, man, I was about to show you my room and stuff, dude!" protested Robby.

"Son, he has to go, maybe right after school tomorrow" interjected Susan.

"Hey man, I got a few seconds before I got to take off, we can run up there for a few minutes" comforted Jake as he draped his arm over Robby's shoulder.

The trio ran out of the house and into the garage. Jake looked over and saw the bright yellow Hummer. He was amazed at the sight of it. They ascended the spiral staircase that led to Robby's loft room.

"Well here is my room, guys" Robby said with a smile.

"Cool stuff!" Jake exclaimed as he looked all around.

Robby showed off his comic book collection, which totally fascinated Madison. Jake walked over and looked at the life sized poster of Titan and almost cringed. He quickly moved away from it so that Robby would not possibly pick up on the connection.

"Man, you have a lot of stuff on that wall, dude" stated Jake.

"Yeah, I guess I do, they are all my favorite baseball players, and my all-time hero: TITAN!" yelled Robby. "I really want to meet him again…"

"Again?" asked Jake.

"Yeah, he saved and changed my life back in Boston when I was eight years old" replied Robby.

"How did he change your life?" asked Jake pryingly.

"Well, you might think it's stupid" uttered Robby as he looked at the ground in embarrassment.

"Dude, nothing about you says 'stupid', bro; what is it?" asked Jake.

"Well…" Robby began. "He made me want to become a hero!" Robby revealed.

Jake was taken and moved that his heroic deed did not go unrewarded with this kid. He had a warm feeling inside about what he had just heard. Jake looked at his watch and knew that he was pressed for time.

"Well man, I gotta go or the parents are gonna kill us" declared Jake.

"Yeah, we gotta go bro!" interjected Madison.

"OK guys, I will walk you out" stated Robby.

The three new friends made their way out of the room and down the stairs. They all three walked in awkward silence as if they were all three lost in thought. As they made their way inside and said their goodbyes, they made plans to meet up and walk to school in the morning.

"Hey, wanna meet Maddie and me to walk to school in the morning, Red?" Jake suggested.

"What did you call me?" asked Robby out of shock.

"Red? Should I not call you that?" inquired Jake.

"No, it's fine; my best friend in Boston used to call me that all the time. It was my nick name from him" he explained.

"So, you do mind if I call you that?" implored Jake.

"Not at all, it would actually make me feel better" responded Robby.

"Cool, Red it is. Well we have got to go, Red. See you in the morning" said Jake as he waved to his new friend.

Robby waved as he got a wave of emotions from both Maddie and Jake. They did not want to leave. He felt as if he could totally trust them as he trusted Derrick. As they left, he felt emptiness settle in on him. He knew that these two would be close to him for life.

Robby closed the door silently and walked back into the dining area. His mother and father were cleaning up after dinner. He had a very sad look upon his face. As usual Susan suspected that something was wrong with her baby boy.

"Son, is there something wrong?" inquired Susan.

Robby looked at her with a tear welling up in his eye, he shook his head no and headed out to his room as fast as his little legs could carry him. He did not know what he was feeling or why, he just knew that he did not want his parents to worry. He ascended the spiral stair case to his room and ran to his bed. Robby grabbed his baseball glove and ball, plopped on the bed and began tossing his ball in the air.

Susan suspected something was totally amiss with her son. She followed after Robby in hopes to talk to him. She made her way to his room and knocked on his door. She awaited him to respond, with no success.

"Son, can I come in?" requested Susan.

"Robby please answer me" she pleaded.

All Susan heard was a muffled sniffle. She carefully let herself in, and gave Robby time to roll over and face away from her, if he wanted to. Cautiously she approached the bed and gently sat down.

"Baby, what's the matter?" She prodded her son lovingly.

"Mom, I miss Derrick, I don't know what is wrong with me. Jake and Madison left to go home and it felt like we were moving away all over again" he answered through his tears.

"Oh honey. I understand what you are going through. This is still all new to you and it's OK to feel like that" she said as she rubbed her sons back.

Robby rolled to face his mom. "It is?" he asked.

"Of course, in fact, I still get teary-eyed thinking about my four boys as we were getting ready to leave Boston" replied Susan.

"Really?" he replied in shock.

"Yeah, it broke me up inside to see you guys like that, so it is totally fine to feel like this, but please understand, we are not going anywhere for a long time. Not to mention, Jake and Madison are here to stay as well, we are secure in that fact kiddo" soothed Susan.

"Thanks mom!" Robby said.

He sat up and hugged his mother tightly. She then got up and left her son to think about what she had just uttered to him. Robby laid on his bed for a few more minutes tossing his baseball.

Robby climbed to his feet. He walked over to the alcove window and stared out into the night. He was wondering what Derrick was up to. Without knowingly doing so, he activated his telepathic power. His eyes shifted from the brightest green to the darkness of the abyss. He was reaching out to his friend.

"WOW! I can sense his thoughts four hundred miles away!" He exclaimed to himself.

Robby shut his eyes and closed the connection. He felt a little more at ease, knowing that he could reach out to Derrick with his powers still. He was, however, amazed that he could do that at such a great distance.

He made his way to his dresser and got his Boston Red Sox sleep pants out. He pulled his shorts off, and pulled his pants on. He walked over to his bed, pulled his shirt over his head, tossed it on the floor, and crawled into bed.

Sleep crept upon Robby McCloud with ease. He drifted off quickly. His dreams were filled with the thoughts and images of his friends from back home, and his new friends in Washington DC. His soul became calm and serene as his mind allowed these thoughts and images to wash over him in a calming flood.

Chapter 29

The alarm clock screeched uncontrollably for a few minutes before it stirred the red head into consciousness. Robby rolled over and looked at the noisy contraption. He reached out and turned it off. Slowly he made his way to his feet. He twisted and stretched his young body to shake off the cobwebs of sleep.

He pondered what he was going to wear to school. He decided on a light colored pair of jeans, a shirt that belonged to his favorite band, Sypher, and a pair of sneakers. He looked in his full length mirror and ran a brush through his medium length red mane. Then shook his head till it looked neatly messy and he was satisfied with its appearance.

Robby grabbed his back pack and headed to the kitchen. As he made his way to the kitchen table, his mom rustled his hair a little bit. He looked up and smiled sweetly at her. He picked his spot as his mother brought over his usual breakfast.

A loud knock was heard at the front door as Susan walked to open it. She disarmed the alarm system and unlocked the door. Gently she opened the door to identify their guest.

"Good Morning Mrs. Susan. Is Robby ready to go?" asked Jake.

"Morning Jake, he is eating breakfast" answered Susan.

Just then a red head popped out from behind his mother. He smiled at his friends who were patiently waiting. Jake flashed a return megawatt smile back at his new best friend.

"Ready to go, Red?" asked the broad shouldered, blue-eyed teen.

"Lemme grab my bag and my bagel and were outta here" responded Robby.

Robby ran in, snatched up his book bag, the remainder of his breakfast, and made his way to the door. He hugged his mother as he ruffled his hair again. Again he looked up and smiled at her. He secretly loved it when his mother would mess with his hair like that.

"See ya, mom" said Robby as he ran out the door.

"Bye, guys" waved Susan.

"Morning, Red" stated Jake with a grin.

"What up bro?" Robby replied as he shook Jake's powerful hand.

"Hey, Robby" said Madison as he jumped on Robby's back almost knocking him down.

"Hi there, oh hyper one!" Robby chuckled.

The terrific trio made their way towards JFK Middle school. They laughed and talked all the way. Robby used this time to get to know his new friends and vice versa. Jake wanted to know everything about the person that set him so at ease. The conversations reflected the inquiring thoughts and sentiments.

They reached the entrance to the school and saw that they still had about fifteen minutes. Robby suggested that they grab a picnic table and hang out till Madison had to head off for the other side of campus. The guys all laughed and joked for about ten minutes.

Robby had this feeling as if he had known Jake for his entire life. Unbeknownst to Robby, Jake felt the exact same way. They both reveled in the fact that they were so at peace with one another and were such close friends in such a short time.

Madison looked at his watch and realized that he needed to go. He stood up and shouldered his backpack. He hugged his brother and bid his goodbyes to his new friend. Madison ran off to the opposite side of the campus.

"Red, I feel like I can tell you this" stated Jake quietly.

"What's up big guy?" inquired Robby.

"Well" he began. "I feel like I have known you my whole life, but it has only been like three days."

"Yeah, I totally feel the same, but, I think that it is because you remind me so much of my best friend, Derrick" declared Robby.

"Really?" he asked. "You think that I remind you of your best friend?" he continued.

"More than you know man" acknowledged Robby.

The two of them left the picnic area and made their way inside. As they walked towards their first period class, Robby could sense that Jake was totally relaxed around him. He still thought that it was odd that he could not get a telepathic, only an empathic reading off of Jake. He just shrugged it off as he had done with his mother's readings.

Once inside their classroom, Jake and Robby quickly took their seats. The teacher already had a writing assignment on the board. The class took out their notebooks and began working on the assigned text. Robby felt the uneasiness in the air over the assignment. Suddenly a wave of nausea hit the red-headed youth like a ton of bricks.

Robby quickly raised his hand to be excused. Mrs. Wade offered him a hall pass and excused him from the room. Robby quickly made for the door and took off down the hall way as fast as he could.

As he had almost reached the boys' restroom, another wave more intense than the first struck him like a bolt of lightning. The pain was so intense that young Robby McCloud doubled over and fell to the floor. It felt as if his insides were on fire.

"Man someone is hurt!" Robby said as he scanned the hallway.

When he was sure that no one was there he focused his highly tuned concentration on teleporting. His eyes gradually shifted from emerald green to coal black. He focused himself with laser point accuracy on the pain that he had felt. A familiar cloud of mist arose and surrounded him. Within a millisecond he the portrait of the school hallway was replaced by the searing heat of an inferno.

Robby reappeared inside the factory where the overwhelming pain was coming from and noticed that he had gotten himself into a slight bind. He quickly surveyed his surroundings and found his target. He ran over to the man that was laying face down and badly burned.

The guardian angel instinct kicked in. Robby placed his hand on the man's head and telepathically eased his pain. Then he implanted an image of the man escaping the fire and running for help. He implanted this memory to cause his "patient" to act quickly once his wounds were healed and he revived from his telepathically induced slumber.

Robby then focused his attention and energy on his victim's injury. He settled his hands right above the man's chest and took in a breath. He concentrated as his eyes shifted to a bright golden yellow. His aura surrounded the man in a blanket of protection. Slowly the burns seemed to disappear. The man was miraculously being healed by his red-headed guardian angel.

Robby felt his energy being drained. He knew that he may have just enough energy to teleport himself and his "patient" to safety, and then "jump" away unnoticed. He had to move quickly or his energy would be completely drained.

He placed one hand on the man's chest and called upon the mist to rise. The two figures were swept away in a cloud only to reemerge outside in the safety zone. Robby staggered to his feet, leaving the semi-conscious worker to his own devices. He mustered all the remaining energy he had left and "jumped" back to the boys' restroom.

Meanwhile, back at school, Robby's adventure to the explosion did not go unnoticed. Jake Knight heard something odd and turned his attention outside. His ultra sensitive eyes saw the radiant heat signature of a major inferno. As he stared out the window he also saw a familiar face appear out of thin air with an injured man in his clutches. He was shocked to see his new best friend emerging out of a fog cloud with another person.

Jake excused himself to the restroom. With a burst of super speed, Jake made his way to the rest room to change into his Titan persona. As he ripped open his sweatshirt, he was met with a startling surprise. A vapor cloud relinquished its passenger.

There Jake was in mid-change as his new best friend emerges out of a fog to catch him in the act.

The two boys stood there for what seemed an eternity in utter silence. Each boy eyed the other up and down with jaws wide open in total amazement of what had just occurred.

"Jake! You're Titan?" questioned Robby with joyful amazement.

"Yeah, you caught me. But you, you're a muta…." He was interrupted.

"A Mutant!" he began to sob "Yeah I am a total freak, and you are probably going to hate me!" Robby continued.

"Well, I'm not exactly normal, either…" soothed Jake.

"You're not weirded-out by me?" inquired Robby as he sniffled softly.

"Not at all, Red, I think it's cool" contested Jake.

"Man, you ARE like Derrick. That's what he said when he found out too" said Robby as he wiped his tears.

Jake walked over and placed his arm around his now super-friend's shoulder. As his skin made contact with Robby's, he felt a slight pull and some energy flowing from him into his friend. Robby was looking rather worn-out and pale before. As Jake's energy flowed into his friend, his color improved significantly.

"You're not a freak, you're a hero, man" said Jake as he released his friend, startled at the energy transfer that had taken place.

"Oh Wow! My hero, Titan, thinks that I am a hero, too? I have prayed for this day since I first met you!" explained Robby as he watched Jake finish his transformation into Titan.

"Well, I would like to talk about this more, but I have a factory to save. Wanna join me?" Titan asked him.

"That would be like a dream come true, let's rock!" Robby exclaimed.

Jake opened the hatch above one of the stalls that only he knew about. He leaped into the sky from there. Robby focused his concentration on "jumping" to the triage station. As he did, the mist rose quickly, he was gone, and reappeared where the medics were.

Robby then focused his attention on creating a mental image that did not include him being there, only that the medics treated all the patients. He began healing the injuries that were there. He found it difficult to maintain focus on the illusion and healing at the same time. Robby knew that it was a matter of time before his energy would ebb away. He hoped that Titan could get this wrapped up quickly.

Meanwhile, Titan used his super strength to bring a water tower over the factory. He had flown over to the tower and with amazing ease he ripped it from its foundation. He then hefted it into the sky and flew back to the site of the inferno. He centered himself over the factory and tore the tank open with his bare hands. As the water poured down he tossed the empty tower to an empty spot on the property. He then focused his plasmoidal blasts to make a ravine for the water to run off of before it drowned the survivors.

Titan was satisfied that the fire had been successfully extinguished by his hands. He scanned the area and found his young friend hard at work. He landed next to his red-headed comrade. Titan then reached out and placed his hand on his friend's arm. He felt that familiar tingle of energy again. Robby straightened his back, as if he was being recharged.

"Hey bro, we are done here, let's bail before someone gets a look at ya" Titan said.

"Sure. Keep holding on, I can get us outta here quick" responded Robby.

Robby's eyes shifted again to the dark abyss that signaled the use of either his telepathic ability or his teleportation. Jake felt a little tickle in his stomach and the mist surrounded them both and they vanished. Back in the bathroom, Robby collapsed into his friend's arms.

"Whoa, tiger! What's up with that?" Titan asked him.

"When I use my powers like that, I get really drained" he answered.

"So," Jake paused before continuing. "What all can you do?" He asked carefully.

"Well, I know that I can read minds, project images and thoughts, block pain for people, and read and interpret emotions. I can also heal people, but doing that just takes a lot out of me, though, and I can teleport myself. I call that 'Jumping', by the way..." Robby explained.

"Man, you can do a lot. That's awesome!" Jake exclaimed.

"Dude, I don't feel so good right now..." Robby uttered.

Just then, Robby passed out and fell to the floor of the bathroom before Jake could react. Jake looked at Robby with utter horror on his face. He knew that he could not just take him to the school nurse; it would be slightly hard to explain. So he shouldered his new ally and launched himself out of the secret door.

Jake knew that there was one person that could help. He aimed himself, and his cargo, towards his family's home. As he flew slowly, he continually glanced down at his friend whom he was carrying. He wondered what was going on. For the first time in his short career, he felt totally helpless.

Jake landed on the balcony of his house and quickly brought Robby inside and laid him upon his bed. He pulled out his cell phone and informed Madison that he was going to have to ride the bus home. He then called his father and requested him to come home for an emergency.

"Robby, man, you have got to wake up!" pleaded Jake.

Madison arrived home after school. He ran upstairs to see if his brother was there. As he walked into Jake's room, his gaze fell upon his new crimson-haired friend who was lying motionless on his brother's bed. Jake turned to Madison with a look of fear on his face.

"Jake, what's wrong with Robby?" Madison inquired.

"Maddie, I think that he's alright. He told me that when he uses his abilities he gets drained, and could pass out" replied Jake.

"Abilities?" questioned Madison.

"Yeah, Robby's what you would call: a 'mutant'" answered Jake.

Just then they heard an audible moan coming from their fallen friend. Jake moved back towards the bed to see Robby open his green eyes and look up. Madison heaved a sigh of relief as his friend regained consciousness.

"Welcome back to the real world, Red!" Jake chuckled.

"Thanks, how long have I been out?" asked Robby.

"Well, about three hours, man" Jake responded.

"Oh man, my mom is going to kill me" Robby exclaimed.

"Relax bro, I called your mom and told her that you were here helping me with my homework" comforted Jake.

"Thanks, I owe you one" uttered Robby.

Jake spent the next few minutes recounting to Madison what happened this afternoon with Robby. He explained how Robby had been skulking around trying to help people without being seen. He emphasized the part when Robby used his teleportation powers.

Robby then described his various powers to Jake and Madison, including the hazard posed by overuse of his powers. He noted the looks of alarm on Jake's and Madison's faces.

"Yeah, I'm real freak, huh?" Robby sighed.

"You're not a freak, Red! Just because you're different, that doesn't make you a freak. Shoot, bro, if you're a freak, I guess that makes two of us. The only one here with any claim to 'normal' is Maddie. And sometimes I wonder about him!" Jake winked at his little brother who retaliated with a playful punch to the shoulder. Jake yelped in mock indignation.

"Hey lil' bro! Watch that! That's a mean right-hook you got there, dude. That hurt!" Jake cried out.

Madison giggled. "Yeah! Right!"

Jake winked again, this time at Robby. "Yah gotta watch out for Maddie, here. He's a lot tougher than he looks. He sure keeps me in line!"

Robby winked back.

Between Jake and Madison with their good natured back and forth heckling, they'd succeeded in lifting Robby's spirits.

Madison brightened as he addressed Robby.

"Man, are you a hero, a Mysterious hero, who pops in and out of mist? Hmm... Let's call you 'Myst!' A misty, mysterious super-hero known only as: 'Myst!'" exclaimed Madison.

"WOW! 'Myst', I kinda like that, but how could I be a super-hero, bro?" asked Robby.

"Just by doing what you do" replied Jake.

As Robby pondered the thought of living his dream, he could not help but remember how his father regarded mutants and meta-humans. He was sure that if his father found out, it would rip the family apart. That possibility was unacceptable.

"Guys, I would love to help, but I can't," said Robby as he looked dejectedly at the floor.

"WHAT?" Jake demanded.

"Robby, you're what my brother needs!" insisted Madison.

"HUH? I don't understand what you mean by, 'what he needs'?" inquired Robby.

"Well, when I was five years old, Mom and Dad adopted me. It was on Jake's birthday. I guess it was like I was sort of a surprise for him. Well, he said the one thing that would make his life a whole lot easier, and that's the power to teleport. I told him, maybe one day he would meet someone that could help with that or maybe build him a teleportation machine" explained Madison.

"Oh yeah, I almost forgot about that, no wonder I think his powers are so cool" laughed Jake.

Robby proceeded to justify to Jake and Madison that he could not operate out in the open as Jake had been doing as Titan. He described his father's blind hatred of anyone with special abilities like themselves. If his father found out, it would destroy his family and Robby assured his friends that he would take his own life before allowing that to happen.

Jake protested, "Robby! You can't do that. My God, your dad might need some time to get used to the idea but he'd come around eventually. I know he would. Maybe he's wrong about us, but if he ever found out, ya gotta know that once he thinks about it, he'll figure it out that he's been wrong. He'd never turn his back on his own son!"

Robby answered Jake's objection with an ice cold glare that chilled the young hero to the depths of his soul.

"You don't know my father. You don't understand how much he hates freaks like me. I don't know everything, but I know enough about his work to know that his job involves tracking and monitoring mutants and aliens. He thinks we're a threat and he's scared to death of what he thinks we can do and will do. And, Jake, you know as well as I do that some really bad things have happened because of the things some renegade mutants have done. So, it's not like my dad doesn't have his reasons. Until this stuff came out in me, Jake, I thought he was right! And even after that, I still believed him until I thought it through and finally figured out that mutants are not different from anybody else. There are good ones and bad ones. Only, because of what they can do, the bad ones are so dangerous, it's almost like any mutant is guilty until proven innocent. And, as far as my dad is concerned, any mutant or alien or meta-human's first and worst crime is that we exist. So, if my dad ever found out, I'd make it so I don't exist anymore."

Jake had no doubt that Robby meant every word he'd said. In his own mind he resolved, "Not if I have anything to say about it." Jake would do his utmost to prevent his friend from harming himself if it ever came to that. He did not share this with Robby or Madison. To Robby he said, "Promise me that you won't ever do anything like that before you talk to me."

At first it looked as though Robby would refuse but after just a moment's hesitation, he answered, "OK." Jake thought to himself, "Does he really mean it? Or is he just saying that to throw me off and give me a false sense of security?" I'll keep working on him to change his mind. Several years before Jake had been born; his dad had lost a close friend and colleague to suicide. Charles had shared the sorrow of this loss with his son on a couple of occasions. "Suicide is a permanent 'solution' to a very temporary problem. There is always another way; a better way." Jake knew that now was not the time to try to change Robby's mind about this. But he resolved that he wouldn't let up and that he would bring him around. Meanwhile, he would watch over his friend like a guardian angel.

Robby sensed Jake's concern but misjudged the reason for it, assuming he was concerned whether Robby, if he were discovered, might reveal his secret too. He looked Jake square in the eye. "No matter what happens to me. I will never, ever betray you."

Jake answered. "Robby, I have complete faith in you. I know you'd never ever betray me. I just hope you know I'll never ever betray you, either."

Then the two boys banged their fists together.

Just then there came a knock at the door. Dr. Charles Knight came into the room. He glanced at the red-headed boy in his son's room and at his son in his Titan persona standing over him. He then looked at Jake with a look of bewilderment.

"Son, what is going on here?" asked Charles.

"Dad, Robby needs our help. He is a mutant and he needs us" Jake stammered.

"You're a mutant, right son?" asked Charles.

"Yes sir, I'm afraid I am" answered Robby with embarrassment in his voice.

"Now Robby, there is nothing to be afraid of or embarrassed about" said Dr. Knight.

"If my dad or mom finds out, he will disown me. Not to mention he works for some people that hate people like me!" started Robby with tears in his eyes.

"Robby McCloud, for one thing, if I told your parents about you, I would be jeopardizing any chance for Jake to have a normal life. Secondly, I am here to help you." comforted Charles. "Look, I have known your father for a long time, son, and the one thing I do know, is that Bob McCloud is a good man. If he is working for an agency that polices meta-humans due to some misguided principles, then it is our job to gently show him the way" continued Dr. Knight.

Jake again retold the events of the day, this time to his dad. He embellished the parts of the story that had to do with what Robby had done. He told his father of him weakening and passing out shortly after the last teleportation.

"Let's get him down stairs, I think I can kill two birds with one stone, you guys!" exclaimed Charles with a grin.

Chapter 30

The four of them went into the basement Sanctum that Dr. Knight constructed. Robby looked around with total amazement at instruments and gadgets that he never thought were possible. Alien technology adorned every nook and cranny of the Sanctum. Robby was in complete awe of his surroundings. He could, however, not help but think what Dr. Knight had meant by the statement "Kill two birds with one stone".

"Welcome to the Secret Sanctum of Titan, Robby" said Dr. Knight.

"This place is amazing" uttered Robby under his breath.

"Yeah, it is pretty cool, huh?" stated Madison.

Dr. Knight walked over to a console and turned it on. He then walked over to a large touch screen panel and began moving dots around a figure that looked like a boy. He would occasionally glance over at Robby as if trying to size him up.

"OK son, here is what we can do. First off, we are going to take a scan of your mutant abilities. What this is going to accomplish is, that we will learn why your abilities drain you so much when you use your teleportation, or healing power, or when you project thoughts for an extended period of time." started Dr. Knight.

"Wow, it can do that?" asked Robby.

"Well, it's going to do that and a lot more, my friend" said Dr. Knight.

"I thought you were an archaeologist, sir." said Robby.

Jake explained a little more about his birth as Titan as it were. He told Robby how he had gotten his miraculous powers. Jake then told Robby that his father was given the knowledge and wisdom of the being that gave him his powers. He had the stored scientific knowledge of an advanced alien race.

"Alien race?" Robby whispered.

"Yup, Zyrtonian to be exact" said Dr. Knight as he glanced at the huge touch monitor behind him.

"OK Robby, what we're going to do here is get a better understanding of your powers, and if you're still wanting to help my son with his day-to-day duties to the world, then we're also going to make you a highly specialized and advanced costume" uttered Dr. Knight calculatingly.

"You do still want to help Titan, don't you, Robby?" asked Madison.

"Help Titan? Are you kidding? That has been my dream since he saved my life almost four years ago!" exclaimed Robby.

"Saved your life?" asked Jake with a look of surprise on his face.

"Yeah, you were flying over Boston, and I wasn't paying much attention to what was going on. There was this crazy guy in a car that almost plowed me over. You swooped down and snatched me from out in front of his path. We hung out in the comic store afterwards, remember?" explained Robby.

"That was you? Man, I have rescued so many people since then, they all seem to run together." Jake replied.

"See, you guys were meant to work together, he is the answer to your wish, bro" said Madison with a huge grin.

"Yeah, I guess you're right, Maddie. He was meant to be the partner that I've been praying about" declared Jake.

"Yeah, now you know why I have all that stuff about Titan on my wall. You're my hero!" said Robby as he looked down and began kicking his feet like a little kid.

"So, the pertinent question for you, my friend, is; are you willing to help Titan, my son, with his duties?" Dr. Knight asked him.

"Yes, sir!" came an enthusiastic reply from Robby.

Dr. Knight walked over and took Robby by the hand. He escorted him to in front of a large white screen. Dr. Knight instructed the boy to remove all clothing with the exception of his boxer shorts. He then walked back behind the control panel with Jake and Madison in tow. He flipped a lever forward and the machine came to life.

"OK Robby, you won't feel a thing. I want you to remain as still as you can. The red beam is going to access your powers and store your unique biological signature in the Sanctum's database" began Dr. Knight.

"OK" interjected Robby.

"The second," Charles continued, "will be a blue beam, and it will take your measurements and body mass index and store it in the database as well. Once this is done, the computer will take into consideration your powers and body form as well as predicted needs that you may have. It will then turn out a costume that you will be able to conceal your true identity with." Charles explained as he activated the machine.

As predicted, a thin red beam shot out of the machine's emitting device. It was aimed at the center of his forehead. Robby was relieved at the fact that he felt nothing, just as he was promised. Abruptly the red beam shut off and was replaced with a bright blue beam. This beam did not just stay in one place; however, it fanned out in a grid pattern all over his young frame. Just as suddenly as the process began, the machine fell silent and the lights in the Sanctum came back on.

Robby was instructed to get dressed and wait a few minutes while the computer analyzed the data. Robby pulled on his Sypher shirt, and jeans. He sat down as Dr. Knight began pouring over all the data.

"Hmm, this is rather fascinating" whispered Dr. Knight.

"Excuse me sir, but what is fascinating?" asked Robby politely.

"Well, your powers are incredible. The computer shows that your body has the potential to generate limitless psionic energy. But it also shows that with the use of your powers you're using your body's own energy stores. If we cannot remedy that soon, you will become totally catatonic, or in lay man's terms, you will fall into a coma near death." Dr. Knight explained.

"What are you saying? My powers will kill me?" Robby asked with a horrified tone.

"Not completely. The data is still compiling. You just have to...wait a minute... this also shows that when you come into physical contact with Jake, your energy levels are restored for a brief moment, to allow your own energy reserves to rebuild. Amazing!" stated Charles.

"Wow! I'm like your battery, bro!" Jake exclaimed.

Dr. Knight kept going over the data to try and find a more permanent solution to this problem. He looked at the screen and the data completed its compilation. His jaw hit the floor when he saw the true readings on this kid's psionic energy levels.

From what the computer displayed, Robby was in fact, the most powerful mutant being to ever be recorded on this planet or on Zyrton. His mental powers were so potent that he could bring the world to its knees if he so thought it necessary. Charles was in awe of this tiny vessel of mutant might. He knew that he needed to aide and guide him in the best way he could to ensure that this being was on the side of Justice.

The machine then made a series of beeping sounds that indicated that the decision was made on Robby's costume. Charles looked at the screen with an inquisitive look. He studied the components of the suit and its physical properties.

"Well this suit is a one-of-a-kind on this planet. It has many great features" stated Dr. Knight.

"What do you mean?" asked Robby.

"Well, from what this says, you will not need another stitch of clothing, other than underwear, ever again" Dr. Knight said.

"How is that possible, sir?" inquired Robby.

Dr. Knight recounted the read-out on the screen. He informed Robby that his costume was made of a techno-organic phase shift type material that responds to the psionic thoughts of its wearer. He told him that it needed to be out in the sunlight to recharge its batteries, too.

"Phase shift? Psionic thoughts?" pressed Robby.

"Yes Sir, this material is a techno symbiotic organism that feeds off your psionic energy and sunlight. All you have to do is concentrate on what you want to wear and it will shift from its natural state, which is your superhero persona, to whatever you are thinking about" explained Charles.

"What, it can transform?" asked Robby.

"To put it crudely, yes" answered Dr. Knight.

"Put it on, Robby" urged Jake with excitement.

Robby walked over to the machine's table. Sitting there was a blue ball, but no clothing. He looked at Dr. Knight with a puzzled look. Dr. Knight instructed him to pick the ball up.

As soon as he touched the ball, it reacted and spread up his arm. Robby began to panic. Charles commanded him to relax, that it was not going to hurt him, that it in fact was a living part of him now. Robby did as he was told and took a deep breath. The blue entity spread all over his body forming the costumed persona of Myst.

Robby puffed out his chest and walked to the mirror. He saw himself for the first time as the costumed hero Myst. He was clad in dark blue, from head to toe. The suit had a bright blue stripe that ran from his mask to his finger tips, down the sides of his rib cage and the sides of his legs. The bright blue also created the division for his boots and gloves. He shook his head and as his red hair was exposed, as a signature of Myst. Upon his chest was a diamond shape that was similar to Titan's. Inside the diamond was the star of life, the symbol that adorns ambulances. Charles thought it a fitting choice for a hero that has the ability to heal people.

"WOW! Look at you, bro!" Jake said as he came up behind his friend.

"This is amazing, look at me, I look like a real hero!" exclaimed Robby.

"Look Like? You not only look like a hero, you are a hero, Red," exclaimed Jake.

Dr. Knight came back towards the duo and took a photograph marking the new union of Titan and Myst. Robby was so happy to be living his dream, and it was with his best friend. How could this get any better?

"Robby, the suit has many properties that will help you out. One thing is that it will store energy every time that you expose it to sunlight. With that energy, according to this read-out, it can act much in the same manner as you touching Jake when you get drained" explained Charles.

"Really?" questioned Robby.

"Yes, but it's not as potent as a prolonged rest for you, or Jake physically grabbing on to you. So, you still have to be careful with how long you use your healing ability" warned Charles.

"I will, Dr. Knight, this is awesome" uttered Robby.

"Now, onto the phase shift properties, son. The suit can mimic the appearance of any article of clothing you can think of" informed Dr. Knight.

Robby thought about that for a moment. The computer had to have taken into account that he was not as fast as Jake, therefore it needed to have been built on that principle. He thought of an article of clothing that he wanted to wear. His eyes shifted to black from their warm familiar green. Suddenly he felt the costume changing.

As his eyes shifted back to normal color, he was standing in an exact duplicate of Titan's costume. Jake began laughing, as did Charles and Madison. Robby joined in with the laughter. All four guys were just relieved that Robby could now be safe to use his powers to help people like Titan does, and still remain anonymous.

"OK, so now all I have to do is think about what I want to wear and it will become that?" asked Robby.

"Yes, that about sums it up" replied Dr. Knight.

Robby concentrated on the clothing he arrived there in. Suddenly he was standing in the Sanctum in his Sypher shirt, jeans and sneakers. Robby was totally enthralled with this costume. Never in his wildest dreams could he have imagined being in this type of costume, let alone, being Titan's answered prayer.

"So from this day forward, bro, you will be known as Myst!" cheered Jake.

"WOW! This is so cool, Robby!" exclaimed Madison.

"Not only will you be known as Titan's partner, I will let everyone know you're my best friend too!" announced Jake.

Robby looked at Dr. Knight and the other boys with a tear in his eye. In a matter of a few hours all of his childhood dreams had been realized. He had helped Titan, his all-time hero. He had just become a hero in his own right. Now he was Titan's partner and friend. He could not believe the luck he was having.

That night Robby lay in his bed with his mind reeling at the events of the day. He had his familiar thinking aide on and was tossing his baseball into the air and catching it. He wondered to himself if he would be a good partner to Titan. He was worried that he would not live up to the high expectations that he thought Jake would have of him.

Chapter 31

The next day came too soon for Robby's liking. He had been tossing and turning all night with plaguing dreams of letting Jake and his father down. He had a dream that in his agitated state, his costume crawled across the floor to wrap him up and try to comfort him.

He got up and stretched. As he did, the costume stirred on the chair as well. He glanced over at the chair and had almost a longing to have the suit on him. Within seconds the suit had made its way over to him. It started at his feet and spread up his body. Moments later Robby McCloud was standing in his room as Myst.

"Is this thing really alive?" he wondered. "I am going to have to get used to this. It is like it knows me and it wants to protect me" Robby whispered to himself.

Robby concentrated and as his eyes shifted, so did his costume. Before he knew it, he was standing there in a pair of jeans, Red Sox baseball t-shirt, sneakers, and his jacket. Robby just grinned at this miraculous piece of clothing.

"Very little laundry for mom to do now and more time for me to play" Robby chuckled.

Jake knocked on the door and awaited someone to answer him. Madison was playing with his trick soccer ball in the front yard as they waited for their red-headed compadre.

"Morning, partner" said Robby as he opened the door to greet them.

Jake just smiled and put his arm around Robby's shoulder. Robby bid good bye to his mother and raced off with his friends. As they

216

walked towards school, Madison was in his own little world with his soccer ball. This gave Robby and Jake time to talk.

"So, how are you feeling this morning, Myst?" asked Jake.

"Man, I am worried, dude!" stated Robby.

"Man, what are you so worried about?" inquired the muscular youth.

Robby told Jake about the dreams he was having. He let him in on the fears he had of letting him down and not living up to the expectations that he probably has had for him. Robby recounted how his dreams had haunted him all night with images of not being able to help, or of failing while helping someone.

"Expectations? Robby, I do not have any expectations of you, or your abilities" stated Jake.

"Well, I just don't wanna let you down" whimpered Robby as he looked down.

"You aren't going to let me down, my brother. We're partners now" reinforced Jake. "We are here to pull each other's slack when the going gets tough."

Robby felt some comfort in the words that his friend had said to him. He concentrated upon the confidence that Jake had in his abilities. He knew without fail, that Titan was a great judge of character. So why should this time be any different? It was no different than the confidence that Derrick, Brandon, Travis, or Peter had in him on the baseball field.

School was a challenge for Robby McCloud today. He sat in his seat with thoughts dancing all throughout his head. The thought, that his new best friend was in fact Titan. The thought, that he would not be able to tell his lifelong best friend, Derrick, anything about this. He also had a warm feeling caused in part by his new "security blanket", as it were.

He felt a mixture of feelings swelling up within his soul. On one hand, he had gotten to realize all of his dreams. On the other hand, he just had to shoulder a tremendous burden in regards to Jake's secret, and of his own. He sat utterly confused and perplexed at the change in events of his life.

Robby glanced over and caught Jake staring at him. Jake returned a kind knowing smile at him. At that moment, Robby felt as if all the burdens and all the possible troubles were worth it. There sat his new best friend, his neighbor, and his hero all in one compact muscular package. He felt a calming wave rush over him as he smiled at his best friend.

The final bell for the day rang. The boys all met up, as they have done for the past five days, at the wrought iron gate that marked the entrance of the school. As they met up, Jake spoke up as if he were invading Robby's thoughts.

"Robby, I've been thinking about this all day. I know that it's a huge responsibility knowing what you know now" Jake said.

"What, you reading my mind now?" giggled Robby.

"No, not at all. It was the same feelings that Maddie had when he learned of my secrets, too" he explained.

"Yeah, it's a big deal keeping a secret like this, man" added Madison.

"Well, I feel better about it, now that I've had time to think" remarked Robby.

As the trio was walking home, Jake's cell phone rang. The police commissioner advised him that there was a hostage situation that was taking place at the DC National Bank. Jake hung the cell phone up and advised his partner of what was going on.

Robby grabbed Maddie's shoulder. His Myst costume appeared as if out of thin air. A cloud of mist enveloped him and Madison and they were gone. In a split second the mist had returned and there stood Myst, facing his partner Titan.

"Time to get to work, partner!" exclaimed Titan.

"Where are we off to?" inquired Myst.

"To the DC National Bank building and I'm going to need your help with any wounded hostages" explained Titan. "And thanks for taking Maddie home. That saved us a bunch of time!"

"That's what I'm here for, so hang on!" Myst said, as he grabbed hold of Titan's shoulder. "We're outta here!" yelled Myst.

He focused his concentration to pinpoint the bank's roof. Robby's eyes shifted to black in a flash. The familiar mist surrounded the two and they were "jumping" in an instant straight to the bank.

"Man that was faster than I could've done it" whispered Titan as they reemerged on the rooftop.

"I need to scan the building to see what we are dealing with" stated Titan.

"Don't bother. You have three guys behind the counter, all with large caliber weapons. One standing by the vault, trying to crack it open. The others are standing guard at all the exits. They seem to have it pinned down, bro" analyzed Myst.

"WOW! You got all that? How?" asked Titan.

"Security guard's mind" replied Myst.

"Man, that is gonna come in handy. And you were worried!" chuckled Titan.

"OK bro, so they have all the exits covered. How am I gonna get in there without any hostages being hurt?" asked a perplexed Titan.

"Easy, I'll jump us both inside the vault. Leave you there to surprise them when the one dude cracks that safe open, and I will jump out to the staging area to await any injuries" offered Myst.

"Now that sounds like a plan" said Titan.

Myst focused his thoughts on the location inside of the vault. He reached over and grabbed Titan's shoulder. He gave it a friendly squeeze as he called the mist to arise. Within seconds the two young heroes were standing within the vault, their only company being the money the assailants were so greedily after, and the sound of the safe cracker's drill.

"OK Titan, I'm outta here! Yell if you need me!" instructed Myst as he teleported from the vault to safety.

Titan stood poised, ready to spring into action as soon as the door swung open. He trusted his partner's location talents, but chose to use his infrared to glance through the door and make out the exact location of the robbers. He located them all, and charged up his plasmoidal energy for six super speed blasts to take them down as quickly as he could.

Meanwhile in the triage area, Myst appeared out of thin air and smoke. The S.W.A.T. commander jumped with surprise at a costumed kid who appeared out of nowhere. He approached Myst with extreme caution, with his gun drawn.

"Son, who or what are you?" asked the commander.

"I am Myst. I'm Titan's new partner. I'm here to help any wounded that we may have in there after my partner cleans up those creeps" answered Myst respectfully with his hands in the air in a sign of compliance.

"Wow, another super-kid" thought the commander as he nodded his approval for Myst's presence on the scene.

"You can put your hands down, son, if you are a friend of Titan's, then you're a friend of ours" declared the S.W.A.T captain.

Inside the bank, the safe cracker was about to get the surprise of his life. As he finally popped the lock off and the door swung open a red blast struck him in the chest. Titan emerged and took aim at super speed on the remaining five assailants. His hands moved in a blur and caught all the thieves off guard with the same kind of blasts, rendering their weapons into melted piles of scrap.

Titan, with another burst of super speed, gathered up all the criminals. He was met with a raucous applause from the hostage victims. He blushed at the accolades that he was receiving. Titan then brought the six perpetrators out to the S.W.A.T. captain.

"Here ya go, captain; that should wrap it up, with the exception of the few injuries on the inside" Titan said.

"On my way, partner!" exclaimed Myst as he vanished.

"Wow, that kid is fast, Titan!" said the captain.

"Not really, since he can teleport; oh and there's no need for ambulances, Captain. Myst has that one under control, he's a healer." Titan explained.

Myst reemerged from the bank on foot; his healing ability had drained him further than his suit could aide him with. He stumbled his way out the door. As soon as Titan had seen this, he ran towards his partner. He grabbed him and placed his hands on his mask, with his thumbs touching his cheek. The pull was instant. Robby's energy levels quickly stabilized.

"Hey, Hey Titan, you saved the day once again, but this mysterious boy that helped you, who is he?" asked a newspaper reporter.

"This, ladies and gentlemen, is my new partner and friend, Myst!" said Titan with a grin.

"Myst, Myst, can we get a picture of you and Titan please?" asked the news photographer.

"Sure, why not?" said Myst with an air of shock in his voice.

As the reluctant hero smiled for the camera, Robby McCloud was lost in thought. For the second time in under a week, he had been at Titan's side helping the innocent, and the weak. He felt a swell of pride rise up within his soul. Myst could not help the huge grin on his face as the camera's flash nearly blinded him.

Titan waved to the crowd and flashed his megawatt smile to everyone. He looked back at his partner with pride too. He now had a best friend that understood him totally, not just Titan, but also Jake as well. He walked over and put his arm around his friend's shoulder.

"Red, are you ready to get outta here?" asked Titan.

"Sure, are you flyin', or am I jumpin'?" asked Myst.

"You look a little worn out, partner, so leave the flyin to me" stated Titan.

Titan took to the sky with his partner in hand; he looked down and noticed that Myst's mask had totally closed over his mouth. He wondered if it was to help him breath at supersonic speed. He did not leave anything to chance.

"Hey what's the deal with the mask?" he asked.

"Well it just told me that it had to protect my breathing at high altitudes" explained Myst.

"It told you?" Titan questioned.

"I know it kinda freaked me out too, until I remembered that your dad mentioned that it was a living extension of me. It has a conscious thought process. It also told me that it adopts the personality of the first person it bonds with. Lucky it was me" continued Myst.

"Well I am gonna hit the super speed to get us home, let me know if it is too much on ya" said Titan.

Robby nodded his head in agreement. Titan poured on the speed. Within a split second the duo were approaching the speed of sound. Before they could reach the breech the sound barrier, Titan was descending onto his balcony, after a quick scan of his surroundings.

After landing, the two of them walked into Jake's bedroom, where they were greeted by Madison. He was happy to see his older brother and new friend arrive safely back home. He ran up and jumped into Jake's arms, trying to tackle him. Unfortunately, no one can move Titan unless he wants to be moved.

"Welcome back, you should have seen it!" screamed Madison.

"Seen what, Maddie?" asked Jake.

"Dude you two were awesome, I mean it was like watching a well rehearsed dance or something" said Madison

"Really, how did you see it?" asked Robby.

"I watched it on TV of course! It was totally awesome!" squealed Madison.

Robby let a concerned look drop onto his face. He wondered if his parents saw that. He wondered if they would put the red hair and frame on his head and figure out his identity. The look of fear gripped the young boy's body.

"Robby, what's the matter?" asked Jake.

"I need to see if my parents are going to recognize me" stuttered Robby.

"Hey I recorded it on TIVO if you want to see it" said Madison in a calming tone.

"OK let's see it" muttered Robby.

Madison led Robby and Jake to the den, where he turned on the television. He grabbed the remote and selected the recordings. As he pushed play, Robby took a deep breath. The newest super-hero addition to the team was worried at what was going to happen.

"WNDC has made a startling discovery! In a recent bank heist that occurred today at DC National Bank, another costumed hero arrived on the scene. A mysterious young fellow seen here calls himself 'Myst'" announced the news anchor.

Robby sat and studied the images on the television. He noticed that you really could not get a good look at his face. This fact totally relieved the new hero. He could not bear the possibility of going home and his father waiting to question him.

Even in the interview, the mask obscured his facial appearance, as to not be recognized. A slight smile crept over his face. He had been so worried about his father finding out his true identity, that he forgotten what it felt like to help others.

"See man, there was nothing to fear. Dad said that costume would do the trick, and it did" reassured Jake.

"Yeah, I guess you're right, Jake" laughed Robby.

Robby focused his concentration on the clothing he was wearing before the bank heist. His eyes shifted to black and his costumed changed appearance back to his school clothes. As his eyes returned to bright green, Robby breathed a deep sigh of relief.

"Man, seeing that costume in action is never going to get old bro" said Jake.

"Yeah, saves me a whole lot of time" replied Robby.

"I have one question for you, Jake" prodded Robby.

"Shoot!" came the one word response from Jake.

"How do you handle it? I mean how do you handle the fame and reporters and people? How do you handle keeping two identities?" inquired Robby.

"Well to answer the first part of that, you just have to be polite. People are going to want to know that they can trust you, and you have to be nice to them. And you can't brag about what you just did, to sum it up, just be humble" explained Jake. "Now, on to the second part. Robby, I am both Jake and Titan, the personalities of the one are just like the other, and I just don't fly when I'm Jake. I'm still me, no matter what" continued Jake.

"But you can be yourself at home. Do you know how hard it is not to use your natural instincts? Do you know how hard it is to act surprised at Christmas, when you know what you have gotten?" Robby asked.

Jake placed his hand on Robby's shoulder. He understood his dilemma, better than anyone. He thought about the first time he went to school, knowing he was stronger and faster than anyone there. He remembered not being able to play a sport for fear of hurting someone accidentally.

"Robby, my brother, I do know how you feel. Maybe not about the whole surprise thing, but I know how it feels to have to not use what comes naturally to you man. If I were to do that people at school would have gotten hurt" explained Jake.

"But your parents accept you Jake, they help you too" rebutted Robby.

"Look I know that it is hard, that is why dad's machine detected your fear and you got a mask" said Jake with a smile.

Robby knew that Jake was looking after his best interest. He knew that he was right; he was given the power and the mask for a reason. That reason was not just to sit back and let bad things happen to good people. It was to help at all cost, and still maintain a powerful family dynamic as well.

"Dude, you are just gonna have to learn that you are Myst and Robby now. You're both at the same time. One is not separate from the other. You have always been Myst. Just as you have always been Robby" He looked at Robby with a different distinction in his face.

"To put it bluntly, bro, one cannot exist without the other. You're a hero, a guardian angel, a baseball player, a son, a best friend, and my best friend, to be exact. Do you follow me?" asked Jake.

Robby pondered what Jake just said to him. "Well you know that does make a little more sense to me now. I wondered how you did it. Now I know, you just totally embrace who you are and watch out for your friends and help people. And you do it just like you would if you were normal" stated Robby.

"Precisely, bro! All I do is what any police officer, or fireman would do. And all we want you to do is the same." added Jake.

Robby was almost elated when the realization, that he could in fact do this, dawned on him. "I will Jake, I see what you mean. It felt good to do what we did today. I know that this was supposed to happen." affirmed Robby.

"Good, I'm glad that you see it that way, because I was beginning to get worried about ya" Jake chuckled.

Robby clashed knuckles with Jake again and bid Madison goodbye as well. He walked across the empty lot to his house. He unlocked the back door to the garage and made his way inside. Sheepishly he made his way into the house.

"Mom! Dad! I am home from Jake's" he announced.

Susan rounded the corner of the kitchen. She came up and ruffled his shaggy red hair as she usually did out of affection.

"Hey sport, are you hungry?" she inquired as she led him into the kitchen.

"I sure am, mom" he replied as he followed her into the kitchen. He sat down, bowed his head and blessed his food. He then began to scarf down his dinner as if he had not eaten in weeks.

"Whoa, tiger, slow down, it's not baseball season yet. You're eating like you just played a double-header, son" stated Susan as she smiled at her son.

"Sorry, mom, I am just really hungry" said Robby. Little did his mother know at the time, it was due to his mutant ability which was draining him that he ate as much as he did in order to restore his natural energies.

He continued consuming his dinner until he heard the key hit the front door lock.

"Dad must be home, Robby" said Susan. Just then, Bob walked in and hugged his wife closely. He walked over and tussled his son's hair, a favorite past time for both Bob and Susan.

"Evening, guys. How you guys making it, tonight?" asked Bob as he sat down to the table. This evening he appeared a little more exhausted than he had appeared in the past.

Robby looked for a split second at his father. "Dad, are you OK?" he inquired as he tilted his head to the side.

"Yeah I'm fine, my boss is just breathing down my neck to get some reports to him by this weekend" said Bob. Robby knew that this explanation was not the truth. He upheld his promise to himself. He would not probe into his father's mind unless it was an emergency. He did not need his power to know that Bob was keeping things from his family. He had to, that was the role of a C.I.A operative.

As Robby prepared to go to bed, he went to the rest room to take a shower. While he let the hot water wash over him, he thought back to what Jake had talked to him about earlier that afternoon. He smiled at the confidence that his hero, Titan, had in him. It was almost a surreal feeling to know that he was at long last working with his hero, as he had always dreamed about. He felt almost as if fate had stepped in and dealt him a winning hand.

Chapter 32

The next morning in the Knight household, it was breakfast as usual. Dr. Knight made his way upstairs from the Sanctum. He was carrying a newspaper in one hand and a cup of coffee in the other. He sat down in his chair and tossed the newspaper opened on the table.

"Well, I see you and Myst made the paper, son" stated Dr. Knight as he pointed out the front page image containing Myst and Titan with the SWAT team.

"WOW! We did! That's a great picture!" Jake chuckled.

"So much for keeping it low key with Myst for a little while, son" Dr. Knight chided with a firm glance towards his son.

Jake was at a loss. He mustered his thoughts and replied.

"Dad, you made the costume so that Robby could work with me. That's what he chose to do. He could've stayed in the shadows, but he knew that he had to risk it" explained Jake.

Dr. Knight continued to read the article. "Well it says here that you two foiled a group of international thieves that have been hitting major banks all across the world, and not one person went to the hospital" uttered Dr. Knight.

"We are so proud of you two, son" said Nancy as she put her hands gently upon Jake's extremely muscular shoulders.

"We really are, son, I am not chastising you for doing what you did. It's just the fact that Robby is worried that Bob, of all people, will find out about him, and the Lord knows what that department that he works for, would do to Robby if they found out." reaffirmed Dr. Knight.

For the first time in his young life, Jake had a dark look on his face.

"No one is going to touch him dad, not as long as there is a breath in my body!" Jake said with a cold tone in his voice.

Charles shivered at the comment. He knew that Jake could and would make good on that promise. His son was, after all, the most powerful being on the planet, with power second only to his partners own. He knew that Jake was really over-protective of Madison, and now that over protective nature was bleeding over to Robby as well.

"Son, you and Robby are close, huh?" asked Charles.

"Yeah, dad, he is the only one, no offense guys, that really understands what it's like to have powers and be this age, too." explained Jake.

"No offense taken, son; I was just wondering what the connection was." responded Charles.

Madison chimed in with his two cents worth. "Dad, Robby and Jake are a lot alike. They both have to be careful with their powers, they both have to hide who they really are from the world, the only difference really in the two, other than their powers, is the fact that you and mom don't hate him for who he is" said Madison.

"I just really have a hard time believing that Bob would hate Robby, even if he found out"

Charles retorted. "Bob doesn't hate Robby. He has no reason to right now, he doesn't know about Robby's abilities. And I want to keep it that way, guys"

"Yes Sir" replied both Jake and Madison in unison.

Later that morning, the boys met up to walk to school. Jake and Madison came up to Robby holding the newspaper article that their father had shown them. Robby glanced at it with a grin.

"Dude, I thought that you would be freaking out!" exclaimed Jake.

"I had a lot of time to think about what you said and what your dad said about it all, bro" responded Robby.

Robby then recounted his thoughts to his friends. He let them into what was running around in his head all night. He told them that he was put on the earth to be a hero, and that is what he was going to be. Ever since Titan snatched him from the impending jaws of death, he knew that his life was never going to be the same.

Whether his father found out about him or not, was not the issue. It was the issue of his ability to act and his willingness to do so. He told his friends that he was not just content skulking in the shadows.

"Are you sure?" asked Jake.

"Look, if dad sees me, then he is going to have to deal with me then and there. I am sure that his love for me will win out over his other feelings. At least I am hoping so" affirmed Robby with a sound resolve.

"Man, I am proud of you, dude! It takes a lot of guts to do what you're doing" remarked Jake.

Jake then handed him the cut-out photograph. "Here put this on your 'wall of heroes'. Let this be the first of many more to come" offered Jake.

"Thanks... Be right back" said Robby as he vanished in a cloud of mist. As the mist rose again, and Robby stepped back out of it, Jake and Madison smiled. "I went ahead and posted it on the wall" Robby chuckled.

"We knew it!" laughed Madison. "I told him that is what you were doing" he continued.

"Am I that predictable?" asked Robby.

"To us, maybe... but to the rest of the world... NEVER!" exclaimed Jake as he bumped knuckles together with Robby and Madison.

School that day, to young Robby McCloud, was a total blur. His thoughts were not with the teachers and the textbooks. Rather they were with his new "family". He could not keep his mind off the second heroic event that he had shared with Titan. Robby was totally enamored with the concept of working side by side with him.

As the last bell for the day rang, Robby and Jake sprang from their chairs and bolted towards the lockers. They got the stuff they needed to complete their homework and hastily made it to the exit. "This day could not have ended soon enough" thought Robby to himself.

Madison approached the duo with a spring in his step. He was always excited to see his big brother, but now he was really excited. He had befriended someone with amazing powers too. He thought that it was totally awesome that his brother was Titan and his good friend was Myst.

"Hey, guys" began Madison. "How are you two this afternoon?" he asked rather formally.

"Good" Robby answered.

"What are you up to bro?" asked Jake.

Madison blushed at the fact that his brother knew him well enough to see that something was working in that marvelous brain of his. "Up to? I am not up to anything" replied the ever moving ball of energy.

"I was just wondering...." Madison began as he was cut off.

"Wondering if I would teleport you home? You are so easy to read Maddie!" said Robby with a grin.

"What? Oh dude you read my mind, didn't you?" asked Madison.

"Well it was not that hard to pick up on what you wanted. And yeah, I will teleport ya home. Just let your brother get changed first and take off, and then we will jump outta here" stated Robby.

Madison was ecstatic that Robby was going to do this for him. Since that first day Jake took Madison flying, he had always wanted to feel a part of the group. Now that Robby had come along, Madison knew that he could hang out with the guys and feel like a part of the team.

"Sweet! This is going to rock!" screamed Madison.

"SSSHHHHH!!!! Keep your voice down bro!" exclaimed Jake as he cupped his mighty hand over his little brother's mouth.

"I'm sorry, guess I got a little too excited" replied Madison.

Jake ducked into the boys' room and changed into his Titan uniform. He sauntered out of the building stretched and flexed his taunt muscles to loosen himself up. He had felt cooped up all day in school and it was past time for him to stretch his proverbial wings.

Robby closed his eyes, ducked his head and concentrated. His jeans and t shirt were replaced with his Myst costume as he reopened his eyes. Madison's jaw dropped when he saw the transformation take place. He thought about the first time that Robby used his costume, about how cool that was.

"Well, young Madison, are you ready to come with me?" said Myst in a fake bravado tone.

"Yes, sir, Mr. Myst, I am ready!" answered Madison in an equally fake meek tone.

All three boys shared a laugh. Myst reached over and pulled Madison's back into his Chest. Titan looked at the duo with a grin. "Race Ya!" petitioned Titan.

"You're on, and hey big guy...We're Gone!" exclaimed Robby as he and Madison vanished in a fog cloud.

"Wow! Robby got the jump on me! Better get a move on!" Jake thought to himself as he leaped into the sky.

Titan streaked across the sky at sub sonic speeds. He gently touched down on his balcony, and opened the door; he looked around and saw that no one was there.

"HA! Beat them" he said aloud.

Titan changed clothes into a pair of shorts and a tank top. He plopped down on his bed reeling at the fact that he had beaten his best friend and his brother home. Suddenly he heard a bump coming from Madison's room.

Jake slowly made his way down the hallway to investigate. As he opened his little brother's door, he saw Robby and Madison sitting on the floor playing a board game. Both boys looked up at the muscular youth and grinned.

"What took you so long, slow-poke?" giggled Madison.

"You guys were here the entire time?" asked Jake.

"A split second after we jumped out, we were here" answered Robby.

"Wanna play?" asked Madison.

"Sure bro I have a few minutes before I go on patrol" responded Jake as he sat down and tussled Madison's long black hair.

"Patrol" thought Robby. That was something that he had not thought of. Using his abilities to seek out those that may be in need of his special talents. He had wanted to keep a low profile as much as possible; however, he figured that the best way to get practice with his powers and train them was in fact to use them on a more regular basis.

While the trio played the board game, Robby continued thinking of ways to do this. He thought that when he went home for dinner that he would look into how Mr. Amazing would do it and put his practice into play for himself. He knew, the better he became the better of a partner that he would be for Titan. That, in itself, was all the motivation that he would have needed.

Titan stood up and excused himself to his duties. Madison cleaned up the board game, and got on his homework. Robby gave Madison a friendly hug and teleported to his bedroom, after he scanned to make sure that it was all clear.

Chapter 33

After Robby reemerged in his room, he made his way to his comic book stash. He grabbed his Mr. Amazing books and started to thumb through them. He knew that if Titan could go on patrol flying, he should use his gifts somehow to seek out those that needed him as well.

"Hmm? It says here that the same way I see if the coast is clear, I can use my telepathy and empathy together to seek out those in pain or worse" thought Robby.

Dinner came and went with the family. Robby told his parents that he was tired and was going to go ahead and head off to bed. He had hoped that his parents would be rather busy this evening. Tonight was going to be the first night that Myst went on the prowl.

Robby scanned his parents as well as he could. His quick peek revealed that his mother and father were busy working on bills. He quieted his mind and soul so that he could feel something. He sensed that his parents would be tied up for hours, and in fact believed that he was already fast asleep.

He then focused his attention outward. He calmly relaxed his mind again. He focused both his telepathy and empathy into almost radar like quality. He plotted out a section of DC and scanned it.

When his mind's eye reached out, he was gripped with pain. What was it that he felt? He fell to his knees. Writhing in agony, he stood back up and singled in on the source. He pinpointed it to one person.

Robby called upon his Myst uniform to materialize. He closed his eyes and pictured the location where the pain was coming from.

A cloud of vapor encircled Robby McCloud and within a second he was gone.

When he reemerged at the location of pain, he probed the persons mind. All he felt was pain, both physical and emotional. Myst stood there in complete horror at the discovery that he had made.

"An elderly lady, oh man, she was beaten badly, and she is in terrible pain" Myst thought as he fought back tears.

Myst was used to seeing an injury physically and healing them. With this method, he made his emotional psyche very vulnerable. He was feeling emotionally exactly what the victims felt. It wreaked havoc on the young man's mind, body, and soul.

Myst knew that it was up to him to save her. He scanned and saw that there was another person in the house. He had to render that person totally unconscious as to affect the jump in to heal the battered old lady. He focused an intense psychic burst on the lady's granddaughter to render her momentarily comatose, but not hurt her in any way. When he projected the burst, he felt her slip into darkness.

Slowly the police car backed out of the driveway, and Robby wondered what had just occurred. "I usually don't like doing this" He thought to himself as his eyes turned black as night. He began peering into the old woman's conscious mind.

"She's been hurt," he thought, "by her own family. How could anyone hurt this sweet old lady?" he pondered as he hid in the shadows outside of the lady's house.

Robby, being the type of person that he was, could not stand to see people in pain, or suffering. It literally wounded this remarkable young man to the core of his soul. He stood there considering his options. He knew he could make a difference here, but how was the best to go about it?

He scanned the victim again. "Oh man, it was her own nephew... he...he beat her badly.....over twenty dollars...I have got to get in there" thought Myst.

He closed his eyes and focused on jumping inside while implanting a dream. As he reached the lady, he placed his hands on her head. "Sleep!" he commanded as she fell limp in his hands. "Now all you will remember is a guardian angel came to heal you" projected Myst with fierce concentration.

Myst took a deep breath and closed his eyes. When he reopened them, they were glowing yellow. He reached out his hands and placed them on his "patient" He saw in his mind's eye, three broken ribs and a fractured collar bone.

"This guy is a monster, this is someone's grandmother" Myst uttered through tears.

As he drew in another breath, he began the process of healing the lady. He focused and mustered all the strength he had in his body. He felt his energy fading the longer he maintained the illusion in his "patient's" mind and the longer he kept contact with her as well.

He held on as long as he could, as he completely healed all of her wounds. Myst staggered to his feet, and as he teleported out of the woman's house and back into the alleyway, where he collapsed, completely weakened to the ground. On the verge of unconsciousness, he wished that Titan was there to help him.

Suddenly Myst felt a pair of strong hands grab him around his waist and hoist him up. He opened his eyes and there was Titan. He saved him again, just as Myst passed out again.

"Robby......Robby......Wake up, man!" urged Titan.

"Wha-....What happened?" asked Robby as he looked his partner and hero in the face.

"I was going to ask you the same thing…" replied Titan. "What was the last thing you remember?"

"I was healing this lady that had been beaten by her nephew, Jake. It was horrible" answered Robby.

"Dude, what in the heck were you doing out here all by yourself?" inquired the massive teen.

"I was trying to help....I was trying to help her, Jake" stammered Robby.

"Did you?" asked Jake.

"I healed her, but I almost could not make it out on my own, I wished you were here" cried Robby.

"Dude, calm down, I heard you calling for me" assured Jake.

"Huh?"

"Yeah, it was like you were inside of my head for a split second and I pinned down your location and flew over here as fast as I could" stated Jake.

"I guess I was lucky" said Robby.

"Yeah you were. Please do me a favor. Don't go out alone without me unless it's an absolute emergency" urged Jake. "At least not until we can get a hold on how to control the whole draining thing."

"I learned my lesson here. Man, I wish I were half as strong as you are, dude, then I would never pass out!" said Robby as he choked back his tears.

"You are bro. You are stronger than you think…"

Titan picked his partner up, instantly recharging his friend with a simple touch. Robby's color pinked up, and his breathing regulated. Titan looked at his best friend with pride and concern as he aimed them toward Robby's house.

As he landed, he looked Robby dead square in the eyes. "Promise me you will never go out without me again, bro" requested Jake.

"I promise man, it was stupid of me to try and go it alone…" replied Robby.

"Not stupid, I think that it was brave, but it was careless" related Jake.

Jake changed clothes; luckily he had a spare set at Robby's just in case he needed them. He sat down on Robby's bed, as Robby's Myst persona melted away. He placed his hand on Robby's shoulder and reassured him that everything would be fine.

"But, Jake, I messed up, some hero I turned out to be, huh?" Robby said as he began to shed tears.

"Robert McCloud, you saved that woman a trip to the hospital, at the expense of your own well being. To me, that's a sign of a true hero!" retorted Jake.

"You…You think…You think that I'm a hero, even after that mess up?" asked Robby.

"Dude, your only mistake was that you didn't wait for me or tell me you were headed out" said Jake.

"I promise I won't let you down again, bro" exclaimed Robby.

"You didn't let me down, you just scared the devil out of me, though" responded Jake.

The two talked for a few more minutes. Jake then hugged his best friend and excused himself to go home. Robby walked him downstairs and let Jake out the back door. He waved to his friend as he watched him disappear into the night.

Robby went in and thought about the encouraging words Jake had said to him. He was happy to know that his hero still viewed him as a hero as well. He knew that he was going to do better and not let Jake down. He just had to keep his wits about him.

Chapter 34

The next day proved to be trying for Robby. He could not keep his mind off last night's events. All throughout the day, he found himself daydreaming about the old lady and her pain. He thought of how it had almost cost him his identity and his very life.

That afternoon the guys decided to walk home from school rather than flying or teleporting. As they passed through the urban terrain of DC, Robby began spilling his guts regarding the thoughts of the day to Jake and Madison. Jake frowned at his comments, and told him that he was proud of his partner for stepping up to the plate.

Robby smiled in an almost fake sort of way. "Stepping up to plate, huh?" he chuckled at Jake.

The boys continued walking towards their houses, as Jake's hearing tuned into the sound of an alarm going off. He informed Robby and Madison of his discovery. Jake quickly dashed behind a dumpster and changed into Titan.

"I will get Maddie outta here, where is the alarm coming from?" asked Robby.

"Another bank, I don't get it. This is getting repetitive, dude" Jake responded.

"OK. Hang on a sec" added Robby

Robby McCloud began concentrating, as his eyes shifted from bright and brilliant green, to ominous onyx black. His Myst costume came into view, as he reached over and took Madison in his arms and disappeared, only to reappear empty-handed.

"There! Ready to go?" asked Robby.

"Sure, partner" replied Jake.

Titan focused his eyesight on the wall of the Bank. He began picking up heat signatures to locate where everyone was. As he did, he looked to his partner for verification. Myst was already on the job. His eyes were black as night as he scanned the people for identification and injury status.

"Jake, we gotta get in there! There is a guard, he's been shot! He's wounded badly. Three gunmen are at the counter and four are at the front door." stated Myst.

"Thanks Partner. I am voting for the direct approach, ya know: wall bashing!" laughed Titan.

"Well, however we need to get in there, I've got to get to the guard, because he's fading fast!" exclaimed Myst.

"OK well stay behind me! When the bullets start to fly, I don't want ya to get hit!" ordered Titan.

Titan took a deep breath, lowered his shoulder and rammed full speed into the wall. As he came crashing through, Myst was hot on his heels. The sound and force of the blast caused the gunmen to spin around and open fire, just as Titan had predicted.

Myst leveled the first gunmen with a psionic burst, which rendered the man unconscious. Titan played clean up using his plasmoidal energy blasts.

"TIME TO TURN UP THE HEAT!!" Titan shouted, as he aimed his hands at the gun men's weapons, and melted them to slag.

"Our guns…. Melted!!" one of the gunmen gasped, as he saw his guns turn to melted balls of metal.

"Show's over, punks. Your little party's a bust!!" announced Titan.

Myst made a mad dash to the guard that was near mortally wounded. Titan rounded the criminals up with a burst of supersonic speed, while Myst focused his healing ability on the wounded guard. The familiar golden aura surrounded the indigo clad hero, and his unfortunate target. This time, something was amiss. As he began the healing touch, he felt his energy deplete faster than what was normally expected.

"AHHHH!" Myst yelled as he collapsed unconscious on the floor next to the fallen guard.

The inexperienced mutant had totally misjudged the extent and severity of the fallen guard. Myst had never come in contact with someone who was so near to death as this man was. The effects of his mortality, combined with his attempt to heal, completely overpowered his energy stores, rendering him catatonic.

"MYST!!!!!!!!!" Titan screamed, as he ran over to him.

As Titan reached his motionless friend, he tuned his heightened senses to Myst's vital signs. He noticed that his breathing was very shallow and slow, as was his heart rate. Titan knew that this fainting episode was much different than the last few.

A rush of emotions hit the mighty hero. Here was the one person that understood the burden that he had to carry as a hero. Robby McCloud became his best friend and confidant in record time. He was worried beyond explanation.

"Myst, wake up, bro!!" Titan urged as he attempted to rouse his best friend.

Titan became fearful of the worst. He began to weep uncontrollably at the thought that his friend was mortally wounded. He attempted to gather his thoughts as best as he could. He knew that there was only one person that could help him. Titan clutched his best friend to his chest and lost control of his emotions.

Titan knew that he had to pull it together for his best friend's sake.

"Oh no... This is not good..." he mumbled to himself as he frantically searched for his cell phone. "This is not good at all... This can't be happening to Robby... Not now..."

He pulled his cell phone out of the side pocket in his suit. He flipped it open and dialed his father's number. He quickly recounted to his father what had transpired. Dr. Knight instructed him to get Myst to the Sanctum immediately, and that he would meet them there.

Jake knew that his father would know what to do. He grabbed his best friend up off the floor carefully. He aimed his hand at the ceiling of the building and blasted a hole, big enough for the two of them, with his plasma beams. Titan, with cargo in hand, took to the skies, and flew towards home.

"Come on, Robby... Stay with me, bro... Don't leave me now!" Jake kept on saying to his friend, whom he held in his arms, while he flew home as fast as he could. "I need you more than ever now!"

Jake flew straight through the secret outside entrance of the Sanctum, and directly into the lab without ever setting down. He placed Robby gently on the table and called his father again.

"Dad, how much longer, this is bad, he has not moved yet, and his breathing is getting slower!" urged Jake over the phone.

Just then Madison let himself into the Sanctum. He saw the red-headed hero lying motionless on the analytical table. He felt a knot form in the pit of his stomach as he looked at his friend lying there, and his brother standing there an emotional wreck.

"Jake, what's the deal with Robby?" shrieked Madison.

"Dude, I have no clue" replied Jake as he choked back tears. "He was trying to heal this guy and then he passed out, and I haven't been able to bring him back!"

Jake heard the upstairs door to the Sanctum open, as he spun on his heel to face his father.

"Dad! Hurry! He's fading fast! Help him!" Jake shouted, as he father came running down the stairs as quickly as he could. "We're losing him, dad! I don't want him to die!"

Dr. Knight did not waste a moment of time. He listened to Jake's explanation as he began connecting Robby to every monitoring device he had.

"His vital signs are weakening... He barely has a pulse..." Dr. Knight said in a somber tone. "He's in bad shape, son..."

He went to the computer terminal and awaited the readings. He could feel the tension emanating off of his son. Charles knew that Jake and Robby were best friends, and he would do whatever it takes to secure the safety of both heroes.

Charles sat behind the computer screen with his hands clasped over his mouth, pouring over the data that the computer had compiled. What he saw frightened this man of science to the core of his being. What he deduced was finite, if he did not come up with a solution to this problem, young Robby McCloud was going to die.

"Is he going to be alright? Dad? Is he?" Jake asked his father. "Please tell me he's okay, dad!"

Dr. Knight kept looking at the computer read-out.

"We need something drastic to change Robby's condition around, or else..." Charles continued.

Suddenly a thought slammed into Charles' skull like a freight train. Jake's powers are recharged and kept stable by solar radiation. Maybe, if Robby were to be given that ability somehow, it would eliminate the taxing drain on him when he utilized his abilities.

"I am a PhD. not an MD, we have got to find a doctor to help with this son, I know the stuff, but the doctor has the techniques that I don't" explained Dr. Knight.

"So what does that mean?" asked Jake frantically.

"I have to get some of your blood and test it to see if it will be compatible with Robby" said Dr. Knight.

"WHAT? I am not sure I get it Dad" inquired Jake with a puzzled look upon his face.

"Jake I need you to go to the local emergency room. Locate Dr. Archer, and bring him here. Make sure that you blind fold him before you land here so that he does not find out who you really are" explained Charles.

Jake nodded his head and raced up the stairs. He took to the skies and flew at supersonic speed towards Washington Memorial Hospital Emergency Room. The one primal thought that drove him, was the salvation of his best friend. He knew that he had act fast or Robby McCloud would be done for.

Titan landed and made his way into the ER. He was mobbed by adoring fans as he landed. Jake felt bad that he had to be distant from people, but Robby was all that was on his mind. He began the long search for Dr. Archer.

"Excuse me Miss, but can you tell me where I can find Dr. Archer?" he asked politely.

"Wow! Sure thing Titan, let me page him for you" replied the young nurse at the admissions desk.

"Please hurry this is a matter of life and death" stammered Titan.

"DR. ARCHER PLEASE REPORT TO THE TRIAGE DESK STAT. DR. ARCHER TO THE TRIAGE DESK STAT" the nurse bellowed over the public address system.

Jake stood there impatiently fidgeting. He awaited the doctor to make his way to him. He wondered if his father had been able to stabilize his best friend. This was the most vulnerable Jake had felt since that fateful day when he had gained his powers.

"Nurse what is the problem here?" huffed Dr. Archer as he rounded the corner.

"Are you Dr. Archer?" asked Jake hurriedly.

"Yes son I am. Can I help you?" retorted the pleasant physician.

"Yeah! My father said that you were a friend of his and we need help like now" commanded Jake.

"Slow down big guy, what is the problem?" asked Dr. Archer.

"My best friend is almost dead and he said that you would know what to do to help" replied Titan.

"OK let me grab my med kit and let's rock" stated Dr. Archer as he ran back to the trauma center.

As Dr. Archer made his way back to the front area of the ER, Titan was standing there with a blind fold in his hand. "I want to apologize in advance doctor, but to protect my identity, I need you to put this on" requested Titan.

"OK I suppose, I need to help your friend if he is as bad off as you say, we need to get moving" replied Dr. Archer.

Dr. Archer put the blind fold on as Titan led him outside. He grabbed him up in his mighty arms and took to the sky. He used caution as not to injure the doctor in transit. He went as fast as he could without making Dr. Archer uncomfortable.

The pair landed at the Knight townhouse. Jake led the doctor down stairs and into the Sanctum. He requested him remove the blindfold.

"Charles?" asked a puzzled Bill Archer.

"Yeah Bill, here is your patient I will explain later. We need help now!" exclaimed Charles.

Dr. Archer wasted no time as he dashed over to the exam table. He pulled out his portable oxygen saturation monitor and connected it to Robby's index finger. He then took his blood pressure and listened to his heart.

"Charles I need some info on the kid" Bill demanded.

"Bill, this kid is an extraordinary specimen. He is a fifth level mutant. He is the most powerful telepath, empath, and a teleporter. What got him into this condition was the other power that he possesses. Robby can heal people" replied Charles quickly.

"That is amazing, he is a healer and he gets to this point?" asked Bill.

"It drains his life force" responded Charles.

"Well I need to get a blood sample. Do you have the equipment for me to analyze it here Charlie?" inquired Bill.

"Yes!" shot Charles.

Dr. Archer pulled out a small vial and needle kit. He walked over to Robby and placed a tourniquet on his left arm. He drew out a vial of the boy's amazing mutant blood. He pulled the needle from the red-headed boy's arm. He looked at the full vial of mutant blood.

Bill walked over to the analyzing station. He placed the vial into the electron microscope. He flipped the switch to activate the apparatus. What was revealed to the doctor's finely tuned eyes shocked him.

"Charles, we are going to have to attack this on almost a cellular level. His X factor that gives him his mutant ability is also killing him. As strong as this boy is, this part of his genetic structure is killing him" explained Dr. Archer.

"What are you saying sir?" asked Jake frightfully.

"If we do not do something and fast, your friend's powers will end up killing him" Bill responded.

"Cellular level?" inquired Charles.

"Yeah we actually need to further the mutation to attempt to alleviate this condition" continued Dr. Archer.

The computer that was continuously monitoring Robby's vital signs emitted a loud beep. Charles and Bill ran to the screen.

"CONSIDER TRANSFUSION" was emblazoned on the screen.

"Transfusion, that's it!" exclaimed Charles.

"What?" Bill asked.

"My son was mutated by outside forces, his blood carries special properties, and just perhaps its properties would heal Robby and further the mutation" explained Charles.

243

"I guess it makes sense. If his DNA was mutated, maybe what did that to him could in turn alter the structure of this boy as well" uttered Dr. Archer.

Charles went to the cabinet and retrieved a special needle. He returned it to Dr. Archer. "This is the only thing that will pierce my son's skin. It is from his adoptive home world" said Charles as he relinquished the needle.

"Son can you come over here?" asked Dr. Archer.

"Sure thing, doc" Jake grinned.

"Son, do you realize what is going to take place here?" asked Charles.

"Yes dad, I'm about to save Robby's life" replied Jake.

"Well more than that Jake. When this is said and done, you guys will be brothers. Your blood type is an exact match to Robby's and furthermore, it will take his already mutant DNA and further mutate it. You will be blood-brothers, in the truest sense of the term" continued Charles.

"Blood-brothers! Let's do it! I will never let Robby get like this again. If it will make him stronger and keep him safe then I am willing to do anything!" urged Jake.

Charles explained that what was going to occur and why. Jake agreed and relaxed on the table, offered his arm and took a deep breath. Bill came over and took out an emergency blood transfusion kit out of his bag.

"So what you are gonna do, is take blood from me and give it to Robby?" asked Jake.

"Yes, that is what we are going to do. I am going to take about two pints of your special blood, then infuse it into Robby. If your father is right, your blood is going to activate another mutation in Robby, this should completely remove that damaged part in his X-factor DNA" explained Dr. Archer.

"Are you serious? I can heal him?" asked Jake with wide-eyed wonder.

"I hope and pray so son" stated Charles.

Dr. Archer placed another tourniquet on Jake's extremely muscular arm. He took the special needle and inserted it with ease. The Doctor then connected the tubing to the catheter that was left in his arm. Slowly the bag filled with Jake's Zyrtonian blood. When the bag filled to capacity, Dr. Archer clamped it off and pulled the catheter out of Jake's mighty arm.

Dr. Archer went back to his bag and retrieved a regular IV needle. He went back to the arm that he had drawn the test blood from. He then picked another vein and inserted the needle. As he felt a slight pop, he slowly advanced the needle. Bill then hung the full bag of blood on the pole and connected a blood transfusion kit to it. He then connected the tubing to the catheter in Robby's arm.

The clamp was released and the blood slowly began to fill the drip chamber. Jake almost held his breath. The blood made its way through the chamber into the tubing and into Robby's awaiting arm. No eyes moved from Robby McCloud's near lifeless form.

Jake bowed his mighty head and prayed. He prayed to God that his father and Dr. Archer were both correct in the assumption that this blood would heal Robby and trigger the life saving mutation that he needed.

Another thought hit Jake like a ton of bricks as he watched the blood flow into Robby. He was watching the proverbial birth of his Blood-brother take place right before his bright blue eyes. He watched intently as his blood entered his soon-to-be brother's veins.

With a guttural grunt, Robby's limp form tensed, rigid as steel. Everyone in the room stared as Robby's arms and legs flexed to the maximum. Jake look in amazement as he saw rope like veins spread across his arm, feeding his cells with the life saving nectar. Jake also noticed his friends already impressive athletic frame gain a more solid, dense and powerful appearance.

"Uhhh! Gah! My head hurts" moaned Robby as he blinked his eyes.

"Robby! Robby! OH THANK GOD!" exclaimed Jake.

"Ohh, don't yell…" whispered Robby.

"Welcome back to reality Mr. McCloud" stated Charles.

"Glad to see that we were right" said Dr. Archer.

"Man, I am glad to hear your voice, dude" said Madison.

Jake walked over with tears flowing from his eyes. "Robby, Oh God I thought we lost you for good! I promise you this; I will never let anything happen to you, man. Today you have become my blood-brother, you are now more than a friend, and you are family. I love ya!" whimpered Jake.

"Blood-brother?" inquired Robby.

Dr. Knight went to the computer screen and scanned Robby's form. As the data compiled, Dr. Knight smiled as he shared his findings with Dr. Archer. His theory was right. Jake's blood had in fact totally recharged his energies and powers, with more speed than he had ever imagined. He had not counted on any other possible side effects to come into play. He was happy to know that his theory and Zyrtonian technology helped heal this boy. Jake, however, was the real hero. Dr. Knight and Madison left the two boys to compose themselves and come upstairs when Robby felt more up to it.

Dr. Archer introduced himself to Robby. He then informed him of what just transpired. He also asked to get a vial of his transmuted blood. Robby agreed to being stuck for a third time. Dr. Archer took the vial of blood back to the computer.

Dr. Archer placed the vial into the microscopic analyzer. As the computer slowly compiled the data, a smile crept across the Emergency Room Physician's face. The computer revealed that the theory is no longer a theory, it was proven, and none too soon.

"We have achieved heightened mutation. The faulty gene is gone" announced Dr. Archer.

"I am so glad" said Dr. Knight.

"Man, I am so glad that he made it" thought Jake.

"I'm glad I made it too, bro" said Robby audibly.

Jake looked at Robby with an intense puzzled look upon his face. He knew that he did not say a word. He also knew that even with Robby's mental powers, he could not read his thoughts. He could only feel his emotions. He wondered if the transfusion actually did what he thought it did. It made them blood-brothers.

Dr. Knight escorted Bill Archer upstairs with Madison. He wanted to give the new blood-brothers a chance to let the emotions to calm down. He knew how upset his son was when Robby was almost lost to his power glitch.

"God, I can't let Robby get hurt like that again" Jake thought to himself.

"Jake, you did not let me get hurt" said Robby.

"I didn't say anything! How did you...?" stuttered Jake. "Are you in my head?"

"I just heard your thoughts for the first time, bro!" exclaimed Robby.

"DAD!!!!" Jake yelled. "Can you come back down here, please!" he requested loudly.

"Dude, what are you doing?" asked Robby.

"Well, we need to know what is going on here Robby; there is no way I'm going to let you get hurt again" reprimanded Jake.

Dr. Knight made his way back downstairs, and looked at the boys with a quizzical look upon his visage. He knew that there may have been a catch to the transfusion, but he had banked on nothing happening.

"Dad, Robby can read my mind" offered Jake.

"Son, Robby is a telepath that's what he does" responded Dr. Knight.

"Dr. Knight, I hate to interrupt, but, I was never able to read Jake's mind, I could only feel what he was feeling" Robby explained.

"Dad, I can hear what he is thinking, too" added Jake.

An alarmed look appeared on Charles' face. "Now that is something that we need to look into, but Dr. Archer said that there could be some changes" said Charles as he walked over to the analytical equipment.

He pulled the scanner platform from the wall and hooked it to the computer panel. Dr. Knight then inputted a series of reading instructions into the mainframe. He paused a moment and faced Robby.

"Son, I need you to stand on this platform. I need to take a full biometric scan of you" ordered Dr. Knight. "I know that Dr. Archer had already done a scan of you before, but I want to scan you one more time, now that we've made this important discovery."

"Yes sir" replied Robby as he slowly stepped up on the raised platform.

He looked down at what appeared to be a target etched on the smoky crystal platform. Fear gripped his soul as he wondered what was about to happen. He swallowed hard in an attempt to calm himself.

"Relax bro!" Robby heard Jake say within his mind. "Now that I have some of your blood in me, I guess it must have done something to your mental powers…"

Dr. Knight then flipped a few toggle switches on the console to the on position. He waited for the apparatus to warm up. As soon as it did, he entered some commands via the keypad into the machine.

"OK Robby, what this is going to do, is to scan you on a DNA molecular level. That way we will know what is going on" stated Charles.

The machine came to life. A semi solid blue cylindrical containment field emitted from the crystalline platform. The machine sent out a red matrix of beams that encased Robby McCloud within the containment field. There were a series of beeps and chirps as the computer compiled the new data that it was collecting.

The computer finished collecting the necessary data and shut the containment field down. Dr. Knight stood poised at the read out screen. What he saw completely startled and amazed him.

"Hmmm, this is really fascinating and perplexing" said Dr. Knight.

"What is perplexing?" inquired Robby with a nervous tone.

Charles thought carefully to choose his words as to not upset Robby or startle him with the findings that were made. He considered what was on the screen. He even thought the discoveries were amazing and startling.

"Son, this states that your body has changed on a molecular level, just as Dr. Archer told us" began Dr. Knight. "I am not sure how far this will go but that infusion of Jake's altered blood has mixed in an extremely favorable way with your unique body chemistry." he added.

Robby cocked his head to the side. "Ummm, what exactly do you mean?" inquired Robby.

"Well, it appears that your DNA mixes well with Zyrtonian DNA, a little too well to be exact. Your natural abilities have been altered at the genetic level. Your mutation has been boosted. Your abilities are getting more powerful every second" explained Dr. Knight.

"I still don't get it." Robby said.

"What's the deal with Robby being able to read my thoughts now?" asked Jake.

"Well, Jake, it appears that now that you two share a similar DNA code, it would appear that you are forever linked to each other. The shared bloodline makes it possible to peer into your mind, son" said Charles.

"But Dr. Knight, I cannot read my parents thoughts that well, either" uttered Robby.

"Well as I said, your DNA has changed. There are other things that have changed too. Not just your psionic abilities, but your physical strength is growing exponentially as well" added Charles.

"What? I'm getting stronger?" asked Robby.

"It would appear so, and you're not going to be invulnerable, but you're not likely to get hurt that easily, either. Things are still changing so it is hard to tell what is really going on with these changes, it is all too new and happening so fast" explained Charles.

"Harder to get hurt? That's a relief" thought Jake.

"HEY! I heard that, Jake!" yipped Robby.

"The transfusion might affect your other abilities as well, but we haven't seen any changes as of yet…" Charles continued.

"So, there may be other changes?" Robby wondered.

"Yes." Charles responded. "So, if you see or feel anything unusual, please let me know immediately!"

"I will, Dr. Knight!" Robby assured him. Then Robby turned to face Jake.

"Well, not only are we gonna be blood-brothers from now on, but we're gonna be linked too!" he said with a smile on his face.

"That's fascinating…" Jake observed. "I guess there must be some invisible link between us now, huh?"

"Yeah… You can't get away from now, dude! I always know where to find you!" Robby laughed. "And, I always know what you're thinking and what you're feeling…"

Jake just stared at Robby for a moment without saying a word, but he just continued to think some thoughts to Robby instead.

"Well, I'm going to do whatever I can to look after your safety and well being from this point forward! I can assure you of it!" Jake thought.

"This is cool; we can actually communicate without saying anything to each other!" Robby thought back. "I guess this must be as a result of the blood transfusion, for we can hear our thoughts. I also want you to know that I do appreciate you looking out for me"

"Oh, yeah?" Jake grinned. "And you are welcome!"

"Yes!" Robby announced. "Plus, I know for a fact you're starting to get a little hungry right now…"

"Well…" Jake said, as he flexed his right arm, allowing a large bicep to show. "I have to feed my huge muscles! Let's go upstairs! I smell pizza!"

Jake turned around and dashed up the stairs, but Robby quickly teleported his way to the dining table. When Jake got there, Robby was already seated next to Madison.

"Grab a slice, Robby" Charles had offered Robby.

"It was about time Jake got here!" Madison mumbled at his brother.

"No fair! I can't teleport the way Robby does…" Jake chuckled, as he took his first slice and placed it on the plate before him.

"No, but Jake can do other things! He can fly, and that is very cool!" Robby admitted.

Nancy sat down and joined them for dinner, and Robby stayed just for a little while, until the phone rang, which Madison quickly answered. He handed the phone to Robby, since it was Susan, his mother. He told her that he was having pizza at the Knight's and asked if he still needed to come back home for supper. Susan asked him to come home soon since they had school the next day.

"Thanks for having me over, Mr. and Mrs. Knight…" Robby said politely, as he finished eating his pizza.

Jake also finished, and offered to help wash the dishes. Of course, he did it at super speed, and he was done washing, rinsing, and drying all the plates, glasses and silverware in less than a minute.

"Hey bro, I'm gonna head on home… I'll see you in the morning, alright?" Robby said to Jake.

"Sure! Call me before you go to sleep!"

"I will… See ya, bro…" Robby smiled.

Then Robby's eyes turned dark, and he disappeared before Jake's eyes.

"Wow... I'm still amazed every time he does that..." Jake sighed, as he stared at the spot where Robby was standing just a few seconds earlier.

Jake went to the bathroom and took a hot shower. Afterwards, he put on his pajamas and sat at his desk, where he did some more studying. He knew he didn't need much sleep, so he could have gone out on patrol of he wanted to. He decided against it, and laid on his bed and read a book. He figured that if he was to fall asleep, he'd go out on patrol a little later.

Chapter 35

Eventually, Jake turned off the overhead light in his room, and switched on his night-light. This didn't give much light, but that didn't matter for him, since he could see very well in the dark. He grabbed a book that he had checked out from the school library, which he needed to read for literature class, and started reading it while he was lying in bed, when a familiar voice suddenly rang in his ears.

"Oooh, reading Huckleberry Finn, are we?" the voice said.

Jake's mouth dropped wide open as he looked up.

"Robby?"

"Cool... I can see what you're reading..." the voice continued. "But, everything looks red to you..."

"But... How...? Are you here? Where are you? Are you in my room?" Jake wondered, feeling like he was talking to himself.

"No, I'm in my own room... But I can see what you're doing... I can see everything... I see what you're reading... Why does everything seem red to you?" Robby asked him.

"I turned my light off, so I'm using my night-vision..." Jake explained.

"Wow... You got such cool powers, Jake..."

"Look who's talking!" Jake laughed. "You can teleport and now you can talk to me without even calling me on the phone! What's up with that?"

"I got you to thank for it, Jake... You saved my life today... I owe you one!"

"Don't mention it, dude… My dad was the one who thought of the blood transfusion, not me…" Jake whispered. "He deserves all the credit for that…"

"Why don't you come over here for a few minutes?" Robby suggested.

"Oh, I might… I was going to get some sleep and then go on patrol later…" Jake said.

Suddenly, he felt an odd tingling feeling in his upper chest.

"Still, it would be cool if you could come over…" Robby said.

Jake noticed that this time, Robby's voice sounded a bit clearer than before. Not only that, but his bed felt like it was a lot harder than it was a few minutes before. Then, he realized that he wasn't laying on his bed anymore, but on a carpet on the floor!

"Huh? I thought I was lying on my bed just now…" Jake thought to himself.

"You're not on your bed, Jake! You're on my bedroom floor!" Robby chuckled.

Jake gasped when he looked around and realized he was in Robby's bedroom, on the floor, and right next to his bed!

"What the heck?" he said, as he quickly got up. "Robby! What are you doing here? Who turned on the light in my room?"

"You're in MY bedroom!" Robby declared. "The lights were on the whole time!"

Jake looked around the room with a very puzzled look on his face.

"Wait a minute… This is weird… How…? How did I end up in your bedroom?" Jake asked his best friend.

"Ooh, boy…" Robby said calmly. "I don't know man. I must have teleported you, Jake…That's the only explanation…"

Jake walked up to Robby's bed and stood right before him, while Robby sat up straight on his bed.

"But… Don't you need to be touching me, in order to teleport me somewhere?"

A wide grin came upon Robby's face.

"Well that is how it is normally supposed to work, but not anymore, it looks like!"

"But… How's that possible?" Jake wondered.

"Like your dad and Dr. Archer said earlier; the blood transfusion may have some additional effects on my mental powers, and since I got your blood, I guess all of my abilities have been directly affected, and the DNA change must have had a psionic type effect on you as well…" Robby mused.

"Wow!" Jake reasoned. "That explains why I hear your voice all the time. I guess it also explains why you can read my mind… That's amazing!"

"Yeah, well, how about we take this teleportation bit for a spin, huh?" Robby grinned. "I need to know for sure, not to mention I need to practice using it…"

Jake suddenly felt the same, faint tingling feeling in his upper chest again. Then he disappeared from where he was standing, right in front of Robby's bed, and reappeared again, standing in the corner, next to his bedroom door, surrounded by a cloud of mist. Slowly the mist faded, leaving Jake standing in the corner of Robby's bedroom.

"Dude, you just teleported me, and you didn't touch me at all!" Jake gasped out loud.

"Cool! I can't believe this bro, let's try this again!" Robby cheered. Immediately his eyes turned black, and Jake immediately was overcome by that tingling in his upper chest again.

Jake disappeared again, and popped up on the other side of the bedroom, standing next to Robby's dresser. As in the case of the first trial, Jake stepped from within the mist cloud that had encircled him.

"Wow!" Jake exclaimed. He was beginning to get used to the feeling of being teleported. "So, is this what you feel like when you do this on your own?"

"Yeah, it is like something invisible tickling the crud out of ya" explained the enthralled mutant.

"This is so awesome!" Robby cheered. "Let's try sending you outside this time!"

"In my PJ's, dude?" Jake questioned out loud.

"Oh! Oh! I got it! Hang on…" Robby said, with an evil grin. Robby's eyes turned black for the third time.

This time Jake disappeared and reappeared in the same spot! The only difference was, again, the cloud of mist that surrounded him.

"Hey! It didn't work this time!" Jake smirked.

"Oh really now?" Robby laughed. "You might wanna look in the mirror!"

Jake turned towards Robby's mirror and saw Titan staring back at him.

"What? You have got to be kidding me! You teleported me into my Titan costume! This is too weird!"

"Yeah, well I did not exactly teleport you into it, I kind of honed in on the costume, and teleported it and you! When you reappeared, so did it, at the same time and same place. Hey I'm gonna try sending you a little further, like maybe to school and back!" Robby chuckled.

Jake stared directly into Robby's eyes as they turned black. Jake watched the smoke surround his frame, and he felt the same strange tingling feeling in his upper chest once more.

Jake slipped through the dimensional portal that Robby opened for him. He flashed out of sight, leaving only the remnants of the cloud of mist behind. A giant plume of smoke appeared in the back parking lot of John F. Kennedy Middle School. The mighty Titan stepped forth and looked around with total amazement.

"Whoa! I can't believe this. So this is what HE must feel like all the time, when he does this..." Titan whispered to himself. "The only difference is, that he can now teleport me anytime and anywhere he wants to, in addition to teleporting his own self!"

Bewildered at his trip, Titan started walking towards the main building when the faint sound of footsteps were heard approaching him from a distance. He didn't want to be seen, so he leaped on to the roof. When his feet touched down on the roof, he spun back towards the source of the sound, looked down, and tuned in his infrared vision to spy the school's security guard, who was making the rounds below.

"Well, sure am glad that he didn't see me! That would have been kinda hard to explain. I guess I'd better fly home..." Titan thought to himself.

"Don't worry, dude, I'll bring you back home right now... Hold on..." he mentally heard Robby's voice whisper.

Again, the cool mist surrounded the teen of might, as the warm tickle crept slowly up his ribcage. Titan smiled as he felt his form slip through space and time, only to reappear back in his mutant blood-brother's bedroom.

"Welcome back, bro!" Robby cheered. "Did you have a fun trip?"

"Dude, that has got to be the coolest way to travel…well maybe the second coolest….I am still kind of partial to flying…I have to say, this is going to come in really handy!" Titan stated.

"Well, I guess we need to call it a night. So be ready around seven-thirty tomorrow morning and I'll teleport you to school with me from now on!" Robby grinned.

"Tardiness will be a thing of the past" laughed Jake. "I will never have to worry about getting mom or dad to write excuse notes."

"Yeah… and Maddie will be über-jealous! He SO hates riding the bus!" Robbie mumbled softly.

"Oh yeah…about that…umm" Jake said sadly.

"Hey, no problem… As you are walking by him, heading for the door, just grab a hold of him. All you have to do is touch him, with this apparent power boost, that's all it takes. He will get the ride of a lifetime…"

"That's awesome!" Jake cheered. "Now there is no place I can't get to as Titan. This is gonna be a blast bro!"

"Yeah…" Robby said, before he let out a loud yawn. "Dude, I'm getting really tired. I need to send you home, okay?"

"Well, I should go on patrol, since I'm already wearing my Titan costume anyway…" Titan chuckled.

"Sure!" Robby laughed, as he got on his bed. "Wanna head over to the Capitol?"

"Go for it…" Titan replied. "I'm starting to get used to being teleported by you…"

"Good night, bro…" Robby said in a sleepy voice. Then his eyes turned dark one more time, and Jake disappeared from his room, only to reappear again in a cloud of mist, standing outside of the Capitol Building in Washington DC. A proud Titan puffed out his ever muscular chest and looked around at the city he called home, in search of anything out of the ordinary.

"Man, I gotta get used to this, but its way cool…" Titan said, as he leaped into the air so he could start his nightly patrol.

Robby closed his eyes and saw his friend flying over the city through the young hero's eyes. For almost a lifetime, he had dreamed of the day he could be like Titan. Now within his mind's eye, he was getting the chance to live that dream. He shifted his frame as he dozed off into a deep, content sleep.

Chapter 36

The very next morning, Robby bolted upright, out of bed. He had awoken this morning feeling more energized, rejuvenated, and full of life, so full of power, than he had ever remembered feeling before. He walked over to the blinds and pulled the cord to raise them. When the suns loving rays danced off Robby's bare chest, he felt a surge of power and strength that struck him by surprise. Unbeknownst to the mutant megalith, the transfusion granted him more than anyone could have expected.

Robby noticed a familiar and warm presence exuding a sense of want. He looked over at the chair closest to his bed, there hung his symbiotic costume. He mentally called to his "friend" as it slinked across the floor, silent and snake like. The indigo extension of his life reached his foot, and warmly greeted its master, by spreading across his ripped body. It spread across his well chiseled legs, making its way up his waist, extending across his washboard abdominal muscles, slowly making its way to his head, where it formed his mask.

"Good morning my friend" Robby whispered to his costume. He knew the costume was as much a part of him now as his own skin, and he always felt secure and comfortable with it on him. On the other hand, when it was not adorning and protecting his frame, he almost missed it, longing for it to once again join him in the adventures of his costumed persona, Myst.

Robby decided to go outside into the crisp morning air for a few minutes. Something was drawing him to the outdoors. Once outside, the sun beamed onto the young man's face. He could feel the warmth tingling against his skin, even through his costume. He could feel the suns energy as if it were charging his body. Never in his life had the sun ever made him feel so good, so revived, and so strong.

"I wonder if this is what Jake feels every time he goes into the sunlight?" Robby asked himself.

"Yes it is bro!" Jake mentally whispered to him.

"Oh wow! I forgot we are linked like that" Robby uttered mentally.

"Yeah! Good morning to you too bro!" Jake said telepathically, or better yet, Robby heard Jake's response.

When the trio had prepared to make their way to school, Jake did as Robby had told him. He walked past Madison and grabbed him in a friendly bear hug. In an instant, the three boys appeared in the vacant back lot of the school. Still having twenty or so minutes before classes were going to start, Jake and Robby began talking about the night prior and this morning. Madison overheard Robby talk all about the changes that had been happening to him and Jake following the blood transfusion. Madison wondered how this was going to affect the relationship that he shared with both boys. He and Robby were pretty close, due to the fact of interests, but Robby and Jake were close for other and more powerful reasons now. Neither Jake nor Robby had any inclination of leaving Madison out of the mix.

Robby decided to just be honest with Madison. After gleaning the emotional information from his young friend he decided to gently confront him. "Dude… Something has changed between me and your bro since I got that blood transfusion from him last night!" Robby whispered to Madison during lunch.

"Why? What are you talking about?" Maddie inquired.

"Last night, when you were already asleep, I actually managed to teleport Jake into my room!"

"Wait, aren't you supposed to be touching him?" Maddie gasped.

"Yeah! That is how it usually works, but it seems things are changing with that, and other things…"

"Oh dude! That's cool!" Madison grinned. "So, you can teleport him anytime and anywhere you want?"

"Yes, it certainly appears that way!" Robby chuckled.

"Oooh… So, if I need him to pick something up for me, you can just teleport him and he can get it?" pondered Madison.

"Very easy…" Robby grinned. "I can practically teleport Jake in my sleep!"

"He can be our own personal courier!" Madison cheered. "Besides, I don't think he'll mind… I mean, does he mind being teleported?"

Robby paused for a moment and pondered his question.

"Honestly, he hasn't said anything either way!" Robby shrugged. "Besides, I know what he's thinking and what he's feeling and I really don't think he cares; actually, he thinks it's kinda cool!"

"It's settled then!" Madison cheered. "So if you want to borrow any CDs or Comics, I can just send them with Jake, right?" Madison asked.

"Sure! That way, I can get a little practice with this boost to my powers, and he can get used to being teleported all over the place!"

"You should send him all over the place when he goes on his patrol!" Madison declared. "Can you teleport him while he's walking, running or flying?"

"Of course!" Robby shrugged. "It's like I have a permanent location-lock on him!"

"You got a permanent location-lock on my big brother? Awesome! And, is this because of the blood transfusion?" questioned Madison.

"Yeah! I guess you could say that we're blood-brothers now…" Robby explained.

"Blood-brothers! That's so freakin' sweet!" exclaimed Madison. "So, where's Jake now?" he wondered.

Robby closed his eyes briefly.

"He's in Room 103 taking his History test. He's on question number 5. He's pretty good; so far he has answered all his questions on the test."

"Dude! Can you see everything he sees?"

"Yeah! I had better not bother or teleport him now! He's taking a test right this minute!" Robby laughed. "But I'm going to teleport him home as soon as school is over so just hold on to him. He told me he knows when he's being teleported because of a tingling sensation in his chest when I'm about to teleport him!" stated Robby

After recess, Robby and Madison made their way to their separate classes. Jake had been filled in at lunch about the plan to teleport all three of them home. The trio awaited patiently for the final bell of the day.

Jake patiently waited for Madison by the back gate to the school, so that he wasn't seen by all the students. Madison met him there and the two walked a little, when Jake heard Robby's voice.

"You ready to go home, little brother?"

"Hold on to me, Maddie!" Jake ordered.

Maddie reached out with his right hand and held on to Jake's arm. Jake felt that tingling in his chest again, knowing that Robby's powers were at work inside of him. Instantly, both boys disappeared and reappeared again inside of their living room back home.

"What a way to travel!" Maddie cheered. "That rocked!"

"It has taken a little getting used to…" Jake chuckled, as he walked over to his room.

"Good! Robby needs to practice his power boost!" Maddie laughed. "So, he needs to teleport you a lot!"

"Oh yeah?"

Maddie came over to Jake and handed him a comic book while holding the cordless phone in his other hand.

"Here, Jake, hold this for a sec…"

"What's this?"

"A comic book. You need to give it to Robby…" Maddie said.

Then Maddie spoke into the horn of the phone.

"Okay, send him over!"

Suddenly Jake was overcome by the familiar tingling in his chest. Like all the times before, he felt the cool mist spilling over his body.

"Hey are you talking…?" he said, before he disappeared.

In a blink of an eye, Jake was standing in Robby's bedroom.

"…to Robby?"

"Thank you!" Robby said as he took the comic book from Jake.

"What is this?" Jake said, as he rolled his eyes. "Am I the mailman, now?"

Robby then handed Jake a CD containing music.

"Can you give this to Madison, its payment for borrowing that comic book" stated Robby.

"You're really enjoying this new power, huh?" Jake grinned.

"Wouldn't you love it if you had the ability to teleport Titan anywhere in the world?" Robby said sheepishly. "I consider it such an honor… I feel like I can help you in such a big way right now…"

Jake just stared at him more a moment, not knowing what to say.

"Please… Don't make me stop using it…" Robby asked him sadly.

Jake walked up to Robby and extended his muscular arms before resting his hands on Robby's shoulders.

"I can't stop you from using your powers, Robby…" Jake smiled. "So, don't worry… You just go ahead and teleport me whenever and wherever you want… I totally trust you… To be honest, I'm enjoying it!"

"Even when Maddie is scheming for me to teleport you all over the place?"

"Yes… He's my little bro and I have to trust him as well. Just do me a favor and use it with caution, though. We can't just abuse this new addition to your power just because you have it"

"Oh good… because he's trying to have me teleport you back and forth between my house and yours quite a few times, you know?"

"That's fine…" Jake grinned. "That gives me a chance to say hi to you and your parents every day!"

"He wants me to teleport you while you're on patrol. He even wanted me to teleport you all over the world while you're flying!" Robby confessed.

"If it allows me to help people all over the world, then you should do that, but like I said, be careful with it!"

"Well you know I will be. You know I would never do anything that would get you into some sticky situation bro" assured Robby.

Jake just smiled back.

"Robby… It's your power. I got the muscle-powers. I'm not going to tell you how you need to use your mental powers. But, I totally trust you, okay? You use your teleportation powers and teleport me wherever you like… Knock yourself out, bro… Teleport me all you want…"

Robby glanced down at his feet. He was at a loss for words. Here he was standing in his bedroom with his hero, being told of the trust that Jake had in him. He felt a swelling of pride and emotions within him.

"Jake, I trust you with my life bro" stated Robby.

"I totally feel the same way, my blood-brother" smiled Jake.

"Well man, I need to get some sleep, ready to head home?" inquired Robby

"Okay…" Jake said, as he braced himself for another jump. "Beam me up, Scotty!" chuckled Jake.

Robby's eyes turned to black and Jake felt that tingling in his chest again. Suddenly, Jake was standing in his bedroom again, where Maddie was waiting for him.

"Finally! What took you so long?" he complained.

"We had to talk about something…" Jake said, as he handed his brother the CD. "I think Robby wanted you to have this…"

"Yeah, I need to see if I want dad to get me this band, so I asked Robby if I could listen to his" responded Madison.

"What band is it?" Jake inquired.

"Robby's favorite band, Sypher!" exclaimed Madison.

"Oh yeah, you will like them. They really rock!" stated Jake.

"Hey Jake, can we go flying? I really need to talk to you about something" asked Madison.

"Sure bro, we can go out" responded Jake with a warm tone.

Jake went to the closet and retrieved Madison's jacket. He walked over and handed it to him. He knew that something was on his little brother's mind. He just was not sure as to what it was. Jake was slightly worried about what it could be.

Jake waited for Maddie to put on his jacket and zip it up. He walked back over to him and grabbed him up with ease. The pair made their way to the window exit of Jake's room. Jake took to the sky with a mighty leap.

"OK little bro, what's up?" he asked with concern.

Madison cocked his head to the side pondering how to ask his older brother something. His emotions began to get the best of him. He shed one single tear as he began to speak.

"Jake, now that you and Robby are blood-brothers, does that mean you are not gonna love me anymore?" Maddie asked solemnly.

"WHAT?!?! Have you lost your mind, bro?" replied Jake.

"Well I was worried now that you have someone like Robby that you will not need or want me anymore..." uttered Madison.

"Maddie, don't you ever think like that again. You're my little brother, and Robby is my blood-brother. We are now one big happy family. I would never replace you, I love you, little brother!" said Jake as he held Madison close to him.

"Thanks Jake! I love you too, I was just worried that I would have to go away or something" said Madison.

"Not in this lifetime!" chuckled Jake.

The duo soared through the open skies over DC. The emotions took a turn for the better as they laughed and cut up all evening. Jake realized that Madison was worried that now that he and Robby were blood-linked, he would lose love and interest in him. He knew that now, more than ever, he was going to have to make Madison an active part of the team.

Madison looked at his brother with wonder in his eyes. He thought about how compassionate he was, and how big of a heart this mountain of teen-aged muscle-boy had. He thought of the times that he used Jake as a courier to Robby. He knew that only with his brother's permission would he use that feature of the side effect again. He loved his brother, and was right there to help either him or Robby.

"So I guess you can say that I have two big brothers now?" asked Madison.

"Yeah kiddo, you sure do, and I know that Robby, for one would be honored to be that for ya" said Jake.

"Really?!?! How do you know? Did he tell you that telepathically?" inquired Madison.

"Yep! He sure did. Just now!" laughed Jake.

"Awesome! I have two big brothers!" yelled Maddie.

"Oh and by the way. Your red-headed big brother just told me that you owe him a hug when you see him next." giggled Jake.

"He did?" asked Madison.

"Yeah, hey I got a great idea Maddie, why don't we get Robby to ship us over to the ice cream place?" inquired Jake.

"When?" asked a startled Madison. "Now?"

"Yeah, sure why not? It'll be fun!"

Indeed… Jake felt the tingling in his chest and in a blink of an eye he and Madison were standing before the Ice House ice cream parlor, in downtown Washington DC, which was over thirty miles away from where they had flown. Jake and Maddie had traveled the distance in a fraction of a second, thanks to Robby's teleportation powers.

"Wow… what a way to get around…" Jake grinned, as he stood before the entrance to the store.

"Get chocolate, dude…" Jake heard Robby's voice ringing in his ears. "Both Maddie and I love chocolate…"

"HA HA HA!!! Hey Maddie, Robby wants us to pick him up some chocolate ice cream, and he said that you loved chocolate as much as he does!" chuckled Jake.

Madison nodded his approval as he and Jake walked into the store and ordered a large half gallon of chocolate ice cream for the three of them to split. When he had paid and walked out, he grabbed a hold of Madison's shoulder and Robby quickly teleported them back to their house. Robby teleported over to the Knights and the three boys enjoyed their ice cream. Jake was slowly getting used to teleporting through the space-and-time-continuum like Robby did. For some reason he felt a huge swell of pride to know that he had a blood-brother that was there for him and could understand being different, and knowing that his adoptive brother is so honest and cool to be around. Jake just smiled at Robby with that pride, as the red head telepath read what he was thinking and feeling, returned the knowing smile.

Chapter 37

When they were done eating ice cream, Robby teleported the brothers and himself back to his room, where they played video games and read comic books, until Jake noticed his father's car pulling into the driveway.

Charles had just walked from the garage into the living room when both Madison and Jake suddenly teleported and appeared standing right in front of him!

"Hi dad!" both boys cheered in unison, the moment they appeared before their father.

"Holy smoke!" Charles gasped. "How did you guys do that?"

"Robby teleported us!" Madison replied.

"Dad! Get this!" Jake said excitedly. "Robby can teleport me anywhere without even being near me!"

"What?"

"Ever since the blood transfusion yesterday, he's been able to teleport me all over the place without touching me or being near me!" Jake explained.

"Wow!" Charles exclaimed. "You mean the blood transfusion has affected you, too?"

Suddenly Robby appeared in the living room in a cloud of mist.

"Good evening, Dr. Knight!" he said politely. "I'm sorry, but I sense your concern, so I decided to come over"

"Jake just told me that you were able to teleport him without touching him or being near him. Is that correct?" Charles asked his next door neighbor.

"Yes, sir. I noticed it last night, when I wished that I could talk to Jake about something. Suddenly, I saw him lying on my floor! That's when I noticed that I had teleported him to my room!"

"That's amazing. I knew you had the ability to teleport yourself and others only when you had physical contact with them, but I did not foresee you having the ability to teleport Jake the same way you teleport your own self…" Charles thought out loud.

"I know! It just happened…" Robby shrugged.

"Do you mind coming down to the Sanctum so I can run a test on you, Robby?"

"Not at all, Dr. Knight…I sort of expected it…Ya know…the whole E.S.P. thing"

"Let's go, Maddie. I'll race you down the stairs…" Robby then stared at Jake with a grin as Madison sprinted past them to the stairs. "I'll teleport you to the Sanctum!"

"Go for it…" Jake shrugged.

Jake felt the tingling in his chest before he disappeared, only to find himself standing alone in the Sanctum just a fraction of a second later. Moments later, Madison and Robby came running down the stairs.

"See? I told you Jake was down here already!" Robby laughed.

"Well, duh!" Maddie chuckled. "Of course, since you can control where Jake is gonna be all the time!"

Jake just laughed at the silliness of the two boys, as Charles made his way down the stairs. He walked over to the computer and started everything up, before he asked Robby to stand on the scanning platform, which was attached to the computer screen.

Charles pressed a few buttons and clicked his mouse on the mouse pad, which started the scanning mechanism on the large machine. After a few moments, the computer displayed its findings on the screen.

"This is interesting…" Charles murmured, as he read the text on the screen.

"What does it say, dad?" Jake wondered as he, Madison and Robby walked up to him.

"The transfusion has altered Robby's DNA completely. This whole process was, in theory, supposed to be more gradual. It has been almost ravenous, but in a good way. Jake's Zyrtonian DNA has blended with your Mutant X-Chromosome DNA to create the most perfect hybrid ever. Robby is getting stronger, much stronger. He is becoming more like you, Jake. And as his powers "see" it, Jake, you are just an extension of Robby. That is why he does not need to touch you, and the mental barriers that you had up, are not a challenge for him now!"

"Say what?" Jake asked.

"That's why Robby sees and hears everything you see and hear. That also explains why Robby can now teleport you anywhere and anytime he wishes. Since he can do that to his own self, he can now also do it to you. Having your blood flowing through his body now has made you a part of him. Robby can now determine where you will be at during any time of the day..." Charles explained.

"Wow! That is so cool!" Madison cheered.

"I like it!" Robby grinned.

"So... I can be anywhere, in an instant?" Jake wondered.

"Well, if Robby goes through training..." Charles laughed. "Just like you need to lift heavy things in order to get stronger, Robby needs to go through practice sessions every week in order to keep his teleportation powers sharp..."

"So if I am the only person that he does not have to touch to teleport..." Jake reasoned, "Then I'm the only person he can practice his teleportation skills on!"

"Exactly!" Charles said, as he walked over to the storage closet and got a can of white paint. He then handed a brush and the paint to Jake.

"Go and paint the numbers one through four on the gray, concrete floor over there in the center of the Sanctum. Make them nice and big so we can see them from far away."

Jake raced over to the center of the Sanctum, which was as big as a basketball court, and he painted the numbers on the floor in white paint, each number about three feet apart. Then he raced back to Charles with the closed can and brush. Jake then washed and rinsed the brush before he came back to the Sanctum. By now, the paint on the floor had dried.

"Alright, now go stand on number 1, Jake…" Charles instructed his son.

Jake walked over to the spot where he had painted the number and stood on top of it.

Charles walked up to Robby, and they stood before the four numbers which Jake had painted on the floor.

"Now, do you see the four numbers on the floor before you?" Charles said, as he rested his arm on Robby's shoulder.

"Yes sir…" Robby said, while Madison was standing on the other side of Charles.

"Now, Robby, teleport Jake from spot number 1 to number 2, then to number 3, and finally number 4…" Charles instructed.

Robby's eyes turned black and Jake's chest was overcome by that tingling feeling again. Suddenly, Jake disappeared and reappeared again, standing three feet away on spot number 2. The same thing happened again, and he disappeared and reappeared again, standing on spot number 3, before he jumped one more time and ending up on spot number 4.

"Wow! Three jumps in a row!" Jake said, now standing 9 feet further from where he started.

"Now, I want you to teleport him back, one numbered square at a time!" Charles instructed.

Jake disappeared again, appearing on spot 3, then on spot 2, before appearing on spot 1 again.

"Having fun yet, Jake?" Madison shouted.

"I'm getting used to this, yeah…" Jake laughed. "It feels great! Do it some more, Robby!"

"Very good…" Charles said to Robby. "But, not fast enough! Can you do it any faster?"

"Yes, sir!" Robby smiled.

Robby drew in a deep breath, before his eyes turned black again. Jake felt the familiar tingling in his chest once more, and the tingling remained. It seemed as if he was going to make one long jump!

Instantly, Jake disappeared from the number one spot. He appeared on spot 2 for a split second, before he disappeared again. Then he jumped to spots 3, 4, and back on spots 3, 2, and finally on spot 1 again, in just four seconds!

"Very good!" Charles cheered.

"Holy cow! That was intense!" Jake gasped. "This is even better than flying!"

"Man! That was fast!" Madison exclaimed. "Robby can make Jake disappear in a blink of an eye?"

"Yeah, I'm getting faster at it... I can feel it..." Robby said. "I feel his jumps... I feel him jumping quicker now... I think I can make him jump even faster than this..."

"I practically don't feel him teleporting me at all!" Jake added. "I barely notice it anymore!"

"Now, make Jake jump from number 1 to number 4 and back repeatedly as fast as you possibly can..." Charles said to him. "Give it all you got..."

"Sure, Dr. Knight..." Robby said.

Robby bit his lips and clenched his fists as his eyes turned black.

Suddenly Jake disappeared from spot 1 and appeared on spot 4, 9 feet away. Then Jake appeared on spot 1 again, for half a second, before he was on spot 4 again. Jake jumped back and forth, faster and faster, until he was jumping so fast, that it seemed as if there were two of them!

"DUDE!" Madison gasped. "I'm seeing TWO Jakes!"

"Amazing... Who says Jake can't be two places at the same time anymore?" Charles said to himself.

Finally, it stopped, and Jake ended up standing on spot number 4.

"What a ride!" Jake shouted. "I loved every minute of it. I love it when you teleport me like that!"

"Whew..." Robby sighed. "That took a lot out of me..."

"You did well, Robby..." Charles said to Robby. "You had us two Jakes for a few moments..."

Jake walked up to Robby with a wide grin on his face.

"Man, that felt awesome!" he laughed. "I was seeing everything double!"

"That's because you were almost two places at once..." Charles said. "Almost..."

"How often does Robby need to practice teleporting Jake?" Maddie asked.

"Oh, I guess for thirty minutes per week is plenty? If he teleports Jake a dozen times a day, he'll stay on top of it..." Charles laughed. "He teleports him at a rate of about one jump in one tenth of a second..."

"One tenth of a second?" Jake gasped. "Wow! That's super fast!"

"Indeed! That means, if we tell Robby of an emergency somewhere, he can have you there as Titan in less than a second..." Charles reasoned. "I like that response time..."

"Robby can send Jake to his house and back in less than a second to get me cookies, video games and comic books..." Madison added. "I also like that delivery time..."

"MADISON, we are not going to abuse Robby's apparent control of your brother's whereabouts. It is not fair to either of them, especially Robby" chastised Dr. Knight, as he glared at his youngest boy.

"AW Dad! I was just kidding anyway" said Madison as he winked at his big brothers.

"It's okay, dude... He can teleport me to his heart's content" Jake whispered to Madison. "And, to your heart's content!"

"Good..." Madison whispered to his big brother. "I need for you to pick up some video games and some comic books at the store tomorrow!"

The boys just laughed out loud following Madison's remark as they walked up the stairs. Robby decided to teleport Jake to his own bedroom, while he and Madison hung out for a while in the younger brother's room. They had a great time at the Knight's, before Robby had to return home for supper that night.

Chapter 38

After dinner, Robby went into his room and closed his door. His parents went to bed, and he decided to spend some time studying for school. When he was finished, Robby just closed his eyes and laid his head on his pillow and a vision came to his mind. He began to see through Jake's eyes.

Jake was also doing his homework, but he was nearly finished. No sooner had he finished doing his math problems, or he began to hear Robby's voice ringing in his ears.

"I think you need to look at problem number 5 again, dude. Your answer is wrong..." Robby's voice spoke inside of his head.

"Oh, thanks for pointing that out..." Jake grinned.

Jake opened his notebook again and looked at the problem and realized that he had made a mistake. He quickly used the eraser on his pencil and erased his answer, before writing the correct answer in his notes.

"Ahh... Nice having my Blood-brother looking over my shoulder all the time..." Jake chuckled to himself.

When he was finished, he closed the notebook and placed it in his backpack.

"Are you going on patrol tonight?" Robby asked him.

"Yeah... I think so, although I have no idea of where to go..."

"Just go outside and start flying... Let me handle the 'where'-part..." Robby continued. "I'm looking up a few places in my geography book right now, just to get some images of some cool places in my mind. I already found some cool places to send you..."

"Oh really?"

"Yeah! I discussed a few spots with your little brother as well! You're gonna love it! I got you on a permanent location-lock, remember? SO….relax a little bit and leave the driving to me, big man!"

"Oh wow!" Jake said. "I like the sound of that…"

"Until I fall asleep, of course… Then you're on your own!" Robby chuckled.

Jake got up from his desk and started walking towards his dresser when he felt the tingling in his chest. Suddenly, he was teleported, but he was still in his room. He looked down and realized that he was wearing his Titan costume!

"Dude! You keep on getting faster at this…" Jake noted. "I barely even notice it anymore…"

"Eventually you won't… You'll be so used to me doing this, that I can teleport you and you won't even feel it…" the voice replied. "I'm gonna start teleporting you everywhere, all day long… You don't even have to walk anymore!"

Indeed, Jake was suddenly standing outside on the balcony and he didn't even feel the jump coming.

"So, where are you sending me?" Jake wondered out loud, as if he was talking to himself.

"China, Egypt, Russia, Australia, just to mention a few…" Robby's voice replied. "Ready for take-off?"

"Yes. Here we go!"

Jake leaped into the air and soared through the sky at high speed. He wasn't in the air for a minute, when the familiar Washington DC streets suddenly turned into the crowded streets of Beijing, China while Jake was looking down from the sky.

"Wow…. I didn't even feel that!"

"Welcome to China, Jake!" Robby said to him. "I'm gonna make you jump around a few countries now…"

Jake just looked down and enjoyed the ride as he continued to fly.

He continued to fly over the large Chinese city. He continued to gaze down at the streets and the buildings from the sky, when the cityscape suddenly changed into the vast Egyptian desert located in the northern part of Africa. Suddenly, in the distance, he spotted a pyramid!

"Oh wow! I guess I'm over Egypt now!" Jake thought to himself.

Jake continued to fly slow and at low altitude over the hot desert for a few minutes, until the entire environment around him changed again. This time, he was flying over the harbor entrance of Sydney, Australia!

"Hey! Is this Australia?" he gasped. Jake had never been to Australia before, so this was a whole new experience for him.

All the flying around had made Titan thirsty, and he began to look for a water fountain somewhere. He slowed down even more, so he could get a better view of the buildings below him. He spotted a public library on a busy street corner in Sydney, so he decided to land right before the main entrance and walked through the main doors at the front of the building.

"I want to get something to drink..." he thought, knowing that Robby would hear him.

As he walked through the doors of the library, he saw lots of people using the computer terminals, located near the entrance of the library. People were standing near a large counter, holding books in their hands, so they could check them out or return them. Several students were standing around a large book shelf, reading the newspapers and magazines that were stacked on the shelves there.

He quietly walked past the magazine rack, picking up the pace even more so when he spotted a teenage magazine which had 'Titan' on the front cover.

Jake had forgotten about the magazines right away, when he spotted a water cooler which was just at the end of the hallway, where the restrooms were. He walked up to it, while trying his hardest not to draw any attention to himself.

He walked right up to the water cooler and pressed the button, which made a small stream of cold water come out of the water spout. Jake drank some water from the cooler, before he turned around and was about to walk back towards the entrance, when a tall, skinny teenage boy walked right up to him and blocked his way.

"Hey, mate! That is one cool suit you're wearing!" the boy said to Jake. "Are you Titan?"

Jake was caught by surprise for a brief moment. He hadn't expected anyone in a library in the middle of Sydney to recognize him like that.

He didn't want to lie to the boy, either, and decided to just be honest and reveal his identity to the curious Australian teenager.

"Yes, that's me!" he whispered. "I just stopped here to get a drink of water. I was on my way home to America…"

"Ooh that's very cool, mate!" the Australian boy said with a grin, as he extended his hand for a handshake. "My name is Edward. I'm very pleased to meet you!"

"Thanks! I'm pleased to meet you, too!" Titan said, as he shook his hand.

"If you ever need to stay Down Under, please come by and give me a ring!" the boy continued, as he wrote his name and number on the back of a piece of paper before he handed it to Titan. "I'd love to have you over!"

"I'll remember that!" Titan said, while he accepted the paper from the teen. He glanced at the number, before he placed it in his pocket. "Well, I have to go now! I still need to finish my patrol. I'll be back some time soon. Can I call you next time I visit Sidney and I stay a little longer?"

"Yes, of course mate!"

"Nice meeting you!" Titan said.

The boys said goodbye to one another before Titan turned around and walked out the door of the library. As soon as he walked out, he leaped into the sky and took high into the air, heading straight north.

As Jake was looking down over the southern Australian shore, the ocean below quickly changed into the vast Russian landscape of Siberia the moment Robby sent him through another teleportation.

"Oh wow… All I see is snow and trees…" Jake thought to himself.

As he continued to fly, he realized that he was flying over mountains and large, extended valleys with miles and miles of forests.

"Slow down, Jake" Robby's voice instructed him. "So you don't come crashing through your living room!"

Jake slowed down and came to a stop, so he ended up simply hovering over one spot in the middle of the sky. Suddenly, the Russian sky disappeared and changed into the familiar living room at his house back in Washington, DC.

"Welcome home!" Robby's voice rang in his ears.

"Thanks, dude... It was great! I even made a new friend in Australia!" Jake grinned.

"Well, I'm going to sleep. Be ready in the morning so that I can send you and Maddie to school, okay?"

"Will do, bro!"

Then Jake ran up to his bedroom and changed into his pajama's. This time, he didn't get teleported; Robby had already fallen asleep next door. Jake crawled in bed; he closed his eyes and let his mind wander about his very first world-wide patrol.

Chapter 39

The next morning, Jake and Madison met up with Robby to walk to school. Robby had a sickly pale look upon his face. Jake felt that something was amiss with his blood-brother. Madison even picked up on the fact that the normally athletically sound teen was looking rather under the weather.

"Robby, bro, you OK?" inquired Jake.

"Dude, I don't really know. I woke up this morning with a splitting headache and with the feeling that I was about to completely lose control" explained Robby.

"Lose control?" asked Madison. "Of... What?"

"I'm not sure, Maddie... It just feels like I'm about to explode or something..." retorted Robby.

"Bro, should you be even going to school at all, while you're feeling like this?"

"I'll be fine... I hope. I'll let ya know if I start feeling any worse" said Robby through a fake smile.

The rest of the way to school the trio remained oddly silent. Jake and Madison were obviously very concerned about their red-headed counterpart. They had never seen their friend in a condition such as this before, and it caused their concern to rise exponentially as they approached the entrance to JFK Middle school.

When they had crossed the gates of the school grounds, Madison hugged Jake and ran off to his class. The super teens quickly transverse the campus and headed towards their first period class. As soon as Jake and Robby walked in they took their seats.

Before the bell rang, one of the boys' friends walked in. It was Piper Brightmore, an inquisitive, intelligent girl who happened to have a crush on Robby, and she sat down right next to Jake.

"Morning Jake" announced Piper.

"Morning Piper" returned Jake.

Piper leaned in to Jake and inquired as to the condition of their red-headed friend. "What's up with Robby?" she whispered.

Jake explained that Robby had not been feeling well all morning, and that there was really nothing to worry about.

"Well, I'm just a bit concerned because he doesn't look himself at all this morning..." retorted Piper.

"He'll be fine" Jake said. "Why you ask?" he inquired.

"No reason" she blushed.

Jake knew for some time that Piper had been eying his friend with a loving gaze. It was almost as if she was smitten by the red-headed baseball player. Jake smiled a sly knowing smile at Piper, which fortunately, she was unaware of.

As the bell rang, and the teacher took her position at the head of the class, Robby's headache steadily increased. He felt like someone was trying to beat him in the head with a blunt ax. He had to get out of the class room.

"Jake; I gotta bail bro, my head is killing me and I'm not sure what's about to happen" Robby mentally whispered to his blood-brother.

Jake got up and walked with Robby to their teacher. Jake explained what was going and requested to walk him to the nurse's office. She agreed and wrote them a pass. Jake took it and hurried Robby out the door.

As the two made their way towards the rest room, Robby clutched his head and fell to the ground. Jake was in utter shock over the pain that his friend was feeling. Robby was on his knees clutching his head. Jake placed his hands on Robby's shoulder while trying to reassure him.

"Jake! We gotta get outta here bro, I can't hold on anymore!" grunted Robby.

"Can you jump us outta here?" asked Jake.

"I think so, not sure where we're gonna end up though…" uttered Robby

Robby tried to clear his head. He focused his mental thoughts to teleportation. The duo quickly vanished in a cloud of mist, only to reappear on an empty hiking trail, several miles outside of the city.

"GOD!!!! JAKE I CAN'T STOP THE PAIN!!!!" screamed Robby.

"Robby, bro are you alright?" asked Jake as he tried to make his way to his fallen blood-brother.

Robby gnashed his teeth and clinched his fists. He couldn't take the pain any longer; he was suffering worse than when his telepathy and empathy had emerged. He opened his eyes and stared into the heavens. Robby then let out a scream of agony which sounded like that of a wounded howling wolf.

"AAARRRRRRGGGGGGHHHHHHH!!!!!!"

Jake watched helplessly as his friend's pain increased. He looked into Robby's normally gentle eyes and noticed that not only were they solid black, but they were almost like they were on fire. The black was surrounded with an eerie red glow!

"Robby? What's going on?"

Just then Jake noticed things started floating behind him and Robby.

"Robby! The trash can… rocks are levitating in the air… What are you doing?" Jake wondered.

Then Jake himself felt his feet leaving the ground. He knew that he had not made the mental push to will himself off the ground. No one could move him and he knew it. He wondered what was going on.

"ROBBY!" he screamed to no avail. "RRROOOBBBBBYYYYY YYYY!!!!!"

More rocks were flying! Jake was almost horizontal in mid air, even though he wasn't flying on his own power at all! He was being pushed 3 feet… 4 feet… 5 feet above the ground, and he couldn't stop it!

"Put me down! Robby!" Jake screamed. "Snap out of it!! ROBBY!"

"AAARRRRRGGGGGHHHHHHH!!!!!!" Robby continued to yell at the top of his lungs.

Robby could not hear Jake calling to him. He could not control what was happening to himself. The moments seemed to creep by as the intensity of the startling psionic explosion rapidly increased. More and larger items were being lifted as Robby's control of the situation completely ebbed away.

"ROBBY!!!!!" Screamed Jake as Robby finally looked at him.

"WHAT?!?" grunted Robby in an almost angry tone.

Everything, including Jake, fell to the ground as Robby turned and ember gaze to his blood-brother. Robby, still holding his head, tried to climb to his feet, only to fall back to the ground.

"Ugh…" Jake groaned as he tumbled to the ground. Luckily he didn't feel anything. He was more concerned about Robby, who was panting on the ground, while his face was completely covered with drops of sweat. His face was completely red, and his t-shirt was soaking wet, due to the sweat.

Robby blinked his eyes in amazement. He looked around wondering what had just happened. Jake walked over to him and extended his hand to help his ailing friend off the ground.

"J-j-Jake, w-w-what h-h-happened?" asked Robby.

"I was about to ask you the same question" responded Jake.

"The last thing I remember was getting here and my head was feeling like it was going to explode" said Robby.

"Well, all I can say is that I couldn't move, then suddenly I was floating, just like the trash cans and the rocks all over the place, man…" continued Jake.

"What? Are you telling me that I was able to stop you and make you 'float'?" asked Robby.

"Absolutely! You had me flying six feet above the ground! We need to get you to the Sanctum and call dad!" exclaimed Jake.

Robby stumbled as he attempted to walk to the park bench. Jake caught him and he gently sat him down on the bench. He put his hands on Robby's knees and knelt right in front of him. He looked at Robby with genuine concern for his well being.

"Are you going to be able to teleport us home?" asked Jake.

"I don't think so, big bro. I'm feeling really weak right now..." stated Robby.

"It's OK. You don't look too good. I'll take care of the travel arrangements, bro..." Jake said in an attempt to comfort his ailing blood-brother.

Jake pulled out his cell phone and called his father. He informed him of what just transpired. Then he folded his phone shut and stored it in his pocket. He gently picked his blood-brother up and took to the skies. His blood-brother weighed nothing to him, however, Robby's well-being weighed very heavy on his mind.

Chapter 40

Jake navigated the skies carefully to get his best friend and partner in the hero realm to the Sanctum as quickly as he could. He looked down at his ailing partner. The anguish that was still apparent on Robby's face was startling to the young hero.

"Hang on bro, we are almost home. Dad will know what to do" reassured Jake.

Jake gently settled on the balcony entrance. He opened the door and speed towards the stairs. He quickly made his way to the Sanctum. He raced towards the analytical equipment. Jake then gently placed his blood-brother on the holographic scanning table.

Robby was writhing in pain. Jake could not stand idly by and watch his best friend struggle. He, in fact, did not have to watch Robby struggle, he could feel it. The bond that was forged between the two boys had created a link that allowed both kids to feel what the other was feeling. These feelings could be either of the emotional variety, or intense physical pains.

Just then the upper door to the Sanctum burst open. Dr. Knight ran quickly to the aide of the red-headed telepath. He placed his hands on Jake's shoulder to ease his tension. He walked over to the analyzing table where Robby was resting.

"Son, are you feeling alright?" asked Dr. Knight as he placed his hand in Robby's shoulder.

"My head is still killing me" replied Robby.

Dr. Knight walked over to the computer console and keyed in a sequence of commands. The table lit up with an eerie blue glow. The computer beeped to signal that its scan of Robby had been completed.

Charles glanced over the data, and compared it to the scans that were taken right after the transfusion.

"OH WOW!" bellowed Charles.

"Dad, what is it?" asked Jake

"Well there have been some major changes of the course of the past few weeks" Charles began. "Your psychic abilities are totally off the charts. I cannot believe what I am seeing here. It is totally amazing. Your mutation has further evolved and gotten stronger. It seems that you have gained another psychic related ability. You've gained telekinesis!" continued Charles.

"What is that?" inquired Robby as he bolted straight upright.

"Well, it is the ability to move objects with your mind. That is not the extent of it. These abilities are growing so strong, and so intense, I believe you have found your counterpart to Jake's plasma blasts" uttered Charles. "Basically speaking, you could use this as a high intensity discharge type weapon. It would be like unleashing all your mental ability in a focused or even bubbled burst."

"WOW! Sounds like more training for ya, bro!" Jake chuckled.

"Dr. Knight? Do you mean to tell me that I can move things with just a thought?" wondered Robby.

"Yes Robby, it seems as if the transfusion as enhanced your mental abilities, and to be honest, they are off the charts. There has never been a case of telepathy or telekinesis that has been this powerful" stated Charles.

"Wow! You got the coolest powers, bro..." Jake chuckled. "You can teleport, read minds, heal people, and now you can do this, too!"

Robby stood there in shock and awe over the revelation that Dr. Knight just leveled him with. The color in his skin completely drained. He slumped down and covered his face. He then let out a soft cold sigh.

"When will this all end?" he asked aloud.

"Bro, what's wrong?" responded Jake.

"What's wrong? You're asking me what's wrong? I am a total freak, and I am getting freakier by the minute, that's what's wrong, Jake!" grunted Robby as he gnashed his teeth in abject anger. The emotions were running so rampant within the boy; he did not notice that tables were sliding across the floor of the sanctum on their own accord.

Jake walked over and placed his hand on his friend's shoulder. "Robby, calm down before you bring the walls down, and I've told you before, you are not a freak!" reassured Jake. "Besides, look at me! Speaking of freaks! What do you think about me? I'm like overly muscular, I'm outrageously strong, and I'm the only kid in the world who can fly! How do you think that makes me feel, sometimes?"

Jake continued to comfort his worried friend as his father kept poring over the computer read-outs.

"Yeah... I guess you're right, bro..." Robby sighed. "That makes us equal..."

"If you think of yourself a freak, than I'm an even bigger freak than you are!" Jake laughed. "And, if that's the case then I guess I'll just live with being a freak for the rest of my life..."

Robby breathed a sigh of relief, hearing that from his best friend and blood-brother.

"I love my powers and I treasure my super strength! So, if people think of me as a freak, then I'm fine with that! Let them call me a freak! I still get to go out and be a hero. If that makes me a freak, then I'll be happy with that, you know?" Jake smiled.

"Yeah... I guess you're right..." Robby grinned softly. "We're both freaks, then..."

Charles cocked his head to the side and rubbed his chin, something he always did when he was concentrating on something major.

"Well it seems that your physical strength is increasing as well, and that physical strength will act as a stabilization of your mental, and teleportation powers. In essence the power drain that you used to experience will be markedly reduced" enlightened Dr. Knight.

"What do you mean?" demanded an agitated Robby McCloud.

"The data is clear son. You are becoming stronger than every single human male on this planet. With Jake and a select few others being the exception" clarified Dr. Knight.

Robby allowed a grin to creep across his face at the news he had just learned. He now felt as if he could physically be the hero that he wanted to be. He knew that Titan was the muscle man on the team, but it did not hurt to have a little more muscle of his own. He knew that Jake would help him reach his full potential when it came to the raw muscle power that he had been granted. He also was aware that Dr. Knight would be the best mentor for his mental powers. That fact was clear after the training exercises that Charles had put him through after he learned he could teleport Jake at will. Robby let his mind wander back to the day after the transfusion. He remembered the look his body had taken on and the feeling of power coursing through his veins.

"Hey, I guess I will be able to keep up with you now, Jake!" Robby snickered.

"Well, I would say that you will be able to hold your own, but never totally keep up with this!" exclaimed Jake as he flexed his mighty right arm and laughed.

Robby returned the flex and laughed in amazement as he glanced at his own arm. It had in fact grown considerably larger and denser since the transfusion. It had also gotten more defined as well. Jake looked at his blood-brother's shredded arm and shook his head in acknowledgement.

"Looking good, bro!" Jake nodded.

Dr. Knight watched his two young heroes laughing and being themselves. He was relieved that Robby had calmed down and accepted the realization that his powers were increasing. He was also happy that Robby did not condemn himself for his gifts as he had done in the beginning of the afternoon.

Robby turned his attention to Dr. Knight.

"So this weakness thing when I use my powers, is it over?" he asked.

"I don't think entirely, son. It will just take a whole lot more to exhaust you" explained Charles.

"Well that's good, I was worried about that" Robby chortled. "You're a great teacher Dr. Knight" he continued.

"Thanks. You and Jake are outstanding students" Charles grinned.

When Robby and Jake reported back to school the following morning, they met with their teachers fifteen minutes early, since they needed to find out about any class assignments they had missed from the previous day. They had missed almost three periods of class, so they knew they needed to make up the extra time.

After they got their assignments, they walked over to their first period class, when they both heard someone call out their names.

"ROBBY! JAKE!"

Both boys stopped and turned around and smiled, when they noticed Piper as she came running towards them from the other end of the hallway.

"I-I saw you guys leaving class early yesterday... I was really worried..." she said, as she turned towards Robby. "Are you alright?"

"I'm feeling much better..." Robby uttered.

"Listen, I have to get my science book out of my locker..." Jake chuckled, as he turned around and casually strolled towards his locker, which was just down the hall. He wanted to give Robby and Piper a moment of privacy.

"I was worried sick about you..." Piper whispered to Robby, as she gently rubbed her hand against his chest. "You looked so pale when you walked out of class yesterday... You looked like you were really sick or something... What was going on?"

"I had a splitting migraine..." Robby explained. "My head was killing me... I just had to get outside for a few minutes and I ended up going home..."

"Oh wow... Do you get those often?"

"I get them every now and then... I use my mind a lot..." Robby sighed. "I just learn to live with it..."

"Well, I'm glad to see you're alright..." Piper said with a sigh of relief, just as Jake came walking up to her from behind.

The group was all together for a brief moment, when the bell rang, signaling the start of the first period. The trio then made a beeline into their classrooms and they took their seats, as Mrs. Wade stepped up to the front of the class to begin her lectures.

Chapter 41

School went pretty much as it always did. Teachers were giving instruction, students steadily taking notes and preparing for the weeks upcoming test. Nothing seemed out of the ordinary today, which for the two heroes was a pleasant change of pace for them.

One of the most ironic things that happened this school year, other than the DNA bond between Robby and Jake, came in the form of Piper Brightmore. She managed to finagle her way into all but two of Robby's classes. Jake was the first to pick up on the fact that Piper was more than just friendly towards the red-headed super-hero.

Jake often had class in other rooms with other teachers, but he still shared the vast majority of classes with both Piper and Robby, and he took note of the fact that Piper and Robby were always sitting together during class.

According to school rules, all students who owned cell phones, had to keep them turned off during class times. Jake had to bend that rule a bit. He had to keep his special cell switched to vibrate in case a need arose and he was to be contacted. Today was one of those occasions.

Jake suddenly felt a slight vibration in his cargo short's pocket. Startled, he fumbled in the pocket to stop the vibration. He knew that it was never a good thing for that phone to be going off at any time. It was always requesting his presence for some reason or another, whether a disaster or a criminal on the loose, it was never a social phone call.

Jake politely raised his hand. The young man hated this one fact of his alter ego's importance to the city. He hated that he had to always run out on his class, and his class work. Making up the work was not a problem, due to his sharp intellect and lighting fast speed. He just hated that he would miss what the teachers would have to say.

"Yes, Jake?" Mrs. Wade asked him.

"Can I have a hall pass to go to the bathroom?"

Mrs. Wade took the plastic pass, which was on the desk, and held it out in front of her, as Jake ambled from his desk and hurried towards the front of the classroom. He took the pass and walked out the door. Scanning the hallway carefully for any sign of life, he dashed to the restroom at near supersonic speed.

The phone was in Jake's mighty hand before the door could securely shut behind him. He dialed his special code into the handset as he made his way to a stall at the far end of the rest room. Nervously he awaited someone to answer his call, knowing that something was amiss in the city he called home.

"Hello, Commissioner? Yes! This is Titan! A what? An eighteen-wheeler turned over on the freeway? Just outside of Washington? Blocking traffic? I'll be right there!" the boy spoke into the small cell phone.

Jake hung up the phone and closed his eyes, concentrating on Robby.

"Dude... We need to get to the freeway... A truck has overturned in the heavy fog and is blocking all traffic... Can you help me out?" Jake thought.

"I'll be right there..." Robby replied. "As soon as I can get out of class..."

Robby quickly raised his hand as well, and signaled for Mrs. Wade.

"Ma'am! Could I get a hall pass please?" he asked her.

"You too, Mr. McCloud?"

"Yes Ma'am! I have to go..."panted Robby as he danced around the desk.

"Can you wait for Mr. Knight to get back?"

"No, Mrs. Cooper... I really have to go..." Robby pleaded with her.

"Alright…" she sighed, as she handed him her only remaining hall pass.

Robby got up and took the pass from her, and then he quickly proceeded to walk out the door. As soon as he was out in the hallway, his eyes turned to black, and Robby disappeared from sight.

Robby appeared standing before his partner, Titan as he waited for him in the rest room. Instantly, he turned into Myst, right before Titan's eyes.

"OK Bro, get us to the freeway overpass! There's an overturned truck out there somewhere! We got a little bit of a situation, there also seems to be a massive fog bank that we gotta work through! I think we are gonna have to split up when we get there and scan the area!" Titan suggested to him.

"Okay… we're outta here!" Myst said, as his eyes turned black.

A fraction of a second later, both boys were standing out along the curb of the highway.

"I'll jump down there, if you fly down that way!" Myst instructed his partner, before he disappeared.

Myst teleported himself to every other mile down one stretch of the freeway, while Titan flew down the other end of the highway; going in the opposite direction. Finally, at one point, Myst saw a large concentration of cars before him. He teleported to the side of the road, where the traffic jam had started, and he gasped when he saw what had happened.

"Oh no!" he said to himself as he reached out telepathically for injuries.

Before him, he saw a massive hulking transport truck lying on its side. The truck had jack-knifed and flipped over, causing a huge pile up of passenger cars on the bridge. That was not the only cause for panic. Adorning the rear of the trailer portion of the wreckage, was a hazardous liquid placard, warning people of possible corrosive, explosive, and inhalation hazards.

Myst immediately closed his eyes and began to concentrate.

"Titan! I need your expertise here, dude! No time for you to fly, I am about to jump you here!" he thought. He focused on teleporting Titan to where he was standing, and instantly, Titan appeared out of nowhere!

"Holy smoke!" the mountain of boy-muscle gasped. "What happened here?"

"The truck must have overturned in the fog, big bro!" Myst said to him. "You gotta get it on its wheels so that the traffic can get through, and before THAT stuff spills out" he continued as he pointed to the diamond shaped warning placard.

"WOW! I gotta hurry! I am on it, bro!" Titan affirmed, as he leaped into the air.

Titan flew to the top portion of the over turned truck. He then placed his hands on the edge of the top, and gently started lifting it up. Slowly, the large eighteen wheeled time bomb began to tilt back towards its other side, so that it was resting on all of its tires. Titan leveled the truck slowly, in hopes to not agitate any of the volatile chemicals inside. He knew full well, that if he accidentally jarred them too much, the effects would be catastrophic. Finally, the truck was settled fully back on its wheels again.

Titan then flew over to the front cab of the truck gently lifting it off the ground slightly. Gritting his teeth, he began to pull the truck so that it no longer blocked any of the three lanes of traffic. Titan pulled the large truck on to the curb of the freeway, so that it was clear and safe for all to pass.

Myst sprang into action as soon as the truck had come to a complete stop. He sauntered up to the driver's door, and with a tug of inhuman strength, tore the steel door from its hinges. He quickly climbed into the cab. Myst reached out and touched the stricken man's forehead. A surge of pain swelled within the young mutant's body as he scanned the driver for injuries.

"Fractured leg, two broken ribs, and a dislocated shoulder. Man this guy is messed up" Myst thought.

"Do you need a power boost from me bro?" asked Titan out of concern.

"I think I may have this one under wraps dude, thanks for the concern though" Myst answered mentally.

Myst focused all his energy inward, and closed his eyes. The protective barrier of his gloves faded away, allowing its master to have full contact with his patient. A soft yellow aura surrounded both victim and savior. The glow grew brighter as Myst began healing the unfortunate man's wounds. One by one, the fractures began to mend, the dislocations reset, and the pain that this driver had felt, slowly dissipated like dew in the morning sun.

Myst, being sure that his patient was fully healed, slowly stepped out of the truck and back onto the pavement. He walked over and rejoined his partner, Titan. There were no audible words exchanged between the two heroes, but Myst was emotionally moved that his partner was still concerned over his well being.

Several police officers, who watched the events unfold from a distance came over and thanked both he and Myst for being there. The driver of the truck finally regained his composure and made his way over to where the officers and the two amazing boys were standing. He reached out and placed his hand on Myst's shoulder, thanking him for helping him. He then turned his attention to Titan. The burly man extended his hand to the muscular teen. The two shook hands out of appreciation and respect.

"Sir" said Myst, as he tugged on truck driver's vest.

"Yeah, kid?"

"Please be careful! Your wife and son would really have been upset if something happened to you, especially with you being so far from home" pleaded the red-headed mutant.

The concern for his family was all the rough-neck trucker could take. With a bear like grip, he pulled his guardian angel to him, and hugged him tightly. The man knew what the young boy said was the truth. What would his son have had to go through, if he would have not made it back home? What would his wife do? These questions stirred emotions deep within the heart of this "Man's man".

As soon as they were done, the boys disappeared from view, and they quickly appeared back at the restroom in school.

"We'd better change, before we miss the rest of this class again!" Robby said to Jake, as they changed from super heroes back to school kids.

Jake and Robby hurried their way down the hall and scrambled to make their way into their seats.

"OK, why is it that you two seem to always leave together? You two are worse than some girls I know" Piper whispered to Robby, the moment he sat down in his seat.

291

"It was just a pure coincidence..." Robby uttered in response.

Later on, during lunch, the sound of clanking silverware and the mass seas of voices filled the cafeteria. The TV sets were on, and the mid day news broadcast had just started. Today the main topic of conversation on the show was reporting on the traffic accident, which had just taken place on the highway during the past hour. Many camera feeds showed Titan, removing the large, overturned truck from the roadway and Myst healing the driver of the truck.

"That's peculiar..." Piper wondered. "This had happened around the same time, when Jake and Robby had left the classroom... While they were gone, Titan and Myst appeared...Could it be...?" Piper started to suspect something about Robby and Jake.

After school was over, Jake, Robby, and Madison had met up and started walking towards the gate, when Piper walked up to them.

"Hey, Jake... Can I talk to you for a moment?" she asked him.

"Sure..." he said. "Why don't you guys walk home...? I'll meet up with you later..."

Madison and Robby continued to walk home as Jake stayed behind to talk to Piper.

"What's going on?" he asked her.

"Listen, Jake... What's going on with you and Robby?" she asked him. "You guys keep on missing class at the same time. Robby keeps on getting sick all the time. What's the deal?"

"Well... He just keeps on getting these migraines, and since I live right next door to him, I bring him home in case I see it getting really bad, you know?" Jake explained to her. "I happen to know his parents really well, plus I live right next door and I know where they keep the key to their house. That's all..."

"Okay... The reason I ask is, Well..." she sighed. "I kinda like Robby, and I'm really concerned about him, you know?"

"WOW! He's a really lucky guy!" Jake shrugged.

"Be honest, Jake..." Piper said in a serious tone of voice. "Is he seeing anyone else?"

"Not as far as I know!" Jake said, as he shook his head.

"Oh good.... What a relief..." she grinned.

"You must really like him, huh?"

"Yeah... I figured he hangs out with you a lot, so you'd know for sure..." she smiled.

"Well, he's free! I can assure you!"

"Thanks, big guy..." Piper winked. "And, Jake... Don't spend so much time in the gym. Go out now and then. That way, you might also get a girlfriend, one of these days, you know?" Piper said, as she started to walk away.

Jake just looked down at his muscular body.

"Time in the gym? Is it that obvious?" he wondered. Then, he slowly started to make his way home.

Chapter 42

School proved to be a challenge for Robby the next day. He was excited at the fact that he had developed such a cool new ability. All throughout the day he had been playing around with Jake, while using his power. Jake would reach for a pencil, as it would mysteriously fly off his desk. Jake looked over at Robby and cut him a sly smirk.

Piper Brightmore, the object of Robby's affectionate eye glanced over at the two best friends and gave them a strange look. She had wondered for weeks what was up with the two friends. She returned her attention to the front of the class and the teacher.

Mrs. Wade walked towards the chalk board. She reached out for the eraser, when it suddenly leapt off the rail and across the front of the room. Jake shot Robby a knowing look as the duo erupted in laughter. The whole class looked at them with odd expressions upon their faces.

The bell could not have ringed fast enough for Jake and Robby. They made their way out of the school and down the sidewalk. Just then Jake's private cell phone rang. The police chief wanted to have a word with him. He glanced around and saw that no one was there, so he changed into his costume at super speed.

Jake handed his backpack to Madison and took to the sky. Madison and Robby continued to walk towards their respective residences. The youngest Knight boy chatted exuberantly with Robby about school and the computer classes that he was taking.

Off in the distance Robby sensed someone in danger. He turned his attention to the direction of the fear that he was feeling. He noticed a young kid skating down the street, completely out of control. He also saw a car racing towards the intersection, unaware of the kid on the skate board.

Robby instinctively activated his telekinesis. His eyes turned coal black as he mentally pulled the kid out of harm's way. Robby was amazed that he could focus his new ability so soon. He realized that it was totally out of instinct. He glanced around to see if anyone had caught him in the act.

Piper had been walking towards the Ice House ice cream shop, when she noticed the one boy that made her heart flutter. She stopped dead in her tracks when she witnessed Robby perform a veritable miracle. Her jaw fell agape as she came to the realization that Robby McCloud may in fact be the hero that she was so infatuated with, Myst.

The next afternoon after school, Piper caught up with Jake. She asked to talk to him alone again. The pair walked off to the picnic tables and found a seat. Jake wondered what was going on with her as she sat nervously across from him.

"So what's up Piper?" inquired Jake.

"Well I asked you here to find out a few things" stated Piper.

"Like what?"

"Well as you may know, I really like Robby. I was wondering if he was seeing anyone" she probed.

"I told you yesterday Piper, he is very single" replied Jake.

Piper beamed with happiness at that news. She had fallen for the red-headed hero the second he graced JFK Middle School with his presence. He stole her heart with his light dusting of freckles across the bridge of his nose and cheeks, his bright green eyes, and his brilliant red hair. She was totally entranced by this boy and was happy to know that she may have a chance with him.

"Well that is good, but I saw something yesterday that made me wonder about him" said Piper.

"What are you talking about Piper?" asked Jake.

"OK OK, I think Robby is that super-hero kid, Myst" exclaimed Piper

"WHAT?!?" returned Jake.

"I saw him snatch a kid out of the way of a car, like with some weird power" admitted Piper.

"OK, Lemme get this right, You think Robby McCloud, Mr. Migraine, is Myst? Yeah I'll believe that when I can fly!" joked Jake.

"Jake, I'm serious" argued Piper.

Jake knew that he had to cover for his blood-brother. He knew what Robby would think if he found out anyone knew his secret. He thought for a split second and tried to ease Piper's thoughts.

"Piper, if Robby can move things with his mind, I think, being his best friend, I would be the first to know about that one" laughed Jake.

Piper slugged Jake in the right pectoral muscle. She recoiled in pain as her fist made contact with solid matter. Jake winced in fake pain to cover the fact that he was in fact Titan. He had to come up with something good to get out of this conversation. He mentally called to Robby and requested him to call his cell phone in two minutes.

"Jake it is not funny, I would not think anything bad of Robby if he was Myst" added Piper.

"Look, Robby is a baseball player. The only power he has is the ability to hit anything thrown at him" retorted Jake with a grin.

Just then Jake's cell phone rang. He fumbled in his pocket and pulled it out. He quickly answered it and gave a complete one sided conversation. He then got up and attempted to excuse himself from the table and Piper.

"Piper, I am sorry, but I have got to get home" stated Jake.

"OK! Please don't tell Robby about this. I want to go out with him Jake, not scare him off" pleaded Piper.

"I don't think this will scare him off!" chuckled Jake.

"Well, I really need to get going…" Jake sighed, as he began to walk home. "See ya later!"

"See you, Jake…" Piper said, as she hopped on her bike and began to pedal on her way home.

She had not pedaled for even ten minutes, when she began to smell smoke. She then looked up and spotted a cloud of black smoke coming from a small building, which was down the street from her house. She came closer, and noticed a small crowd of people gathering in front of a pediatrician's office, which was on fire.

People had to move out of the way as quickly as possible when two fire engines and two police cars and an ambulance pulled up. Right away, people were wondering, if there were any children trapped inside of the burning building?

Suddenly, several kids were running out the back door, followed by Myst and Titan! The two teen heroes were already on the scene, and they had gotten all the kids out of the building in the nick of time.

Two kids were in wheelchairs, but Titan practically lifted them up and flew them out of the building, one by one. Myst had teleported the rest of the inhabitants of the physician's office to safety in a matter of seconds.

Several police officers and doctors attended the children, just to make sure that they were alright, while the firemen took care of the flames. Luckily the roof had caught on fire, due to an electrical short, and the firemen were able to put it out in about fifteen minutes.

The police officers and firemen took time to chat with Myst and Titan for a few minutes until most of the crowd had dispersed. There lingering in the background was a familiar face to the teen heroes. Piper Brightmore stood looking on as Washington's mightiest beings saved the day once again.

When the police and fire personnel left, she walked up to the two super heroes and started to talk to Myst. Piper leaned in slightly to Myst's right ear. "So when were you gonna tell me that you were Myst, Robby?" whispered Piper.

Myst's jaw dropped and his face went flush. Myst turned and glanced at Titan, who just shrugged his shoulders at his blood-brother.

"Miss, what are you talking about?" evaded Myst.

"Myst, please trust me" she pleaded.

"Can you hold on for just a second?" asked Myst.

He turned to Titan and pulled him into the alleyway. They walked over to the curb and Myst sat down. He placed his head into his hands and heaved a heavy sigh.

"Robby, look I know what you are thinking. I did not tell her anything. I promise bro" stammered Jake.

"Then how did she figure it out?" asked the worried red-headed super-hero.

"I am not stupid Robby" whispered Piper as she walked around the corner and sat down next to the hero.

"Hey, I am gonna go make sure that all the loose ends are tied up at the clinic, and let you guys talk" offered Titan as he walked quickly out of sight.

Piper put her arm around the perplexed hero as he sat there in fear of what to tell her. All she was after was the truth and the affections of his heart. Myst was so nervous that he did not even use his powers to find out what Piper was up to.

"Look, I just put two and two together, Robby. You and Jake are always leaving school together, and then Myst and Titan show up nearby" she stated.

"But I was so careful, if this gets out, my father is going to kill me" Robby whimpered quietly.

"Robert McCloud, don't you get it, and for someone who can read thoughts and emotions like you can, I am surprised that you have not picked up on this" said Piper.

"Picked up on what?" he asked nervously.

She leaned in and kissed him gently on his cheek. "I like you silly, I really like you" giggled Piper as Robby's cheeks blushed to match his hair.

"You wha-...what?" stuttered Robby.

"HA HA! For a super-hero you are really slow. I am in love with you, Robby" admitted Piper as she took her turn to blush.

"Really?" asked Robby.

"Yes! That is why I always sat next to you, and kept asking Jake about you. I have been dropping hints since the first day of school" said Piper.

"WOW! I am sorry!" said Robby. "I have to admit, I like you too. Every time you come in the room, it is like my heart jumps out of my chest" he continued.

"Please believe me, your secret is safe with me, and so is Jake's. Do not worry about that, I care about you too much to let anything get out about your secret" smiled Piper.

"Well in that case, I guess there is only one thing left to do" whispered Robby.

"OK, what's that?" inquired Piper.

"Piper, will you go out with me?" stammered Robby under his breath.

"YES!" she squealed as she threw her arms around the young hero's neck and kissed him on the cheek.

"Way to go brother!" Robby heard Jake exclaim within his mind.

"You can stop eavesdropping and get over here" Myst chuckled.

"So, what's the verdict, guys?" Titan asked.

"Well Piper and I are going out now!" exclaimed a relieved Myst.

"Cool! Congrats guys!" cheered Titan.

Myst got to his feet and grabbed Piper by the shoulders. He concentrated as he looked deep within Piper's dark brown eyes. His eyes shifted from green to jet black, this time it was the first time starring into his new girlfriend's eyes. The trio vanished in a cloud of mist, only to reappear at a quiet park on the edge of town.

"That was amazing Robby!" squealed Piper.

Myst concentrated, as his costume faded away into his street clothes. Then Robby concentrated on Titan, and he was surrounded by a cloud of mist. When the cloud disappeared, he was wearing his street clothes, and he looked like Jake Knight once again. Jake then walked away for a few minutes to let the new couple cement their relationship further.

"Robby, I think I can help you guys out a little bit" stated Piper out of the blue.

"What do you mean?" asked Robby with bewilderment.

"Look, I know that Madison has wanted to be a part of the team. I think that he and I can devise a system to keep you guys informed of what is going on when you are out on your patrols or whatever" continued Piper.

Robby thought about it for a moment. "Piper, there is no way I can put you in danger" he said as he put his arm around her shoulder and sat with her on the top of the picnic table.

"Robby, we are not gonna be in the spotlight, baby. Madison and I will be working the police scanners and computers, chasing leads..."

"Oh! I get it, you two will be playing detective, while Jake and I are playing 'good cop/bad cop'."

"Yeah! Now you got it! We will be your information gathering team. What ya think?" she asked.

"Let me talk it over with Jake, just to get his opinion" he said as he hugged her.

"Deal!" replied Piper as she returned his hug with a long embrace of her own.

Robby quickly walked a few yards over to the large fishing pond, where Jake was standing. He was quietly admiring the kids, who were casting their lines into the pond, when Robby approached him from behind.

"Dude! We're going out! She's so cool! She can help us!" Robby said excitedly. Then he quieted down, as he realized that Jake had suddenly become a bit sad. Robby noticed right away what was going on.

"Hey man... If you miss Genny, then you need to fly down to Arizona and you need to look her up, you know? You haven't seen her in over six years!" Robby whispered to him.

"I'm scared... What if she doesn't remember me?" Jake wondered.

"You'll never know unless you try... You rescued her cat, which has the same name as you...and you are TITAN for crying out loud..... you are on every television in the civilized world.... She'll remember you!" Robby assured him.

Just then Piper joined in on the conversation.

"What's going on?" she asked Jake, with a smile on her face.

"Just seeing you reminds me of a girl I met six years ago in Arizona..." Jake explained. "I kinda miss her right now. She lived in Diablo Rojo and I met her on the day when I first became Titan..."

"That's interesting..." Piper laughed. "I have family living in Diablo Rojo. I have an aunt who lives there and a few distant cousins. It's a very small community, so who knows, I might be related to her!"

"Maybe you should look her up again?" Robby said to him. "I think that now's as good of a time as any to pay her a visit!"

"Let me do that. Then the next time I see her, I'll have you teleport us over here, okay?" Jake suggested. "I don't want to rush it…"

Both Robby and Piper just smiled as Jake turned around and started to walk away.

Robby then teleported Jake into the restroom, which was in a building nearby, where he changed back into his Titan costume. He brought his clothes along in a plastic bag, so he could change back. Thanking his blood-brother for the inspiration to go see his long lost friend, he waved and took to the sky. He aimed his mighty form towards the great state of Arizona, hoping that he would not be disappointed.

"Stop thinking like that Jake" whispered Robby, trying to comfort the nervous powerhouse.

Chapter 43

Instantly, Jake was flying over the desert of Arizona. He realized it when he saw the landscape change below him. His blood-brother had helped him out by teleporting him to the Grand Canyon State while he was flying, so he could get there even faster.

"Awesome! I'm here already!" Titan thought to himself, as he prepared to make his descent in Diablo Rojo. Titan decided to land first and then change back in his street clothes, so he won't startle Genny too much. Then, he would tell her his true identity.

Genny stood outside in the middle of the fenced-in, vast back yard, overlooking all the plants and flowers that her mother had planted for her. Her mother loved plants, and it was Genny's task to water them every afternoon. She really didn't mind, however, it was a welcome break from studying. The yard had a tall, wooden fence, so nobody could see her or bother her while she watered the plants.

She had just left the end of the garden hose in one of the potted plants and walked over to turn off the faucet, when she heard a faint noise behind her. Then came that faint, familiar voice.

"Hi Genny!"

Startled, Genny turned around and gasped. Right in front of her was a boy with big blue eyes, brown hair, and a wide grin on his face. He wore a baggy long-sleeve shirt and baggy pants. He was about thirteen years old, and he stood maybe an inch taller than her. She couldn't really tell, because of the baggy clothes, but she guessed that the boy must have been very athletic since they were so wide.

"Remember me? I'm Jake… I rescued your cat from a tree a few years ago…" the boy added.

"Jake?" she wondered. "What… What are you doing here? How did you get here?"

"Oh… I just wanted to come over and say hi… Just like I promised last time I saw you… Do you remember?" Jake asked her.

"Of course! You had rescued Jakie, my cat! That was the first time we had met! My goodness, that must have been over six years ago!" she exclaimed, as she slowly walked closer to him, while examining him from head to toe.

"Oh wow, you've gotten bigger…" she whispered. "A lot bigger!"

"Well… You look the same, but older…" Jake smiled. "You're just as pretty as the first day we met…"

She blushed for a brief moment, before her facial expression turned serious again.

"So, how did you get here? Are you here all alone?" she asked.

"Well…" Jake sighed. "I flew…"

"Really? Where did you come from?"

"Washington…" he responded in all honesty. He decided to be perfectly honest with her.

"Washington?" she repeated in a false tone. "Up north?"

"No… Washington D.C." he said, clarifying that he came from the nation's capital.

Genny stared at Jake in complete disbelief.

"You mean… You came all the way out here, all by yourself… You came from Washington D.C. just to say hi to me? And, you flew in an airplane?" she wondered out loud.

"Genny… I didn't say I came on an airplane…"

"Jake… None of this is making any sense to me!" she said angrily. "Washington D.C is over two-thousand miles away from here! When did you leave there to come over here?"

"Ummm… I left home about five minutes ago…" Jake said sadly.

"What?" she gasped.

"It only took me five minutes to get here… You have got to believe me, Genny…" Jake said calmly.

"Jake! Either you're the biggest liar, or…-" Genny shouted at him, before Jake cut her off.

"Genny! Have you ever heard of Titan?" he asked her.

"Titan?"

"Yeah... You know? The super-hero?" Jake wondered.

"Of course! Who hasn't heard of Titan? He's just the coolest kid ever! And he is like on EVERY TV station and magazine cover" she pondered out loud. "But, what does that have to do with you?"

"Well... Can I tell you a secret?" Jake asked her sheepishly.

Genny walked closer to him and turned her head so that her ear was close to his lips.

"Whisper it in my ear..." she said in a soft voice.

"Okay... here goes..." Jake whispered. "I'm Titan..."

She pulled away and stared at him with a grin on her face.

"That's really good, Jake..." she laughed. "Do you really expect me to believe that?"

Jake looked around and smiled when he saw that the entire yard was fenced in and that they were surrounded by the wooden fence which stood over six feet tall. Nobody else was home, and nobody from the outside could see the two kids standing in the back yard. He quickly pulled the baggy sweater over his head and took it off, revealing his red Titan suit and his muscular physique.

"Umm! Oh God...What is....I mean what is going on..." Genny gasped, as her mouth dropped wide open. "Y-y-you're not joking, are you?"

"No... How do you think I got here from Washington D.C in only 5 minutes without taking a plane?" Jake chuckled.

"No wonder you rescued my cat that day... And no wonder you can come here all by yourself... You just fly on your own..." she said, in complete amazement.

Jake allowed his body to rise just three inches off the ground; just enough, so she could see that he was flying.

"OK now you believe me, right?" as he pointed down at the gap between his feet and the ground.

"Oh wow!" Genny said. "You... You ARE Titan! That... That is so cool!"

"I-I hope we can still be friends..." Jake said sadly.

"Are you kidding me?" Genny said, as she walked closer to him and rested her hands on his shoulders. "I think it's really cool to be friends with the mighty Titan... I have a sticker on one of my notebooks with your picture on it, you know?"

"Really?"

"Yeah... A friend gave it to me!"

"Well, I hope you understand that it's a secret and I really need it to stay that way..." Jake asked her.

"Don't worry... I won't tell anybody..." she assured him. "I just have one question... Should I call you 'Jake', or do I call you 'Titan' right now?"

"When we're alone, and I'm wearing this uniform, you can call me 'Jake'. But when other people are around, please call me 'Titan', alright?" the young hero asked her.

"Wow... This is so cool..." she grinned, as she continued to stare at the floating boy. "Listen, would you like to come inside? Do you want something to drink?"

"Sure!" he said, as he landed on the floor and followed her into the house. She led him into the kitchen, where she quickly poured them two glasses of orange juice, while he removed his jeans as well. He figured he might as well stay in his Titan uniform now, since he had to fly back home anyway.

"I'm so glad you remembered me, Jake!" she continued. "I just hope you won't leave here and stay away again for another six years before you come back again!"

"I won't!" he promised her. "Let me give you my e-mail address, so we can stay in touch..."

Jake wrote down his e-mail address in her notebook and she gave him her address in return. They vowed to remain in touch this time, and to keep on writing each other on a regular basis. Both teens had extremely mixed emotions running though them at that very moment.

"Next time I come over, I'll take you flying, if you want that, okay?" Jake said to her.

"Oh wow! Well, maybe we should do that over the summertime, when it's not too cold outside, especially at night. It's just way too cold now..." she reasoned. "But, I'd love to go flying with you!"

"It's a deal, then! We'll keep in touch, and I'll take you flying next time I come over, if you're not feeling too cold..."

"Do you have to go already?" Genny wondered, since Jake had gotten up from the chair.

"Yeah… But, I could be back as early as next week, if you like!" he said excitedly. "I'll e-mail you as soon as I get home! How does that sound?"

"Sure! I'll go turn on my laptop right now!" she said.

When she returned a few moments later, she noticed that Jake had been waiting patiently for her in the back yard, holding a plastic bag which contained his clothes. A saddened look made its way across both of their faces.

"Okay, Genny… I gotta fly back home again…" he said to her sadly. "But, I'll be back… Just e-mail me…"

She walked up to him and kissed him on his forehead.

"I got to kiss Titan…" she giggled. "You're a true hottie, you know that?"

"Well, thanks…" Jake said, as he blushed a bit. "But nothing compared to the beautiful girl in front of me!"

Jake slowly started to rise up off the ground. Then he blew her a kiss and flashed a pearly white smile.

"I'm on my way to Washington. I'll e-mail you as soon as I get home!" he smiled at her. "See ya next time!"

"Bye, Jake! Thanks for stopping by!" she said, as she looked up and waved at him.

Then Jake circled around the yard, while waving at her, before he shot straight up into the air, before flashing straight heading east at high speed. He was gone in a second.

For Genny, it almost seemed like a dream. Did she just get a visit from Titan? When she walked into the kitchen, it dawned on her that the boy was real, and that Titan had in fact just visited her. Then, she walked into her bedroom, and she launched her e-mail application on her laptop computer.

As soon as the program had displayed on her screen, she logged on and checked her e-mails. She read through her oldest e-mails first, and she replied to a few of them, while she deleted a dozen messages, which she had considered as spam. Then she sent an e-mail to a friend and she read two others. When she was all done, she was about to close the application, when the laptop beeped, indicating that a new messaged had arrived.

As she looked at the contents of her Inbox, she gasped when she read the name of the sender. It was from Jake Knight.

"Oh wow! It's him! He's home already! It's an e-mail from Jake!"

Then she proceeded to read the message.

It read: "Dear Genny: Thanks for tonight! I'm sorry for not visiting any sooner, but I've been really busy doing my hero-stuff. I hope you understand! I wanted to thank you for making me feel almost normal again. I have never had the chance to just be ME in a long time. Thanks so much for that. Anyway, let me know how you're doing and please let me know when it's a good day for me to come see you again! Already missing you, Jake!"

She just smiled as she wrote her reply. She was just happy that her best friend from Washington D.C. was none other than Titan! When will she see him again?

Meanwhile, Jake was back in his bedroom. He was feeling much better now, since he had seen Genny again. Robby noticed it too, and he felt it right away.

"I'm really glad to see that you're feeling better!" Jake heard Robby's voice ringing in his ears, while Jake was sitting at his desk. He had just typed the e-mail to Genny, and he was just surfing the web on his laptop. In fact, he was still wearing his Titan costume. He was so excited, that he had completely forgotten to change clothes.

"She remembered me!" Jake said out loud. "After all these years, she still remembered me! But I had to tell her my secret as well..." he sighed.

"Don't worry, dude... she likes you, she'll keep quiet..." Robby assured him. "Just like Piper will do it for me..."

"I'll fly back there and visit her next week... I promised..." Jake said with a smile, as he finally got up and removed his costume.

Then Jake and Madison had a late dinner and got ready for bed. Jake stripped down to his boxers and pulled on a loose fitting t-shirt and went to sleep. Jake woke up a few hours later and went on his night patrol over the city, while he allowed Madison to sleep during the remainder of the night.

Chapter 44

Several days had passed during what started out as a quiet week for Jake, until a tornado struck a small town in central Tennessee. Jake had donned his Titan costume, while Robby flashed his Myst costume on and the duo flew over to the stricken area, where several homes and businesses had been destroyed. Luckily, people from neighboring communities had donated food, clothing and building materials and supplies to the fallen community, so that new construction could begin almost immediately. They were just waiting for the construction crews to arrive at the scene.

Since Jake realized how desperate these people were and how much they needed their homes and businesses back, he felt the need to stay there and help out as well. Using his amazing powers, he began to rebuild several buildings, under the guidance of the former owners, who used to live in the buildings that were destroyed. They showed Jake pictures of what the old buildings looked like, and Jake was able to rebuild these structures for them in a matter of hours while they looked on as Jake worked tirelessly on the homes, Robby provided much needed medical aid to the stricken area.

About four days after the tornado had struck; Jake had completely rebuilt the town. Robby teleported himself and the drained Titan back to Washington DC to get some rest and see his family. Robby popped in and out to assist, because his parents, not knowing that he was in fact Myst, would have gotten in hot water. Jake could afford to stay and help and the thankful people of Tennessee let Jake stay with them, as Titan, and they provided him food and shelter while he rebuilt their homes and businesses.

As soon as he got back, he was happy to see that he had received an e-mail from Genny! She was patiently waiting for him in Diablo Rojo, and she was wondering when he was going to return to pay her a visit. He e-mailed her back and asked if now would be a good time for him to come visit. To his great surprise, he got a reply from her within ten minutes.

Excitedly, Jake dashed towards the balcony and leaped into the air. He soared across the sky at top speed and reached the small community of Diablo Rojo in a matter of minutes. Once he found her street, he grinned when he spotted her watering her aunt's many potted plants, which were standing in the fenced back yard of their house.

Genny had just turned around, when she spotted the flying boy circling overhead. Her mouth dropped wide open, as she dropped the garden hose and began to cheer, at the sight of her hero. Then, the flying muscular boy slowed and landed right before her, in the center of her back yard, touching down with his white boots just a few feet in front of her.

"Hey there, Muscles!" she giggled, as she ran up to him to embrace Titan.

Titan just grinned, as he was overcome with joy as he got to see the young girl who stole his heart once again.

"How are you, Genny?" he said to her. "It's so good to see you!"

The boy and the girl just embrace one another for a moment, until they pulled away so they could stare one another in the face.

"So, why did you call me 'Muscles'?" he wondered.

"Well... I think that's a good nickname for you..." she replied. "After all, you're the most muscular guy I know!"

Jake began to blush as Genny smiled at him for a few moments.

"Hey why don't we go inside, I need to finish packing for a trip..." she said to him.

Genny and her aunt offered Jake something to eat and to drink, before the two teens walked back out in the yard again. Genny knew that she was going to be in Washington DC for the weekend, just to see how she would like it there. Jake had already told her about Robby and Piper, and he was dying to introduce her to them.

"Okay, are you ready?" he said to her. "I'm going to concentrate on Robby and let him know that he can teleport us. In the meantime, hold on to your bag with one hand, and hold my arm with your other hand and don't let go!"

Instantly, Jake and Genny disappeared from the garden and they reappeared again in Jake's bedroom, where Robby, Madison and Piper were waiting to meet them.

"Hey everybody, this is Genny!" Jake said, as he introduced Genny to the others.

Piper and Genny immediately hit it off, as they started asking about who their parents were. Robby and Madison walked up and greeted Genny as well, but Robby needed to sit down and rest for a moment after teleporting them from so far away.

"Jake! Piper and I are actually third cousins! Can you believe that?" Genny said to him.

"Say what?" both Jake and Robby replied in disbelief.

"Well, it seems that my aunt is a sister of my dad... So we're related!" Genny said excitedly.

"I knew we were related somehow, when Jake mentioned to me that he was going to Diablo Rojo! I know that town and my dad had mentioned to me before that I had relatives who were living there..." Piper added.

"Yeah... So, now I have even more reason to come over to Washington and to visit you guys, and to see Muscles..." Genny said, as she turned towards Jake.

All four of them, including Madison, burst out in laughing.

"Muscles?" Robby chuckled.

"Oh brother..." Jake sighed, as he rolled his eyes.

"New nickname, huh?" Madison chuckled. "So, where are we gonna teleport you to next, Muscles?"

"Alright Red, Maddie... You guys finally have a nickname for me now..." Jake sighed.

"We were gonna call you 'Fly-boy', but 'Muscles' sounds better!" Madison chuckled.

"Yeah, especially since your 'girlfriend' is the one who came up with it!" Robby laughed.

All five of them walked out of the back room and into the living room, where Jake introduced Genny to his parents.

"Dad! This is Genny! I just brought her over from Arizona!" Jake said, as he introduced her to his father. "Genny this is my dad, Dr. Charles Knight."

"Well hello Genny!" Charles said, as he quickly got up from his chair to shake the girl's hand. "I'm Charles, I'm Jake's father. It's a pleasure to meet you," winking back at Jake.

"Nice to meet you Dr. Knight!" Genny said. Then Piper took her by the arm and decided to show her around the rest of the house, where she started off by taking her to the kitchen, where Nancy was busy cooking dinner. Piper and Genny started talking to her, while Charles pulled Jake and Robby aside.

"So, do both girls know your secret identities already?" Charles whispered to the boys.

Obviously they must have known, since Jake was still in his Titan costume.

"Piper figured it out on her own, Jake..." Robby replied softly. "She's like a detective! I think she wants to help us fight crimes and track down the bad guys..."

"Well, I had to tell Genny my secret..." Jake sighed. "It got really hard lying to her about how I ended up getting from Washington to Arizona. Plus, I had to explain the flying bit to her, so it was the easiest way out..."

"They both promised that they will keep our secrets safe from everybody else, Bro..." Robby assured him.

"Oh, well that is good to know!" the elder sighed. "I was getting worried for a moment..."

A few moments later, Piper and Genny came walking back from the kitchen.

"Genny can stay with me for a few days... Besides, we're family!" Piper announced.

"Piper is going to show me around the town tomorrow..." Genny added excitedly. "Being in a big city is so much more exciting than living in a small town... I'm so tired of living in the desert! I might just end up moving over here, if I really like it here a lot!"

"Wow!" both boys exclaimed.

Genny then walked up to Jake and rested her hand on Jake's shoulder. "Then I'll be closer to Muscles here so he won't have to fly so far away in order to see me!" she whispered to him.

"Oh… Genny… "Jake blushed a bit.

"Muscles?" Charles wondered out loud.

"New nickname for me…" his son whispered back. "It's kinda obvious how she came up with that, huh?"

Jake and Genny then walked into the family's Game room, while Piper and Robby teleported to the park to enjoy a much needed break from the past few days. The two couples talked it up and got to know one another better as the moments passed.

As Robby and Piper reemerged in the park, they found a quiet bench and sat down. There had been no time in the past few days for the budding couple to actually sit down and get to know one another better. Robby reached over and took Piper's hand.

"You really amaze me, Piper" admitted Robby honestly.

"What do you mean?" she questioned.

"Well, you found me out, you actually learned who I am, and I let you" retorted Robby.

"Let?"

"Yeah, seeing as though you have done your research, you know that I have a very powerful control over the human mind. I can make people think whatever I really want them to. Now I choose not to use that a lot, because I do not think it is right. I only use it if it protects the person from further harm, or my identity. But you are different" he explained.

"How am I different?" She asked abruptly.

"Well, you told me how much you liked me, and I never got the chance to tell you my side" he began.

"Your side? This should be good. I can't wait to hear this" giggled Piper.

"Yeah, well I have liked you since the first day of school. I was just too chicken to come and tell you, so I avoided it all together" continued Robby.

"You avoided it….ROBERT MCCLOUD!!!! What were you thinking?" prodded Piper.

312

"Well I really wasn't thinking. I was only trying to keep to myself" replied Robby.

"You opened up to Jake, though."

"He is Titan, Piper, he is my hero and I wanted to work with him, and I did not open up, we sort of discovered each other accidently, but he can never be what you are to me, Piper" he said as he reached over and touched her cheek softly.

Piper returned the affection, and closed her eyes. She could not stay mad at the red-headed super-hero. She knew that she loved this boy with everything that she had in her being. She also knew that Robby knew that little bit of information as well with his telepathy and empathy.

Chapter 45

That weekend, Genny and Piper spent some time together while Piper showed her around the city. Genny obviously loved being in Washington, so it came as no surprise that she decided that she was going to come back the following weekend and had contemplated moving in with Piper. After all, Piper's family had an extra bedroom in their house, and was more than happy to let Genny stay with her. All that was left to be done, was for Jake to take Genny back to Arizona, so that she could pack for the trip the following weekend, and discuss her options with her parents.

That Sunday, Robby teleported Jake and Genny back to her home in Diablo Rojo, so that he didn't have to fly her over that long distance. Once they had arrived at the house, she immediately started packing, and Jake helped put together a few empty boxes for her.

"I'm going to fly to Nevada for a few minutes, before I come back, alright?" he said to her.

He wanted to visit Zhango-Rhe for a few minutes, since he was in the area. He took off from Diablo Rojo and made the short flight to the Nevada desert, where he landed at the familiar dig site, where the mysterious space ship was buried in the underground cavern.

The moment Jake landed; he quickly walked into the cavern, which was completely dark. Luckily for him, he was able to find his way around, thanks to his infrared vision. When he came to the ship, the blue light at the front of the small spacecraft lit up, and the familiar voice began to speak to him.

"Greetings, mighty Titan…" Zhango-Rhe said to the boy.

"Hi Zhango-Rhe… I just wanted to stop in and say hi…"

"Titan, I'm glad to see you here, but I'm afraid it might be the last time. The enemy is close at hand. You must be ready to face him. He is very powerful and extremely dangerous, and he is very ruthless. His name is Thadius Malcolm and he is out to destroy everything and anyone that will stand in his way. He was the one that I spoke of that destroyed my home world, and now he has come to destroy the planet Earth as well. You are the only person right now who can stop him. Do you understand that?" Zhango-Rhe explained to him in a serious tone of voice.

"Well... I have my blood-brother Robby, who is Myst... He's helping me now..." Titan added. "Thank goodness I don't have to face him alone..."

"Blood-brother? What is this, Titan?" questioned Zhango-Rhe.

"Oh, I forgot to mention that I had to save his life by giving up some of my blood to him" smiled Titan.

"So this human...." he began.

"Mutant" corrected Titan.

"So this Mutant is now part Zyrtonian?" asked Zhango-Rhe.

"Well, according to my dad, he is about one-half Zyrtonian now. He is stronger than any boy his age, not much can hurt him, and we share this really cool mental link as well. Not to mention he can teleport me everywhere. So it looks like I won't have to face this dude alone, huh?"

"No, and you have your father, who has all my wisdom and knowledge as well. Make sure you ask him a lot of questions, Titan. Soon, I won't be around much longer..."

"Why not? Are you leaving?"

"I must self destruct before my ship falls into enemy hands. I cannot afford for that to happen. Earth may not fall to Malcolm the way Zyrton did, do you understand that, Titan? With your father and Myst by your side, and with all your strength and powers, you will have all the weapons you need to fight Malcolm and to prevent him from turning Earth into a barren wasteland!"

"A barren wasteland?" Titan wondered.

"Malcolm will use alien genetic technology to create an army of creatures, zombies or robots or anything his evil mind could devise, to destroy the earth and everyone on it. His goal is to rob the planet of all its natural resources. He is nothing more than a space pirate or a strip miner. And when he is done with one continent, he will abandon it, and move on until it is bled dry, like a wasted world in space. You must prevent this from happening at all costs!"

"Oh, wow..." Titan gasped.

"I'm sorry that my last conversation with you must be so serious, my young hero, but you must understand that I believed that he had perished in battle while fighting me. Unfortunately, it appears that is not the case. Now, I must pass on this battle to you, my young Titan, and I'm encouraged to see that you've been a great hero so far."

"Well, I've received a lot of help from my parents and from my friends. Plus I have Myst and Genny..."

"Genny?" Zhango-Rhe asked.

"She's a girl. I like her... a little... I met her the day you gave me my powers..." Titan said shyly.

"Having friends and being surrounded by those you care about is good for your soul, my boy. Be warned, for Malcolm is very ruthless, and he will use those that you care about to his advantage. Take good care of them; be strong for them, and protect them. You're the one people will look up to. You will be the mighty one; people will look for, when the city will come under siege. Be wise, and never give up. Never fight any battle on your own! And remember, Malcolm may seem very strong, but you can and always will find a way to be stronger than him!"

"I will... I will always remember that, Zhango-Rhe... I promise!" Titan replied confidently.

"Thank you, Titan. I must shut down now. This vessel has very little power is left. The enemy is close at hand. Agents of Malcolm have been roaming all around this place, looking for the entrance to this cavern. I cannot allow them to get too close to me. If they do, I must initiate a self-destruct sequence. Watch for the one called MACH, his is not what he seems, he has a soul, I have felt it. Malcolm, all but destroyed that being's spirit. Look to him Titan. So, I'm afraid that this is farewell, my dear Titan..."

Tears started rolling from Titan's eyes as he heard Zhango-Rhe's final, desperate words.

"G-Goodbye, Zhango-Rhe" Titan sobbed. "…and thank you for giving me this gift…."

A few seconds passed before the blue light faded for the final time, leaving Titan standing in complete darkness. Even though he had been in this situation before, somehow this was different. In the past, he knew he could always come back. This time, however, he knew he would never hear that voice from the ship again. In this place was where it all began. This was where he became Titan; this is the ship that gave him his wonderful powers and his phenomenal, unlimited strength, and now, the ship's brain was gone. For the first time since he gained his powers, he felt totally alone. Even with Robby's connection to him, he felt very lost and alone.

"Z-Zhango-Rhe…" Titan sobbed, as he walked up to the ship and fell to his knees. "Come back… Please come back!!! I can't do this without you Zhango!!!!"

Suddenly, he felt a void creep within his soul. It was almost as if he lost his best friend. After all, he had inherited his powers from Zhango-Rhe, and now he was gone. Titan felt very lonely in the dark, cold cavern. The spaceship had become nothing more than a small, silent, lifeless metal object.

Titan stood there and the stark realization hit him. The only true connection to his adoptive home world of Zyrton was never coming back. He could not inquire on the experiences that were shared on Zyrton. He knew his father could tell him the history and other things about the planet, and Robby shared his DNA, but that did not replace the stories that Zhango-Rhe could and had shared with him.

"Come back, Zhango-Rhe…" Titan cried one last time. "Please…."

He cried for about five minutes, when he remembered Genny, Robby, Madison and his parents. No, he wasn't alone. Jake just felt so empty with Zhango-Rhe now being gone, and perhaps for good. Then he remembered that he had promised Genny that he would return to her house.

Titan wiped the tears from his eyes and slowly turned around. He couldn't bear to look at the spaceship anymore. He quickly walked out towards the secret opening of the cavern, where he stopped and took a deep breath, once he was outside. It was still daylight, so he had to adjust to the brightness, since he had just come from the dark cavern.

Unfortunately, one of Malcolm's thugs spotted Titan. He was hiding behind one of the rocks. He had spotted Titan coming from the hidden entrance to the cavern.

"Target: Titan.....Acquired!" spoke a raspy voice.

"Good work my friend" the cold voice over the radio uttered. "Any sign of that traitor MACH?" questioned the voice.

"No Sir, but we will stay vigilant" replied the soldier.

Titan leaped into the air and flew back to Arizona, where he landed in Genny's back yard. He slowly made his way to the back door, and Genny noticed him standing there, almost in a daze. He opened the door and let him in right away. She walked him into the kitchen where she waited for him to tell her what the problem was, rather than forcing him to talk with relentless questioning.

Jake sat at the table for a few minutes in total silence. Genny sat across from him, wondering what could be troubling her new friend. Jake took a deep breath and began telling her what happened, and who Zhango-Rhe was to him. He let a single solitary tear drift down his cheek, as Genny reached over and gently wiped it from his face.

"Jake, I am so sorry" was all Genny could manage to find the words to say.

In the meantime, the masked man quietly walked up to the entrance to the cavern, where he saw Titan leave, just moments earlier.

"The boy just took off... He flew heading west... Yes, he's gone now... Yes, I'll try to get to the ship, and take out the main memory module..." the man spoke into the portable radio.

The man slipped into the cavern and switched on the flashlight. As he approached the ship, a red light started flashing on the nose of the cockpit. An audible noise began emanating from the ship as well. As the man stepped closer, the sound grew louder, and more frequent.

"Boss, I really don't like this. There is a beeping noise that is coming from the ship, sounds almost like the tone of a detonator. Do you think I should go any further?" asked Malcolm's henchman.

"Listen here, your moron! Don't you dare come back, without Zhango-Rhe's memory module! Do you hear me?" Malcolm's voice shouted through the radio. "I want it, so I can find out more about that annoying 'Titan' brat! I need it! Grab the chip already!"

"Roger, boss. I'm gonna grab that chip so I can blast outta this creepy place…"

The man took another step closer to the spaceship. The audible noise ceased. Suddenly the ship and all its contents exploded into a massive ball of flame. Parts of the ship flying through the air at neck breaking speed, and embedding themselves in the rocky confines of the cave.

Chapter 46

Genny continued trying to cheer Jake up, but knew that it was a lost cause. She knew that something was really wrong and the only person that could possibly help was hundreds of miles away in Washington DC. She grabbed her cell phone and called her cousin.

"Piper, hey, is Robby there? Yeah I need to talk to him a minute" she said to her cousin as she awaited her intended target. "Robby, hey, look can you get down here, Jake is upset, something about Zhango-Rhe and him dying" she explained.

Suddenly a pillar of smoke began to rise from the kitchen floor. Robby McCloud slowly stepped from the mist to face his blood-brother. He immediately took note of the look on Jake's face and the emotions that were running rampant in the super-powered kid.

Titan got up from his chair when he saw his partner.

"Hey, Red! What are you...?" Titan said.

Suddenly Titan's face turned pale and he stumbled backwards, falling with his back on the floor!

"JAKE!" Robby shouted, as he ran to take a look at his friend. "Are you alright?"

"I felt something..." Titan whispered to him. "I felt like something really bad has happened to Zhango-Rhe!"

"Zhango-Rhe's dead, Jake! He's a computer on a space ship!" Robby replied, as he helped his friend get on his feet.

"I have to go back..." Titan said. "I have to go back there right now..."

"I'll teleport us there...You are not going back there alone...." Robby said. Then he turned to Genny. "We'll be right back!"

Myst and Titan suddenly disappeared from Genny's living room in Arizona, only to appear in the Nevada desert. They appeared at the familiar dig site. This time, something was wrong. Jake saw it right away.

"Oh no... Zhango-Rhe... No... NOOOOOOOOOO!" Jake shouted, as he fell to his knees.

There was fire everywhere. The entire cavern was destroyed from what appeared to have been a huge explosion. Pieces of metal were scattered everywhere. It almost seemed as if a huge bomb had detonated at the place, where the ship had once stood.

"He's gone... He's all GONE!" Jake cried. "Zhango-Rhe is gone...."

Robby just stood next to Jake, who sobbed loudly, as he mourned the loss of his creator and the first guardian of this planet. In this saddened moment, Robby knew why his and Jake's lives were intertwined. He knew that this was the moment his blood-brother needed him the most. Robby wrapped his arms around Jake and hugged his friend, while he cried. Together, they looked over and watched, as the flames spread and consumed the bushes and the scattered pieces of debris. There was truly nothing left of the cavern or the spaceship. Every trace of Zhango-Rhe was completely erased. All that was left was the memory that Jake had, the knowledge, that Charles had, and the powers that Jake now possessed as Titan.

"Come on bro, let's go home....there is nothing we can do here..." Robby said to his friend.

As the duo disappeared, a lonely mechanical humanoid ventured out from the nearby crevice. MACH made his way down to where the heroes had been standing. He used his scanning systems to gather information on the whereabouts of the two heroes.

Robby quietly teleported himself and Jake back to Washington DC, where Jake would recount the events of the day to his parents. Robby called Piper and asked her to relay the message to Genny that they would not be returning to Arizona tonight, due to the circumstances. Piper agreed that would be Jake's best interest and called her cousin to inform her.

"Initiate playback mode" stated MACH.

He stood there and watched as the mighty teen hit his knees in tears at the loss of his creator. He also watched how his friend had comforted him. He stood there motionless, watching the internal playback.

"Such a massive amount of emotions for one so young..." wondered MACH.

The cyborg stood there entranced in thought. His lip quivered as his emotions welled up in his soul. Thoughts of his family began to run rampant in a once void place in his mind. The pain that he once felt, that had been long forgotten, came rushing back like a tidal wave.

"MALCOLM!!" he screamed.

For the first time since his transformation in the shape shifting cybernetic organism that stood in that lonely canyon, he felt emotions. He remembered his past, his family and everything about his former life. The emotions welled up within his chest as he watched over and over the mighty Titan reduced to a humbled ball of tears himself.

A tear slowly formed in his one human eye as he struggled to keep his cyborg monocle eye focused on the playback. MACH dropped to his knees. He grabbed his head and wept softly.

"How can that man be such a monster?" Asked an emotionally ravaged MACH. "He could have left me dead, instead I am this monster that my little girl will not recognize. How did this young man awaken this in me? He really is a hero, and today he is my hero as well" he continued.

MACH used his satellite uplink to run a search for Titan. He got a location match on where Titan is most seen. He got a fix on him and made his way out of the canyon.

"The one thing about Malcolm is his ego" thought MACH. "He implanted in me the most advanced evolving microprocessors ever invented. There is no secret I cannot uncover with this. But Malcolm is in for a surprise, he did not count on my will to survive" he thought.

"I have to find my little girl. Run demographics scan on Genny Williams. Cross Reference Brightmore, Piper. Known addresses and school references as well." MACH said, as he made his way down the canyon.

"ANALYSIS COMPLETE. LOCATION TRIANGULATED. SUBJECT GENNY WILLIAMS: LAST KNOWN LOCATION: DIABLO ROJO, ARIZONA. CROSS REFERENCE MATCH: BRIGHTMORE, PIPER. KNOWN LOCATION MATCH: WASHINGTON DC. MATCH ON LOCATION FOR TITAN: WASHINGTON DC" announced MACH's artificial intelligence.

"Looks like I am heading to Washington DC" said MACH "I have to find Titan, and my daughter" he continued.

After the phone call to Piper, Robby walked over to where Jake was sitting. He pleaded with Jake to tell him to let him in on the last conversation, no matter how hard it may be for him that he and Zhango-Rhe had. Distraught, Jake began the tale that Zhango-Rhe had weaved regarding his last days on earth and the person responsible. Jake then told his red-headed friend that Malcolm had somehow became near immortal and was still alive.

"Jake, dude I know what you are feeling, but you heard what Zhango-Rhe said, bro. We have got to be ready for this Malcolm guy" said Robby.

"Bro, I know we have to be ready. Zhango told me all about this guy, and he is bad news. But part of me is still at a loss after the ship blew up" replied Jake as he straightened himself up.

Just then Madison burst through the front door with a petrified look upon his face. "Guys, have you seen the news or have you been under a rock for the past couple of hours?" he panted.

"Whoa, little brother, what's up?" asked Jake as he put his hand on his brother's shoulder.

"JAKE! There is an army of robots that's attacking the Capital, they are heading to the White House!" exclaimed Madison.

"What? The White House? How do you know that?" asked Robby.

"The news, and oh, I don't know, I followed them" Madison said sarcastically.

"YOU, WHAT? Madison Jacob Wayne Knight, how could you put yourself in danger like that?" interrogated Jake.

"Well, you weren't here. And, I'm part of this team, too!" replied a dejected Madison.

Jake and Robby knew that he was right. He was part of the team. They also understood the importance of getting into action as quickly as possible. The duo opted to discuss Madison's brush with danger at a later time.

"Maddie, we will talk about this later, right now Myst and I gotta get out there!" exclaimed Jake.

Robby immediately teleported him and Jake to the central part of the city where the robots were approaching. There, they reappeared as Myst and Titan, and they were greeted by a crowd of panicked people who were fleeing for their lives!

"Run! Run for your lives!" people were shouting, as they poured from the many homes and businesses, that were on the crowded streets.

"It's the end of the world!" another lady screamed.

Jake and Robby quickly turned around and gasped, when they were confronted by four, ten-foot steel robots, which were marching through the city, and who were crushing anything and everyone that stood in their path!

Chapter 47

"Myst! You take the two on the left, and I'll take the two on the right! I'll try to swing my two against yours, any chance I get!" Titan ordered his partner.

"Roger, Titan!" Myst said. "Let's roll!"

Myst then disappeared in a flash, while Titan leaped in the air and started flying towards one of the robots at full speed!

One robot started walking over the parked cars, which were neatly parked in the parking spots, one next to the other. The robot started crushing each car, one by one! People started fleeing from the scene, screaming out of horror, as the robots continued their path of terror and destruction.

Titan approached the offending robot and aimed his fists at him.

"Fire!" he shouted, as he fired his energy blast at the robot, striking him in the shoulder. The blast knocked the robot off balance for a split second, then it regained its composure, and it continued its rampage.

Titan flew up from behind and gave the thing a mighty shove against its shoulder, causing it to topple over with its face down on the street! The entire robot tripped over the remaining cars, falling head-first on the pavement! When it got up, it looked up in anger, when it spotted the flying boy.

As it tried to get up, Titan fired another blast of energy at it, striking it in the chest. He quickly had to fly away, because the second robot was about to grab hold of him from behind.

Titan flew high overhead and fired bursts of energy at both robots, this time aiming for the heads of both of them at the same time.

"YARGH!!!!" he shouted, as he aimed his left fist at one robot, and the right first at the one who was still trying to get up.

Then he flew right back down and swooped between the legs of the robot, which was still standing. The large, mechanical being tried to slap the flying boy in mid air, like he was a bug, but Titan was too fast for him. Titan continued to fly right between the two robots, making them crash right into each other!

As the two crashed into each other, the one who was standing caused even more damage to the one that was on the ground. Titan saw this, and he fired another burst of energy at that one, striking him in the shoulder once again. This time, he caused the right arm to come off!

"ALRIGHT! I took care of one arm! Now for the other..." Titan cheered.

Titan tried to lure the robots away from the buildings, and he saw that they weren't all too far away from the banks of the river. He hoped that maybe he could get the one with the severed arm to fall into the river, and it would hopefully short-circuit.

Titan, like a bird of prey, dived down again and flew after the robot with the broken arm. This time he reached for the head, and he grabbed hold of the top of the metal head. Then he pulled on it, with every ounce of strength he could muster, lifting the robot off the ground.

The robot began to struggle, moving and shaking its legs and remaining arm, as Titan quickly flew the robot over to the river, a few yards away. Then, he released the robot, and dropped it in the river with a loud plunge. Seconds later the robot emerged from the surface, and tried to come back out of the water. Unfortunately for the tin terror, water had come flooding into the damaged arm, and sparks began to come from the exposed wires. A loud explosion followed, and the robot quickly lost power and sank beneath the surface of the river.

"One down, three to go!" Titan sighed, as he quickly turned around and headed back into the city.

Further inland, Myst was fighting his own battle with his robot. The ten-foot mechanical monster came face-to-face with the planet's mightiest mutant mind, and Myst was ready.

Myst used his telekinesis to lift one of the damaged cars and hurled it at the robot, knocking it over. The robot was in a daze for a brief moment, then it got up and quickly started approaching the teen hero. Bewildered at the resilience of the automated life form, Myst prepared for the worst.

When Myst saw that the robot was stronger than he had anticipated, he hurled telekinetic blasts at it, which slowed it down. The first blast struck the oncoming robot in the chest, and the robot stopped for a moment, before it started its approach again. The second blast hit it in the torso, causing it to bend over. Again, the effect was minimal.

"Darn, I need something bigger!" Myst pondered.

Since the previous robot had already crushed several cars that were neatly parked near the curb of the street, Myst decided to use those to nail the robot. "If one car knocked that thing over, let's see what a bunch can do" thought Myst.

Suddenly, one of the crushed cars started to rise up from the ground, and turned straight towards the oncoming robot. Myst aimed it, guiding it with his hand, and allowed the car to fly straight at the large, mechanical monster!

The impact of metal on metal left a sickening sound reverberating through down town DC. The front of the old vehicle struck the large robot square in the chest, knocking him flat on his back, as both the car and the robot came crashing hard down on the street right in front of a brick wall.

Myst let out a deep sigh of relief, hoping he had finally brought down the mechanical menace this time. However, in his celebration, he nearly forgot about the second robot that he was tasked in destroying.

He looked over and realized that Jake had just come from the river. He noticed that one of the other robots was also gone. First there were four, and now there were two. Myst was about to confront the remaining robot, when he heard a sound coming from the area, where he had just hurled the crushed car. He was completely astonished, when he realized that the car was moving! The robot was still able to push the car out of its way!

"What do I have to do?" he pondered, exhausted.

As the robot started pushing the crushed car out of its way, Myst turned around and extended his arm, pointing his finger at the two other cars, that were crushed by the robot, that Titan had sent into the river. Myst concentrated with everything he had and caused both cars to levitate at the same time, and both vehicles telekinetically started hurtling straight towards the robot, striking it in the chest, and pinning it with great force against the brick wall!

Finally, Myst heard the humming sound from the robot come to an end, indicating that he had delivered a knockout punch to the mechanical menace. Knowing that his first sparring partner was done for, he turned his attention to the other two robots and the inbound Titan.

"I got a plan" Myst whispered mentally to his blood-brother.

"Well, now is the time for something bro!" returned the crimson clad hero.

Titan followed Myst's lead on the attack. He mentally told him to catch the robot to the right, Myst then teleported himself between the two mechanical behemoths. He grabbed his head and released all the pent-up fear and anger in the form of a telekinetic blast.

The robots were caught off guard by the red-head's speed and accuracy. The mechanical vessel of destruction to the right landed in the outstretched hands of Titan.

"BLAST HIM NOW, TITAN!!" Myst commanded.

Titan allowed the eternal cosmic energy to ebb and flow in his body. Titan then, with one mighty twist, sent a supercharged plasma blast through the hull of the third robot. This move rendered it inoperative. Titan hurled this one to the ground and watched as it shattered.

Now it was up to Myst to take care of number four. He glanced around as quickly as he could while attempting to survey the wreckage in order to find something to do this dastardly device in. A thought occurred to him as he looked around.

"The wrecked robot's armor-covered leg is light and sharp" he thought with a grin.

Myst flicked his wrist and a huge metallic dagger levitated off the ground. He lowered his head and gave a wicked grin and gritted his teeth. "Here comes the home run, you metallic freak!" Myst grunted.

With that he sent the severed limb of the fallen robot rocketing towards his target. Like a hot knife cutting through butter, the projectile pierced the fourth robot's power core and sent it toppling.

Titan flew over as fast as he could, and caught the robot before the crash leveled any more of the city. He grabbed it up and yanked it off the ground. He flew the wreckage to the banks of the Potomac River.

As soon as the robots were destroyed, Titan grabbed Myst and flew over to the other end of the street, where numerous ambulances were parked. Many police cars were already leaving, and a dozen ambulances were already parked along the curb of the road.

When Titan and Myst arrived, they heard several of the paramedics talking to one another and over the radio. There were numerous injuries reported to people who were trying to flee during the chaos and the initial panic, when the robots first started attacking that part of the city.

What struck the two heroes the most was when they heard that several people were rushed to the hospital because they were trapped in the cars that the robots crushed. Several people had died as a result of the injuries they had sustained when the robots had crushed their cars.

To make matters even worse, several families were trapped in some of the buildings, which were destroyed by the robots, when they initially started attacking the city. These people were rushed to the hospital, although some had also perished during the attack. This had made a profound impact on the heroes, when they heard this.

Chapter 48

After a few moments of hanging around the firemen and the ambulances, they quietly went back to the Sanctum. The duo felt, even in their victory, as if they had actually tasted their first defeat.

"Robby... Up till now, things have been very easy for us..." Jake pondered quietly, as he paced around the room. "We had to help the police and we were able to catch a few bad guys... But, things have changed. This is different. Zhango-Rhe has warned me about this person. His last words were all about how I had to watch out for Thadius Malcolm..."

"Malcolm?" Robby wondered. "Did he send those robots?"

"Most likely! Zhango-Rhe spoke of robots and zombies and monsters and cyborgs and other things that Malcolm would use to attack us and kill us. This guy is very evil and extremely dangerous and he is out to destroy the world and rob it of any resources he can find, before he leaves Earth behind as a barren wasteland, like what he did to planet Zyrton..." Jake continued.

"Oh man..."

"Several people died today... And it's my fault... I should have been there, Robby... People look at me to be the hero who should protect them, and I wasn't able to save them... And these four robots came and caused all that chaotic destruction, just because I wasn't prepared for this... I need to go into strict training, and I need to be prepared for this, because Malcolm is gonna come after me now with everything he's got, and he's out to kill me. He most likely killed Zhango-Rhe, and now he's after me, so he can destroy Earth and wipe it out! We need to do something... We need to expand the Sanctum and create some serious training equipment, so that we'll be much better prepared next time Malcolm attacks us again…" Jake spoke in a very serious tone of voice, before he sat down on the wooden chair in the Sanctum and buried his head between his hands and started to let the anger build within his mighty frame.

Just then the door at the top of the stairs opened. Dr. Knight emerged from the dark stairs to see his son, mighty as he was, a near defeated mess. He knew that what he had seen on the news really affected the young heroes more than he could imagine.

"Jake, Robby, come here, guys" Charles requested as he opened his arms wide and hugged the two exhausted heroes.

"Dad, we tried! We tried to save everyone, I just couldn't" sobbed Jake.

"Yeah Dr. Knight, I cannot heal everyone, or ease everybody's pain" added Robby.

"Guys, guys, I know. I can't say that it's alright, but I can say that it's going to get better from this moment forward" comforted Charles.

"Huh….What? Dad, what are you talking about?" asked Jake.

"Well, my two heroes, in about twenty minutes, there will be a huge delivery from the hardware store and the electronics store" said Charles.

"What for, Dr. Knight?" Robby inquired.

"We are about to retro-fit the Sanctum. I know that we need a bigger and more advanced place to train. The Sanctum really was too small for Jake alone to start with. Now, with the addition of you, Robby, we need to add some more square footage" Charles chuckled.

Dr. Knight had always known how to bring a smile to his son's cherub face. He knew that the thought of the family pulling together to combat this evil, really settled Jake's emotional state. This emotional state was what Robby had felt from Jake ever since the battle.

"How are we gonna do that, dad?" asked Jake.

"Funny you should ask son. What we're going to do is make the excavation and renovation of the Sanctum your first training session. It is for the both of you. Jake, you knock it out, and Robby, you take it out!" Charles laughed.

"So what you are saying, dad, is that I am gonna break the walls down, and Robby is going to teleport the debris out?" questioned Jake.

"Precisely!" said Charles. "This will teach you a little bit about disaster area rescue techniques and planning" he continued.

Dr. Knight explained in detail that Jake was the one that was to knock out the rock formations and put up the steel beams. Robby is to be the one to teleport the debris to the land fill on the outskirts of town. They would both sit down and go over the plans together.

"Dad, is there going to be a secret outside entrance?" asked Jake.

"Yeah, son, it will be under the pool" said Charles.

Jake's jaw dropped in amazement. "A POOL!" he exclaimed with a huge smile.

"Yes, I'm going to have you put the pool bed on a sliding titanium sheet. When either you or Robby want in that way, you can just make a slight mental push with your mind, as the trigger is geared to each of your unique bio signatures. Think it, and it will open for you" explained Charles.

"AWESOME!" both boys said in unison.

"I purchased all the land that is behind our house" Charles continued to explain to the boys. "I bought it several years ago, and was going to sell it, but I decided to keep it instead. Now I'm happy I did, because it makes for a great big back yard..."

"Well, I know that mom is just going to LOVE our pool!" Jake beamed.

"Oh, yes! My mom is gonna be over more often, I can guarantee you that, bro!" Robby added.

"Well, here come the delivery trucks!" Charles said, as he heard several large trucks pull up just outside. The boys and Charles dashed up the stairs and watched as the delivery trucks came to deliver large quantities of steel, concrete, wood, and other construction materials, which were needed for the building and expansion of the new Sanctum.

Jake immediately started hauling all the expensive equipment out of the existing Sanctum, so that nothing would get damaged during the construction phase. He then set everything in the garage, while he emptied out the Sanctum. Once the equipment and the computers were disconnected and hauled into the garage, he started knocking out the walls, which were facing the large, open field, where he was going to dig and expand the rest of the Sanctum.

Then he flew to the surface and grabbed his father's shovel, and started digging a hole in the yard immediately behind the current Sanctum, at super speed. Jake started digging as Robby helped by either teleporting or using his telekinesis to get the loose sand out, until he had dug a huge hole. After ten minutes, he had dug a hole big enough, to allow for a fifteen-thousand square-foot facility, which was located completely underground, with an Olympic-size swimming pool located on top of the ceiling of the facility.

The next phase was for the boys to start pouring the concrete and placing the steel beams. Once the beams were in place, the concrete was poured, and the walls were put into place. The wood and steel was used to erect the surrounding outer walls, until the walls had reached all the way up to the thirty-foot high ceiling. Then Jake placed six thick steel beams over the walls, placing them horizontally from one end to the other. Once the beams were in place, he covered them with steel plates, and then the construction of the pool started on top of that.

The pool was built on top of the Sanctum, hiding the fact that there was a large, underground facility. It was completely secret and secluded, and the pool was a perfect screen for the large, underground base for the super-heroes.

When the Sanctum was finally constructed, Jake and Robby connected the electrical wiring and the plumbing, under Charles' guidance, along with the air-conditioning unit, which supplied the cooling to the underground facility. Jake hauled all the computer equipment and workout gear from the garage to the new, expanded Sanctum, and they still had lots of room to spare. Madison spent a good part of the evening re-wiring and reconfiguring all the existing computer equipment with all the new computers and monitoring devices he had helped to create.

"I'm going to design a special, electro-magnetic weight-bench for you, Jake" Charles said to his son. "You'll need one, since an ordinary weight bench is much too light for you, anyway. That way, you'll be able to use magnets to adjust the weights of the bars you will lift so that it will feel like you're lifting thousands of pounds, which will seem like only hundreds of pounds to a normal human being…"

"Great!" Jake cheered. "That means I can finally get to enjoy a real work-out!" he said as he flexed his right arm.

"Hey, we need to finish up the pool…" Robby said.

"Let's go!" Jake uttered.

Both boys quickly raced up the stairs as they went outside and went to the pool deck, which was above the ceiling of the newly expanded Sanctum. Once on top, the boys were using the new net to fish any leaves that had fallen into the water, as the water pumps were running and allowing water to flow into the pool, that was still only half-full. Both teens were standing near the edge of the pool, as they were eagerly watching the waterline, as it slowly rose higher and higher.

Meanwhile, above the city was a lone figure atop the Lincoln Memorial. MACH had tracked Titan to his hometown of Washington DC. Using his highly sophisticated scanning sensors, he noted a spike in the seismic activity in a nearby neighborhood.

MACH opted to initiate a scan of that neighborhood. He had found them; the ones that had help awaken his emotional human nature. He wanted to talk to them and warn them of the impending danger that they had in store for them.

Robby and Jake were hard at work putting the finishing touches on the pool. Jake was laughing and cutting up when Robby spotted a large armor covered humanoid standing right behind Jake.

Jake was telekinetically pushed out of the way.

"GET AWAY FROM HIM!!" snarled Robby as he hit the creature with a powerful telekinetic blast.

The blast knocked the creature flat on his back. Robby had since morphed back into his Myst costume. He ran over to the cyborg and kept him pinned to the ground with telekinesis.

"Who are you?" spat Myst.

"I am the Mobile Armored Chameleon Humanoid prototype. But you may call me MACH" stated the cyborg.

"What did you say?" quizzed Jake.

"My name is MACH. You must me Titan?" he returned.

334

"MACH? You were the one that Zhango-Rhe told me about!" replied Jake.

"The entity in the craft. Malcolm sent me to destroy it, before I defected" said MACH.

"WHAT??? I will rip you apart!!!" screamed Jake in anger.

"Young Titan, wait! It is you, I seek; you have helped me to see my life differently. I was not the one that destroyed your predecessor. I was originally sent to engage that task, but the programming that was originally entered into my cybernetic brain was totally eradicated, and the human side of me came about. Thanks to you, Titan..." explained MACH.

"What is your deal, buddy? What are you?" asked Myst.

"I was human once. I was a soldier in the United States Marine Corps. I was stationed in Iraq and my platoon came under fire. That was my last human memory. I awoke with a cybernetic body, the most advanced artificial intelligence, and microprocessors on the planet. I also had abilities that were granted me by my then savior, Dr. Thadius Malcolm" MACH continued.

"Malcolm did this to you? Zhango was right, you are not what you seem" Titan nodded.

"I am a shape-shifting cyborg, but like I mentioned, you awoke my human soul and heart" said MACH.

Cautiously, Robby let up on the cyborg and allowed him to climb to his feet. MACH stood up and extended his hand to the young heroes. They both took turns greeting MACH as a friend.

"If you are human, or were human, what was your name?" inquired Robby.

"Stephen Alan Williams, from Diablo Rojo, Arizona" Replied MACH.

"WOW! My girl friend is from there" yelped Titan.

"CROSS REFERENCING!!!! MATCH LOCATED!!" came a faint voice out of MACH's cybernetic arm.

"That girl would not happen to be Genny Williams, would it? MACH inquired.

"Yeah! How did you know?" asked Titan.

"You have a unique energy signature, son. You said she was from there, I patched into the satellites and retrieved that information" MACH said a little more warmly.

"You can do that?" asked Myst.

"Yes I can. I have a favor to ask and I have to trust you with this." whispered MACH.

"Go ahead MACH, what is it?" asked Jake.

"Please protect Genny Williams, Titan" pleaded MACH.

"I will, but why are you so concerned about that?" asked Jake.

"Titan, she is my daughter. Please do not tell her. It has been painful enough for her, I imagine. I cannot have her see me like this" replied MACH.

"I don't understand, why come find us?" asked Robby.

"Because, someone has to keep you two a few steps ahead of Thadius Malcolm. I know his ins-and-outs and that person to help you, is me" offered MACH.

Both boys stared at the strange man with shock and disbelief, and with a sense of joy and relief at the same time. They have finally met someone, who appears to be on their side and, what a coincidence, that this man happens to know all about Thadius Malcolm, and he happens to be Genny William's father. The ironic coincidences were just unbelievable.

They needed time to regroup and to think things over. Besides, Jake wanted to spend time putting together his new weight-lifting gear in the new Sanctum, which they had just finished building. Madison and Charles had already started painting the Sanctum walls, and Robby and Jake just needed to get back to work and finish the rest of the job. Jake knew he could get it done at super speed, giving it enough time to dry overnight so that the Sanctum could be furnished the following day.

"Well this is my house, so now you know where I live. My real name is Jake Knight, and Myst's real name is Robby McCloud. Robby lives in the house right next door to mine…" Jake explained to MACH. "We just finished building the pool, which is right over our training room, which is located underground."

"Very good. Well, I can assure you that I mean no harm. After all, young man, you're the one who's befriended my one and only daughter, and I really admire you for that."

"Well, I must admit, she's an amazing girl..." Jake chuckled. "I like her very much. In fact, she'll be moving here to Washington this weekend..."

"That's why it's even more important for me that I help you..." MACH replied. "Please understand, Jake... It's personal now... It's not just about how much I hate Malcolm for what he did to me, but I also want to protect my daughter..."

"Alright, Steve... Look if you need to get a hold of me I will give you my number..." Jake said.

Jake leaped into the air and flew back down into the Sanctum. There he found his notepad, where he quickly jotted down his and Robby's phone numbers. Then, he raced back outside and showed up, standing before MACH a few seconds later, holding the small piece of paper in his hand.

"My original scans of you were misleading, you're faster than I imagined!" MACH gasped.

"There you go! This is where you can get a hold of us!" Jake smiled. "I would show you our newly expanded Sanctum, but it's not quite finished yet, and I would have to run it past dad first as well. Next time you come over, it'll be completed, I promise. Then, we'll give you a tour of the place, and you can meet my father, alright?"

"You can check out the computers and all the other equipment we got in there, too. Maddie and Dr. Knight have been working really hard to get them up and running!" Robby interjected.

"Great! Thank you very much, you guys. I shall see you next time around..." MACH said to them.

Then MACH turned around, and started to walk away.

"Interesting character, huh?" Robby said to Jake.

"Yeah... what did you think about him, you read his mind, I know you did!"

"We can trust him. After I shook a couple of his bolts loose, letting him know that I meant business, I looked into his mind. Jake he is telling the truth. That man has been through total hell because of the war, and Malcolm resurrecting him to this life" explained Robby.

"How are we gonna keep this from Genny?" wondered Jake.

"Let's head back into the Sanctum and help Maddie finish painting the walls…We can think of that while we work" Robby suggested.

"Roger, Myst!" Jake replied. "Send us down…"

Myst's eyes turned black and both boys immediately disappeared from the edge of the pool, as Robby teleported them back into the Sanctum.

Chapter 49

Once inside, Jake and Robby grabbed paint rollers and brushes, and they started painting the long, wide walls of the Sanctum. They worked quickly, since Jake made good use of his super speed, while Robby was able to manipulate up to four brushes at the same time, thanks to his telekinesis. Once they were done with that, Jake and Charles started designing the electro-magnetic weight-lifting machines for Jake's work-outs, while Madison and Robby started decorating the training room for Robby where he could practice his telekinesis and his teleportation powers. They painted squares with numbers on the floor, which Robby would use for teleporting objects. They would also hang ropes and balloons from the large ceiling, so that Robby could practice levitating things in-between them. Lastly, there were nine red numbers painted on the floor. He would use them to teleport Jake, or himself, as Charles or Madison would shout out the numbers at random.

The boys were working hard decorating and preparing the Sanctum so they could go into strict training, in preparation for their next encounter with Thadius Malcolm.

As the duo continued to work on the final prep to the Sanctum, Robby's cell phone rang. He looked at the outer screen not recognizing the number. He slowly unfolded the phone to answer it.

"Hello. Yeah this is Robby McCloud. Who? What? Brandon? You're here now? What? Moved? Awesome! When? OK, I will ask mom. Later!" came the one sided conversation.

"Robby, what's up?" asked Jake with a puzzled look.

"Jake, the guy that taught me all about baseball and the one that I always looked to as my big brother, has moved to DC, bro" responded Robby.

"Derrick?" inquired Jake.

"No, this is my big bro, Brandon. Brandon Rathbone. He moved here a week ago from Boston!" exclaimed Robby with a tone of excitement.

"That is awesome Robby, I am glad, I know that you miss your friends from back home" smiled Jake.

"Well, not to worry, bro. No one can replace either you, or Brandon, in my heart" said Robby as he returned the smile.

"Who said I was worried?" returned Jake.

Just then Madison came bounding down the stairs. He was bubbling over with excitement about something. He ran up to Robby and Jake and held out his hands with two small objects in them.

"Here, I did it!" exclaimed Madison.

"Did what?" asked Robby.

"Remember a few months ago when Piper and I were trying to get a way to keep you all informed of what is going on?" inquired Madison.

"UH....I guess" replied Jake.

"Well I built these ear pieces. They fit right inside your ear and work by transmitting the signal from the Sanctum to you, so you can hear us. Then it picks up the vibrations from the sound within your ear canal and translates them into a cellular phone-like signal to be retransmitted to us, and we have, voila! Instant two-way communication on an extremely advanced level" explained Madison.

"So, did Dr. Knight help you with this, Madison?" asked Robby.

"Not at all, Red, I did it all by myself!" Madison said, as he puffed out his chest with pride.

Jake walked over and wrapped his massive arm around his little brother's shoulder. "I am so very proud of my little techno-geek brother" chuckled Jake. "I would have never thought of something like that. You are really proving yourself as an important member of this team" continued Jake.

"What? You really think that I'm a member of the team now?" asked Madison.

"Of course!" exclaimed both Robby and Jake in unison. They turned and grinned at one another at their total one-mindedness.

"HA HA! You two are like sharing a brain" squealed Madison.

Both boys grabbed their communication devices and placed them within their ears. As they slid into place, the ear pieces all but disappeared from view, making them remarkably undetectable to the naked eye. Robby shook his head to see if the ear piece was going to come out. Much to his surprise it stayed in place rather well.

"I can barely tell it's there" stated Robby.

"That is the beauty of the design. It is meant to avoid detection from most conventional methods, guys. So we will be in constant communication!" explained Madison.

Chapter 50

While our heroes were looking ahead to their next battle, deep inside of the remote mountains south of Washington, DC, in a large, remote, underground base, Thadius Malcolm was looking back at the horrible, failed attack of the four robots on the city. Video footage of the attack was playing on a large TV screen, while Malcolm sat quietly in his chair, pondering what had gone wrong.

Jaro, the short, chubby, bald-headed servant, stumbled into the room, hoping that his master would at least give him a smile, for bringing his dinner to him.

"I-I brought you something to eat, Master Malcolm…" he said as he quietly approached the grumbling man, who sat in the chair while he was just staring at the images on the screen.

"Two kids… TWO LITTLE KIDS!" Malcolm sneered. "I send four technologically advanced robots into the city and they get stopped by two… BRATS! How is that possible?"

Malcolm grabbed a fist full of crackers and stuffed them in his mouth. He started crunching on the crackers as he watched images of Myst and Titan, while they battled the robots.

"Ooh look at that… That one kid could fly!" Jaro noted. "Oh my, oh my… Look how that red kid grabbed one of your robots by the head and lifted it up… That's not good, master!"

"The red kid is Titan" Malcolm growled. "The brat is stronger than I thought…. He's just like Zhango-Rhe… He flies like Zhango-Rhe… He has the strength of Zhango-Rhe… He shoots those energy blasts like Zhango-Rhe…"

"Then there's this other blue kid with the mask..." Jaro pointed out. "Who's he?"

"I'm not sure... I heard Titan calling him by the name of 'Myst'..." Malcolm replied. "Other than that, I know nothing about him..."

"Is he like Titan?"

"No, he's different..." Malcolm pointed out. "Look at that! Look what that Myst-kid did to those cars!"

"Wow... He made those cars float into the air!" Jaro described.

"Yes... and he slammed them into my robot... without even touching them..." Malcolm murmured. "This kid must possess some extremely powerful psychic-derived powers ..."

Malcolm pressed a button on the remote and rewound the tape to the beginning of the battle. Then he pressed the button to allow for the video to start playing the scenes over again.

"Look at this scene, Jaro. Here is the street. Here, you see the people, running away from the robots, right?" Malcolm pointed out.

"Look at the street... See over there, on the sidewalk?" Malcolm indicated with his laser. "Now look..."

Suddenly, Myst and Titan appeared, standing on the sidewalk, and walking towards the robots.

"Look how those two BRATS appeared out of nowhere!" Malcolm sneered. "How did they do that? Even Titan popped up out of the blue! Zhango-Rhe never had that ability!"

"Maybe he has a new power, Master!" Jaro replied meekly.

"We need to find out who this Myst-kid is!" Malcolm hissed at him. "And I want to know what other powers this Titan-kid has. I don't believe it! Finally....FINALLY...I rid myself of Zhango-Rhe, and now we have to deal with not one, but two... two CHILDREN!"

"Well, Master, maybe if we send some big monster at them, we can trap them and put them away for good... heheh..." Jaro laughed.

"At least, when I was fighting Zhango-Rhe back on Zyrton and here, I felt like I was fighting a worthy adversary... But, NOW...I'm dealing with these two KIDS! We must terminate them! Immediately! How DARE they interfere with my affairs?"

"We should see if they have any weaknesses, master..." Jaro pondered. "We should capture a large group of people or something.

Or, perhaps we could destroy a large facility, like a school... Then we could throw a large number of kids in our new prison facility, and when they come to rescue them, we will spring a trap for them..."

"Jaro, sometimes I like the way your feeble little mind works... Let me think about that... We'll find a way to get rid of those two brats... and then, once we get rid of them, THE WORLD WILL BE MINE TO ENSLAVE AND DESTROY!!! HA HA HAAA HA HA!!!!"

Both Jaro and Malcolm huddled together laughing as they pondered about their scheme of how to get rid of Titan and Myst. It was just a step for them. It was one step, in their ultimate goal, the complete conquest and destruction of the world. The two heroes were the only ones, standing in their path.

"Jaro, I want every agent that we have on the books to find out what they can about this Titan and Myst" ordered Malcolm.

"You mean the ones that we have on the payroll with the CIA?" asked Jaro.

"Of course you dim-witted buffoon!" yelled Malcolm at his lowly servant.

Chapter 51

Later that night, as Robby relaxed in his room above the garage, there came a knock at his bedroom door. He pulled himself up, commanded his sentient Myst costume to join him and become a pair of shorts and t-shirt. He made his way across the room and opened his door.

His jaw dropped as he glanced at the figure standing before him. Brandon Rathbone was standing in his doorway holding his back pack and wearing a huge smile on his chiseled face. Robby threw his arms around the boy he called his big brother and hugged him hard.

"Easy Red! I would like to breathe a little there" grunted Brandon as he struggled underneath Robby's new-found strength.

"Oh sorry B! Come in, please!" exclaimed Robby.

"Man, it is good to see you, kiddo" said Brandon as he ruffled Robby's fire-red hair.

"Dude, it is great to see you too, Brandon, I have missed you so much. You got your back pack with you, what's up?" asked Robby.

"Well I called your mom and wanted to be here when you got home to surprise you with the fact that I was going to stay the night with you" explained Brandon.

"Oh that is awesome bro. Man, I can't wait for you to meet my blood-brother, Jake, dude" said Robby without thinking.

"Blood-brother?" asked Brandon.

Robby realized what he done. He could not believe that with a matter of seconds he had all but told Brandon that he was Myst and that Jake was Titan. He also thought that if there was anyone that would keep that secret safe, it would have been Brandon. He needed to explain what was going on but he needed to think of the best way to gauge it.

Robby took a deep breath. "Brandon, you and I have been close for a long time, and I have always looked to you as a big brother" said Robby.

"I have looked after you like you were my little brother, dude" Brandon started. "What's wrong, you know that you can tell me anything bro, you always shared everything with me and Derrick" he continued.

"Look, you better sit down" instructed Robby.

Brandon came in and sat at the desk while Robby went and sat on his bed. Robby began recounting the day of his fifth birthday. He told Brandon about the headaches, and how he had to get away from everyone. He told him about being able to read minds, move objects, teleport from place to place and heal people. Brandon sat quietly and listened in shock as his little brother confessed all of this to him.

"So you are telling me that you're a mutant?" asked Brandon.

"Yes, to put it bluntly!" replied Robby.

"But I thought mutants were bad, at least that is what Dr. Malcolm said on that public announcement" muttered Brandon.

"Not all mutants are bad. I am not one of the bad guys, dude. You know me better than that" offered Robby with a smile.

"Good point. But what does that have to do with the fact that you called that guy Jake your blood-brother?" he asked.

Robby looked at Brandon with a very serious tone. "You have to promise to keep this between you, me, and Jake!" he insisted.

"Keep what?" asked Brandon.

"What I am going to tell you, can, if leaked, put you in danger bro, and I cannot and will not live with myself if you get hurt because of me" urged Robby.

"OK, OK! I promise, now what is this all about?" inquired Brandon impatiently.

"Have you heard of the super-hero called Titan?" asked Robby.

"Titan? Who hasn't heard of him? He and his partner Myst are big news back home" Brandon began with excitement. "Wait a minute…" he continued.

Just then Robby allowed his eyes to shift to solid onyx black. As his eyes took on the eerie black glow, his shorts and t shirt slowly morphed into his familiar solid blue Myst uniform. He stood up and walked over to where Brandon was sitting. He could tell that his big brother was in a state of shock.

He placed his hand on his shoulder in an attempt to ease the discomfort that he was feeling. "Brandon, I am Myst. I am Titan's Partner, and after I explain a few more things, I will introduce you to my partner" Robby said as he comforted his baffled friend.

"Wow! I really don't know what to say. You can do all those amazing things that they say you can on the news?" he asked through his amazement.

"Sure can! You thirsty?" he asked.

"Yeah I guess" stuttered Brandon.

"One Pepsi coming right up" Robby said as he glanced at the fridge and with a wave of his hand the door opened. An ice cold Pepsi flew into Myst's outstretched hand. Robby opened it and handed it to Brandon.

"How did you know that I wanted a Pepsi?" inquired Brandon.

"You are an easy read bro, not to mention I do remember that it is your favorite drink" Robby chuckled.

Brandon laughed at the fact that his little brother did know him better than anyone. Brandon relaxed a little bit more. Robby then morphed his clothing back into his shorts and shirt. He began telling Brandon the story about how he gained the strength and added ability due to the blood-bond that he shared with Jake.

"So you see bro, Titan gave me some of his special blood, that cured the weakness that my powers caused, and gave me a slight boost to my body as well. I am nowhere near as strong as Titan, but I am stronger than any human on the planet" explained Robby.

"Dude, I have always been stronger than you" protested Brandon.

"Not anymore!" offered Robby as he picked up an aluminum baseball bat and bent it in half.

"Holy cow! God, you are strong, bro!" laughed Brandon.

Robby then explained about Jake and how he was Titan. He told him about the mental bond that the two of them shared. He also told him that Jake knew all about the conversation that they were having right now.

"You mean to tell me that he can read your mind as well?" asked Brandon.

"No, I am allowing him to hear this, so that he knows what to expect when he meets you face to face" explained Robby.

"When is that going to be?" asked Brandon as he felt a tapping on his shoulder that caused him to jump.

"How about now!" Jake said with a grin on his face.

Brandon spun around to face the short muscular kid that was standing behind him. He grinned nervously.

"Hi, you must be Brandon?" Jake inquired. "I'm Jake, but you probably know me as 'Titan'" he offered.

"WOW! Two well-known super-heroes in the same room and one is my little brother!" stuttered Brandon.

"Brandon, I need to apologize to you. I should have told you a long time ago about this. I told Derrick, but I feel so bad that I did not tell you" said Robby ashamedly.

"Bro, look I am older, and back then I kinda figure that you would have been scared to tell me. I understand why you did that. If I was in your shoes I would have most likely done the same thing" reassured Brandon with a soft smile. "You have to know Red, I love ya like a brother no matter what. That will never ever change. And don't you forget that" reaffirmed Brandon with a stern glare.

"And Brandon, you do not have to worry about him getting hurt, I am always watching him…" said Jake.

"That is good. Because, I can be honest when I say, that I would die if something happened to him. I have lost my parents, and as far as family goes, it is him, his family and my brother. They are all that I have left. Even with his powers I would do anything and everything to protect him" Brandon said with a tear in his eye.

"Wha..What?" Robby asked.

"Red, you gotta know that I think that you are the greatest kid ever, that is why I asked the courts to let me live with my brother here in DC after mom and dad passed away. All so I could get back standing by my little brother" replied Brandon.

Jake stood back up and walked over to Brandon. He placed his hand on his shoulder and gripped slightly. "Brandon, even with all these powers that the two of us have, there is one power that you have that is far superior to any of ours" Jake said.

"What?"

"You have the biggest heart I have ever seen or been around, dude. Your love for my blood-brother is greater than I would have ever thought of. That makes you a hero in my book. Not only just a hero, but you are my hero" urged Jake with a smile.

"What? Your hero? Are you serious?" asked a bewildered Brandon.

"Hey, Brandon, you have always been my hero. I have tried so hard to be like you all these years, and if it were not for you coaching me, I would not be the person and hero that I am today" added Robby.

"Guys, I don't know what to say" replied Brandon with tear and a smile on his face.

"Say you will join the team B" insisted Robby.

"Join Myst and Titan? Are you serious? Of course I will" exclaimed Brandon.

Brandon's chest puffed out and he swelled with pride that his little brother and the world's most popular superhero thought enough of him to call him their hero. Not only their hero, but their team mate. To him there could be no higher honor than that.

The rest of the night, Robby and Jake took turns telling Brandon all about what they had been up to. Brandon chimed in with stories of Robby as a kid. The guys also listened to Brandon's ideas on how to get better as a team and keep going. This night was one that was soon not to be forgotten.

Early the next morning Jake and Robby took Brandon to see the Sanctum of Myst and Titan first hand. Inside the newly expanded Sanctum, Madison, Brandon and Robby were looking on, as Jake was sitting in his newly-built electro-magnetic bicep-curl machine. Jake was grunting as he struggled to lift the bar, which he was holding in the palm of his hand, as his mighty bicep was flexed to its full glory.

"Wow, I'd never imagine I'd see the day that Jake would struggle lifting something…" Madison chuckled, as he turned a large, round knob, that was attached to a control panel that sat attached to the machine. "Jake, do you want me to lower the force a little?"

"Uhhh… Yeah… Just a little… Uhhh" Jake groaned, as he barely managed to lift the bar with his right arm.

"Who would have thought it a few months ago? Me, a kid from Boston, standing in the secret headquarters of Myst and Titan, this country's greatest heroes" said Brandon with pride.

Madison gently turned the dial to the left, allowing the humming sound of the electro-magnetic machine to lower just by a tad. Suddenly, Jake managed to raise the bar completely, before lowering his arm all the way, followed by a deep sigh of relief.

"Okay, that's enough for now…" Jake said, while drops of sweat were pouring down his neck and his forehead.

He slowly turned around, and got up from the machine.

"Wow, according to the machine, you just lifted a seven-thousand-pound dumbbell, bro!" Maddie cheered. "And that's just in one hand!"

"Yeah, and I did over thirty reps, too…" Jake sighed. "That's the best workout I've ever had!"

"Dude, if you keep this up, you're gonna be as hard as a rock!" Robby laughed, as he gently punched Jake in his shoulder.

"Yup… my bro already makes a great punching bag!" Madison laughed.

"You need to start your training, next!" Jake said to Robby. "You need to sharpen up on your telekinesis and your teleportation skills, blood-brother! After all, that's what we built this Sanctum for!"

"Wow, I get to finally see my bro in action, huh?" asked Brandon.

"Looks that way" Robby smirked.

"I wanna help!" Madison piped up. "I'm part of the team, too!"

"Well, I'm gonna shower…" Jake said to them.

Just then Charles walked into the Sanctum, as Jake walked towards the shower, which was part of the weight room. He showered at super speed, so he came out and was all dried off and dressed in no time. Charles joined Madison, Jake, Brandon, and Robby in the Sanctum, where they gathered in the computer room.

"Now that Jake has finally broken a sweat, you are about to join him Mr. McCloud" chuckled Charles.

Robby all of a sudden had an overwhelming feeling of distress wash over him. "What if I let them down?" he thought to himself.

Jake spun around on his heel and stopped dead in his tracks. He glared at Robby with a look of shock. "Robby, you have never, nor will ever let us down" he returned in thought.

Robby slowly grinned. "I hope you're right, bro" he said aloud.

"Dude, I recognize that look anywhere. You'd better get your head in the game, Red. You're not letting anyone down. You're the best!" Brandon reassured him.

"Robby, what I'm going to do is set the weight limit on that block over there" Charles said as he pointed to a large metallic cube. "That thing is tied to the electromagnetic field generator that powers Jake's workout machines. We will use it to measure and train your telekinetic strength and endurance" continued Charles.

"But, Dr. Knight, what about my physical strength and fighting? You said that I was going to be stronger than any human on the planet, thanks to Jake's little boost" inquired Robby.

"Well, Jake said that he wanted to save that for just you and him to do together. He wants to teach you how to use the powers that he passed on to you. I for one think that is a great idea" said Charles with a proud smile.

"Oh yeah and while you slept last night bro, I talked to Jake about the strength part of your training. I am going to be there the entire time to help push you, man. Just like old times" giggled Brandon

With that, Robby turned around and faced the block of titanium. He steadied himself and began to concentrate. His eyes shifted from emerald green to onyx black. He outstretched his arms and the block began to lift off the ground.

Charles began adjusting the knobs on the control panel. The force began to increase, as did the strain on the body and mind of Robby. Robby grit his teeth and balled up his fists as the power began to take a toll on the young telepath.

"That's it bro, you're doing great. The weight is way up there!" cheered Jake.

"Come on little brother!!! Keep it up!" yelled Brandon.

"It....It's getting really hard to keep it off the gr....ground bro!" grunted Robby.

"Robby, we are going to go up a little higher to see how long you can maintain" announced Charles.

"YES S...S....Sir! gnashed Robby.

Dr. Knight then turned the dial all the way to the right. The block got as heavy as they could make it. Robby had no clue that they had turned it all the way up on him. He grabbed his head and concentrated with all his mental focus and tightened every blood-transfusion-enhanced muscle as tight as he could to stabilize himself.

Brandon looked on in amazement. Gone was the young baseball student of his. Now standing before him was a real hero. One, who at such a young age had faced many things that most adults shy away from. Brandon looked at him with a swelling of pride, knowing that just a few short years ago, he had helped mold the hero before him.

Charles flipped the switch off and the machine shut down. The entire Sanctum grew silent. Jake, Brandon, and Madison stood there with their jaws agape at the read-outs on the computer screen. Dr. Knight was also astonished at the read-outs.

"Mr. McCloud, you never cease to amaze me, son. You need to see this, come over here" stated Dr. Knight.

"Look bro...LOOK!" cheered Jake.

"Son, we could not reach the maximum of your telekinetic potential" explained Charles.

"So, what are you saying? This says that I lifted twenty tons just now. WOW!" exclaimed Robby.

"What did I tell you, Red? You ain't letting anyone down!" cheered Brandon.

Jake walked around his father and made his way to Robby. He draped his muscular arm over his blood-brother's shoulder. "I got the body, and he's got the brain!" Jake chuckled.

"Son, Robby also has a body to reckon with. His physical strength is increasing greatly, by what these read-outs are showing" said Charles.

"Robby has mental muscles!" Jake exclaimed, as he burst out in laughter. "Whatever I need to use my muscles for, he can do the same thing, but by using his mind!"

"That pretty much sums it up, son!" Charles replied.

"You two are a major force to reckon with, guys" said Brandon.

"Yeah, my big brother and your little brother...the two blood-brother protectors" giggled Madison.

"So, what's next for me on the program, Dr. Knight?" Robby asked.

"Well, you need to get ready to use your teleportation powers a lot!" Charles explained. "Especially for this coming weekend..."

"What's going on this weekend?"

"You're going to help Genny move!" Jake replied excitedly. "You're going to teleport me, along with all Genny's stuff, from her house in Arizona to Piper's house!"

"Oh wow! That's gonna take a few trips for sure!" Robby noted. "I hope you're ready to make several journeys through the space-time continuum, Jake!"

"I'm ready! Remember, I'll be touching her bags and boxes, too... I hope you can handle teleporting all the extra cargo!"

"No sweat!" Robby grinned. "I can teleport you in my sleep!"

"I know that!" Jake said, as he rolled his eyes. "I think you actually have teleported me across my bedroom several times! It's happened more than once that I woke up in the middle of the night and I found myself floating on the opposite side of the room..."

"Wait a minute, Piper and Genny? Who are they?" asked Brandon as he raised an eyebrow at Robby.

"Well she is, well she is sort of, umm..." stuttered Robby.

"Piper is Robby's girlfriend!" said Madison as he burst out laughing.

"Aww Bro, you never told me about her" Brandon said. "And, I take it that Genny is your girlfriend, Jake?" he inquired.

"You got it. And she is moving in with Piper, who just happens to be her cousin. That was a total coincidence!" Jake chuckled.

That following Saturday, Jake flew to Diablo Rojo to meet Genny. She had packed all her belongings and she set everything on her back patio. As soon as Jake arrived there, as Titan, she said goodbye to her aunt, and she left her Piper's address and phone number in Washington, DC. Then Jake took her hand, and mentally called on Robby to make their first jump, so that Jake didn't have to fly Genny back to DC from Arizona. The two teens disappeared instantly, and they reappeared in Piper's living room, where both Robby and Piper were waiting patiently.

As soon as Piper showed Genny her new room, Robby sent Jake back to Genny's house. Jake took a suitcase by his left hand and a soft bag in his right hand, and called on Robby to make him jump back. Robby teleported Jake back a third time, with the two bags. He continued to send Jake back and forth from DC to Diablo Rojo for another four times, until Jake had finally jumped back with the last of her boxes of books and clothing.

"There you have it! She's all moved in!" he said to the girls.

"Wow that was the easiest move I've ever had!" Genny smiled.

"Thanks for the jumps, blood-brother!" Jake said, as he gave Robby a high-five. "I guess you practiced your teleportation skills for this week…"

"Well, like I said before… You use weights and barbells in your workouts… I just use YOU in mine!" Robby chuckled. "I guess we can go back to the Sanctum now…"

The boys said goodbye to the girls, before Robby teleported him and Jake back to the Sanctum. They had vowed to continue their training sessions, as long as there were no major emergencies to attend to in the city, for they would not know when the need would arise for them to help out during disasters or emergencies, or when they would have to face criminals, thugs, or other robots that were sent by Thadius Malcolm again! Preparation was the key to success and the boys still felt unprepared.

Chapter 52

The next morning all was quiet in the Knight household. The boys were out at the baseball park, so that Robby could warm up for Little League tryouts that were scheduled for later that afternoon. Dr. Knight was in his study going over the data from the meeting of Titan and Myst with the robotic killing machines. A thought dawned upon him just then. He knew that for all the knowledge that Zhango-Rhe had passed onto him, one thing still eluded him. He did not know how to train the boys physically and needed someone to help him.

He pondered a list of people that would fit the training portion, but who could he trust. One man fit the role to a proverbial "T". Tim Marshall, who was and is his right hand man on any archeological digs. He knew that Tim possessed many skills that the young heroes would need to learn to survive the onslaught that Malcolm was throwing out at them.

Just then his cell phone rang, and almost as if it were the result of divine intervention, it was Tim on the other end of the phone. "Hello, Dr. Knight here!" uttered Charles.

"Hey boss, something told me that I needed to call you. What's up?" inquired Tim politely.

"Well Tim I was just thinking about you, as a matter of fact. I am glad you called" replied Charles.

"OK Boss, what's up?" Tim asked again.

"Could you possibly come over here for a few minutes I need to run something by you" responded Charles.

"Sure, I am actually headed in that general direction now, I am on the way to the Metro Baseball Field for tryouts today" said Tim.

"Really, one of Jake's friends is out there today trying out. I did not know that you coached Little League" said Charles.

"This is my second year. Seeing as though Samantha and I have not had any kids yet, it's our way of giving back a little bit" replied Tim.

"Great, so you can afford a few minutes here?" asked Dr. Knight.

"Sure boss, I will be there in about five minutes if that is OK" answered Tim.

"Sure" said Charles as he hung up the phone.

The moments passed quickly as Charles awaited his assistant's arrival. The door bell rang, as Nancy Knight made her way to the door to answer it.

"Oh Hello, Tim" said Nancy as she opened the door for the family friend.

"Hi beautiful, where is your hubby?" inquired Tim.

"You are such a flatterer Mr. Marshall. He is downstairs, let me get him for you" grinned Nancy.

Nancy opened the door of the stairwell that led to the basement. "Charles, honey! Tim is here!" she bellowed down the stairs.

"Tim, he will be here in a second, you want a drink or something?" asked Nancy.

"No thanks!" replied Tim.

Just then the door swung open and Charles emerged from the depths of the basement. "Tim, it's good to see you! Glad you could make it" said Charles as he extended his hand to shake Tim's hand.

"Good to see you too boss! Now, what ya got on your mind?" Tim inquired.

"Follow me, I have a business proposal for you" said Charles as he led Tim to the basement.

The two men navigated the narrow stairwell to the recently expanded basement. Unknown to Charles, Tim was looking around in wide-eyed wonder. He was totally amazed at the sight of a basement that looked as if it took up the whole city block.

"Charles!! What have you done to the place? You trying to build an underground city or something?" asked a shocked Tim.

"Well we have done a little remodeling down here" Charles chuckled.

"That's an understatement!" Tim yipped.

Charles led him to the observation office that he had constructed to monitor the boys as they trained. He opened the door and ushered Tim inside to the seats provided.

"Have a seat Tim" asked Dr. Knight.

"What is this all about?" asked Tim.

"Where do I begin? I called you here because I need your help" responded Charles.

"Charles, you know I am here, and always have been" remarked Tim.

"I was counting on that. We have been close friends since before Jake was born. And you are the ONLY one that I can trust with this, and you're like an uncle to Jake anyway" started Charles.

"What are you getting at?" inquired Tim.

"I'm in need of someone to oversee the training of Jake and his partner Robby" retorted Charles.

"Training? Training for what? Baseball?" Tim smirked.

"Well, not exactly! I need you to think back about seven years ago..."

"What, when we uncovered that space craft?" inquired Tim.

"Yes! See, that night when Jake arrived, and you brought him in. Something happened to Jake and to me that night" responded Charles.

"Okay? This is kind of weird, boss. So, what exactly happened to the two of you?" asked Tim.

"Well, in case you have been living under a rock for the past six or so years, then you may have missed the emergence of a young super-hero, named Titan..."

"Titan! Of course I have heard of him, who hasn't?" replied Tim inquisitively.

"Well Tim, I think it would be better if I showed you rather than tried to explain it" said Charles.

Dr. Knight grabbed his cellular phone off the desk and punched in his son's number. Jake answered quickly as he usually did.

Robert C. Aultman & Rex Torres

"Jake, son I need you and Robby to come home immediately. When you get here, please come downstairs" Charles ordered as he hung up the phone.

"Charles, what is going on here?" Tim asked.

Charles kept quiet as he awaited Jake and Robby to appear. Tim sat in total confusion as to the vague conversation that had just occurred between him and his boss.

Suddenly the stairwell door swung open, and the sounds of three sets of feet could be heard trampling down the stairs. Tim spun in his chair to face Jacob Knight. His jaw dropped as he was looking down at the kid that used to sit in his lap while at the movies and functions. He couldn't believe that Jake had transformed into the muscle-bound mammoth was now standing before him.

"Charles! W-what has happened to Jake?" he gasped.

"Dad??? What is Tim doing down here?" inquired Jake.

"I was about to get to that, son" responded Charles, before he turned to face Tim.

"Tim, I asked you to recall that day seven years ago. Jake and I underwent a metamorphosis of sorts. That craft housed the coded remains of an ancient alien being that possessed a limitless amount of power and knowledge. Jake decided to go exploring that morning, and met this being, who decided that Jake would be the successor to his role as the guardian of the planet" explained Charles.

"Guardian of the Planet?" pondered Tim out loud.

"Let me finish, Tim. That night, this being passed all the physical powers that he possessed onto Jake and all his knowledge and technology on to me..." continued Charles.

"Okay, the technology part would explain why it looks like I am standing in Darth Vader's bathroom here, but I still don't understand why Jake looks like that big wrestler, Batista..."

"Boys, could you go and change quickly please?" Charles asked them.

In a flash, Jake and Robby were replaced with the personas of Myst and Titan.

For the second time since his arrival, Tim's jaw fell agape at the sight of something. Jake walked over to his father and whispered something in his ear.

"Tim, I am here to ask you a favor" said Charles.

Tim stood silent as he stared at the overly muscular youth and his indigo clad partner. Myst walked over to Tim and waved his hand in front of his face.

"Hey coach... Snap out of it!" giggled Robby.

"Tim, I need you help me train these boys. I inherited the knowledge needed to train them in some of the powers that they posses, but you know the physical training better than I do. You were a Navy Seal, for God's sake, and I would hope that you would know how to train these kids to be the strongest and the best fighters around" uttered Charles.

"You mean you want me to train Titan and his sidekick?" asked Tim.

"Uhhh, Coach, I'm NO ONE'S sidekick! I'm his partner!" protested Robby.

"Yeah, Tim! That's my blood-brother, not my sidekick!" demanded Jake.

"Sorry, sorry! You want me to train Myst and Titan?" asked Tim.

"Yes, Tim! I can't do it all, and you know Jake, for he is like family to you. So there's no one better to look after the physical training than you. Would you consider it?" Charles asked.

"Wow! Me, the coach of the strongest boy in the universe, and the most powerful mutant mind on the planet! Charles, Jake, Robby, it would be an honor!" responded Tim.

Jake ran up to Tim and threw his arms around Tim's waist. "Thanks Uncle Tim. I think you will make a great coach!" squealed Jake, while he practically lifted Tim an inch off the ground.

"Whoa, Tiger!!! Easy on that grip!" chuckled Tim.

"So! Not only are you going to be coaching me here, but you're also gonna be my Little League coach as well?" giggled Robby.

"You were going out for the DC Wildcats Little League team?" asked a still shocked Tim.

"Try out? Nah, I was going to amaze ya coach!" chuckled a confident Robby McCloud.

"Well in that case, what position do you play?" inquired Tim.

"First Base..."

"Welcome to the Wildcats, this way I can keep an eye on you all the time!" Tim grinned.

"Wow cool, you guys are gonna have to train your butts off!" giggled Madison from the shadows.

"Jake? How come you're not trying out for the team?" inquired Tim.

Jake quietly walked over to the bat bag and pulled out an old dinged up aluminum bat. He showed it to Tim and commenced to tying it into a knot effortlessly. Then he walked back over and handed it to Tim.

"You tell me, Uncle Tim?" Jake grinned.

"I get the point..." said Tim.

"Tim, he cannot play any sport. As much as he would like to, there is too great a chance, due to his unlimited strength, that someone will get seriously hurt" explained Charles coldly.

"Well, I am not sure what I can do for these two, but I am honored to give it my all!" said Tim.

"You know the basics of physical training, we're just going to elevate that to their levels to get them bigger and stronger and better at fighting!" Charles said.

"Alright, you two..." Tim said, as he looked the two teens in the eye. "I'll come over tomorrow afternoon, and you can show me what your powers are and what you're capable of. I'll train you guys a couple of hours every day, and we'll take it from there!"

"Cool!" Jake smiled. "I can't wait!"

"I'd better get ready to go to baseball practice!" Robby said, as he started to head towards the door.

"Hey, I want to come and watch you guys play!" Jake said to Tim. "Can I watch you guys from the bleachers?"

"Sure! I don't see why not..." Tim shrugged. "Do you know where the practice field is?"

"I know where it is, Coach!" Robby replied. "I can get Jake there! Remember, I'm in charge of making sure that Jake or Titan show up wherever he's needed! That's my job, since I can teleport him anywhere I want to!"

"That's one of Robby's abilities..." Charles whispered to Tim. "He could teleport Jake anywhere he wants to, in a blink of an eye..."

"You don't say?" Tim wondered.

"Hey, Jake! I'm sending you to the baseball field!" Robby shouted, from where he was standing, which was near the stairwell. Jake was standing right in front of Tim, when Robby said that. He was still wearing his Titan uniform.

Suddenly, Jake disappeared into thin air, making Tim jump.

"Charles! Your son! He vanished right into thin air!" Tim uttered.

"Oh, you'll get used to that!" Charles said calmly. "Robby just teleported Jake to the baseball field. He's probably sitting in the bleachers right now!"

"That is absolutely amazing!" Tim continued. "What more can these two boys do?"

"Oh, you'll be surprised! Just wait till you see Jake fly, or use his energy blasts! And Robby has his psychic bursts as well. These kids have a lot of powers, among the two of them! You'll get used to being around them. But you have to remember, they're still kids. Jake is still the same boy you knew from way back. He's just gotten a little stronger, that's all…" Charles laughed.

Chapter 53

Robby and Madison went to Robby's house, where Robby changed. From there, Robby teleported both of them to the baseball field. Tim left the Knight's house, feeling very impressed by the two boys, of course, and he drove towards the practice field as well.

When he arrived there, he glanced over at the bleachers and smiled, when he spotted Titan sitting on one of the top rows of the bleachers, watching the practice session from high above, so nobody recognized that it was him.

The boys' regular training schedule started the very next afternoon. Tim showed up at the Sanctum as soon as the two super-teens got home from school. Brandon made his presence known as well. He was not going to just let his little brother be trained without him there to look after him. Right away, Tim had them spend twenty minutes stretching and running laps around the Sanctum. For Jake, that was easy, since he ran them at super speed. So he made Jake run over 200 laps, before he was allowed to rest.

Then he made Jake use the special weight machines, which Dr. Knight had constructed in the new area of the Sanctum. These were driven by the electro-magnetic device, so Tim was able to increase the virtual weights on these machines, allowing it to become more challenging for Jake to lift them using his arms or his legs. Tim could increase the weights so that the machine would make it seem like Jake was lifting over ten-thousand pounds at a time, or even more. He was doing bicep curls with 12,000 pounds on each arm, and he would do bench presses with over 30,000 pounds on the bar, thanks to this machine! He would use the same for Robby, but Robby would use his psychic abilities to move the weights, rather than his muscles.

Afterwards, Robby demonstrated how he was able to teleport himself around the Sanctum by making himself disappear and reappear at different corners of the room. Then he did the same for Jake by making Jake disappear and making Jake jump to various locations around the vast Sanctum as well. Tim thought this was a great way for allowing Jake to practice his aim at using his energy blasts. Dr. Knight had constructed a metal target that would withstand Jake's weakest energy blasts. Robby would teleport Jake around various positions in front of the target. After each jump, Jake would fire one blast of energy at the target, and Tim would record how often he would strike the target, and how often he would miss. He would do the same for Robby, but Robby would do the teleporting himself, and Robby would use his psychic blasts instead.

Dr. Knight would check in occasionally and observe the training from a distance. He became very pleased with the progress that the boys were making, and Tim would report back to him how the boys were getting faster and stronger every day.

During the first two weeks of training, Tim would come over and help the boys with their agility before leading them into their strength training. This helped the boys tremendously, especially Jake! He grew much stronger, and it showed. He noticed quickly that he had to be extra careful with everything he touched, due to his incredible strength.

Brandon helped Tim keep the logs of the boys training. He also was the one that was instrumental in pushing Robby to the limit, as Tim was with pushing Jake. Brandon was more in tune with Robby's needs when it came to his training. He was the one that got him to be the excellent baseball player that he was, and knew that he could do it here too.

After their training sessions with Tim, the boys would meet up with Tim once again, but at the baseball field. This time, only Robby would participate. Jake would sit in the bleachers, usually by himself, as he watched the boys practice on the field. At first this didn't really bother him, but as the weeks went by, Jake became increasingly quiet and depressed.

Occasionally, Charles and Bob would also come over to watch Tim and Robby during baseball practice. It was during the most recent baseball practice session that Charles took note of the fact that Jake hadn't been himself lately.

Jake was sitting on the very last row of bleachers, just behind home plate, when one of the players at bat had hit a foul ball. The ball flew straight up and into the bleachers, landing practically into Jake's hands. When Jake got up to toss the ball back at one of the players on the field, he unintentionally tossed it much too hard. The ball sailed clearly over the field, bouncing off the wall at the opposite end of the baseball diamond. The ball had bounced just inches from the top edge of the outfield wall, much to Jake's relief. All the boys on the field were in awe of Jake's mighty throw, but the boy, who was standing closest to Jake, just stared at him in anger.

"Good grief! Why did you have to throw the ball so hard?" the boy shouted. "You could have just tossed it to me! What a jerk!"

"I-I'm sorry... I didn't mean to throw it that hard..." Jake replied, clearly feeling embarrassed. "I'm terribly sorry..."

Robby spun on his heels to face the boy. He walked over and shoved the kid in the chest, sending him sprawling in the dirt with his enhanced strength. "What's your deal, Brad? He did not mean to throw it that hard!" scowled Robby as he glared at his rude team mate.

"Robby, calm down!" ordered Brandon.

"McCloud, help Brad off the ground and give me fifty push-ups!" bellowed Tim.

Jake felt terrible. The boy had blond, curly hair with glasses. He looked a little geeky, even. But he stared at Jake as if Jake intentionally tried to show off his strength, and he didn't appreciate it one bit. This had rattled Jake completely, along with his feelings of sadness and loneliness he had been dealing with recently, he had just sent Robby into a rage and got him in trouble with Tim. Jake sat there helpless as he continued to watch his blood-brother play baseball like other normal kids. Jake just sank his head into his hands and felt like he could almost break down in tears.

"I think you and I needed to have a little talk..." Charles said to his son.

Jake looked up and realizes that his father had walked up the steps to come and sit down right next to him.

"What's the matter, son?" he said to him. "You seem kind of down, lately…"

"Dad… I don't know how to explain this… I'm just feeling really alone right now…" Jake replied. "This kid hit a foul ball and I caught it and…"

Jake started to break down in tears.

"I tried to toss the ball back to him and…" he sobbed. "I… I couldn't… even… do that… anymore…"

"It's alright, Jake…" Charles whispered back to him, as he rested his arm on Jake's broad shoulders. "I saw what happened. Having super strength can be a burden sometimes…"

"It's like… Everything I do… Everywhere I go…Everything I touch, I have to handle with kid gloves" Jake continued, in tears. "No matter where I'm at or what clothes I'm wearing… I'm always Titan… Even when I'm asleep, I'm flying across my bedroom… I'm becoming Titan more and more… I have to watch everything I say, everything I do… I have to be super careful… I'm so scared, dad… I'm so scared I'm gonna hurt somebody…"

"Jake…" Charles answered. "I know you carry a heavy weight on your shoulders, son. But, listen to me…"

"Sure, dad…" Jake said, while he wiped the tears from his eyes.

"How many people do you know, who can fly?" Charles asked him.

"Nobody…" Jake replied.

"How many people do you know, who can lift a cruise ship with their bare hands?"

"Nobody…"

"How many people do you know, who have perfect vision in complete darkness?"

"Nobody…"

"How many people do you know, won't get hurt when they get shot, or when they touch a flame or when they cut themselves with a knife?"

"Nobody…"

"And, how many people do you know, who can fire beams of energy from their fists or their fingers so powerful, they can easily level a building?"

"Nobody..."

"You can do all these things, Jake!" Charles added. "You're the only one who can do these things! Most kids would kill, just to have one of the abilities that you have! See your powers as wonderful gifts, not as a heavy burden! I hate to sound like a movie cliché, but with great power, comes great responsibility. You have all these amazing powers and you may feel overwhelmed by them, but, you should enjoy the fact that you have them! When was the last time you've gone flying? Go out and fly around, for crying out loud! You can enjoy the ultimate freedom and be free as a bird! Change into your Titan uniform and have some fun, like you did right after you received your powers from Zhango-Rhe in the Nevada desert! Have you forgotten that?"

"I guess I have... I've been so focused on the training and on Malcolm and I've been thinking about the attack with the robots and so on..." Jake uttered. "And then, when I'm sitting here watching Robby play baseball it just makes me feel a little out of place, because I can't play..."

"Jake, I know that being a normal kid is not an option for you, but you have so much going for you. You have unlimited powers, people love you. Your mother and I love you, Robby and Maddie love you, and your fans love you. What you need to do is embrace the fact that you are this hero, this person that everyone knows as Titan. You should just let it all go and give these kids something to remember and talk about for a long time. You should let these kids watch this baseball team working their butts off with their hero! You should give these kids Titan!"

"It will never be the same again will it dad?" asked Jake as he stood to his feet.

"No son it won't, but it can be an adventure" responded Charles as he hugged his son close and ruffled his hair. "Now go!" he urged.

Jake walked down the stairs towards the restrooms. He quickly changed into his Titan uniform, and he dropped off his clothes in his dad's van. Then he took off, flying low over the baseball field, where

Charles saw him from the bleachers, where he was sitting. Charles waved at his son, who was flying overhead, and he was glad to see the boy smiling again. Then Titan extended his arms fully and headed towards the downtown area of Washington DC, enjoying the cold wind that was blowing in his face.

Titan flew over the big government building and the tall skyscrapers, enjoying the view to the fullest. He had to evade a few news helicopters as well, waving to the cameramen in the process. He realized that he had been filmed, of course. He landed on the roof of one of the tallest buildings, and just filled his lungs with air as he leaned over the edge. What a view it was, to see the people and the cars below!

Then he leaped from the edge of the rooftop, diving straight down, while people on the ground were staring at him in complete amazement. He allowed his body to glide across the sky, flying over the crowds below.

"Look at that flying boy!" they cheered.

"Hey! It's Titan!" another person said.

He flew low and slow, waving at all the kids who were walking on the street. It was time to have fun as Titan again! Everywhere he went, the kids cheered him on and they waved at him. He loved it, and it encouraged him tremendously.

After a few minutes of flying, Titan headed back to the baseball field. He wanted to be with Robby, Brandon, Madison, and his dad, who were watching Robby's baseball practice with Coach Tim. After all, Robby was Myst, his partner, and he didn't want to leave him out there, by himself.

When Titan arrived at the baseball field, he landed on the top row of the bleachers, just out of habit. As soon as he landed there, he heard Robby's voice ringing in his ears.

"Oh no you don't..." Robby spoke to him, using his telepathy. "You're not sitting by yourself again! There's a group of kids sitting in the bleachers in Section C. I'm going to send you there right now! Have fun for the both of us bro, I know you need it!"

Suddenly, Titan was teleported from the top row of the bleachers in Section A, to the middle row of the bleachers in Section C. After the smoke had cleared, Titan was swarmed with a mob of excited kids that were more than ecstatic to see their hero come to visit them.

Brandon glanced at Robby and gave him a knowing smile. He could appreciate his little brother's need to alleviate his friend's emotional stress. After all he had just learned that Robby could feel the emotions of every living creature on the planet if he wanted to. Brandon knew full well that if someone close to him was hurting emotionally, his red headed little brother would be sharing in that dread.

"Titan! That's so cool! How strong are you?" one kid asked him.

"Can you show me your muscles?" another girl asked him.

"Hey, Titan, can I have your autograph?" asked Brad, who was sitting right behind Titan.

"Sure thing Brad!" smiled Jake as he realized that the boy who ridiculed him now wanted his autograph.

Titan had his hands full. Charles and Robby were happy, for Jake had now all but forgotten his concerns about being Titan. He was his old self again.

Chapter 54

Dozens of tall, strange looking men with bright, green eyes and bald heads were wandering around the colossal underground structure, located hundreds of miles outside of Washington DC. The secret facility housed many construction battalions and technology centers. One such facility was an advanced robotics center, which was bustling with activity as its workers attempted to perfect the re design on another giant robot.

A familiar form made its way down a long corridor within the facility. A tall, pale faced man, clad in a black three piece suit was impatiently awaiting a phone call from his field officers. The ominous man would stop, and lean over the railing to gain a better view of the progress being made in the robotics wing.

The men worked the hardest they could, for the man in the black suit was their boss, Thadius Malcolm. And this was already their third robot they were building. The first four robots had been destroyed by Myst and Titan just a few days earlier, but this new version would be much bigger and stronger.

The cell phone rang and Malcolm immediately answered the call.

"Malcolm...Yes, who is this?" Malcolm spoke into the phone. "Yes, Agent Plotzky! I remember you. What have you found out? You've been following those two kids? Good! What have you found out? Two girls? Oooh, really?"

Just then Jaro came from the other direction and walked up to Malcolm. He stopped right next to him and patiently waited for his boss to finish his conversation on the phone.

"My robots will be finished by next Monday! Then, I want you to grab those two girls and take them to my office in the tower, unharmed. I'll have my men prepare my office with the same Zyrtonian ray I used on Zhango-Rhe and our new mind-scrambling machine. We're going to use those two girls as bait, and we're going to catch us two little fish! As soon as those brats are out of commission, then Washington and the rest of this retched planet will be mine!!!!!" Malcolm laughed loudly before he hung up the phone.

"Sounds like you got a plan to get rid of the boys, Boss?" Jaro asked him.

"Yes, my little friend. It won't be long now...." Malcolm grinned, as he stood and looked down at the large robot, which lay on the ground before him. "This time, those brats won't be around to stop my robots. We're going to set a beautiful little trap for them! The minute they walk into my trap, the city, and the rest of the United States of America, will be mine to conquer and destroy. Who will be able to stop us?"

"You're a genius, Boss!" Jaro cheered.

"Of course!" Malcolm sneered. "Zhango-Rhe thought he could outsmart me. Hah! I proved him wrong! Then he sent some little boy to take his place. Well, Titan's days are numbered. He will die in the same fashion that his predecessor did."

Malcolm pulled a small, red stone out of his pocket.

"All we need is a little of this, and a little time. It won't take too long for the Zyrtonium to finish him off, especially if he is anything like Zhango-Rhe."

They were confident, that their plan was going to be a success, and that their robot would be the cause of complete chaos and destruction in the city, for Myst and Titan wouldn't be around to stop the robot, if their trap worked.

Chapter 55

That following Monday afternoon Genny and Piper came to visit the Knight's for an early dinner. They joined Jake, Robby, Brandon, and Madison after school, and the gang just rode the bus home together. They studied in Jake's living room, and they watched TV and hung out, until Charles and Nancy came home.

After diner the boys changed into their costumes. Madison and Brandon joined Charles in the Sanctum's computer lab to go over the training data. Robby teleported Piper and Genny home and they all gave each other hugs and said goodbye.

Robby offered to teleport both he and Jake back home, but Jake decided to fly home instead. So Robby teleported himself, and Jake leaped into the air. He flew over the neighborhood and enjoyed the bird's eye view of the area. He grinned as he looked down and watched the people and the cars from above.

Unknown to Jake, three men were patiently sitting in two separate cars, which were parked a few feet away from Piper's house. They were waiting for the girls to come home. After Robby had teleported away and Jake had taken off, they waited about five minutes more and made their moves. They cautiously approached the house, drawing their weapons, and rang the door bell.

When Jake approached his house from the sky, he noticed an unusual vehicle had just pulled up in their driveway. Jake landed, but he didn't want to be seen. He peered from around the corner and he realized that the person, who got out of the car, was MACH!

Jake then ran towards the back entrance of the house at super speed and he opened the door from the inside.

"Greetings, Titan!" MACH said to the young hero. "May I come in?"

"Sure... I'll let my dad know you're here. I just got home myself!" Jake replied.

"Yes, I know that... Trust me; I have been watching you and your neighbor..." MACH explained to him. "And, I hope everything is alright with my daughter?"

"Yes! She's doing well!" Jake answered. Just then Charles came from the living room. "In fact, she was just here a few minutes ago..."

"Good evening MACH. How are you this evening?" inquired Dr. Knight.

"I am fine sir. I came to deliver you a warning. Thadius Malcolm is working on something really big. You must be ready! My sensors have found that he has completed construction of a large underground facility about one hundred miles south-east of the city. I don't know what he's doing, but considering the fact that he has already sent four large robots to attack the city, you can just bet that this is only the beginning and there will be more to come!" MACH warned Jake and Charles.

"You mean he's built a robot factory of some sort?" Jake asked.

"The purpose of this secluded factory is unknown, but judging the man's past track record, I can almost deduct that would be his intentions. He has hundreds of genetically artificial zombies and smaller robots working for him! Not only that, but he has a large compound outside of the city. I think that's his headquarters..." MACH continued. "I've been using satellite technology to scan the area and I think that's where he's building his robots! He's building more of them, and he's going to attack the city one of these days! You two had better be ready! You're the only ones who can stop him!"

"Well, we've been training hard!" Jake announced. "We're ready!"

Just at that moment, Robby, and Brandon appeared out of nowhere, and they were standing right next to Jake.

"Never mind explaining it all to me. I overheard everything, thanks to Jake!" Robby explained. "We're ready to fight more of Malcolm's robots!"

"Yes, but are you ready to face Malcolm himself?" MACH asked them. "He is very sly and tricky! He will catch you off-guard! I'm warning you guys! I know how Malcolm works! I'm watching you two! You guys need to work together, especially when you're facing Malcolm! You must NEVER face him alone, or he will destroy you!"

Both Jake and Robby gulped when they heard those words from MACH. Could this man really be so evil?

"Who the heck is that?" Brandon whispered to Robby.

"Oh, that is MACH. He is kind of like our guide against this guy that is trying to take over the world" replied Robby.

"Hmmm really? Take over the world? Sounds like he has his hands full trying to do that with you two around" Brandon said quietly.

Suddenly, Jake's cell phone went off and so did Robby's. Genny was calling Jake and Piper was calling Robby, at the same time.

"Genny? What's wrong? You're what? You're where?" Jake was saying over the phone. Genny was clearly upset.

"Piper? Trapped, what? By who? Where? I'm coming!" Robby shouted over his cell phone.

Both boys hung up their cell phones and stared at MACH in anger. Robby's face flushed with rage as he grit his teeth to bite back the urge to scream. He knew that if he gave into the anger that he felt, his powers would wreck the Sanctum.

"The girls have been kidnapped by Malcolm. They're being held at his headquarters on the south-east part of town at the Green Tower on the corner of Olive Street and Park Avenue, they want us to meet them there... Alone!" Jake said in a serious tone of voice.

"You can't face Malcolm alone!" MACH shouted. "You're not ready!"

"But he has my girlfriend MACH! She is in danger! We MUST face him or else he will kill her!" Robby piped up.

"Please... We have to rescue them... That's your daughter..." Jake continued. "We have to go there alone..."

For the moment the two men and the three teens stared at each other in silence.

"Then, so be it." MACH said. "Please, be careful..."

"Look bro I lost my parents, I am not about to lose you. You better be careful" urged Brandon.

"I will Brandon, I promise!" stated Robby.

Robby's eyes turned black. Instantly, Robby and Jake disappeared into thin air.

Charles pondered what had happened, and then looked up and was about to say something to MACH. Then, he realized that the front door to the house was standing wide open.

Charles walked over to the door and was about to close it, when he realized that MACH had vanished as well. That's when he knew that MACH was probably going after the boys. He sighed, as he slowly closed the door. Normally, he wouldn't be worried when Jake and Robby went out on patrol. This time, he felt uneasy and worried. He could only hope for the best.

Chapter 56

When Jake and Robby materialized on the corner of Olive and Park Streets, they found themselves standing before a large building, which resembled a large European castle from the middle Ages. The main gate to the large building was open wide, and the walls were made of large, rectangular bricks.

The boys quickly raced towards the entrance of the large structure. Robby looked at the door with a perplexed glance as the doors blew off the hinges. They walked in brave and bold. As they continued through the building, they came to a long hallway. Suddenly, they began to hear the voices of the girls, which appeared to be coming from the end of the long hallway. Titan ripped the door from the wall and glared inside to see his and Robby's girlfriends bound to chairs inside.

"Jake! Robby!"

"PIPER! Are you alright?" Robby gasped.

"Robby, stay back! It's a trap!" yelped Piper.

As the boys raced towards the girls, they were both caught in the invisible rays, which were emitted from two devices, which were fastened to the ceiling of the room. One machine was emitting a ray of Zyrtonium, and the other was emitting a mind-scrambling ray.

As soon as Robby felt the mind-scrambling ray, he immediately placed the palms of his hands over his ears, and his knees buckled, making him drop to the floor.

"Aaaaaahhhh! What is that noise?" he shouted.

Jake had it just as difficult. He was caught in the Zyrtonium ray, which caused him to weaken immediately.

"Oh no… I'm not feeling too good…" Jake groaned. "I… I… feel weak…"

Jake fell on his knees as well, and then he fell on the floor, barely able to keep his eyes open.

The boys were barely conscious when a sinister figure quietly opened the steel door and walked into the room.

For a brief moment, the two super-heroes weren't aware that they were finally in the presence of the one and only Thadius Malcolm, until they heard his evil chuckle with their own ears.

"Well, well, well, if it isn't the amazing Myst and the unstoppable Titan…" Malcolm spoke with his baritone voice. "How nice of you to drop in? I've been dying to meet you, or should I say, you are dying because you have met me!" cackled Malcolm sinisterly.

Jake looked over and saw Robby on the floor. Robby stared back at him, clutching his head and realized they were both in pain while the Genny and Piper were helplessly tied up in their chairs. Things were not looking good.

Malcolm sauntered over to the fallen heroes. He squatted down and grabbed Jake's face. "I thought you would be a little taller" Malcolm chuckled. "You're rather short for a super-hero…"

"What do you want with us?" asked Titan bravely.

"That is easy, my dear boy. See the thing is I want this planet as my own. You and your red-headed cohort here are the only things that are standing in my way to utter and total global domination" stated Malcolm.

"But Zhango said that you totally destroy planets after you get what you want out of them" gasped Titan, weakened by the red Zyrtonium ray.

"I wish you would not have said that arrogant jerk's name. See, I like this planet, and I plan on calling it my new home. The people of this planet have one chance to live, and that is to bow to me" continued Malcolm.

"I am going to offer you a choice my dear boy. Join me and rule, or stay here and die while I enjoy all the fruits that this planet has to offer" stated Malcolm coldly.

"I will never join you Malcolm, you disgust me!" grunted Titan.

"Suit yourself. You are just as arrogant and just as full of yourself as your predecessor was. You can stay here and die for all I care. Either way, I have disposed of you. But, just think about all that you will be missing out on. All the power, all the fame, and all the control you could have…"

"GO TO HE--……." Titan shouted.

"AH, AH, AH, watch your mouth, there are ladies present, young man" giggled Malcolm.

"But alas, they too will join you in a grave right next to your predecessor. I am leaving and my guards will finish the four of you off. I have bigger fish to fry, and by morning you will be nothing more than a faded memory. Oh, and long after you are gone, people will remember me, and not you or your friend over there" Malcolm said as he pointed at Myst's pain-racked body.

Malcolm turned and made his way to the door. He glanced back over his shoulder one last time, as if checking to see if Myst or Titan would change their minds. When he realized that their collective fates were sealed, he exited his office quietly.

"ROBBY!!!! I think I am dying over here!" screamed Titan to no avail. His screams were falling on deaf ears.

"Piper, we have to help them" urged Genny.

"Cuz there is no way that we can get ourselves free" replied Piper.

Downstairs, MACH had arrived on the scene. He knew something was amiss as he saw Malcolm's limo pull out. The team had failed to stop him. He quickly made his way over to the power coupling box on the outside wall. He pulled a cable from his cybernetic arm and patched into the building's security system.

"Access security camera feed for penthouse office" MACH said coldly as his synapses connected him to the security system.

"Analyzing security feed! There they are. Time to go get those two."

One of MACH's more impressive abilities is that of shape shifting. He concentrated on the form and visage of Malcolm's trusted assistant Jaro. His form slowly adapted to that image. MACH pulled the door open and walked past the guard station with no trouble.

He made his way to the elevator and stepped in. The penthouse access required a security code. MACH relied on his super advanced positronic brain and cybernetic enhancements to over ride the codes.

MACH reached the top floor and raced for Malcolm's office. He flung open the doors and glanced around. He saw both machines that were wreaking havoc on the teen heroes. He transformed his arm into the impressive form of a cannon and fired an Electromagnetic Pulse wave at both machines rendering them inoperative.

"Myst! Get it together! Teleport Titan outside, NOW! Get him into the sun. You follow; you need to charge as well. I will tend to the girls..." ordered MACH.

Robby crawled over to his blood-brother, he was too weak to just teleport him by himself. He grabbed him and teleported the two of them to the roof. Robby nearly passed out from exhaustion.

The rays of the sun bathed down upon Myst and Titan, charging them like a battery. Titan bawled his mighty fists as he sat up and embraced his blood-brother. For the first time since they had known each other, Robby saw true fear in Jake Knight's eyes.

As soon as Robby had teleported himself and Jake from Malcolm's office building, the teens reappeared outside at park which was a few yards away from the Pentagon. This is where they heard that several giant robots were coming!

Chapter 57

"Jake! Are you ready for this, dude?" Robby asked him. Both boys were still a little in a daze following their narrow escape from death in Malcolm's office.

"It's now or never, Robby! This is what we're here for! This is why Zhango-Rhe created me in the first place!" Jake replied, as both boys suddenly saw the giant robots approaching from a distance. Then Jake turned to the bright, blue sky and he glanced at the sun above. "This is why you are here too Robby; this is why that crazy driver almost killed you back then. It brought us together" he said glancing at his partner.

"Alright, Zhango-Rhe. You gave me these gifts. Don't let me down, now!" Jake said to himself. "I need every ounce of strength I can muster... And, please, no Zyrtonium this time!"

Suddenly, the robots started marching straight towards the Pentagon building. They trampled everything that was in their path, crushing cars and buildings that were blocking their way!

"Robby! We gotta stop those monsters right now, before someone gets killed!" Jake said, as he leaped into the air. "I'll take the one on the left!"

"Roger that, dude. I'll tackle the one on the right! You hit 'em high, and I'll hit 'em low!" Robby said, as he immediately teleported into thin air, only to appear right before the giant, thirty-foot mechanical monster.

The robot was about to step on a car! Luckily Myst saw it, and he concentrated on it, making the car roll several feet forward, so that the robot's foot just missed stepping on it. Then he jumped right in front of the robot and aimed his right hand at it, firing his first salvo of psychic blasts at it, causing the robot to lose its balance. The robot then glanced over and spotted Myst, standing on the ground.

Angrily, it lifted its foot and attempted to bring its right foot down on Myst, hoping to crush his body to the ground! Luckily, the second his foot came down, the boy had disappeared.

Suddenly, Myst appeared again, just several feet away from where he was standing. The robot saw that and he lifted his foot again, this time it was sure it had crushed the annoying kid. But when it lifted its giant, metal foot, it realized that there was nothing there.

"Over here, you giant, hunk of scrap metal!" Myst taunted him from below.

The robot then ran after him, as Myst kept on disappearing and reappearing just a few feet away, hoping to lure the large mechanical monster away from the buildings. Finally, Myst appeared in a large, metal garbage dumpster. He hollered out at the robot, hoping to catch its attention. When the robot saw him and came running towards him, Myst just waited patiently while standing on the outer edge of the dumpster. When the robot finally arrived, it slammed its foot into the dumpster, just when he closed the top lid shut. The impact had cut a few wires off the robot's leg, and the robot now had to walk with a slight limp.

Myst hopped off the edge of the dumpster and fired another telekinetic blast at the robot. This time, with a small handicap, it knocked the robot off its feet and caused it to fall over and land on its back with an enormous crash.

But the robot was quick to recover and it quickly got up. As it was struggling to get up on both feet, Myst was making the large, metal garbage dumpster rise up into the air, and hover above the spot where the robot was. Then, he allowed the dumpster to come crashing down on top of the robot with one mighty bang.

Unfortunately, the robot was several times larger than the dumpster, and recovered quickly from the attack. It pushed the dumpster off of its torso, before it got back on its feet. As soon as it was standing, it started charging right at the red headed hero again.

"Oh no! How am I going to get rid of this thing?" Myst gasped.

As the moments passed on, Myst's anger began to swell within him, feeding his psionic powers, causing them to increase tenfold. Unknown to the young mutant, his powers had grown to an almost deadly level.

He glanced at the robot looming over him and gnashed his teeth. He knew that it was going to be him or the titanic metallic brute left standing. He prepared himself for the worst. Something within the young hero caused him to smile.

"Now I get to really let loose!" grinned Myst with an almost sinister smirk.

Myst glanced over his shoulder and saw a fleet of cars that were parked close to where he was standing. He steadied himself and one by one, he pointed his hand at each car, causing them to levitate into the air and fly towards the robot. With a sheer force of will, the teenage mutant made each car slam into the robot's torso, leg, or head. At one point, he forced three cars to hit the robot at the same time, making the robot nearly fall over backwards.

He kept grabbing the cars with his telekinetic vice grip and propelling them with a force that would have rivaled Titan's strongest punch. Shrapnel started flying off the front of the robot. Myst began to see that his attack was beginning to cause some significant damage. When he saw that the robot started to wobble following the attack of all the flying cars, He drew his fists back and let loose a torrent of psionic force blasts aimed at the mechanical menace's chest. Each blast had enough force to topple a city building.

Myst continued the onslaught and hurled his invisible blasts at the robot, much like a baseball pitcher hurling a baseball at the guy at bat. In this case, the baseball was an invisible blast. Each blast caused the robot to take another step back, causing it to inch ever closer to the edge of the lake, which was just a few yards behind where the robot was standing.

"Come on, you big piece of scrap metal!" He shouted at the robot. "I'm taking you for a ride! Up you go!"

Myst aimed his hand at the robot and slowly allowed the robot to levitate off the floor. He had to really concentrate hard, to make the robot rise up above the ground. The robot started swinging its arms and legs around, as it struggled to understand what invisible force was causing it to levitate in mid-air.

"YAAARRRRHHHH! You are MINE!" bellowed Myst as he forced his telekinesis to do his bidding.

Myst released a wicked grin as he spotted a high voltage power line, hanging overhead. He forced the body of the robot to hover motionless above the awaiting make-shift stun-gun. The young hero knew that he had to get ruthless with these harbingers of mayhem. He let the grin spread wider across his face as he lowered the robot's body onto the power line. As soon as the robot touched the power line, it started sparking as it came into direct contact with the power line!

Sparks continued to fly as the robot remained firmly planted in the power line. Finally, Myst let his grin fade into a glare of concentration. He bawled up his fists and cocked his head to the side. Myst then used his telekinetic powers to send the robotic creature jack hammering head first into the ground. The robot came down hard on the pavement, with more pieces of metal flying off the robot's chest, exposing more wires and gears and other electronics.

"If I can just get ole' Sparky to fall into the lake..." He said to himself, as he watched the robot slowly struggle to get back on its feet.

Myst started firing one psychic blast after the other, causing the robot to stumble backwards with each blast.

"Take that, you pile of rust!" He shouted, as he hurled another blast at its head.

Finally, the robot had reached the edge of the lake and started to lose its balance, when it tumbled backwards and plunged into the shallow waters of the lake with a loud splash!

Myst ran towards the lake, panting for a few moments, since he didn't see anything, when the robot suddenly came rising up from the surface! The boy was startled by the robot's sudden appearance, and he took several steps backwards, tripping over some seaweed and falling into the water.

The robot lifted its foot up high and was about to press on down on the almost exhausted teenager's body, when suddenly, the robot's exposed wires and electronics had short-circuited! The robot froze and tumbled backwards, crashing down into the water, as Myst looked on with tremendous relief. For a few moments, there was silence. Then, the robot's head surfaced from the lake again, staring at the boy. Myst stared at him in anger, as he aimed both fists at him.

"You're going down... Now!" he shouted.

Then he glared at the robot with sheer hatred. He pulled himself fully upright and aimed his hands and arms at the robot. He knew the time was at hand to finish the robot off. He closed his emerald green eyes only to reopen them with a coal black stare. He flashed a grin then gnashed his teeth again. He let loose a guttural growl as the robots head sheered from its body at the hands of Myst's telekinetic grip.

"Die!" Myst said. "And never come back!"

The young mutant stood at the edge of the lake, as he watched the robot sink to the bottom of the lake for the last time. He collapsed to his knees with exhaustion. He had fought harder than he ever thought possible. He knew there was more to his powers that he had to discover, but now was not the time to worry about that.

"I'd better go and see how Titan is doing..." Myst whispered to himself, as he climbed to his feet. He scanned for his partner's whereabouts and teleported nearby.

Meanwhile, Titan had wasted no time with the 30-foot robot. He realized right away, that it could have come from nobody else, but Thadius Malcolm. And, since he had nearly gotten killed just a few minutes ago by that same person, he was totally enraged at the thought that he was going to have to fight one of Malcolm's minions.

Titan leaped into the air and clasped his hands together, soaring right for the robot's chest. He slammed right into the robot with a mighty BANG, knocking a sizeable dent into the robot's metal skin and causing it to stumble backwards.

Then Titan flew around and dove right for his head, just as the robot tried to swat the flying boy with its large, metallic hand, barely missing him. He spiraled out of the way, firing a burst of energy right into the mechanical menace's head, striking it into the side of the head. Then he zoomed out of the way again, flying out of range before preparing for another attack.

This time, Titan decided to concentrate his firepower on one part of the metallic menace, with the hope of causing enough damage, to incapacitate it. He aimed at the left shoulder, firing another burst of energy from his fists, as he flew right towards him. The robot swung his hand at him again. Titan flew high above his head, diving behind his back and firing at him from behind before coming from behind and from between the robot's legs. As he ascended, he aimed for the left shoulder again, and he caused a metal plate to come off the robot's shoulder.

As Titan was flying in front of the metallic monster, the robot suddenly reached out with his right arm, and he dove quickly to avoid it, but he didn't spot the left arm. Suddenly, he found his body being engulfed by five, large, metallic fingers! He was caught in the giant grip of the robot's hand!

"Oh no you don't..." Titan groaned, as he felt the robot's grip being tightened around him. "I... must... break... loose..."

With a burst of titanic strength, the super-strength possessing hero pressed his mighty hands against the metallic walls of the robot's hands, forcing the armor plated fingers to spread apart. It was just enough to give Titan the edge he needed. As he leaped into the air, he turned to fly backwards, aiming his fists at the robot's hands. He unleashed powerful plasma energy blasts, to wreak havoc on the robot's appendage that attempted to crush the life out of him.

"It ain't gonna be that easy, you giant hunk of scrap metal!" Titan said angrily, as he shook his fist threateningly at his foe.

Titan decided to concentrate his efforts on the left shoulder of the giant robot. He knew that he had to give it everything he had to topple this creature and put a stop to its reign of terror. He aimed a volley of plasma energy blasts at the shoulder joint, in hopes of severing it from the body.

"YAHHHHH!!!!!!" he shouted, as he cannon balled right into the robot's left shoulder, causing more pieces of metal to shear off. The force of the collision finally knocked the robot off its feet, causing it to topple over and crash onto its back. As it lay on the ground, Titan quickly made his move. He moved with lightning like speed to the fallen being's left side. He reached over, and with both his mighty arms around the wrist of the robot, he pulled with his massive strength. His muscles sprang to life and swelled at the force that their young master was commanding them to do. As he bit his lip and strained more, the left arm tore loose from the shoulder with a loud screech.

"UNNNGHH!!!" grunted Jake as he tossed the severed arm of his foe in to the Potomac River.

Titan took to the sky, as the robot slowly climbed back on its feet. He flew out of reach of the remaining robotic limb. The robot kept swatting at Titan, to no avail. Titan's anger was growing exponentially as the moments passed.

The muscle bound hero decided to concentrate all of his attention on a new target and fire his energy bursts at the robot's head, hoping to cause more significant damage. Suddenly, as Titan attempted to fly into a better vantage point position of attack, the robot's hand came crashing down, and its palm of its large, metallic hand struck Titan from behind, hitting him in the back. This caught him by surprise, sending him crashing onto the pavement. Titan's body slammed into the ground at the robot's feet.

Dazed and disorientated, Titan opened his eyes and gasped at the sight of the giant robot standing before him, the robot lurched forward and lifted its massive foot. He saw the sole of the right foot which about to come down on him, and Jake quickly was rolled out of the way, as the large foot came crashing down, causing the pavement to crack just inches from his head.

"So you want to play rough, huh?" Titan grinned. "I have been waiting a while to really crank up the power, and you look like the perfect punching bag for me to smash to bits" he continued.

The robot attempted to trample Titan again with its foot. He was more than ready for that little maneuver this time.

Titan reached out his huge muscular arms and grabbed hold of the edges of the robot's foot, stopping the foot dead in its tracks as it attempted to crush him, in an incredible feat of physical strength, he grit his teeth, as he slowly made his way back to his feet as he held on to the robot's foot, forcing it even higher off of him, even while the robot continued to try to push down as hard as possible.

"Now... it's my turn... to play rough!" Titan uttered, resolved to put this menace to rest as quickly as possible.

He spotted a three story abandoned building, a few yards from where he was battling the robot. Jake figured that he would give the demolition crew a hand by using the robot to demolish the building. He slowly started rising up, flying above the ground, while still holding on to the robot's foot. This caused the robot to lose his balance and fall over, landing on its back.

Then Titan slowly started spinning the robot in a tight axis. The robot's body went limp from the sheer centrifugal force of Titan spinning him with super-human speed and power. Metallic parts started to tear away from the robot's body as the force of the revolutions took its toll on it.

He spun around at lightning speed, almost like a discus thrower at the Olympic Games, before letting go at just the right moment. The robot's helpless body was catapulted into the abandoned building. The robot's body crashed through brick building with a wickedly destructive tone, an orchestra of twisting metal, breaking glass, disintegrating bricks, and splintering wood could be heard across town.

He hovered, smiling with a sense of satisfaction as he peered through the smoke and dust, at the rubble that once was a building. Then, he saw the robot's head slowly rising up from the rubble, as it struggled to come back on its own two feet.

"What do I have to do? Now I'm gonna finish you off, you bastard..." Titan said angrily.

Titan clasped his fists together and unleashed a continuous beam of plasmoidal energy at the building, setting it on fire. The entire front, side, and rear of the structure were engulfed in a blaze of fury!

Then, when the robot tried to move once more, he focused the beam on its metallic frame one more time. This time keeping the monster robot pinned to the ground with the sheer force of the blast. All the hatred, all the rage that was boiling up within Titan was manifesting itself in the form of the plasma blast he was firing.

"Die, you stubborn hunk of junk...DIE!" Titan shouted, as he the last of his fury came crashing down upon his metallic foe.

When Titan landed he scanned the building. The menace that Malcolm had unleashed finally ceased to function. He saw the last twitch of the robotic hulk.

The young hero stood there in silence as he watched the building burn. It brought him a certain feeling of satisfaction, since the robot was sent by Malcolm. For a moment, it felt like payback. It was a fitting ending to what has been a long, bad day.

"This one... This one's for Zhango-Rhe..." He said solemnly to himself, as he looked on at the burning robot. Malcolm killed Zhango-Rhe, and now it seemed like Titan had finally returned the favor and destroyed something that Malcolm had created.

Brandon, Charles and Madison watched in horror as the News Seven helicopter was broadcasting the mayhem below on the evening news. Brandon sat in fright as he watched Robby do amazing things to put a stop to the robots. Charles was worried at the same time that, even with Jakes power, it would not be enough to overcome these terrors that Malcolm had unleashed.

There came a sigh of relief as the duo emerged from the smoke and wreckage to stand triumphant at the battle's end. Madison had been so worried that he had begun biting his nails in fear. Charles was steadily accessing satellite imagery, while Brandon stood motionless praying that all would turn out well.

Jake took a few moments staring at the burning building, when Robby appeared standing right next to him. He didn't realize it at first, until Robby walked a little closer to him.

"Boy, I'm glad that's over..." Robby sighed.

"Robby!" Jake cheered. "Boy; am I ever glad to see you!"

Jake practically embraced Robby and lifted him off his feet. He was so elated that Robby had also destroyed his robot. Both boys were victorious.

Chapter 58

As Jake was holding Robby in an embrace, he spotted strange looking people coming towards them, coming down the street.

"Robby... Who are those strange-looking people coming towards us?" Jake asked him.

The people were wide eyed, and they looked as if they were in a fixed gaze, as they were marching straight for Robby and Jake. The boys let go and turned to face in opposite directions when they realized that they were being surrounded by hundreds, or maybe thousands of them. The strange people were all marching at a slow but constant pace, and they were looking at the heroes with an odd stare, without even blinking. They showed no expression or emotion, as they approached the heroes.

"That's weird..." Robby said. "I am not getting any kind of reading from them. No thought other than "feed" and no emotion. It is like they are lifeless!"

"Lifeless?" Jake asked. "How can they be lifeless? They're walking! They can't be lifeless!"

"Jake, I think that these things are dead. Ya know, like 'Night of the Living Dead'-dead!" Robby continued.

"What?"

Suddenly, Jake heard MACH speaking to him over his earpiece.

"Jake! You have to destroy them! They are not alive! They are the byproduct of Malcolm's failed attempt at a super army! They are the Dead-Live! They are zombified, mindless slaves of Malcolm's! Shoot them, Titan!"

"I can't shoot innocent people!" Jake uttered. "That's wrong!"

"Titan! You must listen to me. They are not human anymore. They are zombies that are part of Malcolm's army. The only way to stop them is to obliterate them one way or another!" commanded MACH.

"Start firing, dude! They're coming closer!" Robby shouted, as he was standing back to back against Jake.

Jake extended his arms and started firing his energy bursts, knocking down one zombie after another. However, for each one he shot down, it seemed like three more appeared to come from behind it. Robby started doing the same, aiming at the approaching zombies and firing his kinetic bursts at them and knocking them down one-by-one.

"Robby! There are too many of them! They're coming from all over the place!" Jake exclaimed. We can't keep this up!"

"It's a trap!" Robby screamed. "Malcolm's trying to wear us out by trying to get us to fire at each zombie individually! Hold your fire, Jake! Stop firing!"

The boys stood closer together, pressing with their backs against one another as the zombies marched ever closer to them, surrounding the two teen heroes on all sides. It seemed like they were now thousands of them, and they were coming from all sides.

"Robby, what's the plan? You gonna teleport us outta here or something?" asked Jake.

"That is one way out, but that is not going to eliminate these things! I am not really sure what we should do right now" Robby said.

"Jake! Robby! You two need to work together!" MACH ordered, while speaking into their earpieces. "You two must fire at them with everything you got, but you need to do it at the same time. Just blanket the area with plasma and telekinetic energy. And make it the heaviest you guys have ever laid out!"

"Robby! Did you hear what MACH just said?" Jake asked his partner.

"Yeah! Alright, dude… On the count of three… Blast the place with everything you got!" Robby ordered.

"Okay…"

"Get ready…" Robby instructed. "One… Two… Three! FIRE!!!"

Both Robby and Jake extended their arms in front of them and let loose every ounce of fury they could muster. Jake released the mightiest blast of energy burst he has every thrown at anything before, blasting the large crowd of zombies that were approaching before him with blazing fire, causing all of them to burn instantly!

Robby did the same, launching a tremendous telekinetic force wave on the massive crowd of zombies that were gathering before him, leveling the entire field in an instant! It was like a huge bomb had gone off in the center of town, for a tremendous wave of fire and energy flowed over the area, starting from the spot where the boys were standing, and traveling outward towards the zombies like waves in the ocean.

Within seconds, every zombie that was standing within a mile from the boys were either blown to pieces by a telekinetic explosion from within their very bodies or burned from the impact of massive amounts of solar hot plasma beams, and the entire area was covered by the remains of the burned, dead beings.

Both boys were panting as they stood, completely exhausted, and drenched in sweat, as they looked over the field of bodies which lay before them.

"Are… Are they all gone now?" Jake stuttered.

"Bro…I can't detect them because they're all dead…" Robby said. "I-I think so…Hold tight!!.....Myst to control, give me a scan of the area and let me know if ANYTHING is moving…" ordered Myst.

"MACH to Myst.....zero movement in the area.....threat neutralized" stated the cyborg.

"Man, I'm glad that's over…" Jake sighed.

"Me to, bro!" announced Robby.

Jake and Robby just stood there, looking over the carnage and the destruction. It saddened them that Malcolm would go to such lengths to get rid of them. It made them wonder what he would do next, now that they actually destroyed the robots and killed all the zombies. Both boys were very concerned about that, for they realized that Malcolm's attacks would become more vicious from now on.

"You know something, Robby?" Jake noted, as he was looking out over the sea of dead zombies that lay before him.

"What's that?"

"I have to admit one thing: MACH has been correct about every single thing he has told us about Malcolm so far..." Jake announced. "I can honestly say that he is to be trusted..."

"Man, am I glad to hear those words coming out of your mouth, Titan!" MACH spoke out loud.

The duo spun around to see MACH standing next to an SUV. The back doors swung open as Genny and Piper piled out of it and ran towards Robby and Jake.

"Jake! Robby!"

Genny and Piper came running towards the two teen heroes and they each embraced their own hero; Genny leaped into Jake's arms while Piper gave Robby a firm hug.

"We were so worried about you guys! But, you were magnificent! We saw everything on TV from the Sanctum!" Piper cheered out loud.

"You too, Jake! The way you handled the robot and then you blasted those awful zombies! You were terrific!" Genny beamed out loud.

"Ooh it wasn't me at all, Genny!" Jake said calmly. "Robby was the big hero! He saved the day with his awesome psychic powers!" Jake added. He hated taking all the credit for saving the day when he knew he relied on Robby as well.

"No way!" Robby piped up. "There's no way I could have done it all this without my muscle backing me up out there! I'm not taking all the credit for this!"

"You two need to stop it!" Piper injected. "Both of you deserve the credit for saving this town from becoming Malcolm's headquarters!"

"I second that!" MACH added. "These two finally learned that they are unstoppable when they work together... I think they learned a valuable lesson today!"

"So, what do we do now?" Piper wondered.

"I want to go home and rest... "Robby answered. "Then I need to get ready for a baseball game in a few days..."

"I want to get out of town for a few days..." Jake pondered out loud.

"How about we all go to the beach tomorrow? I think you guys deserve a break!" Genny suggested.

"Sure... Let's head back to the Sanctum so we can plan what we're going to do for the next few days, alright?" Robby continued. "Then, we can take it from there..."

"I'll take the girls home, since you two can easily fly or teleport..." MACH said.

MACH then signaled the girls that he was going to head back to the Sanctum and that he could give them a ride back home. Jake and Robby stayed behind, knowing that they would easily beat them home anyway. As MACH drove off with the girls, the teens saw someone else approaching them on a bicycle covered in dust and dirt.

"Oh gosh! That looks like Brandon!" Robby exclaimed. "Brandon!"

Brandon came pedaling on his bicycle and hopped off, just where the two heroes where standing. He looked around and gazed in astonishment at the dead bodies everywhere, before he walked up to Robby, who was still wearing his Myst costume.

"Brandon!" Robby said. "What are you doing here?"

"Are you kidding me?" the young man spoke to the hero. "I'm here to see my little bro! I was watching you on TV! First you were fighting that huge robot, and then you had to face those ugly zombies! There's no way I'm going to allow you to fight your battles on your own, without me being there to help you out if you needed me! So I left the Sanctum against MACH's better judgment and headed here. I had to come to help you Robby. You were always there during baseball season, Red, so now I'm here to help you out when you do your super-stuff!"

"Brandon, you mean to tell me that you came out here to try and help us, knowing of the danger that you would be in?" Jake asked him.

"There's no way I'm going to let you guys fight your battles on your own. I will risk everything to be with you, no matter what you guys are facing!" Brandon replied confidently.

"Brandon, you're one brave dude!" Robby spoke softly, as he embraced his "big bro".

"Brandon, I'm amazed by your loyalty and your courage, man…" Jake spoke solemnly. "Dude, to me, you're my hero!"

Brandon and Jake just stared at one another, while Brandon's mouth dropped wide open.

"Jake… Do you mean that? I mean… You… You're Titan!" he stuttered. "You're everyone's favorite hero! You're the most powerful kid on earth! And you think that I am your hero?"

"Just because you don't have super powers that doesn't mean can't be a hero…" Jake replied calmly. "And, super-heroes like me can also have heroes of their own… You're my hero, Brandon!"

"Thanks Jake, err I mean Titan…" Brandon said, with tears of joy rolling down his face. "Hearing that from you means a lot…"

"B, you have always been my hero. I have always looked up to you all my young life, and even now. You risked getting hurt to come to my side if I needed you. To me you are part of the team" Robby added.

"Robby….I have always loved you like a brother. Heck, you are actually closer to me than the rest of my family is. And you telling me that I am part of your team is the greatest honor I could ever have" said Brandon as he embraced his little brother again and shed a few tears of joy.

The boys talked for a few minutes, before Robby teleported Jake to the Sanctum. He spent a few minutes with Brandon, until they joined Jake, MACH and the girls at the Sanctum as well, so they could plan a fun outing for the next few days.

Before Robby and Brandon went back to the Sanctum, they shared memories of Boston. Robby told Brandon how glad he was to have him by his side again. Brandon returned the sentiments. Robby told him how serious that he was about having him on the team. Brandon was elated at the fact that both heroes thought that.

Chapter 59

As the heroes and Brandon made their way into the Sanctum, they were greeted by a thunderous applause from Charles, Nancy, Madison, Piper, Genny, MACH, and Tim. They had all gathered there to watch the battles on the huge flat screen monitors, and to help them and assist them by way of the new earpieces, which they had made for Titan and Myst.

"Now, before we do anything else, I think we should come up with a name for our group of heroes and their support people who work hard behind the scenes to provide the information they need to fight the evils and injustices that are out there..." Charles announced. "So, does anybody have any suggestions?"

Everyone got around in a wide circle in the center of the Sanctum as they threw around some ideas for a name for the new group.

"The Power Kids," Genny suggested.

"The Super Ninjas," Madison thought out loud.

"The Capital City Crime fighters," Jake had thought up.

"Washington Warriors," shrugged Brandon.

"Well, being a mutant I sometimes feel so different from everyone else, that it seems like I was born an outcast..." Robby piped up. "I think Jake can relate to this, seeing as though he can't do a lot of the things that the so-called 'normal' kids can do. So, why don't we just call ourselves 'The Outcasts'?"

"Ya know that is a pretty catchy name!" Jake chuckled.

"It would describe me perfectly" stated MACH coldly.

"Alright... We'll go with 'The Outcasts' unless anybody objects or comes up with something better..." Charles continued. "Now, we need to elect a leader for our group, so I open the floor for any nominations…"

"I nominate Jake!" Genny said right away, causing Jake to return a startled look.

"Do you accept her nomination, son?" Charles asked him.

"Umm… I appreciate your nomination, but I humbly decline…" Jake replied sadly. "I don't think I'm qualified to lead this group. I'm a servant, not a leader…"

There was a moment of silence among the members of the group as everyone waited for someone else to nominate another person, following Jake's surprise announcement.

"Alright… Do we have any other nominations?" Charles asked.

"Well, in that case, I nominate Robby!" Piper announced.

"Well, Robby… What do you say?" Charles asked him.

"Wow! If my blood-brother feels that he should not lead, then, yes, I will accept!" he replied with a smile on his face.

"All in favor of Robby leading the Outcasts say 'Aye'!" Charles said out loud.

"Aye!" everyone said at the same time.

"All opposed of Robby leading the Outcasts say 'Nay'…"

There was a moment of silence.

"That settles it! Robby McCloud, also known as Myst, is elected by unanimous vote as the leader of the Outcasts!" Charles announced happily. "Congratulations, son!"

Just about everybody took turns walking up to Robby to congratulate him on his new assignment as the leader of the Outcasts. Everyone was talking to Robby except Jake, who silently retreated to the corner of the Sanctum where the computers where. He quietly walked over to the large computer, and just stared at the terminal as he leaned against the desk.

After a few moments, he felt a gentle tap on the shoulder. When he turned around, he saw his father standing before him. Jake briefly looked up and then he bowed his head.

"I guess you're probably disappointed in me, huh?" he said to Charles.

"Why do you say that?"

"Because I got nominated to lead the group and I turned it down…" Jake replied quietly. "I figured that you probably wanted to see me become the leader of the group, right?"

"Not unless you don't want the job, son…"

"So, you don't mind?"

Charles ran his hands over Jake's broad shoulders and then down his arms.

"I can't tell you how proud I am of you right now, Jake…" Charles whispered.

"Really?" the boy wondered, as he raised his head so he could look his father in the eyes.

"You have become so much like Zhango-Rhe, it's scary…" Charles whispered back at him. "You're just like him!"

"What?"

"You talk like Zhango-Rhe! You act like Zhango-Rhe! You think like Zhango-Rhe! And you're starting to even look like Zhango-Rhe, when he was younger…" Charles grinned. "Zhango-Rhe told you that your purpose here was to serve and not to lead or to rule! He would have done the exact same thing! Trust me, I know! I have his knowledge and his wisdom, remember?"

Jake just stared at his father in awe and in wonder as he pondered his words.

"Wow! Thanks, dad… I really, really appreciate that…" Jake said.

"Do you know what some of the teachers are telling their students in school, while using you and Myst as an example?" Charles asked his son.

"No?" Jake wondered. "Where did you hear about that?"

"On the news." Charles responded softly. "They're telling all their students to 'Act like Titan in everything you do, and be like Myst everywhere you go…'"

"Oh, wow… I had no idea…" the young super-hero whispered to his father in reply.

"Well, son, take a few minutes tonight and go out to the dig site alone to meditate…" Charles said softly. "Go back to your roots, and have a talk with Zhango-Rhe tonight, Jake… Trust me; it'll be good for your soul… Come back when you're ready, so you can have some fun with the rest of the group, alright?"

Jake turned around and walked up the stairs. Then he left to go out to the second floor balcony when Robby appeared standing before him, while still wearing his Myst suit.

"I guess you're leaving the party early, huh?" he asked.

"Yeah… I just need to go back to the desert for a few minutes… I'll be right back…"

"I can get you there faster…" Robby stated. "If you want…"

Jake just stared at Robby for a moment, when his sadness turned to a brief smile.

"Sure… Teleport me there… I'd appreciate it, Myst…"

"My pleasure, Titan…" Robby grinned. "I'll come and join you in a bit! Take your time dude; I know that you miss him. I have to say, he gave the world an awesome gift when he selected you to be its champion and guardian. Now GO! "

Myst stared at Titan and concentrated, while his eyes turned black. Instantly, Titan disappeared into thin air, and he reappeared again in the middle of the Nevada desert, thousands of miles away, at the exact location of the dig site, where Zhango-Rhe's space ship once stood. In fact, this was the precise location where Jake Knight had received his powers and where he first transformed into the mighty Titan, over seven years earlier.

The young, muscular boy slowly walked around the site, which was now nothing more that rubble and dirt. There was very little left of the secret cavern, which once housed the sinister space ship that was the home of Titan's alien ancestor.

As the wind blew the young hero's hair, Titan couldn't help but look up into the starry sky and wonder in awe at the bright stars, which were joined by the large, bright moon, which was shining overhead. It almost seemed like Zhango-Rhe was looking overhead, and listening to his descendant below him.

"I miss you so much, Zhango-Rhe…" Titan spoke into the wind. "I know you died a long time ago and that you came here as a computerized remnant that was installed into your spaceship, which was destroyed when Malcolm found you… My father has your knowledge and I have your powers and your strength, but neither of us have your experience…"

The wind kicked up and blew even harder in Titan's face, as if some unseen force had answered or acknowledged the young hero's words.

"I know you died a long time ago, and I know your memory and your hologram has perished when the ship had exploded as well, but I really miss having you around..." Titan continued.

Then the wind calmed down again as everything became quiet around the short, muscular boy.

"I wish there was a way to bring you back..." Titan spoke. "I wish I could speak to you again, and ask you questions and listen to your advice... I wish there was a way to revive your hologram, your memory and your mind in some form or fashion... I'm part of the Outcasts now, and you would be such an incredible part of our little group... We need you, Zhango-Rhe... Please, I beg you... Please come back..."

A violent gust of wind kicked up, engulfing Titan. It almost seemed like someone had listened to his request.

Then, when the wind had died down again, Robby appeared standing next to him once again.

"Jake?"

Titan turned and faced Myst. This time, he was happy to see his best friend again.

"Are you ready to go home now?"

"Yeah..."

"We all got together and discussed our plans for tomorrow while you were gone" Myst explained. "The girls wanted to take us to the beach for a picnic in the morning before we head out to the baseball field in the afternoon to watch my game with Coach Tim. Are you coming along with us?"

"Of course..." Titan replied softly.

"Alright... Let's go home!" Myst commanded.

Titan and Myst disappeared from the Nevada desert and reappeared in the Sanctum in a cloud, while everyone was waiting for them to return. Genny walked up to Jake and softly kissed him on the cheek. Brandon came over and hugged one of his heroes. They all gathered around and had a late dinner, before everyone went home.

Chapter 60

The next morning, Robby came running into the Sanctum with a huge smile plastered on his face. He was holding a small poster in his hand. He ran up to Jake, who was sitting at the control center showing Brandon the computer controls. He handed the poster to Jake, who read it and looked at Robby with a look of happiness.

"You mean to tell me that Sypher is playing in the park on the same day that your game is, bro?" asked Jake.

"Dude, you mean the same band that you have been telling me about for years, bro?" asked Brandon.

"Yes! They are playing early that afternoon for the finale of the Battle of the Bands" exclaimed Robby with a huge grin.

Robby explained that they all could go to the show. He told Jake that it would be one way that he could get all the frustrations that Malcolm had placed on his shoulders, a way that he could let out the anguish that he was feeling about the loss of Zhango-Rhe. Jake thought about it for a moment and decided to call Genny and see what she thought.

As Jake hung up the phone he had a huge grin on his face. He informed the guys that Piper and Genny would love to go to the show. Jake could not contain the excitement that was boiling up within his soul. His face was beaming with glee.

"Robby, this is awesome; I have never been to a concert! And I get to go to your favorite band's show" gasped Jake.

"Well my boy, Mikey from school told me about it. He called me this morning and asked me to stop by his place, well when I arrived, he handed me that poster. So we are meeting up with him there" explained Robby.

"Oh you mean Mikey Mims, the kid from your science class you are always talking about?" asked Jake.

"Yeah, that would be him" smiled Robby.

Later that morning, the adults loaded up the boys and left to pick up Piper and Genny. They all loaded up in the van and drove to the city park where the concert was being held. As they pulled up they could hear the sounds of the local bands blaring over the speakers that were set up.

"Hang on guys let me call Mikey so we can meet up with him" urged Robby.

As Robby hung up his phone, he turned to see his friend making his way towards them. Mikey Mims stood a little taller than Robby. His hazel eyes sparkled with excitement as he ran up to his best friend from school. He took his hat off and shook his shaggy brown hair and replaced his hat cocked a little to the right side. He smiled as he hugged his friend and smiled an honest friendly smile.

"Hey Robby, how are you bro, I see you brought the gang" said Mikey.

"Yeah! Mikey, this is Jake, my big brother, Brandon, Piper, Genny, Dr. and Mrs. Knight, and our trainer Tim Marshall. Guys, this is my best friend from science class, Mikey" Robby said as he introduced everyone.

"Where are your parents, Robby?" asked Mikey.

"They will be at my baseball game later this afternoon" replied Robby with a grin. "You want to go?"

"Dude, I would love to" answered Mikey.

"Oh, I know that you are a really big fan of Sypher's. I was wondering if you would like to meet the lead singer?" asked Mikey.

Robby's eyes grew wide and the rest of the gang let out audible gasps. Robby could hardly believe what he was hearing. For so long he had followed this band, both on the Internet and radio. He bought all the songs off the Internet and ordered t-shirts off the bands Web site. He was so devoted to have never met the band.

"Are you serious?" asked Robby with amazement.

"Yeah, Koren Taylor is a really good friend of mine. His parents were at my parents' wedding, we kind of grew up together" replied Mikey.

"Awesome!" exclaimed the group in unison.

Mikey then led Robby, Brandon, Jake, Piper, and Genny to the band staging area. Mikey left the group at the gate and went in with his pass to find Koren. He was only gone for a few short moments before returning with Koren Taylor, front man of Sypher in tow.

Koren was the same height as Robby, but that was where the similarities ended. He was sporting a close cut Mohawk haircut. He had two large black tribal type earrings in both ears. His eyes glistened with a regal and emotional appearance. You could see why this young man could capture the minds of his audience the way he did.

"Koren, this is Robby McCloud. He is like Sypher's biggest fan" announced Mikey.

"Hi Robby, it is really nice to finally meet you, Mikey has told me a lot about you" said Koren as he extended his hand to shake Robby's hand.

"Hi! Dude, it is an honor to meet you" said Robby.

As Robby shook Koren's hand, he got a flash of something that was different about Koren. He could not quite figure out what it was. He felt the emotions that fueled the amazing rock front man to create the music that he did. He sensed that Koren was a noble soul, but he was also a volatile spirit. The confusion did not end there.

"OK, guys, I have got to get ready. Mikey is going to make sure that you guys get up front, and that Jake, your parents are taken care of" Koren said as he smiled and made his way back stage.

Robby glanced over his shoulder and watched Koren leave. He wondered what it was, about this teen that spiked his curiosity and caused him to automatically read him the way that he did. He chalked it up to the excitement of seeing his favorite band perform.

As the band took the stage, Mikey stood there arm-in-arm with Robby and Jake. He talked about how much that the group was going to amaze Robby and his friends. The intro music hit with an ominous tone, as the band made its way to their respective positions. The first note screamed through the air with piercing precision.

Koren made his way onto the stage and the sheer shock of what Robby was seeing startled him so much that it triggered the connection between him and Jake. Jake looked over at his blood-brother with a bewildered look.

"Robby what is it?" Jake whispered to Robby mentally.

"You can't see it?" returned Robby.

"What?"

"The aura around Koren? He has an aura that is radiating off him, I think I picked up on it earlier, but now I can see it" answered Robby mentally.

"What can it mean?" asked Jake.

"Not sure" answered Robby. "Let's just enjoy this and I will figure it out later" offered Robby.

Everyone rocked out as the clean crisp sounds strummed through the park. They watched as Koren had the crowd eating out of his hands. He pulled out all the stops, as if he was auditioning for Jake and Robby. He was more intense than Robby had ever remembered seeing him. Mikey was totally enthralled with the performance of his close friend.

The concert came to a close and the band left the stage. Robby wondered what was so different about Koren. He decided to scan the young man to see if he could legitimize his feelings. He closed his eyes as to not draw attention to himself. He gently probed the front man's mind. What he saw shocked him, and relieved him at the same time.

"Jake, come here!" requested Robby.

"Yeah, what's up?"

"Koren is a mutant" whispered Robby.

"You sure?" responded Jake.

"I am positive, I guess it takes one to know one" Robby chuckled.

"Is he dangerous?" asked Jake.

"No, he wants to meet us and work with us, I think…"

Jake and Robby pondered what they had just learned about the front man's secret. Robby could not help but wonder if Koren let him see what he was all about. He was happy to know that there was someone else out there that was like him. He could barely contain his excitement.

Epilogue

As the large group moved from the park where the concert was held to the baseball field, everyone decided to sit with their friends and to pick their favorite spot in the bleachers from where to view the game. Nobody noticed at first, however, that Jake was sitting alone, on the top row of the bleachers, with his elbows on his legs and his chin resting between his hands. At first, he seemed like he was bored silly, but a closer look revealed that the boy was deep in thought, and he wasn't thinking about baseball.

The first person to notice that Jake was off and on his own again, was Genny Williams. She was talking to Piper, who was very excited that Robby was playing, of course. Everybody was ready to cheer for Robby and to cheer on the Wildcats. But when Genny turned around and spotted Jake sitting in the bleachers, all by himself, she became concerned.

"I'm going to see what's up with the muscle guy..." she said to Piper, as she turned around and walked up the stairs, which lead her into the bleachers. Then she quickly made her way up the steep stairs, until she reached the top row, where Jake was sitting. She quietly sat down next to him, and placed her arm over his broad shoulders.

"Come on, Muscles..." she chuckled. "Don't look so down, will you? This is your partner's big day! Why are you so down?"

"Oh, Genny..." Jake sighed. "I'm just thinking about all the things that have happened to me lately... About Zhango-Rhe, and Malcolm, and the robots, and the attacks, and the zombies, and the crime in the city, and the Zyrtonium, and the police, and the..."

"Jake!" Genny whispered angrily. "We're at a baseball game. This is not the time to be thinking about all those things! Enjoy the game! Look at Robby! He's a hero just like you, and he's not fussing about those things right now! He's having fun playing baseball! Now stop worrying about these things and enjoy yourself for a change!"

"I know, Genny..." Jake said sadly. "It's just so hard... It's hard not to think about it..."

Genny let out a deep sigh.

"Well, is it ever going to end?" Genny asked him.

"No... I'm afraid not... Malcolm is still out there... Who knows how he will try to attack us next..." Jake replied. "And, Malcolm aside, there is plenty of evil that is lurking in our city and across the planet. Now more than ever, The Outcasts have to be prepared..."

"Yeah... Oh, look! Here comes Robby!" Genny cheered, just as Piper sat down next to Jake.

"Alright Robby!" all four of them cheered at the same time, as Robby walked up to the plate with a bat in his hand.

Robby took his position over the home plate as the pitcher was warming up for the first pitch of the game.

Robby had an unfair advantage of course. He knew that kind of pitch was being thrown before it ever left the pitcher's hand. He grinned slyly as the pitcher coiled back and threw a thunderous fast ball.

"COME ON, ROBBY!!!!" they all cheered in unison.

As the pitch left the mound, Robby tensed his muscles and prepared the swing. He unleashed all the fury he could unleash on that poor unsuspecting ball. His swing met the ball at the perfect moment.

With a mighty swing of his bat, the ball made contact and it was instantly hurled far into the air. Robby immediately dropped the bat and started his dash towards first base, as the crowd went wild.

"Go Robby, go!!" everyone shouted. "GO ROBBY!!"

Everyone on the field held their breath as they watched the baseball soar high over the field. Then, as the ball approached the outer wall, every single person in the stadium gasped in anticipation.

"Is it going to make it?" Piper asked.

Make it, it did. The ball sailed high and strong over the center-field wall. That homerun hit, set a new Little League world record for the longest hit home run by someone under the age of eighteen. Even though Robby had a slight advantage, it still felt good.

"HOME RUN NUMBER EIGHTEEN ROBBY MCCLOUD! THE WILDCATS ARE ON THE BOARD!" bellowed the announcer over the p.a. system.

"HOME RUN! It was a home run!!!" Genny cheered.

Robby continued to run from first base to second base and he continued on to third.

"RUN, LITTLE BROTHER, RUN!!! GO BRO GO!" yelled Brandon at the top of his lungs.

"You better move, man" cheered Mikey.

"RUN, ROBBY!!!!" Piper, Genny and Jake shouted. The crowd was on their feet! Every single person in the stands was standing and cheering for the red-headed baseball player, who had just scored the first home-run of the game.

As Robby ran from third base and cruised over home plate, he turned towards the bleachers and looked into the direction where Piper, Genny, Brandon, and Jake were standing. Then, he used his telepathic powers to send a message that only Jake Knight could hear.

"This run is for all the good guys, Jake!" Jake heard Robby's voice ringing in his ears.

Jake couldn't help but return a huge smile to his partner, who had just walked into the dugout to a standing ovation from the crowd.

Tim greeted the Home Run hero in the dugout with a knowing smile and a pat on the back. Tim knew that this was the closest to home that young Robby McCloud had felt in months. Robby flashed a smile of acknowledgement at Tim. He was right after all. Baseball, Brandon, Piper, and Jake, this was a little slice of heaven for him today.

Then Robby walked into the restroom, and quietly disappeared from site. He instantly appeared sitting among Jake, Piper and Genny in the bleachers, joining the rest of the gang. Brandon gave him a huge hug and ruffled his hair. He was so proud of his former protégé.

They all talked and enjoyed each other's company, as they looked up and wondered what the future held for Myst, Titan and the Outcasts.

To Be Continued In "Myst, Titan and the Outcasts", Book 2: "The Outcasts: Evolution".

Official web site for Myst, Titan and the Outcasts:
www.superfantasystories.com

You can purchase additional copies of this book at:
www.mystandtitan.com

If you liked the story of Myst and Titan, and want to order cool t-shirts and merchandise, plus if you want to be the first to know about the next book by these authors, please go to www.superfantasystories.com

Robert C. Aultman and Rex Torres
December 2007 – August 2008

About the Authors

Robert C. Aultman and Rex Torres both live in Tallahassee, Florida.

Robert, a Hattiesburg Mississippi native, currently works as a wireless consultant and data specialist for Alltel Wireless. He is married to Celina, and has three sons: Mathew, Michael and Madison. Robert spent the past ten years working as an Emergency Medical Technician, before moving to Tallahassee Florida, where he resides currently. He is avidly into martial arts, soccer, which he coaches, and any form of electronic gadgetry.

Rex is a Programmer Analyst for the State of Florida and he has been writing fan fiction stories for young adults since 2003. He was born in Curacao, Netherlands Antilles, but he was raised in Tucson, Arizona. Rex got his Bachelor's Degree in Management Information System from the University of Arizona. He has worked as the Marketing Manager for Caribbean Motors Company N.V., which is a large car dealership that is owned by his father in Curacao, and he also worked for the I.T. Department for the Department of Finance of the Netherlands Antilles. During the past seven years, he has worked as a Programmer Analyst for the Florida Department of Education. Rex plays tennis, writes children's stories and maintains several web sites in his free time.

Printed in the United States
124113LV00001B/154/P